MUCH MORE TRAVEL BY GEORGE

ISBN 0-7414-2600-5

Illustrations by Lisa Hill

To order additional copies of this book, contact:
D. Wesley Coombe
1-760-343-1502
P.O. Box 212
Thousand Palms, CA 92276
NISICOO@AOL.COM

Published by:

INFINITY
PUBLISHING.COM

1094 New DeHaven Street, Suite 100
West Conshohocken, PA 19428-2713
Info@buybooksontheweb.com
www.buybooksontheweb.com
Toll-free (877) BUY BOOK
Local Phone (610) 941-9999
Fax (610) 941-9959

Printed in the United States of America

Printed on Recycled Paper

Published June 2005

MUCH MORE TRAVEL BY GEORGE

GEORGE WESCOOMBE

Also by George Wescoombe

More travel by George

Travel by George: A collection of Whimsical Narratives

The Saga of Ocean Explorer I

To My Wife, Bernice (Nan)

Thanks for Sixty-eight Years of Love and Assistance.

Acknowledgments

Many thanks to daughters, Bette Burke, Marnie Caputo, Patty Warhol and to Kent Warhol, for typing, copying, editing, and engineering.

Undoubtedly errors have crept into this manuscript. The errors are George's fault alone

Contents

A FORTNIGHT IN BAVARIA WITH THE NIGHT BLOOMING JAZZMEN

DAY minus 1—Saturday, September 27, 2003

In order to facilitate an orderly departure for Munich, Bavaria, Germany, tomorrow, Sunday, September 28, 2003, the Wescoombes decided to prevail upon daughter, Marnie, to drive them to the Comfort Inn at 300 Katella Avenue in Orange County this a.m.

This strategic maneuver accomplished several things, or at least it should have. It put George and Nan into position to accompany son, John, who has four tickets to the baseball game between the Anaheim Angels and the Texas Rangers, scheduled for Edison Field this p.m. As Nan is not interested in the baseball game, there will be a ticket available for granddaughter Mary Kay Burke, aforementioned daughter Marnie, grandfather Wescoombe, and last but not least, the provider of the expensive tickets, John Wescoombe.

Furthermore, Marnie will be able to accompany Mary Kay on some kind of a foot race scheduled for Sunday morning.

Also, George and Nan will be in position to be picked up at the Comfort Inn by Janet and Bill Read and ride with them to their home in Fullerton to await the Super Shuttle which will deliver the foursome to LAX by 12:25 p.m., Sunday.

If the foregoing sounds complicated, it doesn't matter. That's probably only half of what will really happen.

It is a typical beautiful day in Orange County, much too bright for comfort in the expensive front row seats. Day games are much sunnier than night games.

Although all have had lunch, George suggested that the group move to the shade of the second deck pavilion where he would buy snacks and also all the beer we could drink. This was in exchange for getting him out of the sun—and an offer too good to turn down--beer for shade. Shade doesn't cost much.

It was an unhappy game for the home team Angels who lost by a lopsided score, but a great game for the many fans who enjoy lots of hits, runs, and errors. What else is there, by the way? And the Angels are already eliminated from contention. So, have another beer, which we did.

Finally as the game subsided, a move to join Nan at the Comfort Inn is in order.

It is time to leave for other venues, but John quickly crossed the street and picked up a jug of Canadian Club for his dad and mom to enjoy in Europe. Of course, it had to be sampled right away. Thanks, John.

Almost before the youngsters drove away, the oldsters were dozing.

DAY 1 and 2—Sunday and Monday, September 28 and 29, 2003—LAX – Munich – Grassau

The Super Shuttle picked up the Reads and the Wescoombes promptly at 12:30 p.m. and expeditiously moved them to LAX by 1:30 p.m. in order for them to be in position to board the aircraft three hours before scheduled flight time. For some reason the government has decided that it is important to keep people sitting around waiting much longer than necessary.

The International Section of LAX is very busy as several large aircraft are loading at the same time, as is the custom.

There are many workers milling around, but none offering assistance to passengers who are also milling around trying to find out where to go. Finally, we are directed to a collection area off to one side, which seemed like a good idea, and in about ten minutes our bags had undergone rigorous inspection and placed in a holding area directly in front of the ticket counters.

It is necessary to join a serpentine line, which wound around and around in the area in front of the counters for one hour and 40 minutes, until 3:20 p.m. The line was moving reasonably fast for such important work. The service was excellent, by pleasant people. We spent less than ten minutes before a clerk and that included boarding a wheelchair, which had been ordered the day before. Robert, the wheeler, moved through customs and onward until 3:40 p.m. at which time we reach the Lufthansa boarding area. However, all the seats are taken. Maybe, if the airlines scheduled flights at various times, things would loosen up and whoever is paying for this boondoggle would save a hundred million dollars cash. And as Yogi says, "That's the same as money."

There is no reason to have Robert standing around leaning on the wheelchair, so he is paid $10 for 20 minutes hard work. He seemed satisfied; and I sure am. I could have walked the distance in a painful hour, maybe.

Jan Read found an empty seat for me, quickly. Thank you, Janet.

Sure enough, after sitting around for another 50 minutes, as predicted, Lufthansa Airbus, Flight 453, boarded at its scheduled time, 4:40 p.m.

Work expands in direct proportion to the time available.

The airbus, a beautiful aircraft, has some 270 fragile humans carefully and tightly packed, row upon row upon row, inside its thin skin. There is hardly room to take a deep breath, and maybe it would be better not to breath.

George has maintained that passenger aircraft are the most viscous carriers of communicable diseases. More times than not he catches a cold, cough, whatever, after a cross-country or longer flight.

George noticed that the coffee-pouring steward, on the left side of the aircraft, pours a cup of coffee, then coughs into the pot with the same motion. He pours "coughee" and "coffs" with the same short stroke. He should not have been at work, but who would pour the coffee. This could be the start of the plague or maybe just the German flu.

This beautiful bird has all the latest aids in the cabin to advise passengers as to the speed the aircraft is moving, how long to the destination, the height above sea level, and maybe other attributes that most people don't give a damn about. A picture of the aircraft is superimposed onto a map of the world, so one may see exactly where one is in the universe at all times, and this is very important. Oh no, they just turned it off to show the news in German.

The young lady wants to know what George would like to drink. "Canadian Whisky" is his request. "We only have Scotch," she admits. "Do you have beer?" was a polite question. She proudly replied, "Yes, we have Beck's." "Better than nothing, please bring one to me," George is fond of Beck's beer, but thought the airline should have at least two beers on board.

Lunch is much better than that served on America's airlines, but not in the same league as the food served on Oriental airlines. "In George's opinion," should be added.

Munich has a sparkling new airport, first class in every detail. George is wheeled to the baggage department by an attractive lady, without putting in a prior request. Maybe the request "Los Angeles to Munich" worked at both ends. She haughtily refused George's offer of payment. He merely wanted to pay her for pushing him around. She momentarily has high color. George wonders what caused that, perchance.

The buses to Grassau are difficult, delay after delay occurred. Even Bill Read had trouble sorting things out. It wasn't the buses' fault, they were the finest obtainable.

Finally, the two buses reached Grassau, and Tom and Gina, from their lists, sorted out the passengers between the Sperrer Hotel and the Hotel Hansback, located about four blocks, 400 yards apart, in the center of Grassau.

The Reads and the Wescoombes are finally allocated to the Hotel Hansback, the Reads in Room 101, and the Wescoombes in Room 204.

The rooms are commodious having feather beds and pillows.

It is necessary to walk from the Hansback to the Sperrer where the dining room is located, a distance of about 400 yards. George and Nan are not looking forward to the nightly walk, but as it has been a long day, decide to enjoy drinks and dinner and think about the problem tomorrow.

Gina mentioned something about trading the Hansback room with someone located in the Sperrer. Let's go to sleep.

Let's take a page from the promotion material of Tom and Gina Crisp, which says it better than anyone else could say it:

Tour Germany & Austria with The Night Blooming Jazzmen Dixieland Band
& Tom & Gina Crisp, your specialized tour hosts for Germany & Austria

Sept. 28—Oct. 12, 2003

Tom & Gina live in Tucson, Arizona and have been conducting tours to Germany for several years. They personally make all tour arrangements and deal directly with the hotels and the bus company in the village of Grassau. Tom is a square dance caller for over 30 years and knows how to party and show a crowd a good time. He is now retired from the USAF with over 14 years of duty in Germany. Gina comes from the little village of Koenigsdorf, just south of Munich. Gina being in the restaurant business really knows how to cater to people. Tom & Gina make great travel hosts. They know the area, both speak the language and can show you local places of interest that most tourists miss.

This is a full two-week vacation, which also allows plenty of time for shopping, hiking, exploring, dining, or just relaxing. It includes round trip airfare from Los Angeles and other US cities, all your breakfasts, nearly all your evening meals, all your transportation, all jazz entertainment, plus *all entrance fees to all the attractions listed. The price is the best part, only $3,895 per person, based on double occupancy. (Subtract $100 per person when registering before March 1, 2003). Compare this low price with any cruise or other European tours and it can't be beat for price, value, and personal attention. Individual extensions or post tours are available upon request. Space is limited to just two buses. With a tour package like this, we expect an early sellout.*

This is not your typical rushed whirl-wind European tour, dragging suitcases on and off buses each day and visiting old city buildings. You'll pack your bags only once. We stay in just one modern Bavarian style hotel with private bathroom and shower in the little picturesque village of Grassau, nestled on the edge of the Alps. It is from here where we'll take daily bus tours to local places of interest. Our goal is to let you learn about the land, its people, their customs, and their traditions. This vacation allows plenty of time to enjoy the very best of southern Bavaria and parts of Austria. You'll experience a personalized guided tour tailored especially for the Traditional Jazz fan at one super low price.

You'll be entertained daily by the superb live music of the ever-popular Night Blooming Jazzmen, from Claremont, California. This Dixieland Jazz Band has been actively featured in every conceivable jazz festival across the nation for the past 25 years. You can always expect the unexpected—both musically and in the dry witty humor of Professor Chet Jaeger. These jazzmaniacs will keep you constantly entertained with their unique blend of hokum and a careful approach to the music they play. Their well-known specialty is the revival of jazz gospel, specifically the Hymn-a-long, a feature regularly requested Sunday mornings at Jazz festivals, overseas tours, and cruises. The band's style ranges all the way from traditional to early swing.

***<u>Here's your itinerary</u>**: Overnight flight to Munich, Germany, 13 nights in the picturesque Bavarian town of*

Grassau, nestled at the foot of the Alps, day tours to favorite places of interest, and return flight from Munich.

Only $3,895 per person—*double occupancy.* ***Here's what you get:***

All ground transportation by modern luxurious motorcoach.

Round trip airfare from Los Angeles and other selected US cities.

Two full weeks—personally escorted with friends with a common interest

Large breakfast buffet daily & all evening dinners are included except two.

Full accommodations in a modern Bavarian style hotel with private shower.

You may choose to stay in a nearby private Bed & Breakfast in a Bavarian home.

Free admission charges to all jazz concerts and all places of interest listed on tour.

City tours with professional English speaking tour guides in Salzburg & Munich.

Tour to Munich for a city tour, shopping, and visit the world famous Hofbrauhaus.

Bus tour to the highest mountain in the Austrian Alps, the majestic "Grossglockner."

You'll experience the original Munich Oktoberfest, the largest beer festival in the world.

Visit the wood carving capital of Oberammergau and the fairytale Neuschwanstein Castle.

Take a dance cruise with our own NBJ on Lake Chiemsee, the largest inland lake in Germany.

Also on Lake Chiemsee, we'll take a boat trip to Herren Island and visit King Ludwig's Castle.

Visit Berchtesgaden nestled in the Bavarian Alps. Also visit Obersalzberg and the famous salt mine.

Travel to the village of Icking for a joint concert with the Veterinary Street Jazz Band from Munich.

Travel to Salzburg, spend a wonderful evening in the renowned Peterskeller for a Mozart Dinner Concert.

Also in Salzburg, City of Mozart, take a guided walking tour and see the impregnable "Hohernsalzburg" fortress.

Attend an evening with the local towns' people for a folklore show with their traditional Bavarian "Schuhplattler."

Enjoy personalized concerts with the Night Bloomers Jazzmen Dixieland Band and local Dixieland bands.

Experience the beauty of the alpine village of Reit im Winkl nestled on the edge of the Austrian border.

Mingle with the local people and tour with friends with a common interest—Traditional Jazz.

Ride a local ski lift to a favorite launching site for hang-glider and parachute enthusiasts.

Enjoy a special "Aufwiedsersehen" farewell banquet with distinguished local guests.

Even Trip Cancellation and Medical Insurance is included with the tour package.

DAY 3—Tuesday, September 30, 2003—Grassau – Sunny, mild

The breakfast room in the Hotel Hansback is ready for action by 7:00 a.m. Five different kinds of cold meats are available along with hard-boiled eggs. Several cold cereals with two levels of milk, and four or five fruit juices are set out for the taking. George and Bill are happy with the assortment of bread and rolls, plus unlimited hot coffee, cocoa, and chocolate. What appear to be homemade jams and jellies are available in copious quantity, not in little plastic packages. All in all, in the bright, sunny, spacious room, breakfast is a delightful repast.

The monetary unit of Bavaria is the euro. The local bank is requesting, no demanding, that we pay to them $1.15

US for one of their damn fool euros. That is highway robbery. How is it possible that any other country could have a currency more valuable than that of the good old USA? There is, no doubt, some kind of a conspiracy at work.

After a conference, the men from the USA decide that their wives would want to do shopping or at least have lunch, so they had better get off the dime and realize that our native land is not tops in the money business at this time, and so they grudgingly invest $100 USA for $85 euro. "It doesn't seem right," said Bill, sobbing.

The bus is ready to move folks to the town of Amerang, not far distant, to visit the FarmHouse Museum of the district of Upper Bavaria. George had been told that Bavaria is a province of Germany. This brochure calls it a district. Maybe they haven't made up their minds. In any event, it doesn't matter. It is an absolutely beautiful, gently rolling, perfectly green countryside. Amerang is about 20 miles from Grassau, and there are two or three villages in between. Everything is neat, clean, orderly, and German.

The Farm Museum is worth a quick look. There are about ten acres on which are displayed farm buildings with equipment as they would have appeared at various times such as 1525, 1567, 1600, 1671, 1725, 1738, 1800, 1808, up to 1920.

Examples are the sawmill 1800, blacksmith's shop 1830, apiary 1889, wind wheel 1900, rope maker's shop 1920, flax kiln 1800, cartwright's workshop 1810, and several types of barns from 1525 onward. A calvary has something to do with religion. Obviously, the Germans of that era were a hardworking, clean living type of people. There are no weapons of mass destruction on display.

The box bed, from which a new little one popped at least once a year, showed that the German male had some strength left after his strenuous working day.

Fortunately, on the museum grounds is located a snack "Parlour" with a beer garden, a delightful place to enjoy a bowl of soup or a sandwich with beer, coffee, or soft drink.

Warm sunshine certainly increases George's enjoyment of a mundane thing, such as "an old barn."

Living quarters for our 100 travelers are divided between the 35-room Hotel Hansback and the 34-room Sperrer.

Each hotel has a breakfast room, but dinner is at the Sperrer which has a larger dining room, a space for dancing, and a bandstand area for our own, for a fortnight at least, The Night Blooming Jazzmen Dixieland Band, under the direction of Professor Chet Jaeger. This collection of seven top-ranked jazz musicians have, for the last 28 years, played in every festival of consequence in California, the US and Canada, the ships at sea, and other important parts of the world. And, as Chet would say, "in some not so important." They are extremely well known in the "jazz world." The Wescoombes and Reads have been interested in jazz music since childhood and jumped at the chance to spend two weeks with this celebrated band.

George has no knowledge of the arrangement between Tom and Gina Crisp and the Jazzmen except that the band will perform almost every other night and sometimes in the afternoon.

It was the presence of the Jazzmen that got the Wescoombes, in particular, on this adventure. George and Nan have been to Germany and Austria two or three times before and had no desire to drag their old bodies to those countries again. Only music as played by the Night Blooming boys could accomplish that feat.

As soon as dinner is over, say 7:30 p.m., the orchestra gathers on the bandstand, Chet raises his hand, and a thunderous cacophony of sound erupts as the band roars into their opening number—Rampart Street Parade.

For the next 90 minutes, hold on to your hats.

DAY 4—Wednesday, October 1, 2003—Sunny, warm

After the usual scrumptious breakfast, the feature this a.m. is a visit to the Salzbergwerk (Salt mine) in Berchtesgaden.

George has no idea what visiting a salt mine would entail, but even though he has not used salt (from a salt shaker) in his life, he and Nan joined the Reads on the 50-mile bus trip to Berchtesgaden.

Yes, it is the same city where Hitler supposedly hung out in WW2. His real playground was in Obersalzberg, but who cares.

First of all, the group was shown how the mined and refined salt was packaged into various sized containers for distribution. This is old stuff. Every product gets that treatment; otherwise it would never reach us, the consumers.

Then we are treated to a mysterious underground tour to view the fascinating world of salt, "white gold." This mine started in operation in 1517 but few were allowed to tour the salt mines until about 100 years ago.

Believe it or not, it is necessary to wear traditional salt miners' dress as one is taken deep into the mountain's interior by a mine train. The route continues via downhill slides and dark tunnels through disused sedimentation works and past an iridescent salt grotto, whatever that is.

Competent miners, still responsible for mining the brine, guide our group and explain everything to us in fluent German. For some reason there is a sparkling salt lake in our way, underground. So we board a handy raft to raft to the other side. George doubts that the miners were moved around on the 40-person rafts, but it is good fun especially as we are dressed up in the spooky outfits.

The guides do show us how the accumulated white stuff is removed from the walls in large chunks and reduced to manageable sizes. Lick your finger, "No doubt it is salt."

In order to entertain the visitors and as the levels in the mine are about 200 yards apart, one above the other, channeled, hard wood polished slides have been built joining the two floors. In groups of four, one behind the other, hanging together, the visitors slide down the 200 yards. Actually, it does give one a momentary rush. George says he wouldn't want to pay for it, it's not that good. But it certainly is more fun than George has had in any other salt mine he has visited.

The best place for the tour to end is where we rid ourselves of the over-garments. George's over-pants were too big, and he had to keep hitching them up. A visit to the mine's pub was most enjoyable.

The mine-owners displayed a great sense of humor.

As it is a fine sunny afternoon, and as there is plenty of time remaining, a visit to the "Eagle's Nest" (Kehlsteinhaus) Hitler's hangout in the mountains is in order.

George seems to recall a change of buses--something about being necessary to park our tour bus and take a city bus to the parking lot where the glass elevator is available.

The glass elevator affords an excellent view of the entire area (the same view as Hitler had) as it rises 130 stories. Today, most of the Eagle's Nest has been converted to restaurants, both inside and outside. The remainder is still in conference room configuration. But George has no idea as to what type of conference is held there. He thinks that they should "glück auf," whatever that means.

Tom, of Tom and Gina, joined the Reads and Wescoombes for lunch, but that did not improve the service. The waiter would have been better off home in bed, probably where he should have been. It took so long, George has forgotten what he and Nan had to eat. Other than the view, the Wescoombes were not impressed by the "Eagle's Nest." George wonders if Hitler enjoyed "nesting."

Fortunately, the Wescoombes care little about food, so George will avoid commenting on that subject as much as possible. At the Sperrer, in George's opinion, the soup is excellent, the salad palatable, and the main course chewy. Others may have a different opinion. Bill is able to finish his own plate, then Nan's plate, then George's, but Janet raises a barrier. Enough is enough. But Bill is a big man with a big appetite, and he seems to enjoy eating.

Dinner seems to be over quicker when one knows that Chet will soon raise his arms and a beautiful sound will once again fill the air. Chet plays the cornet, not the trumpet. The trumpet has a sharper, more shrill sound than the more mellow tone of the cornet. Chet can hike the cornet to a dizzying pitch, if he desires.

The three front men of the Bloomers, Chet on cornet, Jim on sax and clarinet, and Dick on trombone have been together for many years and pass the melody, if one may call it that, around effortlessly, and also back each others solos, seamlessly.

Most of the tunes are upbeat. In fact, most numbers move along like an express train, such as Beale Street Blues, Panama Rag, and Tin Roof Blues. Chet says, "We have to get special permission to play a slow number." He didn't say from whom, but he's the one calling the shots.

The only time this group slows down is when someone has an urge to sing, and sing they do. At least four of them are excellent vocalists.

It's a good thing they have a vocal every four or five tunes so the audience may catch its breath.

DAY 5—Thursday, October 2, 2003—Sunny, warm

We are told that we are enjoying a Bavarian style "Indian Summer" which sometimes lasts until late October—October 12 will do.

Back on the bus with Manfred for a Munich City tour. The famous city is quickly reached and we pick up Kathryn, our guide, for the morning. This lady is a middle-aged, blonde smiler who speaks perfect English. Munich does not display a bunch of skyscrapers, only one or two tall buildings of medium height.

It appears to be a warm friendly place, which one enters through a series of gates, such as the Victory Gate. A building of interest is, of course, the cathedral, which ranks, in height, with the tallest business buildings.

It is a busy city as trucks take up a large part of the main roadways. It is interesting that the large trucks have soft sides unlike the American behemoths, which are solid on all sides.

The Farmers Market indicates that the people of Munich enjoy eating. There is also a line up for day old bread.

Kathryn had the driver drive by Olympia Park, site of the 1972 Olympic Games, which covers 740 acres. More than 15,000 workers from 18 countries transformed the site into a park of 5,000 trees, 27 miles of roads, 32 bridges, and a lake. It also has a 960-foot television tower. The stadium holds 69,000 spectators. The pamphlet George has picked up is enticing us to eat at the tower-revolving restaurant because of the extraordinary view, which reaches the Alps.

The article continues with a description of "Black September," the massacre on September 5, 1972 of two Israelis and the subsequent terrible events culminating in the presiding officer of the Games, Avery Brundage, issuing the famous pronouncement, "The games must go on" and so they did.

Kathryn concluded her portion of the tour, by leading the group to the Hofbrauhaus.

The state-owned Hofbrauhaus is the world's most famous beer hall. If you have only one day in Munich, you must at least visit the famous eating and drinking place, as we did at noon, today.

The first Hofbrauhaus dates back to 1859, with the latest built in 1897 where 4,500 beer drinkers can crowd in, on any given night. Several rooms, including a top floor room for dancing, are spread over three floors. George and Nan, on one of their previous visits, were relegated with the rest of the supposedly over-noisy Americans to the second floor. George can't remember whether that was an honor or not, but it didn't make any difference to the Americans at that time. There is Oktoberfest-type activity throughout the building, including a brass band, sing-a-longs, strolling musicians, and dirndl-clad waitresses moving through the crowded three floors.

It will be the same all day, but we are going to the Oktoberfest this afternoon, and an N.B.J. concert in Wirtshau's zum isartal, this evening. A busy day.

Few cities in the world cling to a beverage the way Munich clings to beer. Munichers, with a little help from visitors, consume a world's record of the brew; 280 liters a year, per capita. It is said that Bavarians never open their mouths except to pour in more beer.

Some of Munich's most notable events have floated on the suds. There was Hitler's beer hall putsch (Hofbrauhaus, 1923), an attempt to assassinate Hitler (in the Burger Braukeller, 1939), and most recently, the Beer Garden Revolution, a 1995 event, when the authorities proposed closing of a neighborhood beer garden at 9:30 p.m. was seen as a threat to the civil liberties of the city's beer drinkers, causing mass rallies by infuriated Munichers, and rightly so.

During Oktoberfest, at least 7 million visitor's flood into the city for two drink-sodden weeks, filling the sprawling network of advertisers' tents set up in the theresienwiese for the event. But while the festival promotes the consumption of millions of liters of beer, it causes but a ripple in the regular rate of consumption in Munich.

Bus driver, Manfried, picked up fifty of our party at a pre-arranged spot at the Oktoberfest at 5:30 p.m. and moved us to the Wirtshaua zum isartal for dinner and then a special concert with our N.B.J. and the Veterinarian Street Band.

W.Z.I. is a nightclub sort of place, half of which has a second deck overlooking the bandstand. People are crowded on the main floor on the same level as the band. We are fortunate to get front seats on the second level.

The Veterinarians are playing a dainty type of Dixieland when we arrive, with their leader playing a creditable trumpet. The rest of the horse doctors in the band follow his lead, but not closely.

As the food is very good, most of the visitors are not paying too much attention to the music but are chomping down on the excellent pork chops or pork roast.

Then suddenly, the roof of the building rises a couple of inches as the N.B.J. blast into action with "That's a Plenty."

The men on the front line, as they exchange leads, do not let the roof come back down in the least. The crescendo holds and magnifies. In fact, the roof stays up while Chet relates one of his comical stories.

Jim, playing harmony on tenor and alto sax at the same time, holds the roof level; then Dick, on trombone, makes the roof bounce up and down with his saucy trombone.

N.B.J.'s "Undecided" completes the set winning the match, if there was a match, by a score of 100-0 on our scorecards, but we are biased, are we not?

The Doctors come back on the stand and join the N.B.J. in a rousing free-for-all with the two leaders dueling vigorously on their horns for ten minutes—it seemed that long, anyway.

Thunderous applause filled the room. However, those of us on the second deck front row realize that we are almost asphyxiated by the cigarette smoke wafting upward from the continual puffing by the German folk sitting below. Some of us made a hasty exit to breathe fresh, cool evening air into our lungs. Remember when the people in California smoked and smoked and smoked. Aren't you glad we quit smoking? It was a magnificent night, anyway.

Good times are back at this year's Oktoberfest

Despite weak economy, tents nearly run out of beer as good weather brings out the visitors

Serving 3 million visitors in one week at this year's Oktoberfest can be a tough job.

Oktoberfest without beer is such a paradox that the operators of Munich's giant beer festival didn't think twice before allowing several breweries blindsided by record visitor numbers to break the rules of beer supply last weekend.

"Suppliers are only supposed to drive up to the tents during certain periods, but apparently this was a real emergency. In the end, nobody had to go thirsty," said Johanna Schicke from the Munich tourist office, which operates the Oktoberfest.

The response during the first week of Munich's 170th Oktoberfest was so overwhelming that some taps actually ran dry on Saturday, the head of the Paulaner brewery, Wolfgang Salewski, confirmed: "That has never happened before." About 16,000 hectoliters of Paulaner beer was poured into the mass, *heavy one-liter mugs, during the first week of the festival, Salewski said – 20 percent more than during the same period last year.*

The first week on the Wiesn, *the local name for the Oktoberfest, was a good one. Three million visitors compared with 2.6 million in 2002, and by last Sunday they had consumed 2.3 million liters – about 580,000 U.S. gallons – of beer. A big finale is expected for the long holiday weekend starting this Friday.*

Visitors not only came in droves, they also arrived in better spirits than in the last two years. The 2002 festival struggled with heavy rain and even snow, and the 2001 Oktoberfest took place in the immediate aftermath of the Sept. 11 terrorist attacks. Before 2001, 6.5 million visitors at this world-renowned event was nothing unusual.

This is why Schicke says this year's success and exuberant atmosphere shouldn't be interpreted as a positive economic indicator: "It would run counter to the facts. The good weather has had an immense effect."

According to Gabriele Weishaupl, the chief Oktoberfest organizer, the economic value of Germany's biggest festival is ∊954 million, or $1.12 billion, not including travel costs of visitors from other German states and abroad. According to the Munich tourist office, Oktoberfest visitors spend an average of 74 euros per person on the Wiesn *itself, plus hotel and other activities elsewhere in the Bavarian capital.*

Munich police have also been a lot busier during this year's festival, with incidents to date up by 14 percent.

Red Cross staff said the number of people needing treatment soared by 80 percent largely because of the higher temperatures. Everyone could be helped, including a 77-year-old man looking for his dentures after four mass and one sobering night in a hospital.

Season spoiler: Bitterness in beer industry

By Mark Landler
New York Times News Service

Munich, Germany The Oktoberfest starts here this weekend, and even before noon on Friday, the vaulted main hall of the Hofbrauhaus was teeming with tourists in boisterous training.

But in Bavaria's breweries, bitterness is spoiling the season. Some of Germany's leading beers have been sold into foreign hands, and to defenders of national pride, something of Germany's birthright has been sold with them.

This week, one of Germany's oldest breweries, Gabriel Sedlmayr, announced it would sell its famous beers, which include Lowenbrau, to Interbrew, the giant Belgian brewer of Stella Artois, for 477 million euros ($538 million).

In previous deals, Interbrew acquired Beck's, the famous northern German beer, while the Dutch beer giant, Heineken, bought close to half of the Munich brewery that makes the locally popular Paulaner brand.

Sedlmayr, which brews the venerable Franzikaner and Spaten brands in addition to Lowenbrau, has long been an anchor of the Oktoberfest. Indeed, Lowenbrau, which is said to date from the 14th century and is known by its golden lion, virtually symbolizes the hallowed tradition of beer in Bavaria.

"The mayor is going to open the Oktoberfest with an Interbrew product," said Prince Luitpold of Bavaria, a descendant of the state's former rulers, who brews beer at his castle 30 miles west of Munich. "What's to stop them from brewing Stella Artois in Munich and selling it at the Oktoberfest?"

Actually, strict laws govern the production of beer in Germany, making it all but impossible for Interbrew to try to pass off a German version of Stella Artois, a mass-market beer it brews in Belgium, at the festival.

Moreover, by city law, only beers that are produced in Munich by traditional breweries can be sold at the festival. That disqualifies microbreweries, as well as dozens of brands from Munich's beer-drenched hinterland—including Prince Luitpold's Konig Ludwig, which he has fought unsuccessfully to sell at Oktoberfest for 20 years.

COMMENT: Prince Luitpold said he did not want Paulaner and Lowenbrau to be banned from the festival. But he said the city should allow in smaller regional brewers, like himself, to offset the foreign-owned players.

"The city of Munich should not defend the monopolies of Interbrew and Heineken," said the prince, adding that his family helped start the Oktoberfest in the early 1800s and had been brewing beer since 1260.

The festival's organizers said the Interbrew deal would not disqualify Lowenbrau or its sisters. "We see no reason not to serve it," said the general manager, Gabriele Weishaupt. "Lowenbrau has been sold, but it is still a Munich beer, made in Munich, according to Munich practices."

RESPONSE: Weishaupt also said the festival would not reconsider its ban on beers made outside Munich. Although she agreed that Prince Luitpold had a distinguished beer-making lineage—not to mention that his forebears ruled the place—she said if he were allowed in, the Oktoberfest would have to accept every pint-sized Bavarian brewery, as well as those from Austria and the Czech Republic.

"It's a pity, but this is a question of principle," she said.

While the Oktoberfest has always been a closed market, the Munich brewers have added reason to be protectionist these days. Annual consumption of beer by Germans has fallen to 32 gallons per person from 38.4 gallons in 1980. Experts attribute that partly to concerns about health. Beer sales have been further depressed this year by a new deposit placed on cans and bottles.

Germany has become a ripe target for acquisitions in recent years because it is a large but fragmented market, with 1,291 brewers producing around 5,000 beers. Interbrew was attracted to Sedlmayr because it gave the company the chance to fill out its portfolio in southern Germany.

"This is the right deal at the right price, in a key market," John Brock, Interbrew's chief executive, said at a news conference.

Interbrew's move vaults it ahead of Holsten of Hamburg as the largest seller of beer in Germany, with a market share of roughly 11 percent. Analysts expect further acquisitions, with attention focusing on three large German brewers: Holsten, Brau and Brunnen, and Radeberger.

At the Hofbrauhaus, however, the talk was of the virtues of local ownership. The house beer in Munich's most famous beer house is Hofbrau, which is owned by the state of Bavaria. Wolfgang Sperger, whose family owns the Hofbrauhaus, said his guests valued the staunchly Teutonic image.

"Hofbrau is identified with Munich, the Oktoberfest and Germany," Sperger said. "The impression people have is that the beer is made in the house," he added, noting that it comes from a brewery within the city limits.

DAY 6—Friday, October 3, 2003—Sunny, warm

After the excitement of yesterday, a drive through the mountains sounded like a pleasant change.

What George did not know was that the Grossglockner High Alpine Road holds second place, after some palace, among the famous show places in Austria, with more than one million visitors annually. And no wonder, the road encompasses the most impressive part of the national park, because at 3,798 meters it is the highest mountain in Austria, and beneath its northern flank lies the pasterze, half covered in scree and Austria's largest glacier.

How does George know all that important stuff? He knows that and more as he bought, for a few euros, a beautiful book full of outstanding photographs plus facts and figures galore.

George says, "I will tell you only the interesting stuff, thus saving you the time required to read the entire book."

The road was first thought of in 1924 but remained in the draft stage due to the depression until the Austrian government financed the construction as a state employment scheme, providing 3,200 jobs.

The road was opened in 1935. The first year, a quarter-million toll payers came, and now the toll of toll payers has reached 1.2 million annually.

Here's an interesting tidbit: Visitors to the Glockner Road travelling from bottom to top, or top to bottom for that matter, cross every single non-tropical climatic and vegetation zone there is. In other words, the journey over a distance of altitude of 1,500 meters is the equivalent in terms of natural science to a 4,000 km. journey to the Arctic. Now that's impressive. George wishes he understood what he is talking about.

He does understand that there are many information stands along the road explaining what is happening in plain German. So they may read the signs, many people get out of their cars and walk, which leads to hiking.

Let's get in the bus, all fifty of us, and hope Manfred can take us up and back safely. One thing in favor of success is that Manfried owns this bus and three more. There must be big money in driving a bus in Germany.

Our attractive leader, Gina, on the first day, devised a scheme whereby everyone on the bus would move one seat forward each day until they reached the front. Instead of getting off the bus, they would start again in the back seat.

Believe it or not, lucky George is in the front seat on the most exciting trip of the tour. Nan is not so pleased but she is a good sport.

German buses are magnificent. The moving parts are made by Mercedes-Benz and the remainder by an outstanding body builder, Schwartznegger. Not really, but it is a similar unpronounceable German name, for George's tongue anyway. Most of the buses are independents, it seems, no greyhounds anyway. Each bus has a toilette, necessarily.

The trip to the halfway point, where the restrooms and sales offices are located, takes about two hours. The reason is that the highway has no idea of a straight line, and evidently to move higher quickly, the road builders use switchbacks, which means the bus literally returns on the same track on which it came down.

This is great fun for the young Germans with their Porches and BMW's, but Manfried has to be somewhat careful moving the long bus around the sharp turns.

George, 87-years-old, is not afraid (much) of the bus toppling, end over end, down the mountainside. On every switchback, and there are eighteen up and seventeen down, (different road), the front of the bus cantilevers over the edge of the mountain and the folks in the front seats can look straight down about a mile (seems like). Manfried doesn't seem to mind—it's all in a day's work to him.

The stop at the restaurant for lunch is disappointing, as the service is so poor. Janet had not received her coffee and cake before word came to board the bus.

The downward trip is as thrilling or chilling as the upward trip, except one is more used to the startling downward view. Seven peaks with heights from 3,261 meters (10,696 ft.) to 3,798 meters (12,437 ft.) are lined up in a jagged row.

DAY 7—Saturday, October 4, 2003—Sunny, warm

The Wescoombes awakened with stuffed-up heads and decided to take it easy throughout the day (at least avoid the water)

George has discovered some interesting information on King Ludwig in Chapter 11 of the Bavarian Alps and hereby passes it on.

The Fairy-Tale King

Often called "Mad" King Ludwig (although Bavarians hate that label), Ludwig II, son of Maximilian II, was only 18 years old when he was crowned king of Bavaria. Handsome Ludwig initially took an interest in affairs of state, but he soon grew bored and turned to the pursuit of his romantic visions. He transformed his dreams into some of the regions' most elaborate castles, nearly bankrupting Bavaria in the process.

Linderhof, the first and smallest of Ludwig's architectural fantasies, was his favorite castle, and the only one completed at the time of his death. His most elaborate effort was his attempt to construct his own Versailles on the island of Herrenchiemsee, but best known is the multi-turreted Disneyland-like Neuschwanstein. From a distance, the castle appears more illusory than real. It's the most photographed castle in Germany, and one of Germany's greatest tourist attractions.

The "dream king" was born in 1845 at Nymphenburg, the summer residence of the Bavarian rulers. A bisexual loner who never married, Ludwig's most intense relationship was his friendship with the composer Richard Wagner. An admirer of Wagner when that composer's music was considered crude, loud, and even demonic by almost everyone, it was Ludwig's enthusiastic and generous support that gave Wagner the opportunity to develop his art.

More and more, Ludwig withdrew into his dream world; he ran up huge debts and refused all advice to curb his extravagant building projects.

Finally, the cabinet decided he had to go—his excesses were too much. He was declared insane in 1886 when he was 41 years old, and his uncle Luitpold was made regent. Three days later, he was found drowned in Lake Starnberg on the outskirts of Munich—he may have committed suicide, or he may have been murdered. His death remains a mystery. On the bank of the lake is a memorial chapel dedicated to him. He is buried with other royals in the crypt beneath the choir of St. Michael's Church.

Today, Ludwig enjoys something of a cult status in Munich. Was he really insane? His theatricality, self-absorbed lifestyle, morbid shyness, and outbursts of temper certainly made him a very strange person, but there is not much evidence of real insanity. He seems mainly to have been an eccentric who had the means and power to try to turn his fantasies into reality.

Unfortunately, as we will not be on Lake Chiemsee, we will miss the Night Blooming Jazzmen concert. Maybe we will find a tape.

Heimatabend in Marquartstein, a local Bavarian folklore show, is the feature attraction this evening. Full buses brought a hundred of us to an already full venue. Although room was reserved for all of us, space was tight, so George and Nan found a table at the far side of the room but with a perfect view of the proceedings.

The show had nothing to do with schooling but is an association of people interested in local art and culture for all age groups. A fine ten-piece symphony orchestra entertained the crowd until it was time to show off the talent.

Once underway, it became fast moving—one group succeeded another in rapid succession performing dances with German names. The dancers were young and old, the movements fast and slow, but none resembled tap dancing or jazz of any type.

Musical renditions interspersed the dancing, mostly performances by individual violinists and harpists, with a few duets, trios, and quartets thrown into the mix. It seemed that all the entertainers appeared twice.

A group of young men, one in each corner of the room, snapped and cracked lengthy whips in the direction of each other, in rhythm with the music. George had never seen a performance such as this and is not sure he liked it. It was impossible, with his one eye, to see how close the cracking whips were coming to the other participants.

There were two empty chairs at the table and as the hall is filling up, two young people indicated they would like to use the seats.

"Of course, happy to have you." A reply was expected in German, but the young lady responded with, "Thank you" as they sat down.

Introductions revealed she was Margaret A. Huschle, born in a small town in Minnesota, now working for a private company, teaching English in Bavaria. Margaret's present address is AAFES, unit 24604, APO AE 09098—

HuschleM@aol.com. Peter has been her companion for several years. They are not married, therefore are very happy.

Peter is employed as an engineer in the construction business. George remarks, "You should be happy. The euro is now fifteen percent above the dollar."

Peter replied, "That is fine, but we also have fifteen percent unemployment, which affects many more people than the value of the euro. Also many of our companies are moving to other countries due to our high payroll-added costs. Our economy is sick."

George consoled him, "We have high unemployment also, but our government doesn't count all the unemployed, so we feel better. Also, when things are tough, the government prints more money."

Peter said, "In Germany, young people are continually reminded of the "thirties" when our money was worthless. That will never happen to Germany again."

George admitted, "It could happen to us unless we get rid of the greedy rotten bastards at the top of business and government. We have maybe three years to straighten out and fly right."

George and Peter had another beer with lemon, called a "Radlermass," and forgot about the state of the economy.

Nan and Margaret continued conversing and agreed to keep in touch.

I forgot to mention that Peter was one of the whippersnappers. He told George the name and purpose of all the whipping and cracking, but, of course, as that was 30 minutes ago, George has forgotten.

It was an unforgettable night, nevertheless.

DAY 8—Sunday, October 5, 2004—Overcast—Mild, light rain

The Night Blooming Jazzmen is a pioneer in jazz gospel, specifically the now famous hymn-a-long. This morning, Chet passes to the assemblage the familiar yellow sheets with the words to the hymns, and 100 folk sing-along with the band.

The front line instruments are able, whenever necessary, to make the sound sublime, delicate, whatever brings smiles to the listeners faces and warmth to their spirit, as the old favorite songs of faith are played in a jazz format. Examples are "Just a Closer Walk With Thee," "What a Friend We Have in Jesus," and "Amazing Grace."

Just as easily, the Bloomers move into a faster but just as smooth gear with "When The Saints Go Marching In," "Swing Low, Sweet Chariot," and "Down By the Riverside." Sometimes, these old gems need a dozen choruses to make their point.

The rhythm section, especially piano and guitar, put so much feeling into their solos, they almost bring tears.

What a religious way to spend an hour or so.

A rain shower causes the visit to the ski lift to be cancelled and for some unexplainable reason, George forgot about the Schnapps party. He must be getting old.

DAY 9—Monday, October 6, 2003—Salzburg—Overcast, cool

It is overcast as Manfried moves the bus from Grassau to the autobahn and on the way to Salzburg, in Austria.

There is no problem crossing the border, as these days, there are no borders.

The bus is left in the downtown parking area and a lady guide moves the group quickly through the crowded streets.

The Wescoombes soon realize that this efficient guide moves much too fast for their limited walking ability. Gina is always ready to suggest an alternative. She points out the entrance to the Stiftskeller, the classy restaurant where the Mozart dinner concert will be held this evening.

The Wescoombes, after examining the Peters Keller, including the second floor historic baroque hall, are seated by an attentive waiter in a favorable location.

Time is not important, so let's linger over cocktails, linger over soup, linger over salad, and linger longer over a luncheon entry for George costing 13.50 euros, and a luncheon entry for Nan costing 11.60 euros. The old folks have forgotten what they ate excepting that it was delicious. The total tab is 54.65 euro or about $63 U.S. Not bad for a two-hour lunch in this classy joint.

It is about time to leave when Janet and Bill arrive, after completing the guided walking tour. They join the Wescoombes for a continuation of the two-hour lunch. George and Nan are beginning to like this elaborate dining place. Nan finds a white wine to her liking, and George decides to sip on a couple of lemon beers.

The Reads join for snacks and drinks, and after another two hours, George is presented with a bill for another 41.00 euro or $47 U.S.; $110 is quite reasonable for lunch in such a quality establishment. Not only that, it kept Nan out of the dampness.

A look outside revealed the sun was peaking through, so a short stroll is in order. A couple of sunny benches were available nearby, one of which was partly occupied by an elderly individual.

Bill said hello and is immediately overwhelmed by the man's life history.

"Al" turns out to be an Austrian who was pressed into service in 1940 by Hitler and served as a mechanic in the Luftwaffe.

He suffered a shrapnel injury to his neck in 1943, which is still clearly visible. Upon recovery, instead of going back into service, he escaped, avoiding detection and capture by devious means, sometimes by the skin of his teeth, and ended up hiding, mainly in Austria. Now he carries a card, which identifies him as Alois Wratscko, Pensioner.

He expressed great admiration for the good things American Generals Collins and Clark did for the Austrian people.

Finally he ended hiding near where we are now, right near the Petershill. One of the waitresses became very friendly and brought him food, very good food, incidentally.

As soon as it was possible, they married and had a good life together. She died about 10 years ago.

Wratscko is eighty years old and has a high regard for Americans. He loves to practice his excellent English.

The entire party of 100 is treated to a Mozart dinner concert by Tom and Gina. It is right here on the program.

Listen to the sales brochure, it sounds expensive:

A seduction in music and the culinary arts in the stylish ambiance of the historic Baroque hall in the Stiftskeller St. Peter restaurant.

Enjoy the most popular compositions by W.A. Mozart by candlelight—with music played by Salzburg artists in historic costumes—and a multiple-course dinner, prepared according to traditional recipes from the 17th and 18th centuries.

Imagine the joy of living of Mozart's Salzburg with all its colorful costumes and its culinary joys let yourself be enchanted, be...a guest of Mozart. The first documented mention of the Stiftskeller St. Peter restaurant was in 803 on the occasion of Charlemagne's visit and, as the most ancient central European restaurant, it enjoys an excellent reputation in catering.

This place is indeed top drawer. George is glad he didn't have to pick up the tab for one hundred people.

We also drew one of the front row tables with Janet and Bill, Joy and Bill McCormack, and Al and Mary Ann Charlberg.

Salzburg's best violin sextet graces the stage and are probably making the finest music possible with violins. A colorfully dressed young soprano appears accompanied by a handsome 17th century baritone. They both sing beautifully while pretending to be in love.

As they stroll off the stage along with the orchestra, a swarm of waiters appear and immediately serve the soup course to the assemblage.

After a suitable wait, the orchestra returns, the same two singers entertain and the waiters return with another serving of delicious food.

Everything moves gracefully and effortlessly through three courses, tastefully presented by people who know what they are doing. After all, they have been in business since 803, which is quite a while ago.

The only reason George isn't a devotee of classical music is because he enjoys the Night Blooming Jazzmen more.

George has a front seat and the young soprano has a great slim body packed into a tight gown. When she fills and empties her lungs with the power necessary to hit the high notes, the muscles of her tummy ripple delightfully.

As it is a long walk from the hall to the bus park, the Wescoombes order a taxi and with the Reads, reach the parking area in a few minutes, even before the buses make it to that spot.

The folks at the Hotel Neutor, near to the bus park, are kind enough to allow us to use their lobby for protection against the chill. Thank you.

Eventually, the tour buses arrive and we are whisked back to Grassau.

DAY 10—Tuesday, October 7, 2003—Laufen—Cool, overcast

This is the time of year when one can almost feel the leaves about to burst into a riot of color. There is very much green in Bavaria all year long but now the leaves have a quince-yellow tinge around the edges.

George's daughter Lisa is a professional artist specializing in landscapes. George was hoping the leaves would turn so he could show off by describing to her the magenta, vermilion, the burnt orange, and also the dark reds if there is any maple in this part of the world.

Lisa would say, "Cool it, Daddy, you don't know blue from green and you know it."

"Yes, but if one is a writer, all he has to do is write the words, not paint the colors."

In thirty-five miles, we passed, at least, five towns with about 3-4 thousand inhabitants each. The area between the towns seemed to be about one-half bush and one-half cultivated land or pasture. Everything is clean, neat, orderly as though put in position by design. Each town has a church. We are told the population in Bavaria is one-third Catholic, one-third Protestant, and one-third Muslim, also, as if by design.

The roads are somewhat narrow; tour buses have to pass carefully.

The houses are generally square or rectangular, two-story with usually a red-tile roof. There is a balcony at the top of the lower story generally along one or two sides. The balcony is completely fronted by a flower box, which is covered by the brightest flowers available.

We must remember that in a month or so the whole place will be covered by snow and ice. The summertime makes things brighter to the eye, unless you are a figure skater, hockey player, or a skier.

The houses appear very solid. It would take a strong wind to shake one of these babies. I am wondering if the flowers are taken inside in the winter. I remember when I was a boy in Canada, my grandpa would take all the geraniums into the house, when the cold weather came.

There is not much new construction in this part of Bavaria. We are talking about rather a small area; say, between Munich and Salzburg.

One notices considerable space between the houses say 15-20 feet, not jammed together as the new developments are in California.

Let's call the houses sturdy rather than stylish. The bus soon reaches the charming village of Reit im Winkl, which is well known for excellent shopping and good prices.

George and Nan are at that stage of life when they are disposing rather than accumulating. A cursory glance reveals many interesting object d'art but all the Wescoombes bought was a $40 summer sport shirt for George marked down to $18. There are not many shoppers from Palm Springs buying clothes in Bavaria.

It is time for Manfried to move bus number one to the Salsach River where the cities of Laufen in Bavaria and Oendorf in Germany are joined by a picturesque bridge built in 1903.

Lunch is at an Italian restaurant on the riverbank, which features an eight-year-old boy playing an accordion. It reminds George of the time he owned, but did not play, an accordion when he was a youngster. After two months, he gave up and sold the accordion at a profit.

The food was excellent, Janet enjoyed lasagna and the others thick, tasty soup, a meal in itself. Bill walked across the bridge to visit Austria, but it was too far for old George, so he stayed in Bavaria. Bill examined a famous old Austrian church and pronounced it still usable, as it was full of people. He said it was the usual--A.D.C.

Laufen is an upscale town with fine goods for sale at reasonable prices. The tour ladies were in their glory, snapping up bargains to take back to the U.S.A. for Christmas presents, maybe.

Dinner is scheduled at the Cloister (it used to be just that) at 5:30 p.m. George spots a fancy ice-cream store and insists ice cream should be an extension of his lunch. He polished off a banana split, the rest had cones.

The town of Laufen is flooded with large posters advertising Dixie Night mit den Night Blooming Jazzmen (U.S.A.) at the Salzach Halle at 8:00 p.m. For those German speaking people who read my narratives, here is the advertising:

Di., 07.10., 20 Uhr Salzach Laufen Halle

Dixie Night mit den Night Blooming Jazzmen

Direkt aus Claremont, California, USA kommt diese Dixie-Gruppe, die schon auf so ziemlich allen namhaften amerikanischen Jazz-Festivals gespielt hat. Seit nunmehr 25 Jahren begeistern die "Night Bloomers" ihr Publikum. Nur für zwei Wochen touren sie durch "Good Old Europe" und machen dabei Station in der Salzachhalle. Bandleader Chet Jaeger ist bekannt für seinen trockenen Humor, was jeden Auftritt der siebenköpfigen Gruppe nicht nur zum musikalischen Erlebnis, sondern auch sehr unterhaltsam macht. In Amerika gelten sie als eine der beliebtesten Dixie-Bands aller Zeiten. Karten Sind im Vorverkauf zu 10, - bei unseren Vorverkaufsstellen (siehe Seite 1) erhältlich. An der Abendkasse kostet die Karte 12, -.

Veranstalter: Salzachhalle Laufen

George knows it is our group as there are pictures of the zany zeven in English, all over town.

The Salzach Halle is next to the Cloister, so it will be dinner then music. As the German folks are paying to hear the band and we get in free, Tom and Gina suggested that we let the paying people in first. Good thinking, we should let people know that some Americans have manners.

In order to get the audience's attention and to let them know they are serious, the band explodes with Larry drumming his way through "Millenburg Joys." That starts the heads bobbing and feet tapping. Everyone is awake.

"It Don't Mean a Thing If It Ain't Got That Swing" is a catchy old thing that had a long run. The Maniacs "Swing" their way along, with an innovative touch. The front line guys vocalize, do-op, do-op, do-op in various places. The crowd gives generous applause, so they are with it.

The Bavarians do not know the words to the American Jazz tunes, but they certainly know the melody, and rhythm. George has forgotten the words to "Doing the Raccoon," "Panama Rag," "Strutting With Some Barbecue," and "Butter and Egg Man," but the audience is cheering, and cheering, and cheering. They certainly love American Dixieland jazz as played by Chet Jaeger and The Night Blooming Jazz Band.

DAY 11—Wednesday, October 8, 2003—Iffy, overcast

Wonders will never cease. This is a day-off day.

Tom and Gina have been working us so hard to make sure we get our money's worth, I go to bed each night exhausted

We are surprised they do not have a dance scheduled each evening from 10:00 p.m. to one o'clock.

What shall I write about, as we do not have the usual bus ride to somewhere? Does Manfred get a day off?

I have been accumulating notes. You never know when something may become interesting or important.

The Germans have a good name for the city hall—it's the Rathaus.

If something is good, the Germans often call it "bad."

The three major religions in Germany are divided—one-third Catholic—one-third Protestant—one-third Moslem.

Many words in the German language have more than ten letters. Maybe more is better.

On Beck's bottle—beer is bier, Birra, Biere,—cerveza.

They drink so much beer in Munich, the prayer books have handles.

Normal Bavarian beer is light beer—Ein Helles—slightly less potent than the beer in North Germany, France, and England.

Beck's beer is dark beer. Ein dunkles.

Russa—Weiss—Wheat beer with lemonade

The autobahn—built in 1935—Munich to Salzburg

Aus fahrt—on. Ein fahrt—off.

Most 18-wheel trucks in Germany have soft sides, probably tarpaulins.

Signs over lanes tell trucks if they may use that lane.

The airline people must take a nap after serving a meal, then pick up the dishes an hour later, leaving the passengers entrapped by dishes just at the time when they need to get out of their seat.

There is still some space remaining. Let's spell out the names of the stars of this narrative.

The Night Blooming Jazzmen:

Leader—Professor Chet Jaeger – cornet

George Olson – string bass

Dick Doner – trombone

Jim Richardson – reeds

Larry Kostka – drums

Vinny Armstrong – piano

Lance MacLean – guitar

636 Alamosa Drive, Claremont, CA 91711 – 909-626-1771

DAY 12—Thursday, October 9, 2003—Rattenberg—Overcast, showers

The destination today is Rattenberg, literally translated, The City of Rats. Not that we expect to see any of the hideous pests.

Even with an overcast sky bearing down on us, Rattenberg is an utterly beautiful, very small Austrian town. Our guide is a pleasant lady, who walks and talks too fast for old George. George is going to give up and turn the background over to the excellent guidebook.

Rattenberg, the smallest town in Austria with 500 residents, is situated in the middle of the Lower Inn Valley. Rattenberg with its completely unspoiled, romantic streets and alleys, bay-windowed houses with marble doorways nestles between the River Inn and the castle ruin. Beautiful churches and recently the Augustinian Museum are some of the sights. Rattenberg is also famous as a glass blowing and glass cutting centre.

Rattenberg is first mentioned between 1000 and 1100. Around the mid-13th C. the Dukes of Bavaria set up a customs station here. Later it developed into a settlement that received its town charter in 1393. Shipping on the Inn provided the most important transport artery into the 19th C. All ships had to pay tolls in Rattenberg. The town became very wealthy through the silver and copper mines nearby which were run by the Fuggers. Rattenberg's importance began to wain with the building of roads and the railway (1858). In 1632 Claudia de Medici had a glassworks built here. In the Bavarian Wars of Succession 1504-1506 Rattenberg, Kufstein and Kitzbühel were ceded to the Tyrol, in other words, to the House of Habsburg. Unfortunately, the castle earned itself an infamous reputation as a prison and place of execution for Anabaptists. In the year 1651 Claudia de Medici's chancellor, Dr. Wilhelm Biener, was also executed here. His official pardon was deliberately held up by his enemies and only passed on later, so that this noble servant had to die on the scaffold in the castle courtyard. 1782 marked the end of the castle's role as a fortress.

On a warm sunny day, dining outside on the main street would have been enjoyable. The downtown buildings are very modern for their time period, maybe 150 years ago. Almost all lower windows are bedecked with flower boxes, as the rain has not as yet become snow. A foot of snow under foot would not be pleasant.

This little town is nestled alongside the Inn River. George wonders if the river freezes and if the citizens skate in bright costumes along the shoreline. It would be fun to watch them from inside a bar or coffeehouse.

As a young man George worked as an accountant for a glass bottle manufacturing company in Canada and is basically familiar with the production of glass. Rattenberg is famous for glass blowing and glass cutting but the taxi driver didn't know what George was talking about. Of course, George was talking English, as he was not able to find Tom or Gina.

The town parish church of St. Virgil, dating back to 1473-1507 is built of local marble and is as good as new, as are the magnificent sculptures and exquisite frescoes. George thinks that if he lived in Rattenberg and was a Catholic, he would spend an hour a week in the church and donate a few euros.

It is really a most delightful village nestled between the river and mountains. George can imagine a golf course in the picture.

Believe it or not, Rattenberg is famous for something very new and modern. Rattenberg rocked the skateboarding community by introducing the world to the first concrete "cradle" a perfect radius capsule with a quarter sphere dome.

Rattenberg's skateboard park has generated tremendous international coverage, including multiple web sites focused entirely upon its existence, such as http://www.skatethecradle.com/

There is a special concert tonight at Hotel Hansback. Grassau grade school music department will strut their stuff for an hour of big band music. Followed by the Jazzmen playing big band music if they have enough big band tunes to last an hour.

The Teachers are decked out in their formals and look real spiffy as a big band should do. Their sixteen-person unit includes four ladies who add a touch of class.

The Teachers are on stage first and start off on the right foot with a solid rendition of Artie Shaw's "Begin the Beguine." The clarinet and tenor men have listened to Shaw's recording intently.

The five-person sax section blends nicely as they swing through Glen Miller's "Tuxedo Junction." Even Miller's trombone can be heard.

Count Basie's "One O'clock Jump" is a little ragged, but Basie's band occasionally was ragged. The trumpet man had trouble soloing like Buck Clayton. As a matter of fact, who doesn't?

The Teachers are performing very well and the crowd is enjoying their work as evidenced by the spontaneous applause.

The Teachers decide to slow the tempo and "As Time Goes By" seemed as though it was never going to go by. It must be more difficult to play slowly as a 16-person unit.

"Stomping at the Savoy" was recorded by many big bands. George cannot identify which band the Teachers are emulating, but they are doing a first-rate job.

All in all, the Teachers are very entertaining.

The Night Blooming boys are also dressed up as their magical music fills the air.

The startling cornet of our leader sets the tone on "Muskrat Ramble" which begins and ends on a high note.

This is big band night so the lovely ballad "Love Letters in the Sand", sung by Jim, fits right in.

Dick is in good voice as usual and his encore asks "What's New?" It is not an easy piece of music, with a couple of chord changes, but Dick is a master.

The whole band keeps the house jumping with exuberant renditions of "Little Rock Getaway," "Joe Avery," and the raucous "St. Louis Blues."

To prove they can play the smooth, gliding stuff, the Jazzmen continue with "Don't Forget Our Sunday Date," "You took Advantage of Me," and while you are at it, "Squeeze Me."

Jim, the reed specialist, thrills the crowd with "Stomping at the Savoy" played on alto and tenor sax at the same time. How does he do that?

The hardworking musicians are still producing "The Sound of Jazz" but George is too tired to continue. These are long days. Good night.

DAY 13—Friday, October 10, 2003—WeisKirche, Neuschwanstein, and Oberammergau

The tour bus will take the group to three locations today. So there will be mucho driving.

The first location is that of a special church known as the WeisKirche, or as Bill is wont to say, A.D.C., another damn church.

The church stands on a mound or hill about 100 yards from level ground, which means the building is elevated about 30 yards. It is a spectacular edifice and George made it inside the church after two rest stops.

The main reason he climbed the small hill was because the sun has appeared and it is a very pretty day, and the church looks nice—so there.

This is how the tour book starts:

A masterpiece of Bavarian Rococo, the WeisKirche stands amid the forests, meadows, and peat bogs whose gentle undulations characterize the final slopes of the Ammergau Alps the Lech and the Ammer. Designed by Dominikus Zimmermann (1685-1766), one of the most gifted members of the Wessobrunn School, who was entrusted with the task of building this pilgrimage church "in der Weis" (in the meadow), and dedicated to Jesus Scourged. The focal point, as in the earlier edifice, was an oval cupola, which lent itself to painted decorations and emphasized the Rococo approach.

George made his way, eventually, to the front of the inside of the church and looked up and back as all were told to do in order to see the gates of heaven. The artists have done amazing work on the entire ceiling and there are certainly gates splendidly painted on the ceiling but there is not a sign on the gate reading "heaven."

The statue of Jesus, crying real tears, had been given away. That's hard to believe, they should have gotten big bucks for that statue.

While we are in the church the sun disappeared and the stupid drizzle returned.

The bus doesn't mind rain. The next stop is at the castle, Neuschwanstein, and we have moved out of the rain area.

The advertising doesn't do justice to this "Fairytale" castle. The castle is about half a mile up in the air and as there is no transportation up close, George will never see it "up close."

Here's a little professional blurbage:

Neuschwanstein Castle, Germany

This is King Ludwig's magnificent and most famous castle, built in the neo-late Romanesque style. With its turrets and mock-medievalism, its interior styles ranging from Byzantine through Romanesque to Gothic it's a real fairy-tale fantasy come true. It was built between 1869 and 1886 for the Bavarian King Ludwig II. A splendid and imaginative "Fairy-tale castle" high above the Alpsee lake with the Alps towering above it.

Tour buses are not allowed to transverse the road up to the castle. The castle people have their own buses. Most of the group, including Nan, Bill, and Janet pay 8 euros each to be taken somewhere near the castle.

George and other folks who are disadvantaged stay behind in the little town, which has cafes, bars, stores, etc. Not a bad place to wait for an hour and a half on a nice day.

The resourceful castle people have four carts holding eight people each pulled by four horses each continually walking to another level about half way to the castle and back down again.

George can't resist and spends five dollars for a ride to the next level. It takes about fifteen minutes for the horses to do their work. There is a restaurant, a bar, and a store at this level. George has never had a pancake stuffed with bacon before, but it works with a Beck's beer.

In half an hour, George grabs a cart and pays two-fifty to come back down. This time he is lucky. He takes one of the two remaining seats. The next passenger is a pretty Oriental girl. Nosey George asks, "Are you from China?" With a radiant smile, she replies, "No, I'm from L.A. I'm on my honeymoon." George, looking around, "Where is your husband?" "He's in the back row, it was the only seat left." "Maybe I should trade with him." "Don't bother, it's only a few minutes." "Well, I should thank him anyway."

George heads for the bus parking area and there is Nan noticeably distressed.

Evidently when the castle bus reaches a certain point, there are still 170 steps remaining to the castle. Nan couldn't climb 170 more steps, so she turned back to a bridge across a deep gorge where others were taking pictures.

The best view of the castle and a 45m waterfall is from the nearby Mary's Bridge (Marienbruecke), which spans a deep gorge. On the path between this bridge and the castle is a wonderful view of Hohenschwangau and the Alpsee. Guided tours take about 35 minutes. You have to walk 170 steps up and down, a lift is not available.

Nan got somewhat lost and it was a tough walk for 20 minutes down to the bus park. No where was it made known beforehand that old people would have to climb 170 steps.

Anyway, she made it safely and a couple of glasses of wine helped her regain her composure. It has been a long day and we still have to visit the woodcarving village of Oberammergau.

By the time we reach this interesting city, the miniature train that runs the mile from the car park to the carving village has finished its work for the day, and is closed down.

A little thing like a mile walk does not deter lady shoppers.

Nan, still a good flat walker, makes the trek with Janet and Bill to the stores but does not buy anything.

George is happy to find a bench and is contentedly dozing when the others return an hour later.

The trip is so late, the group go directly to dinner.

After eating, the Wescoombes go directly to bed.

DAY 14—Saturday, October 11, 2003—Warm

This morning is free for last minute shopping, packing, and maybe a late leisurely breakfast and/or lunch. George thinks breakfast has been the best meal of each and every day.

The Night Blooming Jazzmen are treating the tour group to a request concert at 2:00 p.m. this afternoon. Some of the folks have been enjoying the Jazzmen for many years and have favorite selections. In fact, the band issues a blurb periodically letting the folks know when their upcoming concerts are scheduled and where.

After each concert, much of the recorded work of the N.B.J. is available for immediate purchase. There are records, tapes, CDs—probably a few 78s and 45s.

The band opens with the "Original Dixie One Step" in order to raise everyone's blood pressure.

"It Don't Mean a Thing If It Ain't Got That Swing," "How High the Moon," and the "Song of India." Everyone knows the gamut of tunes so let them roll along.

This is the last concert and the musicians are in fine fettle. A couple of the tour members sing with the band and do a fine job. George knows Kathy but not the male vocalist. Evidently they had filled in on prior occasions.

All checked baggage must be in the lobby by 5:00 p.m. in order to be ready for transfer to the buses.

Tom and Gina have a gimmick, which has become a favorite of their tours. When all are assembled for dinner, a microphone is passed around so everyone may tell what feature of the tour pleased them the most.

Of course, the Jazzmen drew the most plaudits, followed by the good work of Tom and Gina. Many of the folks came up with humorous remarks, too numerous to mention.

George's favorite was the lady who said, "The toilet paper was the softest she had ever experienced."

German money is more valuable than that of the good old U.S.A., now the toilet paper is better, so there is no doubt we are becoming a third world country.

George told the folks that this "Whimsical Narrative" would be available for the asking, in about a month.

Dinner was served by the regular young ladies, expeditiously as usual.

Tom put two baskets, in plain view, so the folks could contribute to the servers, bus boys at both the Sperrer Hotel and Hansback Hotel. After contributing, the Wescoombes left early and made the Hansback without the aid of "Uschi" and her new car. Thanks anyway, "Uschi."

DAY 15—Sunday, October 12, 2003—Munich to LAX—Sunny

This is getaway day. Breakfast is scheduled for 6:00 a.m. The bus leaves Grassau at 8:00 a.m. for Munich airport. Flight 452-Lufthansa, scheduled to leave Munich at 11:15 a.m. to LAX—scheduled arrival in Los Angeles 2:30 p.m.

Our major bags left Room 204, yesterday at 5:00 p.m. Hopefully they are on the bus ready to accompany us to Munich airport. Those are things the Wescoombes take for granted.

Plenty of time for a leisurely breakfast and good-byes to new friends. Nan always thinks of the girls who make the beds and clean the room. For 14 days she leaves them $28.

George talks to the waitresses more than the maids, so they received $30 last evening. One of the maids, Uschi, received extra dough as she drove the Wescoombes from the Sperrer Hotel to the Hansback Hotel on dark and damp nights, a distance of 400 yards in her new BMW. George thinks Uschi likes him as one evening all of a sudden, she asked, "How old are you, anyway?" He told her the truth—too old.

The airport in Munich is brand spanking new, modern in every respect. For some reason, it doesn't seem crowded. On the second level, a wheel chair appeared for George. The in-charge lady moved us with dispatch from check-in to check-in. A couple of times a slowdown occurred but not for long. Even the inspection did not take long. However, something ingenious occurred as we approached the loading gate area, a second inspection occurred. This was speedy and thorough. As soon as the inspectors were through, we ended up in the boarding area never to return to the moving around area again. The wheelchair lady did not enter the final boarding area. She was happy with ten dollars and left. We all found seats and boarded smoothly and quickly.

There must have been fifty folks from the tour on the flight. George is wondering why we are scattered throughout the cabin, as very few are seated with their spouse. George is seated beside a nice lady, Jean, from the tour, and Nan is about five rows ahead. It is a twelve or so hour flight but we will have to put up with the oddity. The tickets were purchased many weeks before departure time. Maybe Lufthansa likes to mix up Americans.

It was a smooth flight, arriving at LAX just about on time and the Super Shuttle moved us to Bill and Janet's house only a little late. Nothing is ever on time. The important thing is to get there.

And daughter Marnie is waiting in front of 860 Glenwood Circle, Fullerton, CA, ready to drive us to the desert.

Thanks, Janet and Bill, it was a wonderful adventure. Thanks, also to Tom and Gina Crisp for giving us so much.

Nan is enhancing the scenery in Bavaria.

THE

MISSISSIPPI

FROM

THE SOURCE TO THE GULF

FEATURING

THE GREAT FLOOD 1993

This narrative relates The adventurers of two odd and old fictitious couples, George Wescoombe and his wife Nan, and Barclay Allan and his wifey Juney, on a recent motor trip.

Juney is George's young sister which makes Nan and Juney, sisters-in-law, Barclay and George, brothers-in-law and Nan, Barclay's sister-in-law and Barclay, Nan's brother-in-law or thereabouts.

Any resemblance to anyone living or dead is purely coincidental.

D. Wesley Coombe

PROLOGUE

It's the middle of January 1993 and Nan and George Wescoombe are at the condo of George's sister, Juney Allan, and her husband Barclay in Florida. This visit is one of a long series of enjoyable annual events.

Juney and Barclay will be married fifty years this coming summer.

Barclay says, "We would like to take a trip with you folks this summer, if possible. You have been almost everywhere in the world, what do you suggest?"

George replies, "A trip to England or a cruise anywhere would fill the bill."

Barclay admitted, "I was in the Navy for three years and was sick every day, so more than a day on the water is too much for me." Juney admitted that just thinking about flying to England made her nervous.

"That leaves only a motor trip unless we can get on a submarine," George summarized.

Barclay said, "We are glad you agree. I love to drive and we could take our car. Any suggestions as to where we could go?

The Wescoombes had wanted, for some time, to drive from the source of the Mississippi in Northern Minnesota all the way to the Gulf staying as close to the river as possible. The Allans agreed that suited them fine. Barclay wanted to know how long it would take.

George said, "It's about 2500 miles so at 125 miles per day, it would take about 20 days. We would have to slow you down. You could do the whole trip in four days. "

Barclay thought he would like to take his time, stay off the freeways, and stop at small towns.

Juney and Nan, avid Bridge players, suggested that Bridge could be played every evening. "We would love to trounce you guys each day."

George summarized, "We will have the longest floating Bridge game in the world, drive about 175 miles per day, play some golf, take day cruises on the river when available, and no freeways.

All agreed and George was appointed to determine the dates for departure, "It' s so damn hot in Indian Wells in July and August, you can be sure we will want to be some where else, so it will be sometime in those months.

On February 27, 1993, George and Nan sent the following letter to the Allan's.

Dear Juney and Barclay:

You have probably been thinking that I have been ignoring our Mississippi adventure, in favor of the India, Nepal trip. Not so, I am quite able to think about both. What follows is a "First Pass" Itinerary.

Day 1 *MSP to Itasca State Park - where Miss. begins This is by freeway - Stay Bemidji*
250 miles

Day 2 *Bemidji to Brainerd - St. Cloud*
125 miles

Day 3 *Brainerd - St. Cloud to MPLS*
125 miles

Day 4 *MPLS*

Day 5 *MPLS to Lacrosse*
185 miles

Day 6 *Lacrosse to Dubuque*
185 miles

Day 7 *Dubuque to Keokuk*
190 miles

Day 8 *Keokuk to Hannibal*
70 miles

Day 9 *St. Louis*
120 miles

Day 10 *St. Louis to ½ way Carruthersville*
125 miles

Day 11 *Carruthersville*
125 miles

Day 12 *Carruthersville to Memphis*
180 miles

Day 13 *Memphis*

Day 14 *Memphis to Greenville*
190 miles

Day 15 *Greenville - 1/2 way to N.O.*
175 miles

Day 16 1/2 *way to N.O. to N.O.*
175 miles

Day 17 *N. O. to Gulf and back*
200 miles

Day 18 *N.O.*

Day 19 *N.O.*

2,520 miles

Average 180 miles per day for 14 driving days, 5 city days

All of the foregoing is tentative and approximate. I still have a great deal of interesting work to do. You could follow the trip on the map and come up with suggestions and revisions.

I won't be doing any more until we return from India, near the end of March. Please let us know when you go back to Canada. There are many, many details to be worked out but we have lots of time.

It looks like approx. July 22 for a start date from M/SP. Juney said she wanted to go part July, part August.

Approx. cost will be as follows:

19 nights at $48 average	*$900*
food, drinks, etc.	*1,000*
misc. expenses	*400*
	$2,300
gas, etc., one-half	*200*
	$2,500

We can add or subtract days or add side trips as we go along.

We will both have the cost of getting to MSP and back from N. O. But this is at least something to think about. Don't hesitate to say if it is too much or too little.

Love you both,
George and Nan

In March there were reports of flooding along the "M" due to excessive rain and run-off but it seemed to have subsided by May.

On May 16, 1993, the Wescoombes wrote to the Allans as follows:

Dear Juney and Barclay:

Moving forward to our expedition, a gigantic step has been accomplished.

You suggested I should block out the time for the trip, so here goes. We will leave L.A. 7:00AM on Northwest flight 302 and arrive in MStPaul at 12:00 noon on Thursday, July 22.

We hope you will be waiting for us at the airport and that we can drive the same day to Itasca State Park for the night, about 200 miles, so we may start our sight-seeing the next day as per the schedule we already sent to you.

We also hope you will take us to the airport in New Orleans on Tuesday, August 10 to catch Southwest flight 1449 to L.A. at 11:10 AM.

As you will be driving and using your car, we suggest we pay for all the gas.

You will have to plan the time required, Hamilton to MStPaul for the meet on July 22 and also the time required N.O. to wherever you wish to go after you get rid of us.

We sure hope this adventure is a success. We are counting on the enjoyment of your company, Bridge, Scrabble, Good Morning Americas, some golf, and many laughs. So the trip is secondary to the company.

Love you both,
George and Nan

Several telcons followed, in which Barclay refused to accept the Wescoombes offer to pay for the gasoline. It was agreed to eat only one large meal per day preferably at noon to avoid further obesity. It was also agreed that all were too old for nightlife so a dawn to dusk schedule was approved. Juney thought this was great as it would leave more time for Bridge.

Barclay suggested that he continue his custom of preparing "Good Morning Americas" (vodka and orange juice) each morning. Nobody opposed that suggestion.

Heavy rain had started all along the northern "M" valley at the time the next letter was written on June 18, 1993.

Dear Juney and Barclay:

It's getting closer and we are so excited. Nan has had an epidermal block, which means a shot of cortisone in her lower back and is about 75% better. Another shot is due next Thursday which if like the first would make her 150% better. We hope.

I suppose it's time to start discussing details.

We will stay at a hotel in L.A. on Wednesday night July 21, so we will be in position to catch Northwest Air, flight 302, at 7 AM Thursday morning, July 22.

We are to arrive at MPLS/StPaul at 12:20 PM, just after noon.

It would be nice if you could pick us up at that time so we could begin our 250-mile trip north to Grand Rapids or Bemidji where the "M" starts.

I will make room reservations in one of those towns for Thursday, July 22 night. It's nice to be sure for the first night. Then we can slowly but surely wind our way along the "M" all the way to the Gulf--sounds good.

After you pick us up, maybe we could drive an hour out of MPLS/StPaul on Hwy. 94 and then stop for lunch and to reconnoiter, whatever that means.

Usually when we travel with our family, we have rules and you are family.

RULES

1. ***Money.*** *We estimate $2,000 per couple for all the things we do jointly, like motels, food, gas, exhibits, fees, etc.*

   We propose Barclay be pilot and Treasurer. We will give Barclay $500 and he can put in $500 if he wishes, and he pays everything until the $1,000 is gone. Then we replenish. Sounds easy. We will probably need $400-$500 extra for personal things, but that is not mandatory. Of course, if the ladies decide to buy a pair of $100 earrings each, then each of the guys have to wear a pair, also, to keep things even.

2. ***Motels.*** *We propose that George be Vice President and navigator. He will be responsible for picking out motels in the average of $50 per night. Barclay can then, as Treasurer, go in and make a deal. Mostly ground floor, with senior discount. Anyone who doesn't like George's choices can have the job.*

   George will make arrangements for good weekend rates in the cities.

3. ***Food.*** *Juney as President and Nan as her Assistant*

will be in charge of picking out places to eat. This is a three time a day job. Anyone who doesn't like the places Juney chooses can go hungry.

4. ***Clothes.*** *Attached is a list of suggestions, one for the ladies and one for the men.*

5. ***Luggage.*** *It is suggested that each couple have one suit case plus each person may have his make-up kit. The pilot is in charge of storing the luggage and no one may interfere or their stuff will be left behind.*

6. ***Golf.*** *It is suggested that the Allans bring one of their large bags with clubs for both inside. The Wescoombes will bring one small carry-on golf bag with maybe 4-5 clubs and will use the Allans' clubs if the Allans will let them.*

7. ***Games.*** *The Allans will bring cards, score cards for Bridge and Euchre. The Wescoombes will bring a Scrabble board. Nan and Juney should bring a lotta money to pay for their losses.*

8. ***Laundry.*** *About every 5th day in some small town while we are having drinks or dinner. This is a fun job, so lets put Nan in charge. Don't forget you can wash and dry things in the hotel room, in necessary.*

9. *Everyone is responsible for their own glasses, cameras, hearing aids, false teeth, etc. Don't expect the Treasurer to buy you new sunglasses.*

10. ***Music.*** *Each traveler is allowed to bring 4 tapes only, which will be played in rotation by the pilot. All the tapes must be played, even if obnoxious, so bring earplugs. If someone wants more, bring your own Walkman.*

11 The Navigator is responsible for anything not on this list. Please let him know what is missing.

The above looks like a good start. We will call you in a few days for comments and suggestions.

Love you both,
Nan and George

MENS' CLOTHES

1 pair good slacks
1 good jacket, foldable
1 pair good shirts
2 pairs wash & wear pants
2 pairs wash & wear shorts
5 wash & wear shirts
2 wash & wear tee shirts
5 pairs underwear - sexy
5 wash & wear sox - misc.
1 pair P.J. 's
2 pairs hats
1 pair reasonable shoes
2 pairs casual shoes--good for golf

All the above will pack in one half suitcase.

Juney--I'm already getting the rules and was told to make out a list of clothes, something 1 never do. Usually just leave a suitcase handy and drop in anything that looks useful and washable.

Will wear pants to travel on the plane (of course) might throw in a polyester dress in case we eat in some exclusive restaurant.

List as follows:

2 knit pants
2 slacks--1 white--1 black 2 shorts or culottes
1 sweater
1 nylon jacket
3 bras - 2 P.J. 's
1 It rain cape that has traveled everywhere and never worn white shoes -- I'll be wearing tennis shoes. flats

Nan

On July 10, 1993, George wrote a letter to the Wescoombe family outlining the upcoming trip. This was his usual custom. The Allan's were included in the mailing.

Dear Family and Allans:

So you will be aware of what we are planning to do on our upcoming trip:

Wed., July 21 *- Hacienda Hotel, 525 N. Sepulveda. Leaving old car there until Tues., Aug. 10.*

Thurs., July 22 *– Northwest flight 302, 7 AM to MSP. Arriving at 12:20 where we will be picked up by Barclay and Juney. Travelling in Barclay's car from MPLS north to Bemidji, Minn where we stay at Comfort Inn on July 22, 218-751-7700.*

We will wend our way along the big "M" (Really Big "M") wherever possible, in short stages, with unpredictable stops, all the way to the Gulf and back to New Orleans from where we depart Tues., Aug. 10 at 11:16 AM on Southwest flight 1449, arriving L.A. at 3:45 AM. The flood will make the trip more interesting for us, not for the poor folks who live there.

Barclay will be the driver in his car. We have no fixed schedule from July 22 to Aug. 10. Just a lazy summer like we used to do, Good Morning Americas, Bridge, euchre, scrabble, beer, wine, golf, flies, mosquitoes, history, cruises on the river and Barclay's jokes. I know and believe that something outstanding will happen every day.

Love to all,
George and Nan

As the Taoist philosopher, Sun Tzu, said, **"Be prepared and you will have Good Luck."**

We are prepared.

DAY 1 - WEDNESDAY, JULY 21, 1993

L.A. - Sunny, 85°

The Wescoombes have a leisurely three-hour drive from Indian Wells to the Hacienda Hotel in Los Angeles near to LAX.

The Hacienda has a large parking lot where one can leave his car for a week free, as part of the hotel rate. Days in excess of seven are charged at a fee of two dollars per day. The Hacienda has a bus to the airport every fifteen minutes and will also pick-up and return customers to the parking lot if they phone when they arrive.

Daughter Bette, granddaughter Pat and Bette's friend George arrive at the Hacienda about 6 o'clock to have dinner with the Wescoombes.

Pat Burke reveals that she is moving to Boise, Idaho, to attend Boise State full-time, in order to get her degree in a couple of years. She is through with getting an education in bits and pieces. Good girl Pat, let's just do it.

Bette is her usual busy self, happy with all her activities, including George.

George entertains with tales of his movie career. He really is a talented individual and it would be great if he could land a speaking part. Someday it will happen, for sure.

Early to bed for the Wescoombes as they must take the 6 AM conveyance to LAX to catch their 7 AM flight to MPLS.

DAY 2 -THURSDAY, JULY 22,1993

L.A. to St. Cloud, Minn. - Rain in MPLS.

Code - Mississippi - "M" Minneapolis - M.P.L.S.

The Wescoombes were ready to leave for LAX on the Hotel Hacienda bus at 6:00 AM to be on time for Northwest flight 302 leaving at 7:00 AM for MPLS/StPaul.

Smooth transfer from the bus, through check-in, and on to the 757 which departs the gate promptly at 7 AM.

Immediately after take-off, Nan, a very experienced flyer, told George about a strange noise that she thought she heard. George was half-asleep by then and replied that aircraft are always making strange noises, same as he does.

The captain is trying to get to cruising altitude but the 757 is swooping up and down like a big bird, playing games. After about twenty minutes the captain announces that one of the flaps on the right-side wing is stuck in a closed position and that he has been advised to return to L.A. for repairs.

When a flight manages to leave at its appointed time, as this one did, "Something untoward is bound to happen." That's Coombe's Law, whoever he is.

By 8 AM we are back in L.A. airport, lined up at a special Northwest counter, 200 deep, waiting to be reassigned to another flight. Nan finds a comfortable spot with the newspaper and her book, while George patiently stands about thirtieth in line.

There is considerable complaining in line but there is nothing that can be done by anyone except Northwest personnel. Really, it's not Northwest's fault that a Boeing aircraft developed a fault. Northwest is in such poor financial shape, everyone having taken a 10 percent pay cut, that maybe the people who inspect the planes before departure only do a 90% inspection. George hopes they didn't cut the pay of the guys who drive these things, as it would not be nice to land 10% short of the destination.

Northwest started the reassignment process with only one clerk who would have taken at least 10 hours to finish, but after one-half hour they increased the clerkage to four.

George finally managed to appear in front of a nice young lady who read him his options. There was another Northwest flight out of L.A. at 11:30 but it was now full. Some option.

There were Northwest flights from Orange County

and Ontario also leaving at 11:30 and arriving in MPLS at 5:00 PM, four hours and forty minutes later than the scheduled arrival time of flight 302. Buses were available to transfer the reassigned folks to their choice of O.C. or Ontario.

George suggests that he might stay overnight in L.A. and take the same 7:00 AM flight the next day. The lady is happy with that until George suggests maybe payment for a hotel and meals would be in order. She counters with, "We can't do that, Northwest has no money. All of us took a pay cut."

George knows there is going to be a long wait in any event so he requests an audience with her supervisor. The supervisor says, "We do not have to pay for your hotel and meals if we have alternate flights, which we have. "

George counters, "Regulations say you have to get us to our destination within three hours of our original arrival time. "

The man doesn't know whether George is right or not but tells the girl, "Give the man a hotel and meal voucher."

That was too easy so George reconsiders as the Allans are waiting at MPLS airport and they may have a problem. George agrees to leave from Orange County. Northwest will page the Allans telling them the Wescoombes' new arrival time. George knows that Barclay is an experienced traveler and probably already is aware that Flight 302 has been canceled.

George has at least two more options. He could have tried for a free ticket to anywhere but Northwest could be out-of-business before he used it. If Nan had been in 100% shape and able to stand in line, George would have scurried around and maybe found another airline which could have taken the Wescoombes to MPLS/StPaul within 3 hours. Northwest would have been bound to accept the transfer, thus losing a fare.

But why kick someone when they're down. A few years ago the Wescoombes had a great flight on Northwest,

L.A. to Tokyo and return. They were upgraded to business class and had seats in the bubble on the 747.

Our driver on the conveyance from L.A. to Orange County is an attractive, outgoing, black lady named Marcie with an outstanding sense of humor. Obviously she likes her work and covered the 50-minute trip in 45 minutes. Our country needs more people like Marcie.

John Wayne Airport in Orange County is about two years old and has a capacity about 10 times its needs. It is a beautiful facility and a pleasure to use as it is like having an airport all to oneself.

John Wayne lived in Newport Beach and was one of the most vociferous complainers about the noise of the aircraft in and out of the airport. The authorities got even with John by naming the new airport after him. Wherever he is, he probably doesn't give a damn, frankly.

The authorities (don't you love them) made one concession to the rich folk in Newport Beach. The aircraft are required to fly almost straight up and down when arriving or departing John Wayne Airport, thus minimizing the amount of noise, or so they think.

Those reassigned from Flight 302 are further inconvenienced by having to fill up those usually unwanted center seats in the row of three. George and Nan are seated a row apart but George is able to continually gaze at her beautiful blonde hair. What a lucky guy.

The lady with the drink cart asks George for his preference. Northwest has got off so light that George suggested that he may be entitled to a free Crown Royal. The lady said she would ask her supervisor. She immediately came back with half a tumbler of Crown Royal, extra ice and water. It seemed the supervisor hoped that George would not tell the other inconvenienced people. He probably should have asked for a case of C.R., but enough is enough.

The half tumbler lasted almost to MPLS/StPaul where the 757 landed at 5:00 PM, about five hours late.

Juney and Barclay Allan were waiting at the gate,

smiling, and as happy as though nothing had happened.

The Wescoombes apologized for the delay but Barclay said, "Think nothing of it, we found out about the problem immediately and took the bus to the new MPLS shopping mall where we had lunch and had a good time looking around. Then back to the airport lounge for a couple of drinks and here we are."

It was too late to drive to Bemidji, so George canceled the hotel reservation before the 6:00 PM deadline and made a new reservation at the Comfort Inn at St. Cloud about fifty miles from MPLS/St.Paul.

It rained for the entire fifty miles so the travelers were happy to be ensconced in the hotel and settled down to a couple of hours of wine, beer and conversation.

The Wescoombes had brought as gifts California tee shirts and a tape of Bing and Basie.

Juney is an expert at needlepoint and gave the Wescoombes eight beautiful coasters with a butterfly design on each.

Barclay has become an excellent wood carver since his retirement. He presents George with a wood carving of a golfer, the printing on which commemorates the 77 George scored on May 26, 1993 when he shot his age. George is delighted with this treasure.

Barclay said he would produce "Good Morning Americas" each day before breakfast. All agreed to play two rubbers of Bridge each night. Both these items are "given" and need not be written about each day.

George soon realizes that Juney and Barclay have the same problem that Nan has, *"Slightly Hard Of Hearing."*

Juney, like Nan, wears her $800 hearing aid in her purse most of the time.

Barclay cups his hand around his ear, hoping to pick up the spoken word more clearly. George says he will look for an ear trumpet for him.

There is nothing funny about being deaf, any more than there is about a flood, but "slightly hard of hearing" can be comical if the ones with the problem are not seriously inclined. This group is not serious at all, thankfully.

The Navigator points out the directions and soon realizes, he will have to "Take the marbles out of his mouth" and "speak up" as each of his three companions hear something different.

Through long association, Nan can read George's lips, if she tries, but Juney and Barclay do not have that facility.

As an example, George says, "There are many casinos in this area. The ladies will be able to play the slot machines."

Barclay asks, "What are they going to play with, sausages?"

And so it goes . . . .

DAY 3 - FRIDAY, JULY 23, 1993

St. Cloud to Bemidji, Minn. - Overcast, warm

The coffee shop at the Comfort Inn was crowded and George, who was the first to arrive, shared a table with a young man named Bob.

George mentioned that he was on the way to the source of the "M." Luckily, the man turned out to be a representative of Cenex Oil Company, which operates 150 service stations in Minnesota. His job was to visit each station.

Bob was interested and went to this room to get a Cenex map, on which. he detailed the back route to Itasca State Park. By the time Nan and the Allans arrived at the coffee shop, George was an expert on the back roads of Minnesota.

Although it was early, our travelers drove around the City of St. Cloud. The National Hockey Center was open as two arenas were being used by about forty young boys dressed in their full hockey gear, with four coaches directing hockey practice. This is the 23rd of July. These people are serious.

An area was devoted to pictures of N.H.L. players who were born in St. Cloud. George was familiar with Frankie Brimsek, an outstanding goalie, and Herb Brooks who coached the U.S. team when they defeated Russia in the 1980 Olympics.

The Cenex map directed the travelers along Hwy. 10 to Little Falls, Rte. 371 to Brainerd and Walker, then Rte. 200 to Itasca State Park.

Little Falls is on both shores of the "M" which is quite wide at this point. This route is up-river to the source. There is not a falls but rapids sufficient to supply power to the town and surrounding area.

Charles A. Lindbergh was born in Little Falls. There is a center devoted to his life, but the travelers passed it up.

All of this area is heavily wooded and splattered with small lakes and rivers.

Brainerd is known for the lore of Paul Bunyan and his ox. They must have been out of town at this time, as we did not see them.

Walker on Leech Lake is a favorite vacation spot with fishing, boating, swimming at Walker Dam. We are still travelling up stream.

At the edge of Itasca State Park is an eating place known as the Headwaters Inn at which our hungry travelers enjoy sandwiches, beer and wine and information. In Lake Itasca State Park, we are soon at the spot where the mighty "M" is a little stream about 5 yards wide, escaping from the Northwest end of Lake Itasca. The water is transparent and beautiful, not muddy as it soon becomes down stream.

George and Barclay walk atop the log, which stretches across the stream. This is the humble beginning of the mighty river as it starts its 2552-mile journey to the Gulf of Mexico.

It's a puny beginning for such an awesome body of water farther downstream. One can almost spit across it in normal times. **This** is the cause of so much destruction and despair in the Midwest, at this time.

At least the water is clear in the land of Sky Blue Waters, no silt, no pop cans, and no oil rainbows, just plain water.

The initial direction of the "M" is northwest as though heading to Manitoba. Then it meanders in an easterly direction through Lake Bemidji before heading southward. If it had flowed a few miles northeast, instead of curving southward, it may have emptied into Hudson Bay.

Surprising how many people are at the source, many children paddling in the water which must be cold.

The travelers decide to take the cruise on the "Chester Charles," the length of Lake Itasca and return. The vast pine forests surrounding the Lake house osprey, bald eagles, and the shoreline's herons, loons, whip-poor-wills and more.

It was when paddling his canoe on Lake Itasca, that Henry Schoolcraft in 1832 discovered the 2-3 yard wide stream dribbling from the north-end of the Lake. The exit had gone undetected for some years as wild rice grows in profusion along the shores of the Lake and the height and thickness of the rice obscured the small stream.

The water in Lake Itasca is quite high due to the excessive rainfall. Nothing seems to overflow in Minnesota as 10,000 lakes and as many rivers probably make the state as much water as land, so how would they know.

It is a short drive from Lake Itasca to Bemidji, where the weary travelers check-in at the same Comfort Inn they had reserved for the night before, but were forced to cancel due to their late arrival in MPLS.

DAY 4 - SATURDAY, JULY 24, 1993

Bemidji to MPLS, Minn - Overcast, warm

Bemidji got its name from the Chippewa word

meaning, "Lake with river running through." As, indeed, the "M" flows into the south end of Lake Bemidji and out again on the eastern side.

Bemidji is known as the *"first city on the M"* and is famous as a vacation spot not only for the woods, water and wildlife, but as a center of culture, education and history. Evidence of primitive Indian village sites and earth mounds, estimated to be from 500 to 900 years old have been found nearby.

The travelers decide to move along Hwy. 2 to the City of Grand Rapids. Not far out of Bemidji a sign indicated that there is gambling at Cass Lake nearby. Nan insisted the men should have another breakfast and was backed up by Juney. The Palace Bingo and Casino is a Las Vegas style gambling emporium way out in the woods. The ladies are excited about losing their $20.00 worth of nickels. The food is excellent. George ate a ham and cheese omelet with wild rice throughout. One can't get wild rice back in civilization.

Grand Rapids with 12,000 people is the navigational headwaters of the "M" and also the birth place of Frances Gumm (Judy Garland). The Blandin Paper Mill dominates the river shoreline and also the city and is probably the reason for the prosperity of the city.

It is hard to believe that seemingly, staid, solid states such as Minnesota and Wisconsin would be hotbeds of casino gambling. There are no less than 27 Las Vegas style casinos in the two states. Billboards along the highways point out the direction to those "dens of iniquity."

Nan and Juney are two of the most rabid nickel slot machine players in the world.

A sign advertises the Grand Casino Hinckley and Barclay feels so much pressure he is forced to stop.

Hinckley was famous for the forest fire, which destroyed the town in 1894 and took 400 lives. Now, it's famous for casino gambling. These places have dinner shows, hook-ups for motor homes and even a two state-wide casino magazine, published out of Waseca, Minn., wherever that is.

Here's a poem which was featured in the August issue.

"INSPIRED WINNER"

I went to the casino just to look around
And picked up a nickel I found lying on the ground
I put it in the nickel slot, it gave five nickels back
By golly! it was easy, I think I've got the knack.

So I tried my luck at quarters and slowly put one in
It gave back twenty quarters, looks like I win again
I played one game of keno, bet my height, my age, my weight
Then raked in fifty dollars, I think this place is great

Went onto the bingo parlor, thought I'd give it a whirl
when I won I called my boss at work and said, "Get another girl,
I'm here at the casino and I'm no longer poor, so tell the
Folks I work with I' ain't comin' back no more."

I've never had a better time, that was so much fun
The dealer at the blackjack table dealt me 21
I didn't spend a penny but I won enough to buy some clothes
And that quilted country bedspread with the little purple bows

A hot tub and a bedroom set, a boat for the old man,
Groceries for a year or two and a fancy ceiling fan.
Next weel O'll be comin' back, I've got a lucky star
Gonna play the dollar slots and bring home that new car

I found a coupon in the ladies room, good for one free drink
So I went into the lounge just to sit a spell and think
I felt a little guilty as I headed out the door
So I'm sending back the nickel that I picked up off the floor!

These two states will soon have a reputation for wild living like California and New York. Next thing will be legalized prostitution as in Nevada.

Casino Magazine has an article describing how the federal government in Canada **sold** gambling to the provinces for $100 million dollars.

The ladies lost their $20.00 in an hour or so but returned to the car happy and smiling for some reason.

Freeway 35 took the travelers the short distance to MPLS in a hurry where the Best Western Bradbury Suites is home for the next two nights.

A drive downtown revealed that MPLS is a complicated place in which to drive, as it seems to have too many freeways. At least the Hubert Humphrey Metrodome is easy to see from most of the city so hopefully it will be in the same place tomorrow.

Close to the hotel is Byerleys, one of those sensational grocery stores that stock everything that is edible in the world. A barbecued chicken, several cheeses, several fruits made a fine repast.

Bridge - today - 2 rubbers - Men 50
to date - 2 rubbers - Men 50

DAY 5 - SUNDAY, JULY 25, 1993

MPLS - Minn. - Cloudy, warm

Sunday morning is not the most exciting time to visit downtown MPLS, as not much is open until noon except the churches. At least the travelers could walk about "River Place" at Butler Square. This is an area of renovated warehouses on the riverfront, transformed into several blocks of quaint shops, parks, and restaurants.

The "M," alongside, is up in volume due to the rain but there is little evidence of flooding.

St. Anthony Falls nearby, a drop of about 18 feet is the only falls on the "M." There is a lock which permits river traffic to reach commercial and industrial sections of MPLS.

The upper "M" from MPLS at Lock #1 to Lock #27 near St. Louis is a series of twenty-seven steps. The 669 miles of river fall about 420 feet while maintaining a navigable channel depth of nine feet. The Locks are mostly the same size, 110 ft. wide and 600 ft. long and are activated by the latest high-tech equipment.

In the old days freight was moved by steamboat with a maximum capacity of 2400 tons. Now 20,000 tons are loaded on 12 or 15 barges, all powered by one sturdy diesel towboat and moved 1500 miles from Baton Rouge to St. Paul. The barges are specialized and are capable of carrying diverse products, the same as specialty built trucks do on the freeways.

Barges also make possible the economical shipment of bulk commodities. Petroleum products and coal are the largest single bulk items moving northward and grain and scrap iron are the largest moving in a southward direction.

Due to the flooding and high water, all the barge traffic has been stopped for over a month; causing an immense loss of jobs and shortage of materials. 50 towboats and 2500 barges are tethered to the vanished shore, costing the industry $4 million a day.

After a tour of St. Paul, the travelers find the Metrodome for the 1:05 PM game between the Twins and the Orioles. The Dome, as it is affectionately known by the locals, is a fine place to watch a game, except when something happens, the noise level reverberates around the building. The hot dogs, beer, nachos, peanuts, and ice cream are vended continually so one does not have to "go get it."

The Twins' fans do not want anything to happen in the early innings, as they are too busy eating to have to cheer.

There is nothing to interrupt the dining today as Jim Deshaies kept the Orioles in check throughout. Ben MacDonald pitched well for the Orioles, but Kirby came through in the late innings for 4-3 Twins lead. Ripkin hit a couple of long fly balls, but the Orioles did not really threaten. Just a dull game until Dave Winfield hit his 449th home-run in the eighth as icing on the cake.

Juney learned how to keep score, but was most happy, as the Orioles do not gain on her beloved Blue Jays.

Getting out of the Dome and finding the car was a cinch but the most innocent looking streets are traps that lead to freeways. This city is a maze of freeways and although we saw 35 west which goes north and south, many times when we didn't need it, it took about twenty frustrating minutes to finally head south on 35 west to the Best Western Bradbury Suites. All the time the Metrodome was in clear view. At the next city we will get a map.

Drinks and snacks left over from the previous night preceded the usual Bridge game accompanied by Sunday night baseball on mute TV.

Bridge - today - 2 rubbers - Ladies 360
to date - 4 rubbers - Ladies 310

DAY 6 - MONDAY, JULY 26, 1993

MPLS - Minn. to Lacrosse, Wisc. - Sunny, 85°

Amazing! It's 6:00 AM and the sun is shining in all its glory, not a cloud in the sky. The folks in this part of the world have had overcast and rain for 45 days, so today must be a welcome relief.

The Best Western has the same generous buffet breakfast everyday, which the "Ws" and the "As" enjoy in a leisurely manner along with the USA Today.

Breakfast is a relatively new feature in many of the medium-priced hotels. It started out as coffee and donuts.

Now it has expanded to several juices, coffee, cocoa, milk, 3 types of dry cereal, toast, many types of muffins, and donuts, waffles, oatmeal and instant grits, and bowls of different fruits. Certainly more than most people need.

To George, medium priced means $45 to $55, plus tax, less senior discount. This is George's level of affluence and includes Comfort Inns, Hampton Inns, most Best Westerns and probably others.

There are stories *of* cresting at Hannibal, only two or three days down stream.

George has decided to start out on the Wisconsin Great River Road heading south to Lacrosse, Minn. Barclay skillfully drives the Chrysler through the early morning business traffic in MPLS along 474 for 5 miles to Route 10, then southward for 10 miles into Wisc., at the town of Prescott.

Prescott is at the confluence of the St. Croix and the "M." One can clearly see the color line in the water where the blue waters of the St. Croix meet the muddy "M." There is evidence of high water, but not much flooding. In the bright sunshine, it is a pretty drive along the east side of the "M" through several small villages.

Red Wing, Minn. on the west side is appealing so our travelers cross the bridge to this obviously affluent city, which is about an hour south of the Twin Cities. In the heart of town, the St. James Hotel, built in 1870 has been restored to its full Victorian elegance. Many shops line the spacious lobby, displaying clothes, arts, books, gifts, etc. The St. James and Red Wing would be a great place to visit for a longer time..

Back to the Wisconsin's Great River Road with a short stop at the Nelson Cheese Factory to stock up on old Wisconsin and more.

At Alma, we took a look at Lock and Dam No. 4 from the observation deck. This procedure is carried out 27 times in the upper "M" to control the river and to maintain a 9-foot navigational channel. Although the river is high at this point there is little evidence of flooding and all bridges are open. However, there is extensive areas of casual water along the roadways, but this is little problem as one can take a free drop from casual water, in golf, anyway.

Our food lady, Juney, suggests we cross the river to Winona. She has a hunch there will be a riverside place for lunch. "Finn and Sawyers" could not be better. Excellent view, friendly service and great catfish for George. The rest had the lunch specialty--beef stew. Along the wall, behind the bar on the lengthy mirror was a leaded design which outlines the "M" from the source to Winona, 750 miles down stream. Barclay took pictures with his camcorder.

Back across the bridge to Wisconsin for the short drive to Lacrosse.

Lacrosse, located at the confluence of three rivers, the Black, Trempealeau and the "M" is Wisconsin's largest city on the "M". Usually it is a very busy part, but due to the high water there is no river activity.

Our travelers stop at the well located Exel Inn, not far from beautiful Riverside Park, which lines the "M" for several miles.

Heileman Brewing Company, the largest business in Lacrosse, is located on the city side of Riverside Park.

As it is a fabulous sunny day, it would have been nice to cruise on the "Lacrosse Queen," but everything is shut down.

Lacrosse is named after the Indian game of the same name. In Riverside Park is an intricate statue of three Indians engaged in the game. Also nearby is a thirty-foot high carving (probably with a chain saw) of Hiawatha. Barclay, whose hobby is woodcarving, is always on the lookout for interesting subjects and takes many pictures of both these statues from all angles.

"Moxies Key, North Deck," overlooking the Black River is fine for drinks and snacks but if we wait for sunset it would cut into the Bridge time.

The T.V. and newspapers tell of the cresting further south, but all we have is a lot of surface water. After 45 days of rain these folks must be glad we brought California sunshine. George is claiming the credit.

We have not caught up to the **real** high water as yet.

Bridge - today - 2 rubbers - Ladies 460
to date - 6 rubbers - Ladies 770

DAY 7 - TUESDAY, JULY 27 1993

Lacrosse, Wisc. to Dubuque, Iowa - Sunny

It is a fine sunny day as we continue from Lacrosse along Hwy. 35 which skirts the "M" on the east or Wisconsin side. The river, which is still high, crested here a week or so ago and is evidenced by standing water a foot deep along the sides of Hwy. 35. Weather like today will soon dry it up by evaporation.

Soon the travelers arrive a Prairie Du Chien or Prairie of the Dog named after the chief of the Indians who lived here and who looked like a dog.

St. Friole Island, the oldest part of town, is an island in the "M." This island was flooded and much water is visible. The attraction is Villa Louis, the Estate of Co!. H.L. Dausman, who became very wealthy in the fur trading business. H.L. was a very interesting individual having had at least two children, by liaison, as they said in those days. His son Louis inherited all the money and built this Victorian-style mansion in 1870. It contains the finest collection of Victorian decorative art and furnishings in the country. The carriage house has been converted into a museum, depicting the early history of Prairie Du Chien.

Both father and son gave lavish parties for famous artists, financiers, traders, politicians, soldiers, and other people of quality. To ensure that the guests were properly satiated during the visit, H.L. would weigh the visitors upon arrival and departure.

The guides were dressed in period costumes and were

humorous as well as informative.

When the "M" crested, the water rose to within a few feet of the Villa Louis, which was closed for two weeks.

The bridge across to Marquette, Iowa is open so we cross over to Hwy. 52 to travel to Dubuque. The countryside is rolling and water is lying in all the low areas along the highway, several feet deep. It is a good thing the roadbeds were raised when they were built.

The travelers find the Comfort Inn on Dodge Street without a problem.

Dubuque is the oldest city in Iowa. In the early days great wealth was made in lead mining, lumbering came next, and now Dubuque is known for meat packing and heavy machinery manufacturing.

We took a drive through the historic district, which was full of restored ancient buildings, but had no bars or restaurants worth visiting. The lower area of the city near the bridge was still under water and the better eating places located there, were closed. The crest had passed a couple of weeks ago but the businesses in the river area were still mopping up.

The Silver Eagle, a cruising gambling ship, sails out of Dubuque and the gambling ladies were disappointed as, like everything else, the Silver Eagle was not operating due to the high and treacherous water. The markers, which indicate the channel in the river, were underwater by several feet. Juney, the director of food made an excellent choice. The Best Western Midway Hotel, not far from the Comfort Inn, featured the Hoffman House, which claimed to have the best salad bar in Dubuque and were able to prove it. In addition, three travelers had liver, bacon and onions, and one ate catfish.

Iowa used to claim it was a place to grow, now it is a place to row. That's their joke.

<u>Bridge</u> - today - 2 rubbers - Men 1360
to date - 8 rubbers - Men 590

DAY 8 - WEDNESDAY, JULY 28,1993

Dubuque, Iowa to Burlington, Iowa - Sunny

This beautiful weather will soon dry up much of the water or at least make the folks feel better.

Hwy. 52, although several miles from the river, is flooded on both sides, with water two to three feet deep. The fields look like mirrors.

The government estimates one and one-half billion dollars as the loss on the corn crop in Iowa. Most of that money will go to the large corporation growers, of course, and the small farmer will get a buck and a half.

There is an old saying in this part of the world, "If your corn is knee-high by the Fourth of July, you are in good shape."

Much of the corn here was knee-high by that date but unfortunately still is. Too much water is as bad as too little.

Looking at a field of corn along the highway it is apparent how far the flooding went by the height of the corn. The rains came in the summer instead of late winter and early spring for the first time in years. Summer is usually hot and dry, <u>not</u> rainy for 45 consecutive days. Water, which has no constant form or shape, is a successful force, which prevails over everything in spite of its apparent weakness. It changes and adapts as necessary in order to succeed in its objective.

Not far from Dubuque is the pretty town of Bellevue, situated on a high bluff overlooking the "M." A park extends along the river, high above the flood line. It is a lucky town as there is no serious flooding. Breakfast in Bellevue was at Riverview Cafe and Bar. The waitress had seventeen grandchildren and five great grandchildren, no wrinkles, and had a good sense of humor.

Barclay is able to get a battery for his watch at Doland Jewelers. The people are happy to live in Bellevue, safe and dry, and with a fine river view.

Around noon, the travelers reached the Quad Cities. This is a unique community as Bettendorf and Davenport, Iowa, and Rock Island and Moline, Illinois, combine to create a major commercial and industrial complex on the "M." Davenport and Rock Island are on the river.

As the travelers are always looking for eating places near the river, Juney spots an advertisement for the "Dock" in Davenport, which must be on the water. About three weeks ago the crest went through Davenport and Rock City. The street on which the "Dock" is located is still under water and that business and others will be closed for months. The baseball stadium is through for at least a month as is the Band Shell and other recreational areas within a quarter mile of the "M."

A Best Western has a restaurant open in the area and the help tell us they were closed for two weeks as no one could get to work. One lady produced pictures showing water rushing through the streets. This is the worst we have encountered so far. However, only 3% of Davenport's total area was flooded, 97% completely escaped the river's wrath.

The river roads between Davenport, Iowa and Burlington, Iowa are still closed, but Hwy. 61 about 5-10 miles west of the "M" is in good shape as it is above the water, which has flooded that far. This is one of the new lakes, which the river created. The lake was sixteen miles wide in some areas. The trees will survive as long as most branches are above water. If this water does not go somewhere before winter, it will be an immense skating rink. The crest was three weeks ago and almost reached Hwy. 61. Interstate 80 at Davenport was closed for three days. There is much knee-high corn all the way from Davenport to Burlington.

Burlington is a busy spot as the Red Cross and others helping the flood victims are located in that city. The travelers are able to get the last two rooms at the Comfort Inn. Burlington is higher above the river than Davenport but the streets adjacent to the river are still barricaded.

The Holiday Inn near the Comfort Inn has two restaurants and two lounges so there is plenty of activity, food, beer, and wine.

There is an interesting debate, covered by T.V., from Davenport discussing whether they should build a levee. After the flood of 1973, Rock City on the other side of the river spent $25 million on a levee and in 1993 had little damage. Davenport did not build a levee and was flooded out again. Those citizens who live away from the "M" do not want to pay the $50 million, which a similar levee could cost today. They say it only floods every 20 years or so, so what's the problem.

The most important problem is that the "President," the City of Davenport's gambling showboat, was damaged and taken out of commission. The "Casino Rock Island" not only stayed in operation, but also picked up all the "President's" business.

It will be interesting to see the result of the voting.

Bridge - Today - 2 Rubbers - Men 2020
To Date - 10 Rubbers - Men 2610

DAY 9 - THURSDAY, JULY 29, 1993

Burlington, Iowa to Hannibal, MO - Sunny

It is such a beautiful day, it is hard to realize that these folks suffered through a year's rain in 45 days.

Keokuk, Iowa is the next stop. Keokuk in Indian means "Where The Water Runs Shallow." The Keokuk Dam and powerhouse is one of the world's larger hydroelectric power stations.

Mark Twain lived and worked in this city and there is a Mark Twain Center, at the Public Library.

Warm, sunny weather has brought many people to the

main street where merchandise is displayed outside the stores. After so many days of rain, there is probably much stored up buying power.

The bridge at Keokuk is open, one of the few for many miles. Normally there would be much river traffic through Lock and Dam Number 19, but due to the high water there is zip, da nada, none.

Keokuk, Iowa to Hannibal, MO, is about 70 miles along Hwy. 61, with knee-high corn on both sides.

The travelers made a reservation at the Best Western Hotel Clemens in Hannibal only to find this usually busy city almost deserted. The bridge is out and unfavorable publicity has destroyed the tourist business. Hannibal, itself, has no flooding as all the Mark Twain, Tom Sawyer, Huck Finn exhibits are protected by a well constructed and expensive sea wall. It is the approaches to the bridge on the Illinois side, which are flooded and must be repaired.

Quincy is on the Illinois side, ordinarily about 10 miles from Hannibal. Now travelers from Hannibal to Quincy or the reverse, must travel north to Koekuk and back, a round trip of about 160 miles.

The River Front Inn, which used to be a whorehouse, is excellent for a repast. It was known as the "Bordello" when built in 1917, by Sarah Smith, an enterprising madam from Chicago. It is only two blocks from Mark Twain's home, which probably doesn't mean anything.

All the river activities are closed so the travelers settle for a bus trip around the city. The very pretty guide, who once played Becky in the annual Mark Twain Show, is informative and also wears attractive short shorts. Barclay is busy with his wit and camcorder. Hope he got some shots of the shorts.

The bus takes us to Lovers Leap, where the flooding can be seen north and south of the city. Riverview Park, 400 acres donated to the city by W.B. Pettibone, has beautiful tree lined drives, featuring two scenic overlooks which are worthwhile. A statue of Mark Twain overlooks the river from a 300-foot bluff.

Barclay takes several pictures of the Tom and Huck statue, which he may carve in wood. It is the first statue in the U.S. to honor fictional characters.

The Molly Brown Theatre is not operating due to lack of business. The proprietor told George he had only 24 customers last weekend and was losing his a - - .

The travelers have all the Mark Twain historical exhibits and shops almost to themselves, which is not all bad.

What a pretty day to wander about this interesting city.

Bridge - Today - 2 Rubbers - Men 410
To date 12 rubbers - Men 3020

DAY 10 - FRIDAY, JULY 30, 1993

Hannibal, MO to St. Louis, MO - Sunny

The scenic route from Hannibal to St. Louis is Hwy. 79, but Barclay, with his camcorder, recorded how the beginning of 79, just south of Hannibal, was under three feet of water.

Hwy. 61, the old standby, moves along about 15-20 miles from the river in this area.

It's time for laundry, so Bowling Green, Iowa, seems a likely spot. Bowling Green is tiny but has a laundromat only a block from Terry's Cafe. The men walk the laundry over while breakfast is being prepared. The waitress is somewhat reserved, but Barclay soon has her laughing.

A hardware store nearby, which sells everything, even extenders for the tire valves on the Chrysler, takes up the drying time.

Some towns are so small that when an eighteen wheeler goes through everyone watches the event. Bowling

Green is one of those towns, but is so friendly.

Next stop on this beautiful sunny day is at Troy, MO, where the merchants display their goods on the street. It's such a fine day that all the neighbors are out and about, happy that the rain has gone. George, of course, tells everyone that the Wescoombes brought the sunshine from California.

There were great bargains, Juney bought a suit. Barclay bought three sweaters for his grand kids and Nan bought a blouse.

While the ladies continued shopping, the men enjoyed a beer at Barb's Bar, where Barclay entertained the folks with Canadian and Florida humor. Also Scotch and Irish jokes.

St. Louis is easy to reach on Hwy. 61 and the Fairfield Marriott on Dunn Road off 270 is a cinch. Just before reaching St. Louis near St. Charles where the Missouri joins the "M," there is much evidence of flooding. We have now almost caught up to the cresting. St. Louis is scheduled for cresting on Monday.

In St. Louis, all one needs to know is Interstate 70, its offshoots, 170 and 270 and Interstate 55 and 255 and Hwy. 44, to make it through and around the city.

In a few minutes, the travelers are parked downtown near that engineering masterpiece, The Arch. The park on which The Arch stands is at least 50 ft. above the river.

The Gateway Arch was designed by Finish born architect, Eero Saarinen, built in 196365 and cost 13 million dollars. It's shape is a "classic weighed catenary curve." The height is 630 ft. and its span is also 630 ft. The Arch is designed to sway 18 inches and does move 3/4 of an inch in a 20-MPH wind, imperceptible.

It takes about 10 minutes for a tram ride, round trip and costs $2.50.

The access road below is flooded and the MacDonald's and Burger King fake riverboats are tied up 10 yards from shore in 10 ft. of water, unreachable. The gambling and cruise ships are also tied up and not operating.

Time for lunch at the palatial Adams Mark Hotel only a block or so from The Arch. On the way, we were interviewed by a T.V. lady and a cameraman from the local station, supposedly for the 6 PM news, asking questions as to what we thought of the flood. It did not make the news, but George would love to have a copy, as it was hilarious. Barclay was in good form.

We took the elevator to the 18th floor of the Adams Mark, from where the flooding to the north of St. Louis is apparent.

Back to the Fairfield for a rest before returning to Busch Stadium for the Cardinals-Mets at 7:35 PM. Expected crowd 49,000.

The game was boring, a no hitter through three innings. Sid Fernandez for Mets, Allen Watson for Cards. Todd Zeile hit a short home-run in 4th for 1-0 Cards. In 6th Mets scored on walk, passed ball and single. Ozzie Smith took charge in Cards 6th with a lead-off drag bunt, stole second, third on ground out and scored on Zeile sac. fly. Cards 2-1.

In the 7th, Card pinch hitter doubled and Ozzie doubled him home - Cards 3-1.

Dull game to this point, but baseball usually has a turning point.

Mets scratch two on with two out in the 8th. Eddie Murray batting against closer Lee Smith. A Murray homer would win it for the Mets. A Murray walk would bring up Bobby Bonilla. Murray and Smith battled for about ten pitches, with Murray finally flying out to the wall. Cards breathe sigh of relief. Bonilla leads off 9th with meaningless tape measure home run, but Cards hold on 3-2. Good pitching, both teams, but combined 13 hits is pitiful this season. 13 other games this night averaged 19.3 hits per game. No doubt, baseball has gone back to the lively ball.

Barclay has the St. Louis freeways figured out, so it was easy to reach the Fairfield Marriott.

DAY 11 - SATURDAY, JULY 31, 1993

St. Louis, MO - Sunny and showers

Early Saturday morning, with very little traffic, the travelers reach Laclede's Landing on the river front by about 9 AM. Laclede's is a group of renovated, turn of the century buildings, with cobblestone streets filled with shops, eateries, and offices.

"Muddy Waters," a restaurant bar right on the river has a flooded basement and many people are sand bagging to prevent, if possible, further encroachment, as the river is rising.

George knows Barclay will use his camcorder, so he grabs a shovel and starts to fill bags held open by a row of pretty young ladies. George hopes he is going to be a judge at a wet "T" shirt contest, but these girls want him to keep shoveling. One girl turns out to be Kristen who lives in La Jolla, California on Rosemont Street near Wind and Sea Beach. George soon gives up, replaced by Juney. At least we helped a little. That sand is damned heavy. These folks will have backaches, but longer arms. What are they going to do with 30 million sandbags? So far there has been many volunteers to help with the sand bagging. One wonders how many will want to help with the messy clean-up.

The bar at "Muddy Waters" is open so it's time for a drink. Some folks at the bar tell us about the new Metro Link Line, which is opening today at Civic Center at 11:00 with a stop near Leclede's Landing. Travel on the Line today is free so it will be crowded but we wait with a hundred others just to be first on something.

The Metro Link will be a boon to the people of St. Louis as it will travel from east St. Louis to the airport with 18 stops with trains every five minutes.

We are planning on a 6-stop ride to the Convention Center Station. Our waiter yesterday, at the Adams Mark, suggested we go to an Italian restaurant with a name something like "Kemools" for lunch today. It is supposed to be between the Convention Center and Busch Stadium, quite a large area.

After waiting for 45 minutes, Nan, Juney and Barclay decide to leave the Metro Link Station and find "Kemools" by car. George decides to stick it out and meet the others at "Kemools" wherever that may be. As she leaves, Juney looks as though she may never see her big brother again. Nan is not worried, she knows he has his credit card.

The Metro Link arrives five minutes after the three leave. George boards the crowded train, crosses the river to east St. Louis, and returns to Convention Center Station, all of which takes about twenty minutes. A phone book in the Convention Center reveals the name to be "Kemolis" at Metropolitan Square, wherever that may be. George asks a black man in the wash room if he knows the place. Sure, he says, "Three blocks left to Broadway, then right four blocks and you'll see it on the right. Also Busch Stadium further along." George covers the half-mile with a few rest stops in about twenty minutes and there is the group waiting for him, having just arrived.

It sure is easy to get around a strange city, if one is lucky.

Kemolis is closed Saturday, but no matter. George noticed Caleco's Bar & Grill a couple of blocks away on Broadway and it turned out just great.

Barclay got us back to the Fairfield in short order. He didn't have to do even one "U" turn.

The Bridge game is interrupted by a magnificent thunderstorm with great lightening.

Shortly after the storm ends, a loud siren sounds. George goes outside the hotel door. The man in the next room is also outside. "What the hell is that noise," asks George. "Oh, that is a tornado warning," was the reply. "What do we do now," was George's next question. "Just make sure you have plenty of booze and stay in your room," was the practical reply.

There was no tornado.

Bridge - Today - 2 rubbers - Men 300
To Date - 14 rubbers - Men 3320

DAY 12 -SUNDAY, AUGUST 1, 1993

St. Louis, MO to Sikeson, MO - Sunny, warm

This is the day the river crests in St. Louis. George suggests that the travelers stay another day to watch the happening, but is out voted. It is just as well as at least 100,000 people were gathered at Gateway Arch.

It may be well to talk about what is meant by cresting.

When the media say the "M" will crest in St. Louis on Monday at 49.0 ft., that means it will be 19 ft. above flood stage which is set at 30 ft. in St. Louis. Each city has what is known as flood stage being the height at which the levees and walls are estimated to hold fast. In St. Louis all the businesses on the lower level are flooded, but the city itself is about 50 ft. above flood level so there is little problem now the rain has stopped.

Some cities such as Des Moines, Iowa, and Davenport were badly battered.

The crest is not like a tidal wave, but builds up slowly from the excessive rain and over filled tributaries emptying into the "M" as the river proceeds south. In some areas the "M" has been so full that the tributaries had no place to go and backed up.

When the crest reaches Cairo it will practically disappear. The upper "M" to Cairo is like a two-lane highway and below Cairo it is like a four-lane expressway.

Last night, the levee on the Missouri River side of St. Charles, about 40 miles from St. Louis, gave way and the downtown area of the city is flooded, including Hwy. 40.

The flood is giving plenty of warning. Although thousands had to evacuate, there were no casualties. This is not like a flash flood or an earthquake. St. Louis does not know what to expect until tonight.

It is another beautiful day as we travel south on I-55, about five miles west of the "M." Hwy. 61, the original route south from St. Louis is closer to the "M," but is closed in many locations.

At the town of Arnold, our Food Director, Juney, spots the Cracker Barrel Restaurant for breakfast. The Cracker Barrel, as its name suggests, is part of a small local chain of unique eating spots. There is a homey, old-fashioned air about the place even to the serving girls' costumes. The food is excellent and the large gift shop interesting.

After travelling another 30 miles, we decide to visit the city of Festus, which is located right on the river. Barclay maneuvers the Chrysler past some barricades and with a couple of "U" turns is able to park about fifty yards from the water on a street on which the water is rising. It is interesting to watch the water slowly inching higher on the pavement. There are myriad's of minnows swimming in the shallow water.

MacDonald's, Shoney's and other businesses closer to the river are 3-4 ft. deep in water and much sand bagging is going on around other stores.

Another 50 miles south, we drive to the City of St. Genevieve, also on the "M."

We are not allowed to get close to the river. Signs are posted threatening arrest if one enters streets leading to the water. We wonder what the reason may be. George reads in a local paper the next day that the inmates from a nearby correctional institute are helping with the sand bagging and the officials wish to keep onlookers to a minimum.

Cape Girardeau, another 50 miles south, has a pretty good system of levees, but most of the neighbors are rallying together to sand bag the weak spots.

Cairo, at the confluence of the Ohio and the "M" is another thirty miles ahead. We do not know what to expect at the juncture so we decide to stay at Sikeston, MO on I-55 about 20 miles west of Cairo and the river, and drive to Cairo if the roads are open.

The Hampton Inn people tell us the roads and bridges are open, just don't drive through the fields.

Merv Griffin, that great entrepreneur, has opened a gambling joint on a riverboat at Metropolis about 30 miles east of Cairo on the Ohio River. It's a hundred-mile round trip, but the gambling ladies insist and, of course, get their way.

"Players River Boat Casino," at Merv Griffin Landing in Metropolis, Ohio, is a 1400 passenger authentic side wheeler river boat replica which makes six, two and one-half hour gambling cruises on the Ohio each day.

Strange laws are in effect. One can not gamble on land, but may do so on the river. Griffin has the boat docked at an immense building which has coffee shops, dining rooms, gift shops, bars, etc., in which the people hang around while waiting for the next cruise. Incidentally, Merv Griffin charges $10.00 each for the privilege of losing one's money.

Unfortunately, we have just missed the 3 o'clock cruise and decide not to wait three hours for the next. We have a buffet style meal but no alcohol, as it is forbidden, on land, in this county, on Sunday.

The ladies are disappointed, but it is an outstanding drive back to Sikeston on this sunny day.

At Cairo, one crosses a high bridge over the beautiful Ohio River and immediately over another high bridge crossing the "M." The Ohio, which is much more peaceful than the "M," has risen somewhat, but not to the flood stage. The Mississippi Queen and the Delta Queen are still operating on the Ohio, but of course, no further north. A third riverboat, The American Queen, the largest of the three, will sail next year.

It is a spectacular sight to see the blue waters of the

Ohio mingle with the muddy "M."

Bridge - Today - 2 rubbers - Men 410
To Date - 16 rubbers - Men 3730

DAY 13 - MONDAY, AUGUST 2,1993

Sikeston, MO to Blytheville, ARK - Sunny, warm

The T.V. news reveals that the "M" and Missouri are cresting this day and the area around St. Louis is bracing for who knows what. George wanted to stay another night in St. Louis to watch and maybe fill a few more sand bags at Laclede's Landing, but was overruled. Later, news reports indicate that the crest did not reach the City of St. Louis itself, and "the city breathed a sign of relief." The surrounding low areas were badly flooded and several thousand people were evacuated.

Sometimes, George wonders why natural disasters usually strike where the poor people have to bear the brunt. A similar situation occurred in Florida when Hurricane Andrew cut its swath. George and Nan saw miles and miles of tract homes de-roofed and mobile homes overturned.

Wonder what God has against poor folks. Surely, he is not on the side of big government even though George Bush maintained he was.

Sikeston is about twenty-five miles west of the "M," so there will be no flooding here.

The day dawns sunny and warm so golf is in order at Sikeston Golf and Country Club. From about this point south, the folks have been praying for rain, whereas north of here, the people have been inundated. The sprinklers have kept the course green and pretty, however.

The course is flat, 6019 yds. from the whites, with very little rough so everyone had a good game. The ladies had 58's, Barclay a 48 and George had 4 pars and five bogies.

The price was right also, $11.00 each for nine holes including cart.

In the Pro Shop George found the worldwide-advertised copper bracelet by Sabona of London. Over 4 million of these bracelets have been sold to arthritis sufferers including Seve Ballesteros. This should put an end to Nan's arthritis pain and for only twelve dollars, plus tax.

After golf a short drive took the travelers to New Madrid, normally a port town on the "M," but with the high water nothing is moving. New Madrid was hit both in 1937 and 1965 and now has quite high levees, on the top of which Barclay drove the Chrysler. The top was about twenty feet above the river at this time.

A short distance further south along the "M" is Carruthersville, which has elegant homes on the approach to the city, but a badly beat-up downtown. Many vacancies and run-down stores line the main streets.

The "Round House Inn" was recommended for lunch and was passable. Juney tried catfish for the first time and enjoyed it. George had not eaten fried bologna before and will not again. It's quite a favorite in this area, however.

Along the river is a dike built to protect the businesses from the floods of 1937 and 1965. The dike is about fifty yards from the river, the fifty yards being a park along the riverbank which is quite pleasant when the "M" behaves. The dike has two opening for cars to drive through about ten feet wide. The wall has slots in each edge into which 4 x 12 boards, 10 feet long could be quickly inserted, thus securing the area should the river rise. A bell is in a tower on the wall, which is rung to tell the townspeople to get down to the river to put the boards in place. Maybe they will have to perform in a few days.

Blytheville, Arkansas is a few miles south and the Comfort Inn is the destination. Drinking in this part of Arkansas is done in clubs so our travelers join the Holiday Inn Club which is nearby. The fee is supposed to be $5.00 per person, but as business is slow, the fee is waived. The drinks are fine, but the snacks are no roaring hell so it's not long before the Bridge game is underway, back at the Comfort Inn.

The Blytheville Courier News, dated August 2, 1993, has a headline, "Freedom March Attracts Support, Much Opposition." Two front-page photographs show the divided lines. Under the left photo it says, "Witches, warlocks and pagans from Memphis, St. Louis, Jonesboro and Blytheville joined together for an expression of 'Freedom of Religion' during a Sunday March in Jonesboro. The pagans met with opposition from Christians who lined the street screaming accusations and holding banners of scripture. "

Under the right photo it says, "Steven Branch of Osceola leads the rally against the pagans and read scriptures from the bible denouncing witchcraft, as Terry Riley and his group of pagans silently passed by."

George figures the travelers had better leave this area quickly as this "Dark Ages" stuff is potentially much more dangerous than the flood.

Eighty policemen were able to control the crowds. Chief McCann was concerned that it cost the city "$1500 in overtime today." Almost everything can be equated to money. There is not much "blithe" in this city, more like "blight."

Bridge - Today - 2 rubbers - Men 380
To Date - 18 rubbers - Men 4110

DAY 14 - TUESDAY, AUGUST 3, 1993

Blytheville, Ark to Memphis, Tenn - Sunny

South of Blytheville, the travelers pick up Hwy. 61 which is closer to the river than Freeway 55. It is a fine sunny day with the cotton fields coming into bloom along the highway. Also alongside are pecan groves with a nut house in the center of the grove.

There are many small towns along Hwy. 61, Burdette, Wilson, Joiner to name a few. These towns are about 5 miles west of the "M." Each seems to have been built around a factory. If the factory is doing well and looks prosperous, then the town is the same. If the factory is run-down, so is the town. The economy of the town is tied to the success of one business.

Oscoela is on the river and being larger has several factories. The water is high, but no sign of flooding.

Memphis is not far and by noon we are in the Hampton Inn. Time for lunch and laundry, and as is the custom, these events are combined. "Earl's Hot Biscuit" is nearby featuring, what else, biscuits, popular in the south. George is introduced to turnip greens, but would rather eat the turnips, which are not available. Probably the animals get the turnips. A laundromat close by does its part adequately.

Downtown Memphis is about 10 minutes away and soon we are parked just off Beale Street.

W.C. Handy, composer of St. Louis Blues and many more hits is commemorated by a statue and a museum containing his memorabilia. The entry fee is but $2.00 and well worth it.

The most famous spot for pork ribs is the Rendezvous located on a side alley in downtown Memphis. This most popular eating place is underground and is huge, probably using the basements of a half-a-dozen stores. There is comfortable seating for 760 eaters, a very limited menu, speedy service, and the greatest pork ribs, at a reasonable price. If you wish to linger over dinner, this is not the place. It would be interesting to know how many meals are served in a day.

Back to Beale Street for some music at the "King's Palace Cafe": this is the home of championship gumbo, but we can't eat again, yet. Charley Wood, working alone this evening, is a blues singer and pianist. He is quite listenable, especially as a white man, doing black blues.

Sitting nearby is a group from North San Diego, San

Marcos and Vista. It's a small world.

After an hour, Barclay can not resist a small order of oysters on the half shell and George has a cup of creole gumbo, with hot cajun spices from a N'Awlins winning recipe.

It's not far over the bridge to the Hampton Inn.

DAY 15 - WEDNESDAY, AUGUST 4, 1993

Memphis, Tenn - Rain, then sunny, hot

Heavy rain during the night and morning, until 10 AM when the travelers departed the Hampton Inn for downtown Memphis. There is a trolley, which runs about three miles along Main Street every 10-15 minutes. Fare is 50 cents each way, only 25 cents for seniors.

Barclay parked the Chrysler near the Holiday Inn Crown Plaza, which is near the west-end of the trolley line.

In about 10 minutes the east-end of the line is reached. The driver points out the Lorraine Motel where Dr. Martin Luther King, Jr. was fatally wounded, April 4, 1968. It is now a historic sight, preserved as it was on that fateful day, complete with the two cars that Dr. King was using, a Cadillac and a Dodge. The motel lobby houses the National Civil Rights Museum.

The trolley takes the group back to the west-end of the line to an area known as the "Pinch." The Pinch was settled many years ago by Irish people who came to America after the potato famine in Ireland. They were so skinny, their belts pinched at the waist, hence the name.

It's 11:00 AM and being in an Irish part of town, it is time for a drink or maybe it's too late.

George spots a sign "Jake's Tavern" and exclaims, "That is the one for us."

The help are preparing for lunch. Barclay spots a friendly looking gentlemen and says, "Is that you, yourself,

Jake?" Jake replies, "It tis, would you like a drink?"

As luck would have it, Jake's Tavern turns out to be a somewhat famous place. It was used in the filming of "The Firm" as the bar in Boston where Tom Cruise worked as a waiter while in college.

It is also the hang-out for the students at Memphis State. Jake sits with the group and is interviewed and cam corded by Barclay and the rest. He is a very friendly and low-key individual, who also owns the "Carriage Tours of Memphis," which is located only a block away from the Tavern at 356 N. Main Street. Jake Schorr offers to open up this establishment. Inside are 4 cats, 5 dogs, mostly collies, and 14 horses which pull the old fashioned carriages. The carriages are also there along with a large tack room. In the evening the carriages move people, especially tourists, along Beale Street and other downtown attractions.

One of the horses "Dan" appeared in "The Firm," but doesn't know he is a celebrity.

It is time for lunch. Jake suggests "The Barge" on the river about a mile distant. He is a partner in that location. The trolley drops the group within two blocks, which is easy walking down hill. The "Barge" is really a barge tied to the shore, converted into a many-level restaurant. We are greeted by Jake's partner, Mike Baldridge, another friendly individual.

Barclay enjoys his favorite oysters on the half shell and George again tries seafood gumbo. The ladies are more conventional. The gumbo was first class. Nan and Juney enjoyed for dessert a hot fudge pie with french vanilla ice cream topped with whipped cream, a specialty of the house. George and Barclay could not resist a few bites. The luncheon is on tape on Barclay's camcorder.

Jake also suggested that we visit "Mud Island." Mud Island is located near the middle of the "M" which is quite wide at Memphis. It was probably mud at one time, but is now a beautiful and spectacular recreational area for citizens and tourists. Connected to the downtown by a two-minute monorail ride, which runs both ways every five minutes and costs $2.00 for every thing except the museum, which is $5.00 extra.

A feature is a five block depiction of the lower 900 miles of the "M" in three dimensions. It takes about 90 minutes to walk along both sides of the marvelous concrete exhibit. Horizontal is 30 inches to the mile and vertical is one inch to eight feet so one is able to visualize changes in depth and width of the river and also see the curves, dams, bridges, and cities along the 900 miles.

Alongside the Miniature River, which has water flowing through it, are various species of trees and beds of many kinds of flowers. The Miniature River finally ends at the Gulf, which is a gigantic swimming pool. What a great place to bring the family on a hot, humid day in Memphis.

Incidentally, the monorail was used in the chase scene in the movie "The Firm."

Memphis is also the home of "Grace Land," dedicated to the life and memorabilia of Elvis. The travelers decide to bypass this much visited shrine.

Back downtown, the trolley takes the travelers to the Holiday Inn near the car park. The ladies use the Holiday Inn to freshen up and discover that it is happy hour in the lobby bar. George will bet that you know that we had a couple of drinks and some finger food.

It is 10 minutes to the Hampton Inn, for a rest, and then the usual two rubbers of bridge.

Bridge - Tonight - Men 90 - 2 Rubbers
Score To Date - Men 4200 - 20 Rubbers

DAY 16 - THURSDAY, AUGUST *5, 1993*

Memphis, Tenn. to Vicksburg, MS - Sunny

The ladies learn that there is a river boat casino, called" Splash" at Tunica, MS about 30 miles south of

Memphis on good old Hwy. 61.

The men are out voted so let's dash to "Splash" for breakfast and slot machines. Somewhere in Memphis, the ladies have picked up coupons for a free breakfast, featuring a 10-oz. New York strip steak. Most of the new casinos charge $10.00 each for the privilege of losing one's money and "Splash" is no exception. Barclay says, "At least we'll get a steak."

The casino is not easy to find as it is five miles out of Tunica on Lake Tunica, as required in order to have gambling. Crazy laws allow gambling on boats, but not on land.

"Splash" is a 10 month old replica of an old-fashioned river boat sitting just on the water's edge with a fifty foot gang plank (fancy, of course) to get aboard. It is as flashy and elegant as the casinos in Las Vegas.

The ladies only nibble at their breakfast and then dash to the machines. The men linger over the "not bad" steaks.

Barclay inquires, "Do you ever play the slots?" George replies, "Maybe once a year. I think it's silly to gamble for nickels or even quarters. Whether one wins or loses makes little difference in ones life. I can think of more beneficial ways to spend my time."

Barclay said, "That sounds like a superior attitude." George replied, "You are right, sorry. So I'll buy 100 dollar chips and we can watch them disappear."

The first 40 chips were swallowed up quickly and then a strange thing happened. The machine poured out 320 chips and people are congratulating George with "nice hit" and other slot machine verbiage.

George distributes some of the winnings among the group for further play, keeping a $200 profit and that's the end of that little episode.

Nan and Juney are soon cleaned out and the travelers return to familiar Highway 61, heading toward Vicksburg, on the east side of the "M."

Not Pittsburgh, Juney, Vicksburg.

A stop in Clarksdale, MS, famous for the birth of the

blues. W.C. Handy spent much time in Clarksdale in his younger days, along with local artist Muddy Waters and several others. The Delta Blues Museum commemorates the history and development of the blues in its displays, recordings, and programs. It was well worth an hour's visit. George bought a book, "Like Jazz," with drawings of and poems about famous performers.

Before reaching Clarksdale, we passed through the factory town of Leland, famous for Lazy-Boy chairs. Needless to say, Leland seemed quite prosperous.

The travelers left Hwy. 61 on Hwy. 82, headed to Greenville. Greenville is normally a busy port on the "M," but like everywhere else, so far, there is little traffic on the river which is fast and high, but not flooding.

Somehow or another the Navigator became confused and instead of continuing south on Hwy. 61, he directed the pilot north for about five miles before noticing the mistake. The Navigator came up with a lame excuse; "as it was noon, the sun was directly overhead and with two choices he guessed wrong." The travelers wrote Greenville off the list. Juney vowed to never go back there again. Barclay made several of his classic "Ewe" turns. What a driver!

Vicksburg was an important battleground during the civil war and withstood the siege of Grant's army for 47 days. There are several military monuments about the city, but the Antebellum mansions are much more pleasant to look at. At least a dozen mansions are open for viewing and have been restored to their former glory, including the landscaped grounds.

A drive along the River Road brings the hungry travelers to the "Top of the River," which specializes in catfish exceptional, served family-style, same as Murphy's serves chicken. One can also take the excess away, again the same as Murphy's in Palm Desert.

George was interested in the corn bread which was baked with jalapenos in the mixture. He took some for later consumption during the Bridge game.

The restaurant had an excellent view of the "M," but nothing was moving, not even a duck.

This is a lucky day for George as he had Barclay bid and made a small slam.

The "M" is cresting in St. Genevieve today. That's the place where the authorities kept strangers out by threatening arrest. The citizens and inmates of the correctional institution have been working for 35 days anticipating this day. Good luck to them.

Bridge - 2 rubbers - tonight - Men 870
22 rubbers - to date - Men 5070

DAY 17 - FRIDAY, AUGUST 6, 1993

Vicksburg, MS to Baton Rouge, LA - Sunny

The travelers are back on Hwy. 61, heading south to Natchez and Baton Rouge.

About halfway to Natchez is the city of Port Gibson, which General Grant spared on his march to Vicksburg, saying, "It was too beautiful to burn." Again there are many Antebellum mansions open to the public. There must have been a lot of rich people around prior to the civil war. They should have been rich, they got their labor for free.

Port Gibson is on the Natchez Trail Parkway so the travelers drive the forty miles to Natchez on the former ancient Indian trail. The trail extends from Natchez to Nashville, a distance of 500 miles, of which about 80 percent is open. This part of the world brings to mind,

From Natchez to Mobile
From Memphis to St. Joe
Wherever the four winds blow,

That Jo Stafford classic, "Blues in the Night"

Near mile post 10.3 on the trail, is "Emerald Mound," the second largest Indian temple mound in the U.S.A. It was built between 1300 and 1600 by the Natchez Indians and used probably for religious purposes.

The Great Primary Platform is 770 feet long, 435 feet wide, and 35 feet high. At the west end of the Platform is what appears to be a stage, facing east. It is 30 x 30 and 30 ft. high. Nobody seems to know what happened or where the Indians went. Maybe the U.F.O.'s had something to do with the disappearance. Let's blame them anyway.

Natchez is famous for its horse-drawn carriage tours on top of the hill. The travelers were fortunate to get a lucid and informative guide. Besides pointing out and describing the Antebellum homes and buildings, the guide was full of history.

Natchez, prior to the war, was one of the wealthiest cities in America and was known as the pre-war Beverly Hills. The Jewish synagogue was built in 1840 and many Jewish people settled in Natchez, including the ancestors of the Monsanto family.

Another thing of interest is that many freed slaves lived in this area and they, themselves, had slaves. One of the most famous of the freed slaves was William Johnson, probably an ancestor of Magic Johnson. He started as a barber, soon had several shops, and amassed a small fortune, buying and selling property. There is a book about William called, "The Barber of Natchez," and both Barclay and George bought a copy.

All the foregoing is on top of the hill. "Under the Hill" is an area much closer to the level of the "M." At one time it was the bordello area, whatever that means. Probably wicked and fun.

Now "Under the Hill" has a six-month-old river boat casino called, "Lady Luck." The ladies dashed to the machines while the men visited the bars along the shore. The bars featured paintings of naked ladies. The men did not look at the paintings and concentrated on their drinks.

This casino, for some reason, did not have an admission fee. The group got together for an excellent buffet lunch, overlooking the vacant river.

After lunch the ladies returned to their gambling, and Juney, with great skill, pulled the handle and won $90.00 in quarters. She was so excited, she forgot to clear the machine, just cashed her chips. Her hearing aid will be on the wrong channel for awhile.

On to Baton Rouge on Hwy. 61, still on the east side of the "M." Accidentally, when nearing Baton Rouge, we got on 61B, somehow losing 61. It was an hour's scenic trip throughout downtown Baton Rouge before the Hampton Inn came into view.

Then it turned out to be the wrong Hampton Inn, so back on the freeway to the right Hampton Inn about three miles away. These people should know better than to have two places so close together. Barclay was in rare form with his "Ewe" turns, but it took a lot out of him as he stayed at the motel while the rest visited the large recreational park next to the hotel.

Among many other attractions, this place had batting cages. George was able to swat the 35-mile an hour pitches all over the field. Juney wanted to hit and as George did not want her to show him up, he fitted her with a batting helmet much too large, so she couldn't see very well. She cracked out a few good ones as the helmet slipped past her eyes.

George tried the 60-mile an hour machine and did not see the first half-dozen balls, only heard them. Finally, he got to the stage where he could foul each pitch. That, in it self, was an accomplishment.

What a great baseball race in the American League East. Four teams practically tied for first. Hang in there, Blue Jays.

Bridge - 2 rubbers - tonight - Men 750
24 rubbers - to date - Men 5820

The ladies are much better Bridge players than the men, but have had no luck. After 24 rubbers they owe the men $5,820.00 each, and decide to quit. Also, we are on Bourbon Street, tomorrow.

DAY 18 - SATURDAY, AUGUST 17, 1993

Baton Rouge, LA to Venice, LA and New Orleans, LA - Showers, hot

Showers, on and off, as the travelers leave Baton Rouge on Hwy. 61 and join with Freeway 10 just before New Orleans. The object is to stay on 10 through New Orleans and pick up Hwy. 23, on the south side of the "M" over the bridge. Hwy. 23 is the only road to the end of the "M" where the "M" joins the Gulf of Mexico. It is hard to say something a mile wide is flowing into something; joining seems more appropriate.

This is Petro Chemical Alley as the whole peninsula is lined along the river with the big names in the oil industry. These are gigantic refineries such as Chevron, British Petroleum, Texaco, Mobil, and some smaller companies. A few small towns along the way such as Empire have little attraction.

As it is Saturday, there are very few workers around. Barclay, with his expertise at the "Ewe" turns, drives the Chrysler out on the last pier before the Gulf. It was a Chevron installation, but no one is there to complain.

The mileage indicator read 2520 miles from the Source to the Gulf. The camcorder was used to record the momentous accomplishment.

About 10 miles from the Gulf, the Food Director noticed, in the town of Boothville, a likely looking place for lunch. Juney went inside to check it out and was gone a long time. It seems she had already made friends with the owners.

It was called the "Little Fish Restaurant and Motel"

and was operated by two divorced sisters and their widowed mother who did the cooking. The more attractive. sister (little to choose) Dianna Barrois, who was once an airline hostess, tel. no. (504) 534-2086, was anxious to chat. A regular customer, "Boopie" Hoskin, a contractor, also joined in.

It's obvious not many people visit this out-of-the-way strip of land, which sticks out in the Gulf. Barclay has the camcorder working and humorously interviewed both Dianna and Boopie.

The food was quite good so it was a fun stop. Juney scores again.

Fort Jackson, a remnant of civil war days is a few miles north. Barclay drove over the DrawBridge, under the Portcullis and into the middle of the fort. The folks didn't like that, so it took a few extra "U" turns to get back out.

The main reason they didn't appreciate the intrusion was that the Fort was now used as a base for drug-busting helicopters. In fact, two were circling above waiting to land on the spot where Barclay had stopped the car. The man in charge suggested we walk back in and watch the helicopters land. One of the drug-busters was a female. She could certainly handle that helicopter.

Nothing further to see on the peninsula, so back to New Orleans where we easily find the Prince Conti Hotel. It's in the middle of the French Quarter on Conti Street, half a block from Bourbon Street. One drives the car right inside the hotel. The valet takes it from there and one doesn't see it again until ready to leave. The fee for parking is $8.00 per night.

The "Famous Door," a renowned jazz joint since 1934, is on the corner of Conti and Bourbon. Before rock and roll, when jazz was king, all the big names played "The Door." A scroll on the wall lists all who worked there and it's a Who's Who of Jazz.

Jazz is not as popular with young people as it once was, so there are many outstanding players who do not get the recognition once accorded the stars.

Tonight, there are four black men beating their brains out. A drummer, a keyboardist, a tenor man and an exceptional trombonist. Our group of old people sip their drinks and sop up the sound, thoroughly enjoying themselves.

After an hour, a little food is in order at a nearby specialty house, then a walk up and down Bourbon Street, then back to the "Famous Door" for another hour before going to bed early by "French Quarter" standards.

DAY 19 - SUNDAY, AUGUST 8, 1993

New Orleans, LA - Hot and humid

The Prince Conti is one of a group of three hotels located in the heart of the French Quarter. The Valentino Family purchased three old properties and converted them into tasteful small hotels in European pension style, reminiscent of 18th Century New Orleans. Classic guestrooms, with poster and canopied beds, including period furnishings, complete the 18th Century decor.

A free continental breakfast is served in a period breakfast room. One does not help oneself, but is served gracefully by a charming black lady, Dolores, who treats each guest, as she would in her own home. No standing in line or having someone push by to the front. Something like this makes tipping a pleasure, instead of a requirement.

It's laundry day again, and Dolores, by telephoning, finds a laundromat, which is nearby and open on Sunday. The travelers decide to drop the laundry off, then stroll through Jackson Park.

The laundry is operated by three assorted, quick-witted men who make a living by charging five dollars per load. It's a bargain as everything is neatly folded. George, on picking up the bag, remarked, "Great, everything is folded." The man said, "If you don't want it folded, it's easy to unfold.

Louis Armstrong Park is a block away, but the travelers are advised by the laundry folk not to go there at 10 am. "It's Strong Arm Park until noon."

Jackson Square has the usual street musicians and dancers who are camcorded by Barclay. It was decided to ride the quaint street cars adjacent to Jackson Square to the "Riverwalk." The "Riverwalk" contains 200 shops of all types, restaurants, a food court, a market place, a dockside promenade, all overlooking the "M" on the site of the 1984 Louisiana World's Fair.

At the food court George buys "Alligator on a Stick," so everyone may try it. No big deal tastes something like chicken or maybe frog legs. Remember when it was mandatory for Catholics to eat fish on Friday and some used to skirt the issue by eating frog legs. Alligator could have been substituted for fish also, but there were not many alligators in Canada. It seems the church threw out the fish on Friday regulation some years ago. Maybe the meat industry complained.

While the ladies browse and shop, the men enjoy a quiet beer overlooking the "M."

The streetcar takes our travelers back to Jackson Brewery, a complex of shops and eateries where George got mixed up with Cajun chili. It was very tasty, but soon caused a tummy ache. Creole is a combination of French, Spanish, and African cooking based on subtle seasonings and delicate sauces. Cajun cooking was born on the Bayou, where the Acadians from Nova Scotia settled. It, too, is a blending of French, Spanish, and African, but is heartier and hotter than Creole, characterized by sausages and hot peppers. It's somewhat too hot for George's stomach. He has been doing all right with Creole, but Cajun is another matter. In fact, let's go to the hotel and watch golf, until the fire goes out. Maybe a few beers will douse it.

Iax Brewery is not only a place to eat, but also a place to shop. The Allans find several suitable gifts for their grandchildren. The Wescoombes have given up on that idea, too many grandchildren.

Larry Mize wins the Buick Open and Bob Betley, a club pro, wins the senior event.

Back on Bourbon Street for another hour or so of jazz at the "Famous Door." There must be more good jazz in New Orleans, but it's not on Bourbon Street. The real fashionable clubs do not get started until 10:00 p.m., at which time these old-timers are fast asleep.

Al Hirt is not working at his club. We were told he had become ill yesterday.

Nan persuaded George to take in the female impersonator show and he must admit, it was excellent. Three men, two white, one black, did the whole show without uttering a word. Everything was on tape. The costumes were realistic and acting or mannerisms superb. Tapes of the stars were played and the actors lip-synced and moved about the way the star would. The black man did Billie Holiday, Diana Ross, and Whitney. The last brought down the house. One white man did Mae West and Bette Midler complete with tapes of part of their stage shows, including jokes and patter. The other white guy did the Mistress of Ceremonies, Patsy Cline and Marilyn Monroe. The Mistress of Ceremonies in her (his) patter made it quite clear that the girls were guys. Well worth the two-drink minimum. The men came on stage after the show. One said he had not told his mother what he was doing for a living.

DAY 20 - MONDAY, AUGUST 9, 1993

New Orleans, LA - Hot and humid

George is still having trouble communicating. If he had known about the problem before the trip, he could have had Gary, Bob, or Ted design a transmitter through which he could speak to each hearing aid individually, without wires. Those friends could do it easily, but it would take a day or so from their busy schedule. Anyway, Juney is back on the right wave length. Today at 11:30 we are going to cruise on the "M" for the first time, on the famous steamboat, "The Natchez."

There are few of these old paddle wheel jobs left. This one can travel with 1500 people, plus crew, on board.

The "M" is very big at this point having absorbed water from 31 states. It is 200 feet deep so although it will crest on August 17, there is little chance of flooding.

New Orleans is the second largest port in the world, behind Amsterdam.

It's a great two-hour trip, with a good commentator, lots of drinks, and also a buffet lunch. George stayed away from the Creole and Cajun dishes.

The "M" has many curves so it's hard to tell which way we are moving. The captain must have been watching Barclay drive, as he is also an expert on ewe turns. The captain also plays the calliope.

Sitting near the group were Nigel and Brenda, "Ben Wright," whose accents betrayed an English heritage. They thought America was the greatest and spent every holiday exploring part of the U.S.A.

Nigel is an aircraft engine designer with Rolls Royce. Barclay interviews .the couple with his camcorder. Their English humor combined with Barclay humor is delightful.

As this is the last day of the expedition, the Treasurer is asked for a report. To this point, each couple has contributed $2,000.00 to the fund for joint expenses, which was the estimated budget. The Treasurer, emphasizing that he has not attempted to skimp, revealed that he has $150.00 still in the fund.

This group is not addicted to expansive meals in expensive restaurants, having passed through that ego trip many years ago. However, as this is the last night, George suggests a steak place, "The Embers," which overlooks Bourbon Street from a balcony. George and Nan were there a couple of years ago and escaped at about $30-$35 per person.

It is agreed to enjoy an hour's jazz and drinks at the reliable Famous Door, then proceed to "The Embers" at 7:00 p.m. and hope they would consider serving us at that very early hour. In the meantime, the Allans and Nan go to Jackson Square for more camcording and shopping. George returns to the Hotel Conti for rest and the newspaper.

There is a movement to establish a Jazz Hall of Fame in New Orleans. The problem is that four factions have different ideas and as yet have not come to terms.

In Armstrong Park, the Black Music Hall of Fame is scheduled to open next year. Some want to renovate the Perseverance Hall complex, also in Armstrong Park as an adjunct to the Black Music Hall of Fame. Another group wants the National Park Service to fund a site near Armstrong Park and make it a National Jazz Park, under government supervision. This would be, of course, inexpensive for visitors, but a further drain on Federal taxpayers.

The State is supporting Buddy Bolden Place, which is in the planning stage and is to be located on the riverfront. This is a large undertaking, including beside a Music Hall of Fame, recording and sound studios, a radio station, theatres, retail stores, and offices. Buddy Bolden, a New Orleans cornetist, is considered the first jazz musician. All these things should be done except the one in which the Federal government has a role.

It is apparent that gambling is rampant in most of the States through which was have passed. Allowing gambling on the river, but not on the land, is not even a subtle form of subterfuge. Gambling is a symptom of a desire to get something for nothing, an attitude that has become more and more prevalent in the last two decades. It is difficult to pinpoint a date, but maybe it coincides with the advent of inflation, 1973.

Government sponsored gambling in the form of State lotteries is another form of taxation. The proceeds, after prizes, are supposed to supply funds to pay for services usually paid for by direct taxation. The sad part is that the proceeds are reduced by the usual bureaucratic overhead, so the designated service receives 25% of the profit and the overhead (operators) 75.25%. If the profit from a lottery, after prizes, is 8 million dollars, 6 million is absorbed in operating expense and 2 million is the amount reluctantly given to the needed service; in some cases, education.

Private gambling in the form of the many casinos along the river is better than having the government involved. After the initial payment is made to the politicians to obtain a license, business people or even the mafia, do not have the layers of bureaucracy that pervades the government. Hence, through private casinos, many jobs are created in a less expensive manner than by government inaction.

The banks are competing for the loans required for casino construction and operation, and for the loans required for spin-off businesses, such as hotels, motels, land acquisition, offices and apartments. A bank president states, "Gambling has helped create a demand for real estate, boosted employment and wages, and funneled business growth." George doesn't know what "Funneled Business Growth" means, but maybe the banker does.

Sheraton and Bally manufacturing have joined the stampede of companies planning to open riverboat and dockside gaming facilities. "Lady Sheraton," a 1450 passenger riverboat casino and a dockside area near the French Quarter in New Orleans, is only one of the Sheraton projects.

After leaving the Famous Door, our group becomes the second table on the balcony overlooking Bourbon Street at "The Embers." As the restaurant does not get busy until 9:00 p.m., the group is able to linger over, before-dinner drinks, wine, very good salads, small filets, baked potato (or potatoe as Dan Quayle would say) and after-dinner drinks. Barclay had his usual half dozen oysters on the half shell. A very pleasant way to spend the last evening of the trip.

Each couple had to contribute an additional $20.00 to

cover the bill and tip. Thus, the entire cost per couple was $2020 for shared expenses, pretty close to the estimate.

DAY 21 - TUESDAY, AUGUST 10, 1993

New Orleans - Phoenix - LAX - Sunny

This is get-away day. The travelers feel they have seen about all of the "M" they need to see. It is another beautiful day, continuing the streak that began the day after the Wescoombes arrived from California. George and Nan experienced a small sample of what the 45 days of continuous rain meant to the area. It poured when they landed in MPLS and all the way to St. Cloud where they spent the first night. However, the next morning the heavy rain was over. Since then, there have been scattered showers and great thunderstorms, which is normal for this part of the country, but mostly sunshine. When the Wescoombes leave, the rain will probably return, but we sincerely hope not.

The Wescoombes' flight 1449 on Southwest Airlines leaves New Orleans at 11:10 with a stopover in Phoenix. Barclay has the car parked and ready for the 30-minute drive to the airport by 8:00 a.m. He wants to make sure George doesn't miss the flight by being late. That's what George accused him of, anyway.

New Orleans Airport is quite pleasant and two and a half-hour wait goes quickly. Southwest flight 1449 leaves on time. They are using what appears to be an old 737 on this "No Frills" flight. Pay less, get less is their slogan. We are setting down in Houston for a few minutes to drop off about 100 people. This is a real milk run. George is not complaining, as Southwest is a very efficient airline, having the best "on time" record in 1992.

We are soon landing in Phoenix where the temperature is 103°. The stopover in Phoenix is one and one-half hours. Arriving at the departure gate, George notices that another Southwest flight is leaving for L.A. in 15 minutes from a nearby gate.

"Any space on that flight?" George inquired. "Yes, you've got it, and we will work on transferring your bags," was the cooperative reply. The Wescoombes did not know the bags had made it until reaching LAX when their bags were first down the chute. Thanks, Southwest.

A call to the Hacienda Hotel was sufficient to have the Hacienda bus pick up the Wescoombes at Southwest in 15 minutes.

It was easy to find the car in the Hacienda parking lot, pick up the bags, and begin the 3-hour drive to Indian Wells by 3:30 p.m. A welcome rest stop for dinner and drinks at old familiar San Gorgonio Inn, then home by 7:30 p.m.

It was a very successful, satisfying, relaxing, interesting and educational trip, as well as great fun with two humorous and loving companions.

EPILOGUE

The Great Flood of 1993 was a disaster of epic proportions. Continual rain for 45 consecutive days throughout the upper Mississippi Basin raised the already swollen "M" beyond anything the levees and flood walls could contain, except in some cities and towns.

Fortunately, it was a scheduled drama. Unlike earthquakes, flash floods, or airplane crashes, there was plenty of advance warning. Therefore, the loss of life was minimal considering the vast scope of the flooding. The loss of one life is one too many.

Due to evacuation plans, people in the path of the flood were able to remove belongings from their homes and to move livestock to safe areas. No doubt, wild animals and birds will adapt.

The lower "M" from Cairo south has a flood control system that has not failed since 1927. The upper "M" north of Cairo is a hodgepodge of reservoirs, lakes, and levees. The U.S. Army Corp. of Engineers have spent billions on flood control. Like most government projects, the effort has backfired. The natural flow of the "M" has been blocked by levees causing the pent-up river to rise higher and cause feeders to back-up like a clogged drain. The water has to go somewhere and if it can't go sideways, it will go up.

Protecting cities and towns is appropriate, such as Hannibal, but the natural flood plains should not be protected, just don't use them. The river will go where it wants to, anyway. Replacing the natural flood control system by an artificial system may increase the number and volume of floods. It is hard to outguess Mother Nature. The "M" says, "Dam me and I will damn you."

We did not see a levee yield to the power of a fist of water. We did see the water rising inexorably on roadways and on the sides of buildings and markers. We talked to many of the victims who exhibited good humor, a neighborly spirit and who joked about their problems.

The Great Flood of 1993 is the champion in height of flood crest, in area and in property damage, but thankfully, not for death toll.

Evidently the Clinton Government is acting speedily with aid, having learned a lesson from the slow reaction of the Bush Administration to Hurricane Andrew.

The government is estimating the loss at fifteen billion dollars. How any estimate in the billions can be made accurately boggles the imagination. George is an accountant and a half-assed mathematician, but has no idea of what fifteen billion is.

U.S. and France say a billion is a thousand million, but England and Germany say a billion is a million million, a major difference.

The national deficit of the United States is $4.2 trillion. In the U.S. and in France it is written as $4,200,000,000,000. In England and Germany it is written as $4,200,000,000,000,000,000, if anyone cares, except the government.

The point is, that the **interest** on the U. S. deficit is almost one billion dollars per day. This is the amount U. S. taxpayers must pay each **day** to cover the excesses of former administrations. So, the enormous loss from the worst flood in history is only the equivalent of fifteen days' interest.

A further complication is the fact that to get 4 billion dollars aid to the sufferers, a more reasonable estimate, would cost taxpayers sixteen billion, due to the layers of bureaucracy unnecessarily used to get the money to the needy. Furthermore, one can rest assured that the large corporate growers with friends in government will receive one hundred percent of their loss immediately, whereas the lowly individual farmer may get $1.75 in six months.

Finally, it was sad to see the Mighty "M" devoid of traffic.

HOTELS, MOTELS, BY CITY, WITH RATE AND TAX

Date			Rate	Tax	Total
7/22	St. Cloud, MN	Comfort	$40.50	$4.65	$45.15
23	Bemidji, MN	Comfort	48.00	5.22	53.22
24	MPLS, MN	Best Western	49.95	6.24	56.19
25	MPLS, MN	Best Western	49.95	6.24	56.19
26	Lacrosse, MN	Exel	42.00	4.20	46.20
27	Dubuque, IA	Comfort	44.95	5.90	50.85
28	Burlington, IA	Comfort	52.00	5.20	57.20
29	Hannibal, MO	Best Western	55.00	5.53	60.53
30	S. Louis, MO	Fairfield	50.35	6.54	56.89
31	St. Louis, MO	Fairrleld	50.35	6.54	56.89
8/1	Sikesron, MO	Hampton	44.95	2.80	47.75
2	Blytheviile, MO	Hampron	*40.00*	3.40	43.40
3	Memphis, TN	Hampton	45.00	4.73	49.73
4	Memphis, TN	Hampron	45.00	4.73	49.73
5	Vicksburg, MS	Hampton	43.95	3.60	47.55
6	Baron Rouge, LA	Hampron	49.00	5.39	54.39
7	New Orleans, LA	Prince Conti	59.00	7.49	66.49
8	New Orleans, LA	Prince Conu	59.00	7.49	66.49
9	New Orieans, LA	Prince Conti	59.00	7.49	*66.49*
			$927.95	$103.38	$1031.33

Average - 19 nights	$48.34	$5.44	$54.28

Daughter Bette telling her Dad where to go…and he loves it.

Barclay Allan, Nan Wescoombe, George Wescoombe
and Juney Allan preparing for the Mississippi trip.

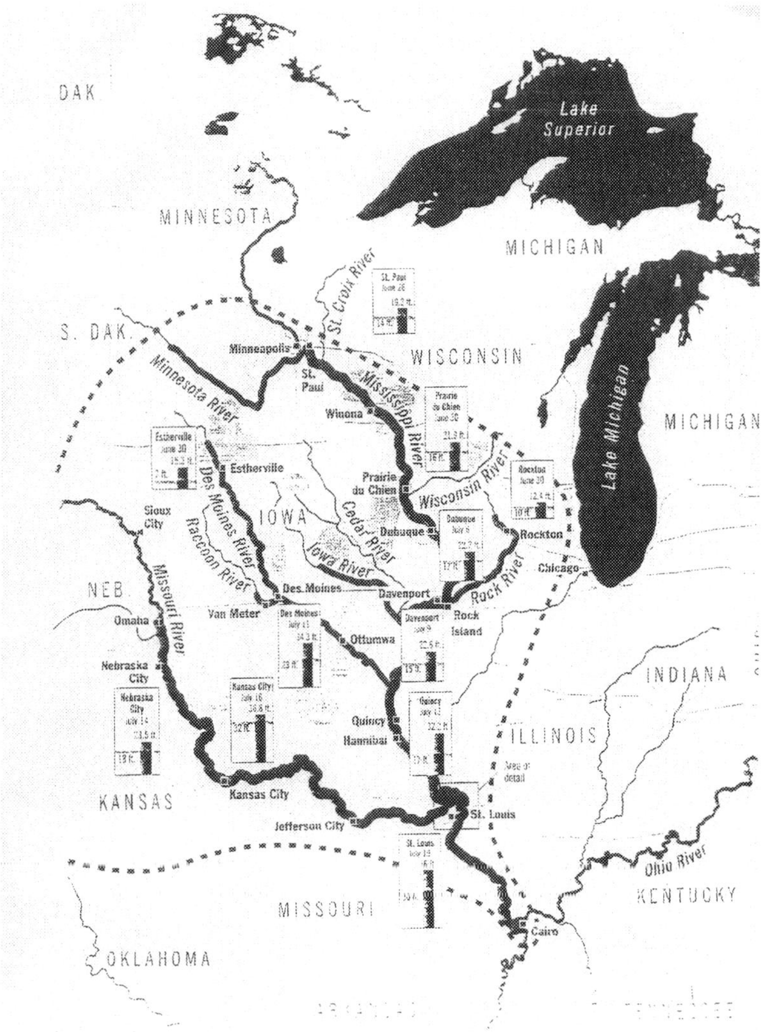

DAK
Lake Superior
MINNESOTA
MICHIGAN
St. Croix River
St. Paul
S. DAK.
Minneapolis
WISCONSIN
St. Paul
Minnesota River
Mississippi River
Winona
Prairie du Chien
Lake Michigan
MICHIGAN
Estherville
Estherville
Des Moines River
Prairie du Chien
Wisconsin River
Rockton
Sioux City
IOWA
Cedar River
Dubuque
Dubuque
Rockton
Raccoon River
Iowa River
Chicago
NEB.
Missouri River
Des Moines
Davenport
Rock River
Omaha
Van Meter
Des Moines
Davenport
Rock Island
Ottumwa
Nebraska City
INDIANA
Nebraska City
Kansas City
Quincy
Quincy
Hannibal
ILLINOIS
KANSAS
Kansas City
St. Louis
Jefferson City
St. Louis
Ohio River
MISSOURI
KENTUCKY
Cairo
OKLAHOMA

Coast to Coast and Back—Almost

FOREWORD

For many years, Wesley Coombe has been writing, what he calls, whimsical narratives about traveling with his wife, Bernice, throughout the world.

Once upon a time during his lengthy business career, Wesley made a call on a customer and the following conversation ensued:

Wesley – "I wish to see Mr. Washborn, if I may."

A beautiful English accent replied, "May I tell Mr. Washborn who is calling?"

"Yes, of course. Please tell him it is Wes Coombe."

"May I tell him your first name, Mr. Wescoombe?"

Without thinking, Wesley replied, "George."

"Mr. Washborn, Mr. George Wescoombe is here to see you, sir."

I had always been an admirer of the popular name George, as many English kings, George Washington, and other important people had used the moniker. So it slipped from my mouth accidentally on purpose when the lady asked for a first name.

When I heard her say George Wescoombe in that splendid English accent, I thought, "That sounds classy."

So at that moment, in my narratives, a family of Wescoombes came into being.

Nan Wescoombe—Bernice, my wife of 67 years.
Bette Wescoombe Burke—daughter Elizabeth
John McAllister Wescoombe—son John
Marnie Wescoombe Caputo—daughter Marilyn
Lisa Wescoombe Hill—daughter Alyson
Patty Wescoombe Warhol—daughter Patricia

Readers may find that the old man sometimes becomes confused and changes the name and/or the voice indiscriminately. The foregoing table may be of assistance.

Nan, Marnie, Bette and George surrounding columnist John T. Kitching in Texas.

DAY 1 – Sunday, August 3, 2003 – Thousand Palms to Mesquite, Nevada—Car Mileage 150,168

The first stop, in five minutes, is at "It's a Grind," a neighborhood coffee shop privately owned by Jim and Carol and patterned after "Starbucks." George, Nan, and Bette were at the opening on March 1, 2003 and have coffeed at "It's a Grind" at least every other day since that time.

The proposed destination for this, the first day of a 7,000-mile trip, is Mesquite, Nevada. The Wescoombes stayed in Mesquite about fifteen years ago, when returning from a visit with Judi Ryan and Ted Andrews at their new home in Vail, Colorado. There was only one hotel in Mesquite in 1988, the Oasis, which featured full scale gambling and an 18-hole golf course. The Oasis has 952 rooms at this date.

Marnie, at the wheel, proceeded along I-10 toward Blythe. George is supposed to be the navigator but fell asleep thus causing Marnie to speed by Highway 177 and miss the turnoff to Desert Center. She went out of the way for ten miles before the sleepy navigator helped her correct his mistake. Highway 95 is a smooth drive to the outskirts of Las Vegas. Marnie spotted the Boulder Station Hotel from Highway 95 and it became the destination for lunch and for Nan to win seventy-five dollars.

The outstanding skyline of Las Vegas is clearly visible. Caesar's Palace built in 1966 is the forerunner of all the amazing hotels dedicated to gambling and sin. The following have opened since 1990: Aladdin 1999, Bellagio 1998, Luxor, Mirage, Excalibur, Mandalay Bay, MGM Grand, Monte Carlo, New York New York, Paris Las Vegas, the Venetian, plus many smaller edifices. It would be interesting to know how many rooms opened each year. Probably that information is readily available on the Internet, but George does not operate a computer.

Furthermore, many, many people gamble their money away twenty-four hours a day in perfect freedom. No one tells them what to do. What a wonderful country!

The city of Mesquite, now with ten thousand population, has at least six elegant hotel casinos and, we are told, four 18-hole golf courses. Nan picked out the Virgin River Hotel Casino as the venue for tonight. This 713-room edifice opened September 1, 1990.

DAY 2 – Monday, August 4, 2003 – Mesquite to Grand Junction, Nevada – Mileage 150,572

Freeway 15, north out of Mesquite, takes the travelers past St. George and Cedar City to the junction with Freeway 70. Freeway 70 has superb and stunning scenery mainly due to the area's seismically active past and scarcity of vegetation. The landscape provides scientists with a remarkable record of the earth's geological history. Countless unusual rock formations inspire one's imagination; maybe it's an ocean reef or a bowl-shaped valley. "A world of grandeur surrounds us."

Colorado, the color red in Spanish, has fifty-eight mountain peaks surpassing 14,000 feet. Utah, not to be outdone has five National Parks and at least a half a dozen National Monuments. Utah also has more than two million Mormons living within its boarders. Brigham Young, leader of the Mormons, proclaimed in 1847, "This is it." Young became governor of Utah in 1850. The Mormons are the religious cult that believed in multiple wives. Wonder why they gave up that splendid idea?

The old navigator missed the freeway entrance to Grand Junction. Marnie drove the length of the city without finding the Comfort Inn. She knows the old man had screwed up, so upon reaching Freeway 70 again, she returned westerly for about five miles and there was the Comfort Inn right where it was supposed to be. George blamed the original construction of the freeway for screwing up this pretty city.

Marnie found the Olive Garden Restaurant and Nan found a bottle of Lambrusca, which is now her favorite wine with spaghetti, anyway.

Near the Comfort Inn, Marnie and George entered an ice cream store on this beautiful evening. A couple of nice people in the store told George and Marnie about their peach orchard, located about 14 miles farther along toward Denver. Would you believe it, the man brought two peaches from his car. The peaches were not the dry California types, but were equal to the peaches grown in the Niagara Peninsula in Ontario, Canada.

DAY 3 – Tuesday, August 5, 2003 – Grand Junction, Colorado to Cheyenne, Wyoming – Mileage 151,012

The Volvo left Grand Junction at 7:00 a.m. proceeding easterly toward Glenwood Springs. A short stop is made at Green River to buy a couple of the sweetest melons in the world for later use.

George has been anticipating the 12.5 miles of double-decked freeway construction clinging to the side of the Glenwood Canyon with the Colorado River flowing along the bottom of the canyon. It took almost 12.5 years to complete the monstrous project. The Wescoombes were able to view the progress during visits to Judi/Ted when they lived in Vail. The highway Department with some ingenious turns, made it possible to switch from side to side and view the immensity of the project from all angles. Marnie and George wanted to make the trip both ways, but Nan said, "Let's go, it's only a road."

Further along, Freeway 70 passes the cities of Edwards and Vail, which have grown immensely in the last ten years.

Marnie expressed a desire to drive through Rocky Mountain National Park. George and Nan agreed that they would be most happy to make the trip if Marnie did all the driving.

Junction 40, on Freeway 70, leads to the entrance to the park. At Granby, one is relieved of $15.00 per carload, in order to experience this hazardous adventure. The snow-mantled peaks of Rocky Mountain National Park rise above verdant valleys, twisting rivers, and glistening lakes. One-third of the park is above the tree line where tundra predominates, an amazing fact. It is a sensational and scary drive with each hair-pin turn outdoing the last, especially as the engineers had not heard of guard rails. The city of Estes Park, around 7,500 feet high, is swarming with visitors. The entire park is interlaced with hiking trails, 60 miles in total. People may avail themselves of camping, horseback riding, fishing, and climbing, many ways in which one may become injured.

Marnie's good driving prevails and soon the travelers are settled in the Quality Inn in Cheyenne, Wyoming. George devours a few too many ribs at Applebee's and needs a nap. Recovering in an hour or so, George and Marnie repair to the hotel lounge for beer and baseball.

DAY 4 – Wednesday, August 6, 2003 – Cheyenne, Wyoming to Valentine, Nebraska – Mileage 151,443

Cheyenne has a population of 53,000 hardy folk, out of Wyoming's total population of 494,000. Wyoming has within its borders 98,000 square miles. One could not consider the state overcrowded. It is the ninth largest state, area wise.

Breakfast is in a Chinese restaurant which is located in the Quality Inn but which is not a part of the hotel. It cost the reasonable sum of $2.75 for cereal and unlimited coffee; a bargain.

Nan sometimes mistakes the price of gas for the time of day. We think she does it on purpose. The advent of bottled water combined with old age has mandated more pee stops for old George.

Marnie has the Volvo cruising along smoothly on Freeway 80 toward North Platte. Shortly after crossing into Nebraska, George has the bladder problem. Marnie stops at a roadside market and gas station at the town of Sidney. Upon leaving, George picks up the free four-page newspaper.

The Sidney, Nebraska, Sun-Telegraph Weekly dated August 6, 2003, had two items of special interest to the Wescoombes.

Being lifetime ardent golfers, George and Nan enjoyed reading about seventh grader McKenzie O'Connell, aged eleven, who won first place with a 61 in the seventh grade division of the Panhandle Juvenile Golf Tournament at Mountain Shadow's Country Club in Gering. McKenzie has won six tournaments this year. She says, "I've been practicing to improve my driving and it has made a difference. I made a 210-yard drive on the fifteenth hole. My goal is to play professional golf, so I'm going to a golf school in Phoenix next year. It's exciting."

The second item of interest to George and Nan was about Ima and Stan Sparrow who travel from county fair to county fair, in their nerdmobile. "So what?" you say. But the nerdmobile turned out to be a 1951 Studebaker Champion. The 1951 Studebaker was known as the bullet nose model. In 1951, George was the auditor for Studebaker dealer, Lynnhurst Motors in Burlington, Ontario, Canada. Bernie Hurst gave George a ten-percent discount from the list price of $1,643.00.

The Sparrows have been touring in their 1951 Studebaker since 1979 and have performed in 22 states and three provinces. Their act is known as "The Nerd."

By the way, Sidney, Nebraska was a Pony Express Station, a hundred years ago. In a pretty park, the threesome finished off the leftover ribs for lunch, cold but delicious, and also ate the world famous melon from Green River, Colorado.

At North Platte, the Volvo leaves friendly Freeway 80 and heads north on Highway 83. North Platte appeared to be a fine little city as the travelers looked it over, from the railway bridge. Another pretty park appeared but the leftover ribs had already disappeared. Highway 83 passed much beautiful country, which was inhabited only by cows, mostly brown beasts.

George suddenly remembers that this is summer and the land which today is green, grand, glowing, gorgeous, glorious, for most of the year is covered by a deep blanket of snow. Forget it, let's stay in California.

Soon Valentine, Nebraska is reached. The ladies suggest a change to a single story motel so the car may be parked in front of the motel room door.

A short search found the "Trade Winds Lodge," a privately owned forty room single story motel complete with all amenities, larger rooms and perfect air-conditioning, and twenty percent less expensive.

A visit to downtown Valentine (not much there) produced Subway sandwiches, beer and Lambrusca, a soft red wine, all of which quickly disappeared.

DAY 5 – Thursday, August 7, 2003 – Valentine, Nebraska to Watertown, South Dakota – Mileage 152,165

The ground floor motel "Trade Winds Lodge" supplied a complimentary continental breakfast.

Another beautiful day in big sky country. Highway 83 continued from Nebraska into South Dakota. It was difficult to tell the difference.

Yesterday, as George was trying to make a reservation at the Quality Inn in the town of Mission, South Dakota, the cell phone was cut off. It is a long way out in the country, so maybe no transmitters. This a.m. Highway 83 runs through Mission and sure enough, there is the Quality Inn. Don't tell Nan but the Rose Bud Indian Casino is next door. She could have lost her recent winnings. Nan is an absolute rosebud.

Everywhere there are motorcycles. Sturgis, South Dakota is the home of the Sturgis annual Motor.cycle Rally. Two thousand or more big men and big women are in the area wearing big black outfits and riding on big motorcycles. They are from all parts of the country. They smile politely at old folks rather than gunning their machines. All these people assemble together 24/7 in perfect freedom with few restrictions. What a wonderful country!

The travelers enjoyed driving alongside the majestic Missouri River but avoided the Tractor Museum. George signed up for the ice-fishing contest to be held next December but failed to pay the entry fee.

Nebraska means "flat water" in Indian—flat as a platte.

At an antique sale in Henry, South Dakota, George was able to buy Marnie a thirty-year-old "Barbie Doll," and for Kent and Patty, a martini shaker activated by a well-endowed blond lady doing all the necessary moves. The Lewis and Clark information center in Chamberlain has a plentitude of exhibits and artifacts dating back to 1804 when the explorers lived with the Indians of the neighborhood.

The Redlin Art Center is a highlight in Watertown. Famous painter Terry Redlin financed the outstanding museum building, filled two floors with his paintings, opened on June 6, 1997, and has welcomed to date nearly two million visitors. Incidentally, Redlin's son designed the ultramodern building. Visiting the art center was an unexpected treat.

Businesses left their brochures at the art center. Marnie picked up a brochure advertising the Drake Motor Inn in Watertown. George's cell phone was back in business and he was able to make a reservation for tonight, Thursday, August 7, 2003. The rooms, bar, and dining room were decorated in the style of the fifties. The rooms were not modern but were large and comfortable. The Thursday night special was prime rib which George and Nan shared. Marnie is a liver and onions fan.

DAY 6 – Friday, August 8, 2003 – Watertown, South Dakota to Amery, Wisconsin–Mileage 152,448

Another beautiful day, as Marnie drives the Volvo out of South Dakota along Highway 212 into Minnesota.

This part of the country is "corny." It is completely covered on both sides of the road by what the Indians, who once owned our wonderful country called "maize." It grows profusely and it is a large part of the diet of our animals as well as of our own.

Driving along Highway 7 toward Minneapolis, corn is all that can be seen as far as the eye can see. Hurrah for corn!

Freeways 694 and 494 completely encircle the cities of Minneapolis and St. Paul. It is a marvelous way to find one's way. The two cities are within the encircling roads, which leave the circle to service outlying areas.

We must stay on 494 until Freeway 94 reappears from the city. Then leave the circle to the right and stay on Freeway 94 until Highway 63 appears which travels north joining Highway 46 into the city of Amery.

With the aid of Kent's map, Marnie was able to find Kent's house and there was Patty standing in front of the house, 2,380 miles from 32380 Miguelito, in Thousand Palms.

Kent joined Patty and welcomed us warmly. It turned out that Kent's parents had both passed away in the short period between March 1999 and June 2000. Kent's father had retired from the hardware business about thirty years ago. Being energetic, he did something he had always wanted to do: build a house. As he owned a piece of land on the shore of nearby Lake Wapogasset, he followed the example of many of the citizens of Amery and had two homes, one in town and one on the lake. In addition, Mr. and Mrs. Warhol spent the winter months in a mobile home in Cathedral City, California. Meanwhile, Kent and his younger brother Larry were working in the engineering field somewhere in the world. Both would return to Amery on vacation.

The main house reminds the Wescoombes of their home at 305 Brant Street in Burlington, Ontario, Canada. Conversation revealed that both houses had been built at relatively the same time thus displaying the design of that period. Both were split-level, for example. As George and Nan have lived in California since 1956, it was like stepping into the past. George and Nan had one of the two bedrooms on the main floor. Marnie had the lower floor all to her own little self. As was the custom at that time, the home had only one bathroom. We all lived through that period; not realizing that life would have been easier with two or more.

There are many fine eating places in this area, ninety percent of which are "on a lake." The five-some are joined by friends Dave and Bonnie, and have supper at Meister's located on Cedar Lake only about ten miles from home. This excellent eating place features beef and fish. George has one of the best hamburgers ever and Nan has a local fish with beer and wine.

It has been a long great day, with wonderful company.

Subject: The Year is 1902...100 years ago!!!!
This ought to boggle your mind, I know it did mine!

The year is 1902, one hundred years ago, what a difference a century makes. Here are the U.S. statistics for 1902...

1) *The average life expectancy in the U.S. was forty-seven (47).*
2) *Only 14 percent of the homes in the U.S. had a bathtub.*
3) *Only 8 percent of the homes had a telephone.*
4) *A three-minute call from Denver to New York City cost eleven dollars.*
5) *There were only 8,000 cars in the U.S. and only 144 miles of paved roads.*
6) *The maximum speed limit in most cities was 10 m.p.h.*
7) *Alabama, Mississippi, Iowa, and Tennessee were each more heavily populated than California. With a mere 1.4 million residents, California was only the 21st most populous state in the Union.*
8) *The tallest structure in the world was the Eiffel Tower.*
9) *The average wage in the U.S. was 22 cents an hour.*
10) *The average U.S. worker made between $200 and $400 per year.*
11) *The competent accountant could expect to earn $2,000 per year, a dentist $2,500 per year, a veterinarian between $1,500 and $4,000 per year, and a mechanical engineer about $5,000 per year.*
12) *More than 95 percent of all births in the U.S. took place at home.*
13) *Ninety percent of all U.S. physicians had no college education. Instead, they attended medical schools, many of which were condemned in the press and by the government as "Substandard."*
14) *Sugar cost four cents a pound. Eggs were fourteen cents a dozen. Coffee cost fifteen cents a pound.*
15) *Most women only washed their hair once a month and used borax or egg yolks for shampoo.*
16) *Canada passed a law prohibiting poor people from entering the country for any reason.*

17) The five leading causes of death in the U.S. were: 1. Pneumonia and influenza 2. Tuberculosis 3. Diarrhea 4. Heart disease 5. Stroke

18) The American flag had 45 stars. Arizona, Oklahoma, New Mexico, Hawaii, and Alaska hadn't been admitted to the Union yet.

19) The population of Las Vegas, Nevada was 30.

20) Crossword puzzles, canned beer, and iced tea hadn't been invented.

21) There was no Mother's Day or Father's Day.

22) One in ten U.S. adults couldn't read or write. Only 6 percent of all Americans had graduated from high school.

23) Marijuana, heroin, and morphine were all available over the counter at corner drugstores. According to one pharmacist, "Heroin clears the complexion, gives buoyancy to the mind, regulates the stomach and the bowels, and is, in fact, a perfect guardian of health."

24) Eighteen percent of households in the U.S. had at least one full-time servant or domestic.

25) There were only about 230 reported murders in the entire U.S.

Just think what it will be like an another 100 year. It boggles the mind.

DAY 7 – Saturday, August 9, 2003 – Amery, Wisconsin

Kent's house is located on a bank facing the Apple River. On one side is "No Name" creek. The front or back faces Cross Street and the property adjoins a neighbor to the north. George guesses that the property is about two acres, covered mainly with grass. Many mature trees stand on the property. A feature is two immense trees that lean on each other. A sturdy oak is falling but manages to support a delicate willow, which is also losing its upright stance.

George inquires, "Kent, what do you have in mind for those two."

"Nothing in particular. They will do what they want to do, when they want to do it." Was Kent's noncommittal reply.

George to Marnie, "Now that Mark is a tree surgeon, let's have him take a look."

Marnie answered, "You pay and I'm sure he'll be here." There is plenty to do and see in this outdoor Wisconsin wonderland.

Kent's brother Larry suggests that Kent and Patty bring the visitors to his house on the lake. Joyce will do a roast with all the trimmings. We can sail around the lakes in the meantime.

Larry's house is on Bear Trap Lake, which is separated from larger Wapogasset Lake by about a 200 yard opening. Both lakes are surrounded by the summer homes of maybe a thousand lucky city dwellers. It is an idyllic life style. George is suggesting a move to Amery when Nan remarks, "No way! For most of the year, it's covered with ice." Her remark ended that conversation.

A pontoon boat is very popular in this part of the water world. They evidently come in various sizes. Larry's boat is a 24-footer and holds twelve passengers comfortably. These are basically party boats, but folks can be seen trying to catch a "muskie" whatever that is.

As Kent's and Larry's father had a home on the lake for many years, both boys, now men, are very familiar with the two lakes and know the owners of the homes, which line the shore. Of course, every house has a boat, which is lowered to the water in sort of a chute.

Cabins which were popular along the shore 30-40 years ago, have gradually given way to more pretentious, commodious dwellings, constructed by the lucky folk who got out of the stock market before it collapsed a couple of years ago.

Many of the cabins still remain, upgraded, and are neat and serviceable. It reminds George of the upgrading at Newport Harbor. The old gives way to the new.

George and Nan are tired from the sun and water and fall asleep in Larry's house after the boat ride.

They wake up to a sumptuous repast prepared by Joyce who is a gourmet cook. Larry brought to the party a succulent roast of beef, which Joyce roasted to perfection in the oven, surrounded by potatoes and several other veggies. It was topped off by Yorkshire pudding and brown gravy. Let's not forget the outstanding salad and strawberry shortcake for dessert. Thank you, Joyce and Larry, for a feast fit for a king.

DAY 8–Sunday, August 10, 2003 – Amery, Wisconsin

When George looks from a window or takes a walk around the property, it reminds him of Burlington. Believe it or not, Amery, Wisconsin and Burlington, Ontario are just about at the same latitude. There must be a feeling of sameness in the air that makes George think he is in Burlington. Let's say it is a good feeling.

Kent and Patty are helping George put a third book together. The manuscript is typed on a regular typewriter, not on a word processor. Thus the pages have to be retyped or scanned in order to be in the format required by the printing company.

George has brought with him the narratives needed to complete the entire book of about 300 pages. Kent and Patty have supplied the needed expertise, and the manuscript is ready to be copied and sent to George's old friend, Robert Scott, for editing. The copying will be done at Office Depot in St. Paul, Minnesota on Monday next.

Bob Scott lives in New York State, is 85 years old, and has been in every facet of the book business. He thinks

George could do better and barely charges him for advice. Does anyone think George is improving?

Kent took the folks on an extended drive to see the surrounding area, including the county seat of Balsam Lake and ending up at Shoreview Supper Club, which opens at 11:00 a.m. on Sundays and serves an excellent brunch featuring Bloody Mary's at $2.00 a pop. Everything was first rate.

Back home to watch Davis Love win the International Golf Tournament. It's the tournament that features a weird scoring system. George is glad they play only one per year.

As is normal these days, the Indian tribes are allowed to operate gambling casinos. The white man took their land so this is their chance to take the white man's money. Nan loves to participate. She usually loses but it's good fun for her. While the ladies play the slots, George and Kent nap in the car.

The Wescoombes suggested that Kent pick out a first rate Supper Club for dinner tonight and to ask Joyce and Larry to be guests.

The Caulderwood Lodge on beautiful Bone Lake is one of Kent's favorites and after dining there, it is easy to understand why. Caulderwood has been in business since 1978 and has a reputation for fine casual dining in "an old world atmosphere."

Joyce and the men have steak, Patty and Nan split a walleye, Marnie also had walleye which was good but too much. George had a superb beef sandwich with mashed potatoes and gravy, which was perfect but again too much. Don't forget the salads and dessert. It would be hard to beat the Caulderwood for quality and service. George was pleased to be the host of a delightful party.

DAY 9—Monday, August 11, 2003—Amery, Wisconsin

Patty and Marnie took the rubber boat up river from Kent's house for about a quarter mile and floated with the gentle current back to the house. Patty had a paddle with which to maintain control. If the boat got away, they could have floated to the Mississippi, then all the way to New Orleans, maybe.

All were hungry enough to visit Gramma Bonnie's Coffee Shop and put away cinnamon buns, bearclaws, etc. George had his favorite raspberry scone, a special in Gramma Bonnies. It cost a couple of bucks for each pastry and $1.50 for regular coffee. This is a better business than selling eggs and toast.

Why not have ice cream for lunch? Kent and Patty have a favorite shop in a small town, Stillwater on the St. Croix River. It is Nelson's and serves heaping helpings of Brown's splendid ice cream in about thirty different flavors. George had a banana split without bananas as they were out of stock. Instead of ice cream, George had peach yogurt. It was covered in chocolate sauce like a banana split, anyway.

A nice lady in Office Depot made two copies of the manuscript of George's latest group of whimsical narratives. She sent one copy by UPS to George's editor, Robert Scott, which will be in his hands in three days. George kept one copy of the manuscript for the file.

The immense Office Depot store is in a large mall in the St. Paul suburb of Roseville. George needs a new pair of summer sandals as the old ones are falling apart and his feet may get cold. Believe it or not, he was able to buy a pair of Teva's on sale for $29.95 in the Maplewood Mall. This must be a lucky day. They were getting rid of their summer shoes at a discount. Not many people are here from California wishing to buy summer shoes.

Kent and Patty remember visiting the 125-year-old Hammond Hotel, built in 1879 and which is opened on a partial scale. The bar is in full swing but all that can be obtained is a 95-cent hamburger in the way of food. If one wishes mustard, onions, pickles, lettuce, etc, the price may reach $1.25. The total bill for five people was just under $6.00 in total. George, as usual, ordered a slice of onion with his hamburger, which was delicious.

DAY 10—Tuesday, August 12, 2003— Amery, Wisconsin to Norway, Upper Michigan—Mileage 152,718

Norway is a small, clean, pleasant city. At 4:00 p.m. we had driven 270 miles. It is the usual beautiful day, with not a cloud in the sky for the past 12 days.

Sadly, we said good-bye to Patty and Kent. They have been so good to us. In fact, their favorite blue heron was displaying itself on the lawn, on the creekside, when we drove away.

George used his cell phone to call Eileen, and Nan brought her up to date. We intend to be in Burlington on Friday next and wish to meet her and Judi/Ted at the "Thistle" for supper. We will keep in touch as we cross this wonderful country.

George called his sister, June, who reported that she had done good work on the family party scheduled for August 17. Twenty-nine people will be attending, including Eileen, Judi, and Ted. Thanks, Junie, you are a gem.

Marnie has been her usual efficient self—helping the old folks with their packing and moving the packed suitcases to their assigned places in the Volvo.

On the way out of Amery, George visited the post office to mail a book to editor Robert Scott for his perusal.

At 9:30 a.m., Marnie inquired "Which way, Poppers?" George, covered in maps, replied, "As we are not taking the magical way Kent discovered on the computer, let's take Highway 8 all the way across Wisconsin. Looks simple to me."

Amery, the City of Lakes, is on Highway 46, which meets Highway 8, which goes to Turtle Lake, about 20 miles northeasterly. In Wisconsin, lake is the most common word.

Next to lake, the most common word is tree. There are so many trees along Highway 8, it is difficult to see what the countryside looks like. The towns along the way are small, clean, and busy. In fact, everything in Wisconsin looks prosperous, or maybe well off. Marnie bypassed Barron and Ladysmith in favor of Prentice for lunch.

Prentice is a manufacturing town with several factories. Marnie suggested lunch at the Golf Club but although she found the course, she couldn't find the clubhouse. She found the Prentice Café, complete with tablecloths. We settled for a light lunch, soup, and sandwiches, but we discovered that a light lunch is not the norm in Wisconsin. All the customers are large and happy, the highlight being two couples grossing at least 900 lbs., laughing their heads off. Good luck to them.

The trees along 80 are becoming more coniferous as we approach Upper Michigan. George doesn't know if that means anything, but it is a fact.

The town of Norway has a 20-unit motel, the Viking on the main street. It looks clean and has about twenty rooms. An Italian lady owns the motel and is happy to rent George a room for three, for $50.00 including tax. Aha, maybe there is no room tax in Michigan. The weather is so beautiful at 6:45 p.m., let's have cereal on a bench in front of Room 5. George finished the Crown Royal and will soon be asleep.

DAY 11—Wednesday, August 13, 2003—Mackinaw City, Michigan

It's 2:00 p.m. and here we are at the Comfort Inn Lakeside in Mackinaw City, Michigan. The mileage meter reads 152,933, which means we have driven 215 miles this morning.

It is another beautiful day, the eleventh in a row. Where has all the rain gone? Marnie has been driving with alacrity. It's time she had a rest—and a drink. Why is there always maintenance on a bridge?

We left the Viking Hotel behind in Norway, Michigan at 8:00 a.m. But before Marnie moved the Volvo out of the driveway, it became 9:00 a.m. eastern time. George has never been happy with the arbitrary man-made time changes. As Bush does not give a damn what the rest of the world thinks, why don't we have one national U.S.A. time zone. The Central Zone will stay as it is. The Eastern Zone will move one hour forward or backward. The Western Zone will move one hour forward or backward, whichever fits, and all of us in the good ole U.S.A. will be on the same time. It might take a month to get used to being all together. Imagine Tom Brokaw, Sixty Minutes, and all the sporting events on at the same time, countrywide.

There are sandy beaches along the shore of Lake Michigan, close to Number Two Highway, at Manistique, a resort area with many hotels. Manistique is on the underside of the Upper Peninsula of Michigan, thus forming Lake Michigan. The topside of the Upper Peninsula of Michigan faces Lake Superior, or thereabouts.

Mackinaw City is a destination for thousands of vacationers. The city is connected to the Upper Peninsula by way of the Mackinac Bridge. This is one of the longest suspension bridges in the world, stretching for five miles. The imposing structure was built in 1957, providing a convenient means of transportation between the two peninsulas. The toll is a buck and a half to cross over.

The Comfort Inn is one of many which line the shore of Lake Michigan at Mackinaw City. The soft sandy beach and the shallow water make it an ideal spot for children to play and for adults to frolic in the warm water. Nan and Marnie are on the beach and George is sitting on the room patio, sipping a vodka tonic.

The water in Lake Michigan, at this location, is warm and shallow. George thinks the elderly folk look somewhat strange standing ankle deep in water about 200 yards from shore. They move slowly about, neither in nor out of the water, something like a stork. At least, they are in the water, which is more than George can say for himself. He has an excuse, "I'm on my eighty-eighth trip around the sun."

Marnie asks, "Dad, do you know what a pastie is?" George says, "Yes I do. It is an item of food, which we ate in Canada. I always thought it was a Scottish hamburger. Or it could be what topless dancers cover their nipples with." "Silly man, you can buy pasties to eat in a shop across the street," daughter Marnie brought her dad up to date.

"Let's go," offered George. "I didn't know they made pasties in Michigan, but I'll try one or two."

So it is across the street for pasties for supper. Nan had a slice of pizza. The pasties were reasonably tasty. George has forgotten how they tasted in Canada, England, and Scotland.

DAY 12—Thursday, August 14, 2003—The Comfort Inn, Mackinaw City, Michigan to Sarnia, Ontario

There is something wrong. This is the twelfth day of the trip and there has not been a cloud in the sky (other than an occasional gentle wisp). It is 6:28 a.m. by my Verizon cell phone, and it always knows the correct time, even when there is a man-imposed time change. The sunrise is beautiful as the sun pokes its head up through a surface bank of clouds. It's working, I have been trying to jinx this perfect weather for several mornings. We are sitting on the verandah of Room 116 on the shore of Lake Huron, about 100 yards from the water's edge. The water is perfectly still, not even a suggestion of a breeze.

Oops, there it is. It is exactly 6:43 a.m. and the golden orb is sitting on the surface of the lake in all its magical glory. The sun wins again. It is another beautiful day.

When making the reservation for today, I wondered why I agreed to pay twice the usual Comfort Inn room rate because we were to be staying in Mackinaw City. Now I know why. The hundreds of hotels that line the shore of Lake Huron were all full last night and are probably full for every night of their short season, 6-27 to 8-16. If anywhere is perfect weather-wise, this is it.

Do you know where Lake Huron becomes Lake Superior and visa versa? Directly under the center of the Mackinac Bridge. George would like to know at what moment in time that was decided. Get a computer, George.

There is something wrong, nevertheless. TV Guide is on the table in Room 116. Opening the first page, an article revealed that Jay Leno is paid at least thirty million dollars a year. Something is really wrong with the world.

George remembers that for some reason the roads in Michigan are always rougher and bumpier than in any other state. Maybe they don't have money to fix them, or don't give a damn.

Marnie decides to drive from Mackinaw to Port Huron by following the shore of Lake Huron. It is slower but prettier.

In Harrisville, a sign reads "Coffee Talk Café." Marnie says, "That's for us." The brochure describes a unique sidewalk café located in downtown Harrisville overlooking beautiful Lake Huron.

After we are served coffee and goodies, George, looking around, notices a picture of a man in a baseball uniform. Curiosity aroused, he finds it is Kiki Cuyler, one of his first baseball heroes. Cuyler was born in this area in 1898. George discovered baseball and newspapers when he was nine years old in 1925. Cuyler was the hero of the 1925 World Series. Playing for the Pirates, he hit a home run off Walter Johnson, pitching for the Senators, with the bases loaded in the last of the ninth to win the Series for the Pirates. The Pirates became George's favorite team, and Cuyler one of his baseball heroes.

A friendly lady, Angela Orozco, P.O. Box 126, Harrisville, Michigan, 48740, owns the "Coffee Talk Café." George promised to send her a copy of this narrative.

The year 1925 reminded George of the Pony League, a league composed of teams from small towns in P-Pennsylvania, O-Ontario, and N.Y. New York. George called Kent on his cell phone with the request that Kent check the Internet for information on the Pony League. Kent quickly replied that the towns in 1925 were Saginaw, Bay City, and Flint in Michigan, Hamilton in Ontario, Bradford in Pennsylvania, and Jamestown and Olean in New York, seven teams in all. Hamilton was in for only 1924-1925. Many other small cities were in and out of the league through those tough times, as it cost $630.00 to join the league. George was pleased that he remembered Hamilton was in the league in 1925 when he was only nine years old. It was his ambition, at that time, to play in the Pony League.

Sometime later, Kent called George with more information. While talking to Kent, George heard Marnie say, "Dad, I'm lost in Bay City. Ask Kent how I can get to Highway 15, going south. Kent is at his computer in Amery, Wisconsin. George relays the message to Kent, who asks where Marnie is at the moment in Bay City. George passes the information on to Kent. The reply comes back in a couple of minutes. "Go five blocks north to 24th, turn right, and in about half a mile you will meet Highway 15. I will stay on with you."

Sure enough, Marnie finds 24th and follows it to the right and in a few minutes happily calls out, "I've got it. There's Highway 15."

George says, "Make sure you go south." Marnie replies, "Thanks, Kent, for setting me on track."

After being part of this exhibition, George decides to get a computer, one of these years. Thanks, Kent and Patty.

Marnie has been hugging the shore of Lake Huron on Highway 23, past Alpina, Oscuda, and Tawas, and others. A beautiful drive. Most of the homes are located on large lots. About every third lot has a used car for sale on it. Car salesmen would be out of luck in this area.

Finally Marnie reaches Highway 69, turns right and soon Port Huron appears.

After stopping at "duty free," and wasting forty minutes in line at inspection, the land of our birth is reached. Immediately lost, we rely on Highway 402 to find a motel, which it does in ten minutes at the Country View Motel. The power is off all the way to New York. We have to find the bed in the dark. How helpless we are without electricity.

Hey ladies, here's one for you!!!!
BLOOD PRESSURE!!!!!
Dear Friends,

It is important for men to remember that as women grow older, it becomes harder for them to maintain the same quality of housekeeping as they did when they were younger. When men notice this, they should try not to yell. Let me relate how I handle the situation.

When I got laid off from my consulting job and took "early retirement" in April, it became necessary for Nancy to get a full-time job, both for extra income and for the health benefits that we need. It was shortly after she started working that I noticed that she was beginning to show her age.

I usually get home from fishing or hunting about the same time she gets home from work. Although she knows how hungry I am, she almost always says that she has to rest for half an hour or so before she starts supper. I try not to yell, instead I tell her to take her time and just wake me when she finally does get supper on the table. She used to do the dishes as soon as we finished eating. It is now not unusual for them to sit on the table for several hours after supper. I do what I can by reminding her several times each evening that they aren't cleaning themselves. I know she appreciates this, as it does seem to help her get them done before she goes to bed. Now that she is older, she seems to get tired so much more quickly.

Our washer and dryer are in the basement. Sometimes, she just can't make another trip down those steps. I don't make a big issue of this. As long as she finishes up the laundry the next evening, I am willing to overlook it. Not only that, but unless I need something ironed to wear to the Monday lodge meeting or to Wednesday's or Saturday's poker club, or to Tuesday's or Thursday's bowling, or something like that, I will tell her to wait until the next evening to do the ironing. This gives her a little more time to do some of those odds and ends things like shampooing the dog, vacuuming, or dusting. Also, if I have a really good day of fishing, this allows her to gut and scale the fish at a more leisurely pace. Nancy is starting to complain a little occasionally. For example, she will say that it is difficult for her to find time to pay the monthly bills during her lunch hour. In spite of her complaining, I continue to try to offer encouragement. I tell her to stretch it out over two or even three days. That way she won't have to rush so much. I also remind her that missing lunch completely now and then wouldn't hurt her any, if you know what I mean.

When doing simple jobs, she seems to think she needs more rest periods. She had to take a break when she was only half finished mowing the yard. I try not to embarrass her when she needs these little extra rest breaks. I tell her to fix herself a nice, big, cold glass of freshly squeezed lemonade and just sit for awhile. I tell her that as long as she is making one for herself, she may as well make one for me and take her break by the hammock so she can talk with me until I fall asleep. I know that I probably look like a saint in the way I support Nancy on a daily basis. I'm not saying that the ability to show this much consideration is easy. Many men will find it difficult, some will find it impossible. No one knows better than I do how frustrating women can become as they get older. However, guys, even if you just yell at your wife a little less often because of this article, I will consider that writing it was worthwhile.

Signed, Bob

BOB'S FUNERAL was on Saturday, January 25th

NANCY was ACQUITTED Monday, January 27t

DAY 13—Friday, August 15, 2003—Sarnia, Ontario to Riviera Hotel, Burlington, Ontario

Awakened this a.m. in Sarnia, Ontario, in the Country View Motel. The mileage is 153,296.

When we arrived here last evening, after crossing the Blue Water International Bridge and telling the customs man we had purchased two 1.14 liter bottles of Gibson's finest, we stopped in Sarnia at the Country View Motel. We paid the lady $86.00 Canadian, and then she said the power is off. "In that case," George asked, "surely we must be due a discount?" She evidently thought he was kidding and ignored his request. He was probably kidding on the square.

The gas station store at the corner supplied ice, milk, and ginger ale. As we bring our own cereal, we will not be hungry, especially as Nan bought a year's supple of licorice All Sorts at the duty free shop.

After the sun set, about 8:30 p.m., there was no doubt the power was off. The air-conditioning and the refrigerator were useless.

Nan had her tiny battery radio tuned to the local station in Chatham, nearby. The announcer didn't know what was happening except that the power outage extended throughout eastern Canada, including Toronto and Montreal, and also New York City. About 10:00 p.m., the announcement came on the air that Burlington had power. That is where we are headed on the morrow.

The humidity made it somewhat difficult to sleep and George's lack of mechanical ability prevented him from opening the screened windows. When Marnie got up at daylight, she opened the windows in two minutes.

George was embarrassed, but pretended not to be. "When you can't see, you can't see," was his lame excuse. "I'll bet a lotta folks had it worse than we did."

The freeway, probably 403, is not crowded, so Marnie proceeds at a comfortable pace. We don't believe the radio report that Burlington has power. In two years, they have built many more highways in Ontario and before we know it, on freeway 403, we are near the Hamilton/Burlington area. At Burlington, the stoplights are working which made believers of this threesome.

Peter, in charge of the Riviera Motel, knows we will be at the hotel this day, but 10:00 a.m. is a little early.

"Give me another hour and both your rooms will be ready," is a fair request as normal check-in is not until 1:00 p.m.

The Travel Lodge, formerly the Venture Inn, located next to the Riviera is available for breakfast. It is an upscale hotel for this area. The Wescoombes have stayed at the Venture Inn but would you believe, although the hotel is situated on the shore of Lake Ontario, only a smidgen of rooms face the water. It is George's opinion that it will have to be torn down and rebuilt. What an error in judgment!

However, the food is excellent and the Wescoombes make use of the Travel Lodge's proximity. It is easy to spend an hour on a leisurely breakfast, reading the Toronto newspapers reporting on what is headlined, "A Power Outage." When the power comes back, will they call it "A Power Inage." Details are lacking except, "It is dark."

The following was written by Lisa Wescoombe Hill and describes the Hills' experience with the power outage:

Rob and I flew to the Big Apple and got there 20 minutes after the East Coast blacked out, which was not good timing. We arrived to emergency alarms sounding all over, in a dark and hot terminal (it was well over 90 degrees and humid that day). My first thought was...terrorist attack. In fact I wasn't the only one to think that. Rob was hungry (eat first before you panic) so we paid cash and got some food, then sought out our luggage. The screaming woman on the loudspeaker announced to all of us to "GO HOME! And come back this weekend to pick up your luggage." Rob and I thought that was not a good idea, even though the noise of the alarm was driving us nuts. We roamed for awhile, and luckily so as they finally announced that the only plane whose luggage that wasn't stuck in the system was ours. After a long wait, the few of us left at the airport got our stuff. Then we had an hour wait to take a cab to the city. Our driver went the long way to avoid the massive traffic jams, which was hard to do.

After landing at Newark at 4:00, we arrived at our hotel in Weehawkin (across the river from the city) at about 7:30. The Sheraton is directly behind the ferry to the city, so we arrived in the middle of a mass exit. There were people everywhere, walking the streets, in our hotel, sitting, lying down, etc... We didn't know if that was normal or as a result of the blackout. It was the latter.

We finally got our room, climbed 8 stories in the dark, put our stuff down, and looked out our window to see all of Manhattan in a dark silhouette against the moonlit sky. Wow! I took a few photos, then we left our room unlocked, of course, and headed for the bar to wait for Robbie, or at least for a phone call. Having a beer by candlelight amidst chaos is really kind of fun! Rob didn't think so at all, but I, in a perverse way, enjoyed the crazy time: no phones, no cell phones, no atm, no nothing except beer, a tiny piece of cheese and a slice of tomato (for $10), and people-watching. We come to find, the next day, that Robbie was stuck in New York. He *chose to stay, instead of walking several miles to and across the bridge, or wait four hours for the ferry. He and his friends bar hopped until the beer ran dry or got warm, and stayed with Bryce Clemens in the city. As worried parents, we decided to try to find his house in Weehawkin, since there was nothing better to do. No one even knew the street name, and we walked along with tons of grumpy but talkative folk, not knowing where we were going. Around 11:00, discouraged, we headed back to our room. We had climbed the 8 floors several times already that night, but (stupidly) we put a card to hold the door closed, but not locked in our door. Well it slipped out, so down we go, for the fourth time, to wait for a sweaty hassled employee to take us up and open the door with a master key. On our way down, we talked to a family of 10, including grandmother and lots of children, who were stuck, after spending a hot walking day in the city. We invited them to share our room with us, and they would have had they needed to. They finally got a ride somewhere, very late that night. We had one tiny candle and a bottle of water for the night, and wondered what the hell we were going to do if this disaster lasted much longer. Luckily for us, New Jersey's power came on first, then New York's slowly came back on Friday throughout the day. Around 5:00 in the morning, the air conditioning came on and the lights...and our peace of mind. However, in the meantime, I developed a sore throat and sinus congestion, probably from the plane trip.*

Robbie and Bryce showed up around 9:00 the next morning and we had breakfast at the hotel. I was hungry enough to take a bite of an egg, and that's all I needed to have the runs and a headache the whole weekend! Hmmm, this blackout wasn't so fun after all, but again, I wasn't the only one who got sick. Oh well, it was great to see Robbie and spend the weekend in the city, and watch his friend Ames Crawford do his comedy act at one of those cool little theaters. We took in some sightseeing, lots of walking and cab riding to see ground zero, battery park, and all the boroughs, including East Greenwich Village where Robbie is moving with two girls next weekend. We took the ferry each day to and from the city, experienced a great thunderstorm, almost got beaten up by two thugs who tried to attack our cab driver for cutting them off, and basically enjoyed the complex and insane lifestyle of too many people in too small of a space, without power. However, we are soooooooo glad to be home where the air smells fresh and there's room to move.

What did you do last weekend?

Luvleeeeeeeeeeee

Peter has Rooms 22 and 23 ready at the Riviera. Marnie is pleased to have a room to herself.

As we are staying five nights, Peter gives us a rate of $65.00 per room, per night, including room tax. The view alone is worth that amount. Remember George grew up within a quarter mile of the location of the Riviera. We have plenty of time to unload the Volvo and pack the drawers and cabinets for the five-night stay. The weather is delightful with a cool breeze blowing from the calm lake.

Nan calls Eileen to tell her of our arrival and confirm that dinner is at the Thistle at 4:30 p.m. with Judi and Ted. The Thistle is one of the finest fish and chip restaurants in the world and has at least three seatings every night. The Thistle has had excellent business since Burlington was half as large. George cannot imagine why the owners have not opened two or three more "Thistles."

Judi, Eileen's daughter, arrives with her husband, Ted Andrews. They are Friday regulars at the Thistle and are greeted accordingly. Judi raises Irish wolfhounds on her ten-acre estate near Guelph, Ontario. Judi and Eileen just returned from a drive to somewhere in Pennsylvania where Judi bought a beautiful, few-month old girl dog. George just can't call her a "bitch."

George says when Irish wolfhounds are babies, they are lovable, but when they grow up they are too large and powerful for old folks. When he pets one of the eight, presently in residence, it nearly knocks him down.

Ted Andrews, Judi's husband of 20 years, is a retired judge who loves Judi and all the dogs, and is capable of settling any and all disputes with dispatch. He is a perfect foil for energetic Judi. The Wescoombes enjoy being with Judi/Ted as there is not a dull moment. They have been invited to visit the estate, Tuesday next.

DAY 14—Saturday, August 16, 2003—Riviera Motel, Burlington, Ontario

It is 6:15 a.m. and the amazing streak continues. The sun is rising out of Lake Ontario as it has done since the big bang or thereabouts. This is fourteen days of continuous sunshine. Marnie says it sprinkled for five minutes yesterday, but George maintains, "Some guy left his garden hose on."

Burlington is the town where George spent his growing up years. Both he and Nan were born in the neighboring metropolis of Hamilton, but George's grandparents moved to the small town when George was three years old.

For some reason, not yet explained, when the power outage which put most of the north and eastern parts of Canada and the U.S.A. in darkness, Burlington and immediate surrounding area was shut down from about 4:00 p.m. Thursday to approximately 9:00 p.m.

George's friend Gene Yachetti celebrated his 90th birthday on July 31 last. Gene is George's oldest friend, still in existence. They will meet for breakfast today at 8:30 at the Travel Lodge (formerly the Venture Inn).

Sure enough, there is Yachetti in the front seat of a car now pulling up in front of the hotel. Gene's daughter, Geraldine, and her husband, Stanley, are bringing Gene to meet George.

Gene has lost sixty pounds in the last two years, but still looks good as a "smaller man." Geraldine says that Gene has lost weight continually since Erma, his wife of 65 years, entered a Home for Alzheimer's sufferers two years ago. He visits the Home every day and obviously misses her very much.

The two old friends have much old stuff to talk about, but not much new stuff. Stanley, Geraldine's husband of 27 years, has read all of George's writings and says he is happy to meet the writer. After all these years, Geraldine looks great, just like George imagined she would. The Bamford, Coombe, and Yachetti kids often vacationed together with their parents at Sauble Beach. One time they were tossing a baseball around and Nan's swimsuit top fell off. Yacketti said, "I didn't know which ball to catch."

Marnie and Nan joined the group for a short while before Gene decided two hours was enough and he had to leave to see Erma. The two old friends enjoyed reminiscing and hugging each other. George has the feeling he may never see Gene again. Let's hope he is wrong on that one.

The sunny weather streak is broken with a bang at 10:30 a.m. Evidently thunder and lightening have been saving up for some time. The electrical storm was a pleasure to watch from the porch behind the hotel room, overlooking the lake. It lasted for a magical half-hour, vicious in its intensity and power, landing many blows and drenching the area with water. This sensational event seldom happens in the desert in California. Thanks, Mother Nature.

At noon, in the dining room of the Travel Lodge, George greets his old friend Kay Purser. Kay was married to Butch Bamford, George's boyhood pal, until Butch's demise in an unfortunate accident in 1976. Kay is with Fred Purser, to whom she has been married for 25 years. Fred, among other things is a world class tenor sax player, now retired. George asks, "Fred, why aren't you still playing?" The answer was surprising, "My old partners, the Washington Brothers, both died." "I could play part time but it's hard to keep the embrouchare in shape, at my age."

Fred, with his two black partners played great subtle jazz for many years, around town. Nothing commercial about Fred.

Kay and Nan, great friends for over 60 years, are head to head bringing each other up to date. Kay brought daughter Dyanne along for the lunch. Dyanne grew up with the younger Coombe kids, and she and Marnie had plenty to talk about. Among other things, Dyanne is a professional figure skater and appears on a commercial as a stand-in for Dorothy Hamill. She is as sparkling and vivacious as her mother was at Dyanne's age.

George sits quietly taking it all in, thankful that he and Nan are still around and, due to Marnie, are able to visit friends from their younger days. It is a pleasurable afternoon. Everyone hoped to be able to do it again. George, ever an optimist, said, "How about next summer?"

George's sister June, along with husband Al, have done all the legwork on this trip. June has arranged the family brunch, doing all the telephoning. Al has made the hotel and brunch reservations, and things are all in order.

Let's drive to Al and June's, have a couple of drinks overlooking the city of Hamilton from their apartment, then take them to the Tartan Toorie for a Scottish supper. George and Al had talked about dining at Shakespeare's, but Nan didn't think she could handle a heavy meal and suggested the Tartan Toorie where such a good time was had two years ago. Al was in good form and the Scottish jokes were flying. Al suggested Marnie drive his new Lincoln Town car, as he and George are comparing the merits of Gibson's Finest and Crown Royal. They are both rated tops in Canadian whiskey and priced the same. George and Al had difficulty making a decision and drank half a bottle of each before settling on a tie.

The shepherd pie and Scottish pie were also adjudged a tie. No one could equal Al's jokes. Marnie did a great job driving home and parked inches from the pillars in the underground garage despite following Al's zany directions.

She had no trouble finding the famous bridge over the Ship Canal and reached the Riviera as though she knew how.

DAY 15—Sunday, August 17, 2003—Riviera Hotel, Burlington, Ontario

The thirty-minute storm yesterday p.m. broke the sunshine streak, but today starts a new streak. The glorious sun is in business as it should be at 6:30 this morning.

Nan is always up with the sun and she is dressed, looking beautiful, ready to go across Water Street (Lakeshore Boulevard, No. 2 Highway) to the "Donut Delight" for a donut and coffee. George staggers along behind, admiring her beautiful legs.

This is reunion day for the Coombe family, scheduled to begin at 10:30 a.m. at the "Water Street Cooker," which back in George's boyhood days and for many years afterward, flourished as the fashionable "Estaminet." Everything of importance that occurred in the area, which included a meal, was held at the Estaminet. Nan's sister Eileen was married to musician Jack Ryan, at that location, on November 11, 1936.

Eileen, a widow for three years, still lives in Burlington in the summertime, and Marnie and Nan have driven to pick her up for the brunch.

George, who is an amateur writer, has brought along a couple of dozen copies of his new hardback, "The Saga of Ocean Explorer I" for distribution to his best fans, his relatives.

The Water Street Cooker is very popular for Sunday brunch, and has set up two long tables overlooking the lake for the Coombe party as arranged by June and Al.

Surprise, George's youngest brother Frank who was stricken by an embolism on August 3, 2000, and who has not walked since, was carried to the second floor along with his wheelchair by four strong young men. Al was able to make the arrangement which pleased George and Frank immensely.

George had a chair next to Frank where he could sit and chat from time to time. Frank's head seems to be fine, but his body has deteriorated. He was minutes from death when the aneurism of the stomach happened. The medical people kept Frank alive but he has been confined to a wheel chair and in a nursing home ever since. His wife Irene, daughters' Cindy, Cheryl, Jackie, and son Stephen take good care of their dad.

Nan, Eileen, and Marnie have arrived and help George greet all the relatives, who only see each other when the Wescoombes come to Canada and arrange a gathering. Diane Fonagy, George's brother Roy's daughter, and Lynda Hanco, wife of George's sister Hazel's son Mark, both take charge ladies, have agreed to make certain a family party will be held each year.

This place serves an amazing brunch. Nan, who is an expert in Sunday brunches, pronounced this as the best in the U.S.A. and Canada, regardless of the price. This one is not cheap even with the rate of exchange.

Susan, Sales Coordinator at The Cooker, helps George set up a table at which he can sit and autograph "The Saga of Ocean Explorer I" for all the folks who think they can read George's signature.

As the nephews and nieces sit with George, much merriment ensues. They don't see their uncle very often but it is obvious that they enjoy his company. The reverse is true, as George loves all the young people dearly.

A stranger asks the Barclay's daughter Beverly, "What is going on?" Bev, in her usual casual manner, replies, "He is a famous writer from California and not only that, he's my uncle."

The party is winding down and the group of four young men carry Frank and his wheelchair to the ground floor. On arriving on the ground floor, Frank, who still has a sense of humor, announces, "Boys, we will have to go back up. I forgot something."

It was a great reunion. Niece Diane has promised to send George a list, with addresses, of all the attendees. Diane, with the help of Lynda, decided to hold a reunion each year and invite the California Coombes. Let's hope they follow through on the idea.

It has been a big day and the Wescoombes need a nap. Upon waking up, it was decided an ice cream cone from the store next door, would suffice for supper. George has noticed that many localities call lunch-dinner, and dinner-supper. Sounds Englishy, but who cares.

The following was prepared by Diane Fonagy. Thank you, Diane.

The following family members attended a wonderful brunch at the Water Street Cooker on Sunday, August 17th at 10:30 a.m.:

Mr. & Mrs. Scott & Jan Barclay
579 East 27th Street
Hamilton, Ontario L8V 3H4

Mr. & Mrs. Paul & Bev Lehman
1161 Fourth Concession
W. Waterloo, Ontario

Mr. & Mrs. Frank & Irene Ashby
76 Terrace Drive
Hamilton, Ontario L9A 2Y6

Mr. & Mrs. Charles & Cheryle Gent (Charles did not attend)
94 Horizon Crt.
Hamilton, Ontario L9B 1X2

Ms. Cyndi Gee & Mr. Mike Szabo
36 Tivoli Drive
Hamilton, Ontario L9C 2E4

Mr. & Mrs. Mario & Leesa Peschynski
66 Lehman Crescent
Markham, Ontario L3P 5W7 (905) 294-6978

Mr. Darryl Fonagy
202-215 Wilson Avenue
North York, Ontario M5M 3A9

Ms. Sharon Ashby
812-1868 Main Street W.
Hamilton, Ontario L8S 2J2

Mr. & Mrs. Ron & Diane Fonagy
13 Sandy Cove
St. Catharines, Ontario L2N 5Z3

Mr. & Mrs. Alex and Janet Dawes (Alex did not attend)
19 Ferncroft Avenue
Scarborough, Ontario M1N 2X3

Mrs. Hazel Hanco, Mrs. Eileen Ryan, Mr. & Mrs. Al and June Barclay

For those who did not attend, I have listed more addresses below:

Ms. Jacki Ashby
56 Woodbrooke Drive
Mount Home, Ontario L0R 1W0

Mr. Stephen Ashby
90 or 10 (?) West 1st Street
Hamilton, Ontario

The following were some comments made in the year 1957:

1) *"I'll tell you one thing, if things keep going the way they are, it's going to be impossible to buy a week's groceries for $2000.*
2) *"Have you seen the new cars coming out next year? It won't be long when $5,000 will only buy a used one."*
3) *"If cigarettes keep going up in price, I'm going to quit. A quarter a pack is ridiculous."*
4) *"Did you hear the post office is thinking about charging a dime just to mail a letter?"*
5) *"If they raise the minimum wage to $1.00, nobody will be able to hire outside help at the store."*
6) *"When I first started driving, who would have thought gas would someday cost 29 cents a gallon. Guess we'd be better off leaving the car in the garage."*
7) *"Kids today are impossible. Those ducktail haircuts make it impossible to stay groomed. Next thing you know, boys will be wearing their hair as long as the girls."*
8) *"I'm afraid to send my kids to the movies any more. Ever since they let Clark Gable get by with saying damn in "Gone With The Wind," it seems every new movie has either hell or damn in it."*
9) *"I read the other day where some scientist thinks it's possible to put a man on the moon by the end of the century. They even have some fellows they call astronauts preparing for it down in Texas."*
10) *"Did you see where some baseball player just signed a contract for $75,000 a year just to play ball? It wouldn't surprise me if someday, they will be making more than the President."*
11) *"I never thought I'd see the day all our kitchen appliances would be electric. They are even making electric typewriters now."*
12) *"It's too bad things are so tough nowadays. I see where a few married women are having to work to make ends meet."*

13) "It won't be long before young couples are going to have to hire someone to watch their kids so they can both work."

14) "Marriage doesn't mean a thing any more. Those Hollywood stars seem to be getting divorces at the drop of a hat."

15) "I'm just afraid the Volkswagen car is going to open the door to a whole lot of foreign business."

16) "Thank goodness I won't live to see the day when the Government takes half our income in taxes. I sometimes wonder if we are electing the best people to Congress."

17) "The drive-in restaurant is convenient in nice weather, but I seriously doubt they will ever catch on."

18) "There is no sense going to Lincoln or Omaha anymore for a weekend. It costs nearly $15.00 a night to stay in a hotel."

19) "No one can afford to be sick any more, $35.00 a day in the hospital is too rich for my blood."

DAY 16—Monday, August 18, 2003—Riviera Hotel, Burlington, Ontario

The rain on Saturday was an aberration. This is day two of the new streak.

This old motel (how old?) has a perfect location. It is the only hotel-motel overlooking the water in Burlington, population 155,000. Maybe Canadians don't appreciate the value of waterfront property. In California, the value is appreciated as it is the only thing that can't be replaced.

Coffee this a.m. with Nan's great friend, Maddie, is at "The Second Cup." Maddie looks great although her husband John is in the hospital with quadruple heart by-pass surgery. He is doing satisfactorily and will be released in a couple of days.

Nan and George stopped at Wellington Terrace located at 410 John St. to visit George's cousin Evelyn. She has a fifth floor unit #502 with a living room, bedroom, bathroom, and kitchen, very spacious, with a large porch. She and George are within a month of each other in age. George has not seen Evelyn looking so happy for a long time. It must be the apartment. Her memory is perfect. She remembered that George, when they were kids, suggested she step on the slippery rocks so she would fall into the creek. George countered with, "I pulled you out, didn't I?" The visit was too short.

Eileen invited Nan to play bridge with her and her friends at her home at 5070 Pinedale, Apt. 104, Burlington. George invited his sister June and her husband Al to lunch at the Swiss Chalet if they would pick him up. Al liked the deal and picked up George at 1:00 p.m. and found the Swiss Chalet on Appleby Line.

Do you know the distance between the Guelph Line and Walker's Line and also the distance between Walker's Line and Appleby Line? The lines are a mile and a quarter apart, for some unknown reason.

When George was a youngster in Burlington around 1920, according to his memory, the population was about 1,500 people. He lived with his grandparents at 40 Elgin Street. The town was growing slowly and by 1930, George had entered high school, was still living at 40 Elgin Street, and estimates the population at 2,400 people. George Wescoombe was married in 1937, and moved with his wife Bernice (Nan) to Indian Point and rented an apartment from A.B. Coleman for $25.00 per month. An estimate of the population of Burlington is 4,000 people in 1940.

Wesley and Bernice (George and Nan) moved back to Burlington in 1950 having purchased 86 Locust Street from Harry Saunders for $5,200.00. He estimates the population at that time to be 5,000 people.

In 1953, the Wescoombes purchased 305 Brant St. from Harold Eagle for $9,000.00. The town was growing rapidly and when the Wescoombes sold 305 Brant St. to Bill

Hourigon for $14,900.00 in 1956 and moved to California, an estimate of the population is 6,000 people.

After the Wescoombes emigrated to California, a dramatic change ensued in Burlington. In 1958, the then still small town of Burlington annexed part of East Flamborough and all of Nelson Township. This amalgamation made Burlington the largest town in Canada at that time having over 90 square miles or 55,000 square acres of area.

There have been many street name and number changes. 305 Brant St. became 566 Brant St. and 86 Locust St. became 577 Locust St. As the two houses are almost back to back, the street numbers should be almost identical. Evidently the new system is working.

An examination of the latest street map of Burlington reveals there is a one block long Wesley Street running between Prospect and Barclay St. Imagine a corner street sign, Wesley and Barclay. It is true.

Believe it or not, the town of Burlington has a population of 155,000, as this is written.

DAY 17—Tuesday, August 19, 2003—Riviera Hotel, Burlington, Ontario

The sunrise is well worth the price of admission. This old motel was built in 1953, George is told. The Wescoombes lived on Brant Street about a half-mile inland from the lake. In 1953, George was 37 and Nan was 34. They were blessed with five children and had no reason or time to watch construction of anything. The manager says 1953 or thereabouts. It is very old, in any event. No hotel built since has an equal view.

Tim Horton, the coffee and donut king of Canada, has not received any of our business as yet. It is time for a scone, donut, muffin, whatever, at Horton's. This excellent operation, now a part of Wendy's in California, has so many outlets, they are used as a guide for directions, such as, at the second Horton's, turn right.

Nan and Marnie need a good walk, so they choose the Mapleview Mall at Maple Ave. and Fairview as a good place for exercise. They usually say "just for a walk" but they always buy presents for the grand- and great-grand kids.

George is not a fan of Macdonald's but recently he has enjoyed one of their new items, a fruit and yogurt parfait, sprinkled with nuts. So far, he has not found any grease in the parfait.

Judi and Ted have invited the travelers to spend the p.m. at their estate located in the vicinity of Guelph, Ontario, where they have lived for the past ten years. We have visited many times but the directions are somewhat complicated. Since Jack left three years ago, Eileen has done a great job as navigator. All George knows is take the Guelph Line to No. 1 side road, then hunt. It is really easy, they say. Anyway, a visit is well worth the effort.

The original log cabin house located on the ten acres has had many changes and additions through the years. Ted Andrews, formerly Chief Justice of the Ontario courts, since retiring, has become a master carpenter, plumber, electrician, etc., etc. There is nothing this talented gentleman can't do with his hands, or his head, for that matter.

He probably did not build the large swimming pool, but he is in charge of its maintenance. He built a large tool shed several years ago, but the shed is now the home of Judi's eight Irish wolfhounds. So he has built another similar tool shed, plus a hot tub and shower room, plus a Japanese Tea House, which Judi uses as an office. Plus a screened in porch, enclosing the front door, plus laying out a walking and training ring for the dogs, and surely other things George has forgotten.

Up until a year or so ago, Judi had an office in Toronto where she practiced as the number one expert in family law in the U.S. and Canada. Now, supposedly semi-retired, most of her clients visit the Guelph estate where they are received in the Japanese tea room office. This office is open only in the summertime, however.

From October to May, Judi entertains her clients at her estate in Palm Desert, California. This property overlooks the entire Coachella Valley from a 3,000-foot level. Ted Andrews spends the winter months making improvements, upgrades, etc. to the spectacular home and grounds. Judi's mother, Eileen, has a self-contained apartment within the main building and spends the winter months in that location.

Back to this day, the ladies, including Eileen, have had a swim. George and Ted have put away a few beers while lying to each other. Now, Judi, who is a gourmet cook, serves a delightful repast on the veranda. What a treat!

George notices that there are no mosquitoes this year. Let's hope Judi/Ted didn't move the pests to California.

Marnie was able to find the way back to Burlington easily. It's usually faster to come back than to go somewhere. If that is true, why is it so?

DAY 18—Wednesday, August 20, 2003—Riviera Hotel, Burlington—Liverpool, New York

Another beautiful morning in the place of our birth. It is 9:00 a.m., we have had coffee, etc. at Bennies and pretty soon Marnie will be singing "On The Road Again." The mileage is 153,614, as we leave for Niagara Falls.

The Wescoombes were in this area two years ago. To George, it seems as though the province of Ontario has built many more highways. Certainly the town of Burlington has grown considerably, especially in the downtown area. It has lost its quaint charm now, replaced by six story buildings. It is a shame, but one cannot stop progress.

There is no hurry, this day or any other for that matter. The border is reached and after a little indecision, Marnie decides to cross the bridge at Niagara Falls.

George still has about a hundred Canadian dollars. The duty free store will gobble up that amount quickly. George has been across borders so many times, he knows that there are no bargains in duty free stores. Today he buys a special carrying bag, pretty but useless, with three bottles of Crown Royal therein for $62.00 Canadian or $46.00 U.S., about the same as in California. He is ahead, one pretty bag. Three bottles is the limit in the liquor department.

Nan picks up a few souvenirs, then turns to the food department. How about several cans of red salmon–tins in Canada. They come in sets of three so Nan buys enough to last the Wescoombes the rest of their lives. It's better than having a handful of loonies and toonies. Wonder what they will call the upcoming five-dollar coin.

Marnie has been driving in Canada for six days, so she has trouble finding the New York thruway, out of Niagara Falls. It finally shows up, thankfully. She doesn't like thruways, freeways, etc. but forgets the secondary roads, for the moment.

Nan, the Scrabble expert, has discovered a single-handed Scrabble game, which is played against the house. She has bought several, one for Eileen, Bette, Marnie, and Patty, as gifts. She sits in the front seat, as Marnie drives along, playing what must be a fascinating game. George hasn't tried it, as yet. He is glad Marnie doesn't play it while driving.

California, as well as other things, is screwed up politically. Evidently, the folks who vote don't like the guy they elected so they have elected to get rid of him. This opens the door for a plethora of miscellaneous candidates. Not that anyone has to be smart to be governor or president for that matter.

The leader of the pack is a German (Austrian) movie star who will win, as did Ronald Reagan. Californians love celebrities. George prefers Arriana, also from somewhere other than the U.S. as she is cute and clever. The only candidate worthy to be governor is Peter Uberoff but as he is the best man for the job, he hasn't got a chance. Thankfully, this mess will be over quickly, or will it?

The New York thruway, No. 90, is monotonous but speedy. Marnie sees Syracuse on the board, which reminds her that we had planned to stay in Liverpool, a suburb of Syracuse this evening.

Liverpool has a busy freeway exit with many motels, restaurants, etc. This area is where Indian chief Hiawatha located the capital of the Iroquois confederacy in 1570. At one time, the bulk of the salt used in America came from Syracuse.

Colorado Mine Company, a steak house, is the venue for dinner tonight, as our hotel offers a free drink at the Mine Company. All the attractive, personable, waitresses are outfitted in skimpy cowboy outfits. Somehow they caught George's eye. George and Nan share a combo, ribs and chicken, and Marnie has salmon. Much too much excellent food and too little exercise does what?

DAY 19 – Thursday, August 21, 2003—
Liverpool, New York to Goshen, Massachusetts

Another sparkling morning as Marnie loads up the Volvo in front of Room 306 at the Knights Inn. The Inn has many rooms, all on the ground floor, which helps. The mileage is 153,853 as we leave for Goshen, Massachusetts where Mark's new home is located.

Most of the hotels these days supply a continental breakfast, which is enough for the Wescoombes and Marnie. Poor Marnie, George lets her do all the heavy lifting. She says, "No problem, Popper."

The towns along Thruway 92 go by as though they are standing still. In no time, Albany appears on the board, and Marnie realizes she had better leave the "raceway." Old Highway 20 parallels Freeway 90 and also goes into Massachusetts reasonably close to Goshen, maybe.

The objective is to leave Freeway 90 at Amsterdam, New York, wend our way along Highway 30 to Esperance where Highway 20 lives. Unfortunately, Marnie turned onto 159 and soon we were in a honeycomb of thruways, freeways, highways, low ways, and overheads, even the Hudson River. Sometime take a look on a map of the Schenectady, Albany area and you will see a rat's nest of roads. Once you are on the road you want to be on, don't leave it. For some unknown reason, we found ourselves on NY Highway 7 heading east. George remembers that Schenectady, 75 years ago, was big in the initial days of radio, something about a General Electric factory there. Never mind, we pass it very fast and find we are on Highway 2, heading for Petersburg. George hopes it is not St. Petersburg in Russia. Marnie is happy when Highway 2, New York, meets Highway 7, Massachusetts. She thinks she knows where she is, removes George as navigator, and appoints Nan in his place. Usually Nan only navigates for laughs. Everyone agrees, "If you are lost, ask Nan which way, and then go the other."

Patty's husband Kent, a computer expert, has given Marnie blow by blow directions from place to place. The directions developed by computer are very accurate, and also speedy. However, they may be boring. Marnie doesn't like to be bored, so she develops a few wrinkles not known by mapmakers.

George was aware that when Highway 2 met Highway 7, we were within 50 miles of Mark's new home. In the back seat, the curvy drive through the Berkshire Hills was enjoyable, if that is where we were.

Finally, US 7 became MA 9, and Marnie said, "Eureka, we have found it!" She was right, as 30 minutes later, she turned left onto Sears Road.

Catherine and the beautiful little girls, six-year-old Hope and two-year-old Willow, are around the compound. Mark and Catherine have just purchased a three and a half-acre estate hidden in the trees. The 2,000 square foot house needs extensive work to make it complete, plus the grounds and trees require attention. George estimates that if Mark and Catherine spend all their spare time working on the property, no vacations or any of that foolishness, in ten years the estate will be worth a million dollars. A worthwhile objective.

Mark returns from work and is welcomed by his three girls. He is wearing or carrying his loggers' gear, complete with spikes for climbing trees, belts for holding on to trees, lines for swinging through the trees like Tarzan, and nets for catching falling fellow workers. It sounds like dangerous work, worth more than what they pay him. However, he is extremely happy doing what he wants to do, working with his hands.

Catherine has found a car for Mark to get back and forth to work, and it is ready in Grandy, Connecticut, about 60 miles away.

George is a card-holding member of Choice Hotels. Marnie calls the secret number and chooses the Clarion Hotel in Northampton, about 30 minutes from Catherine and Mark's estate. As they have to pick up the new vehicle, it is decided that they should take on food somewhere on their own, leaving the older folks in Room 109 at the 122-room Clarion.

It has been a long day, so cereal satisfies the Wescoombes. George is immediately asleep. Nan and Marnie are playing electronic Scrabble

OLD COWBOY

An old cowboy went to a bar and ordered a drink. As he sat sipping his whiskey, a young lady sat down next to him. She turned to the cowboy and asked, "Are you a real cowboy?"

He replied, "Well, I've spent my whole life on the ranch, herding horses, mending fences, and branding cattle, so guess I am."

She said, "I'm a lesbian. I spend my whole day thinking about women. As soon as I get up in the morning, I think about women; when I shower, watch TV, eat, whatever, everything seems to make me think of women."

The two sat sipping in silence. A little while later, a man sat down on the other side of the old cowboy and asked, "Are you a real cowboy?"

He replied, "I always thought I was, but I just found out I'm a lesbian."

DAY 20—Friday, August 22, 2003—Northampton, MA 01060, Clarion Hotel

Yesterday was a long one, George was asleep by 9:00 p.m. Today is a continuation of the unbelievable weather. Mark says it has rained every day, except five, since June 1. The mileage is 154,116 and will remain close to that for a couple of days. We intend to stay at the Clarion, 1 Atwood Drive, Northampton, MA 01060. The Clarion is part of Choice Hotels, the same as Comfort, Quality, etc. The Choice Hotel group supplies a generous continental breakfast.

Sitting next this a.m. is Ralph Derose and his wife Janet. Ralph is sales manager of Curvet, U.S.A., Inc. which produces bent-tempered glass, used for display cases, furniture, sinks, etc, etc. George is an expert on all types of glass, from that used for beer bottles to the exotic glass used in electrodes for measuring pH. He and Ralph have a great time lying to each other about their extensive knowledge of the glass business. Ralph, as a salesman, thinks a glass is for holding a drink, and George thinks a glass is used to look at oneself. They agree to meet again tomorrow.

Room 109 on the ground floor, opens onto a porch that opens onto the indoor swimming pool area. This is ideal for Hope and Willow, as the elders can keep them under continual surveillance while still enjoying the porch area and/or the pool area. George is able to sit at a desk just inside the poolside door where he can survey the whole scene including several young bikini-clad mothers looking after their siblings. Nan and Marnie are happy tending Hope and Willow.

Catherine is busy taking care of everything, including arranging for George to pick up his Palm Desert medical prescription in Northampton later today. She also found a barber shop close to the pharmacy, close to the ice cream store, close to the used book store, so all will be able to read while George's locks are neatened. Catherine is a take-charge lady.

Mark is able to take a half-day off work, so he spends the time in the pool playing with his red-haired daughters, Hope and Willow. This certainly is a perfect hotel for people with children, especially if they have a ground floor room.

Marnie has been in touch with Julie and Robbie, trying to arrange a meeting with them on Sunday next.

Catherine is brought into the mix and discloses that she and Mark also have a desire to spend a day in New York. In fact, Mark has never been to the Big Apple. Catherine says she will examine train schedules, distances, etc. and report back tomorrow noon. She works on Saturday morning for Sylvan Learning Center, as well as on a couple of nights during the week.

This hotel has an outdoor pool as well as the indoor pool, which George is surveying. The outdoor pool has an adjacent snack bar, making it ideal to feed the children. George manages to move to the snack bar, and the five adults and two little ones have their own table while waiting 30 minutes for the short-staffed snack bar to provide hot dogs, hamburgers, yogurt with fruit, and a few fries and chips. If one has to wait a long time, the food usually tastes better, when it finally arrives.

Mark brought some beer, Sam Adams Summer Ale–wheat ale brewed with grains of paradise and lemon zest, says the advertising.

It rained nearby but not on us, so George considers the streak intact.

Northampton, about fifteen miles from the town of Goshen, could be called the cultural center of the valley, with a population of 29,000 and five colleges: Smith, Amherst, University of Massachusetts, Holyoke, and one George has forgotten. It is a busy college and tourist city. Museums, art galleries abound as the little city is overflowing with intellectuals.

It is time to pick up George's prescription, browse the used book store, eat ice cream while George's hair is cut at Shear Xtreme, Inc., and then wend our way back to the Clarion for another swim in the indoor pool.

The swimmers finally slow down, the little kids start to doze, George and Nan are starting to nod, so Marnie and Catherine telephone the best pizza maker in Northampton. In 30 minutes, the deliveryman drops off a large vegetarian with pineapple, and a small without cheese or meat. Little Hope cannot eat cheese or dairy products. Bread, tomato sauce, olives, and mushrooms are staples in Hope's diet. She is healthy and very smart.

Only half the pizza is eaten, so Mark stored the remainder for the morrow.

DAY 21—Saturday, August 23, 2003—Northampton, Massachusetts, Clarion Hotel

New England weather is entirely different from the desert where the Wescoombes live in Coachella Valley. There are a few light clouds sailing serenely across the sky, but, as yet, they refuse to gather into a rain cloud. It is humid but no precipitation. The streak is still intact.

Mark and the little girls are at the hotel early to enjoy breakfast and the swimming pool. They join Marnie in the pool. Marnie also has three grand boys in California, so she is doing well in the "grand" department.

This hotel, with an outdoor pool that is indoors, is about all one could ask in the bathing business. Nan is usually in with the kids, and George enjoys watching.

Northampton has many strange places to eat. The choice for lunch is the Vermont Country Deli and Café. Upon reaching the second floor, one finds three more similar floors above. Let's say it is not fancy but commodious.

Catherine arrives from work and is ready for lunch. Good timing. Back at the hotel, Catherine's mother, Karen, has arrived and is sharing the little girls with Marnie. Many people spend the weekend at the Clarion, as it is so well laid out to entertain children.

Finally, all have been swum out, and it is time for the evening meal. George, magnanimous as usual, offers to host dinner at the Clarion, in Montana's Steak House. This must be a high-class place, if the prices are a criterion.

George has been drinking Sam Adams Summer Ale in the bottle all day. When the waiter says Montana's has it on draft, he decides to start on a keg.

Wow, one taste and this has got to be skunky. The waiter can't believe it. George offers to buy him a glass so he can try it himself. The waiter tries the stuff, gets the bartender to drink some, and they all pronounce it skunky. The bartender offers to replace George's, but George says, "Give me a Bud Lite instead." George was not aware that draft beer in a keg could become skunky. Something strange is going on here.

The food is excellent. Several had steak, some had salads, Nan had soup, and George had a Caesar's salad with sirloin slices. Catherine is a vegetarian and found something to her liking.

All in all, it was a perfect ending to a perfect day at the Clarion in Northampton. George got away light, $135.00 for six adults and two children.

Up early tomorrow morning for a visit to New York City.

DAY 22—Sunday, August 24, 2003—Northampton, Massachusetts, New York City—Danbury, Connecticut

The entire group assembled at 7:30 a.m. in the Clarion Hotel breakfast room. Catherine has set 8:00 a.m. as the preferred time to leave this location and head for Danbury, Connecticut. It is a chilly but clear morning, not much chance of rain.

It turns out that Mark Caputo has never been to New York City and he expresses a desire to make it a group visit. Mark's wife Catherine is a native of New England and is very familiar with the New York area.

She suggests that as today is a Sunday, we drive for an hour and a half in tandem to Danbury, Connecticut, then board what is normally a commuter train to Grand Central Station in New York City. Catherine and Marnie calculate that Grand Central Station would be reached by about 12:15 p.m. today.

Leaving Northampton at 7:45 a.m. along Freeway 91, Springfield is 16 miles along Highway 91, then 27 miles to Hartford, switching to Freeway 84, Waterbury is reached in another 28 miles and still on Freeway 84, here is Danbury in another 25 miles.

Catherine has decided that Danbury, Connecticut is the place to board a train to Grand Central Station. The Connecticut Commuter Rail Company has a train scheduled to leave Danbury at 10:17 a.m. The 96 miles from Northampton to Danbury took 90 minutes. It is necessary to wait about half an hour for the train. The station is not open on Sunday (no commuters). The weather is perfect but chilly. Waiting in the shelter of the Volvo and Honda is okay.

In old England, the 10:17 would have left Danbury no later than 10:18, but in New England it pulls away from the station at 10:20. The electric trains are quite smooth, like large streetcars. They can stop and pick up again speedily.

They are much like the radial cars that operated in the 1920's, which were replaced by buses at the request of General Motors. At South Norwalk, it is necessary to change to a train operating on the next track, for no obvious reason. George made conversation with Frank, a conductor on this line for 29 years, but forgot to ask him why the change. Frank loves his job. He says, "I stand on the train and watch the world go by." Frank charges regular people $20.00 return, and seniors $13.00 return, a reasonable price. Maybe the fares are higher on weekdays. Frank, hang around, will you?

Suddenly, the train reaches Track 19 in Grand Central Station. After a short walk, there is beautiful Julie and handsome Nathan. Julie Coombe and her best friend, Nathan, were alerted by Marnie that she and the Wescoombes will visit them in New York today. Julie then notified Robbie Hill, who lives in New Jersey, that Nan and Gramps would arrive in Grand Central Station at 12:15 p.m. today.

Julie and Robbie were also told that their cousin Mark Caputo, with his wife Catherine and daughters Hope and Willow, would be with the Wescoombes and Marnie, at Grand Central Station.

The Wescoombes do not wish to walk, just sit, and visit for the afternoon. Julie has never eaten at the "Rink at Rockefeller Center" but has heard it praised. A taxi moves the Wescoombes, Julie, and Nathan to that splendid location in ten minutes. Marnie and Catherine are experts on New York, and, with the children, walk for 30 minutes. Mark gets to see the skyline for the first time, rather than the inside of a taxi.

Robbie Hill joins us almost immediately so there is a fun table of eight adults and two children. The large restaurant area is used for ice skating in the wintertime or visa versa.

Julie is going to school, not working at the moment. Nathan has a permanent job in a brokerage house. Robbie has a permanent job with a leasing company, but doesn't get paid until he closes a deal. He is upbeat, optimistic, and enjoys the bars and pretty girls. George volunteers to help him, especially as Robbie is moving to New York City to share an apartment with two business ladies. George breaks into his old song, "Oh, to be 80 again."

Julie is very happy with New York, and George tells her she looks like a New York girl. She is probably the best looking female in the city, and that's not grampa talk. She and Nathan are an outstanding couple. The young folk at the table are talking up a storm. George and Nan love to listen and watch them. Marnie, as usual, is the intermediary sibling.

When four o'clock comes, the restaurant people want to change the table to evening status and will not sell the table any more drinks. They want us to leave, but Robbie and Nathan manage to secure one more round.

George and Nan love to treat their grandchildren, so they pick up the itemized bill—food and drinks, $275.50 with tax $23.88—gratuity, $49.49—total $349.87 for eight adults and two children. Quite reasonable for New York City.

So our Canadian friends will know how good they have it in Canada, last Sunday, George and Nan hosted a brunch at the best restaurant in Burlington for twenty-six cousins at a cost of $663.00 Canadian, or $450.00 U.S. dollars, which included champagne.

Julie and Nathan return with the old folks to Grand Central station in a taxi and Marnie and the rest enjoy the walk, looking at the skyscrapers.

There was time for a drink in Michael Jordon's restaurant, but it was a tough walk, so George gave up and decided to wait at Track 19. Julie and Nathan had been so kind to meet the grandparents. The Wescoombes are content to wait at Track 19 of the New Haven Line to Danbury and suggest that Julie and Nathan wend their way home. Thanks very much to you both.

The train arrives as scheduled, and Danbury is reached after the usual transfer.

Marnie has made a reservation at the Quality Inn in Danbury, located only a short distance from the railway station. It has been a long day and the bed at the Quality Inn is inviting.

DAY 23—Monday, August 25, 2003—Danbury, Connecticut—Mercer, Pennsylvania

We awakened this a.m. to a typical eastern morning. The clear sky has disappeared as Marnie heads west on Highway 84 for somewhere around Scranton, Pennsylvania. The mileage reads 154,229.

It is still overcast as we pass Wilkes-Barre and the tail end of the Poconos. The green, hilly country is a pleasure to drive through. Highway 80 crosses Pennsylvania without passing through large cities, and this is what Marnie likes. Interesting stops, a relative term, are made at Bloomsburg, Lamar, and Dubois, but George is unable, a day later, to remember any distinguishing feature of any one of the three. Is this known as middle America? The people are friendly and the sky has cleared, no rain today.

George has his eye on a town named Mercer as the stopping point for tonight for two reasons. He used to know a guy named Eddie Mercer, and also in Mercer, according to the AAA book, is a single story motel, the Colonial Inn. Marnie should be able to park in front of the hotel room, as George needs to move some clean clothes from the large bag to the small bag.

Also, and this is really important, a town by the name of Wesley is shown in the AAA book, 20 miles before Mercer. Each town is the same distance, five miles, from Freeway 80, with a road shown connecting Mercer and Wesley.

As it is early, let's visit Wesley and then on to Mercer. Wesley does not have a store or a post office, but has a dozen or so well tended large homes. The only street sign read "Bullshit Avenue." George wondered how they knew he was coming. Would you believe, instead of turning left at Wesley, George was so excited, he told Marnie, "Straight ahead, please." We were close to the town of Franklin, before discovering the mistake. Then we couldn't find the road between Wesley and Mercer, so it is back to Freeway 80 and on to Mercer.

Mercer is not much except as a hub for about six side roads. The Colonial Inn Motel is hard to find, of course, and we are getting tired of Mercer.

Finally, the Colonial Inn is located. It is owned by a nice Indian man, Sam, who recently bought the place, and has his family installed. The motel looks good, but George notices a lot of deferred maintenance. Sam is not a Patel, but a slightly higher caste, a "Thakar." The smell of curry has not taken over the office, as yet.

Now, some good news; the only restaurant in town, the Country Kitchen, has a special tonight, lamb chops, which Nan and Marnie order. George opts for the six-ounce sirloin. The meals are $6.95 each, and are better than the twenty-dollar variety we have been exposed to lately. The waitress was delightful, and George, of course, has to meet the cook, a nineteen-year-old young lady who loves preparing food. Nan and Marnie were served two chops each, so one is for lunch tomorrow.

George still has a desire to find the road to the town of Wesley. A customer in the restaurant overheard the discussion and offered to help. He has delivered fuel oil for thirty years and knew every blade of grass in the area. He drew Marnie a map. But even with a map, the road to Wesley is not found. After half an hour, the decision is "screw it."

DAY 24—Tuesday, August 26, 2003—Mercer, Pennsylvania to Elkhart, Indiana

Another overcast morning. One of these days, it is going to rain, for sure. George has a quick cup of coffee with

Sam, who also has cupcakes and orange juice available. George tells Sam about the lack of power plugs, shortage of toilet paper, and the paucity of towels. Laundry is inexpensive and necessary.

Marnie heads for the freeway. Mercer in Pennsylvania is only a few miles from the Ohio border, so it looks like a straight shot to the Toledo area.

The navigator decides to stay south and come close to some large cities but skirt them. There is no compelling reason for driving through Youngstown, Akron, Findlay, or Fort Wayne. They are probably interesting cities, but not as easy on the eyes as the Ohio countryside.

The old Volvo is getting close to thirty miles per gallon, but it has to have a fill-up nearly every day. Service stations supply almost every need. The driver picked a station with a large parking lot so we could finish the delicious pork chops without other folks wanting some. Marnie has set up a cooler arrangement so the food is piping cold.

The old navigator thinks it may be better to approach Chicago from the South Bend, Elk Hart area, and also maybe catch a glimpse of Notre Dame in South Bend. George thinks he remembers that a company famous for making saxophones is located in Elk Hart, but that is a long time ago. Maybe the name was "Conn."

What we have been expecting for some time happens suddenly. The sky swiftly darkens. Marnie heads for the Elk Hart exit; pulls into the nearest motel, the Days Inn, just as the sky opens up with the loudest claps of thunder and brightest and closest bolts of lightening that the travelers have seen since leaving Ontario, Canada for the pleasure of the silky smooth weather in Southern California. Marnie remembers, as a child, when a storm broke, her Nana would say, "God is moving the furniture around."

Watching the storm from the window is fine, but in 30 minutes it is all over and the sun is trying to have a look. A man on TV is reporting that the damage in South Bend, maybe 30 miles ahead, is extensive with trees and power lines down. The news people make up most of the news; probably two old trees fell down, frightened by the thunder. The only thing one can believe on the news these days is the scores of the baseball games.

There are usually many things happening at a freeway exit. We could have stayed at the Comfort Inn a block away if we had seen it. This area is loaded with motels, restaurants, etc.

Across the street is a nice looking place with a Chinese name. It is only 4:30, but they will welcome us. Sure enough, an attractive Chinese lady is ready for business. George decides to be friendly. "Knee how," he exclaims. She beams and comes back with "I am fine, thank you." George thought he had said, "Hello, how are you?" and evidently did.

The lady and her husband are from Hong Kong. The husband cooks, and Helen works as a waitress when the place is not busy, but as cashier and hostess most of the time. She has a pretty Chinese name, so Nan and Marnie say, but Helen will do for George as he watches her walk away. Brown rice with shrimp is George's favorite. Nan has chicken chow mien, and Marnie has shrimp cashew. The man knows how to cook Chinese. George used his only Chinese word, but it was enough to make friends.

Subject: Church Bulletins

FW: church bulletins. Thank God for church ladies with typewriters. These sentences actually appeared in church bulletins or were announced in church service:

1) *Bertha Belch, a missionary from Africa, will be speaking tonight at Calvary Methodist. Come hear Bertha Belch all the way from Africa.*
2) *Announcement in a church bulletin for a national PRAYER & FASTING Conference: "The cost for*

attending the Fasting and Prayer conference includes meals."

3) *The sermon this morning: "Jesus Walks on the Water." The sermon tonight: "Searching for Jesus."*
4) *Our youth basketball team is back in action Wednesday at 8:00 p.m. in the recreation hall. Come out and watch us kill Christ the King.*
5) *"Ladies, don't forget the rummage sale. It's a chance to get rid of those things not worth keeping around the house. Don't forget your husbands."*
6) *The peacemaking meeting scheduled for today has been canceled due to a conflict.*
7) *Remember in prayer the many who are sick of our community.*
8) *Smile at someone who is hard to love. Say "hell" to someone who doesn't care much about you.*
9) *Don't let worry kill you off—let the Church help.*
10) *Miss Charlene Mason sang "I Will Not Pass This Way Again" giving obvious pleasure to the congregation.*
11) *For those of you who have children and don't know it, we have a nursery downstairs.*
12) *Next Thursday there will be tryouts for the choir. They need all the help they can get.*
13) *Barbara remains in the hospital and needs blood donors for more transfusions. She is also having trouble sleeping and requests tapes of Pastor Jack's sermons.*
14) *During the absence of our Pastor, we enjoyed the rare privilege of hearing a good sermon when J.F. Stubbs supplied our pulpit.*
15) *The Rector will preach his farewell message after which the choir will sing "Break Forth into Joy."*
16) *Irving Benson and Jessie Carter were married on October 24 in the church. So ends a friendship that began in their school days.*
17) *A bean supper will be held on Tuesday evening in the church hall. Music will follow.*

18) *At the evening service tonight, the sermon topic will be "What is Hell?" Come early and listen to our choir practice.*
19) *Eight new choir robes are currently needed, due to the addition of several new members and to the deterioration of some older ones.*
20) *Scouts are saving aluminum cans, bottles, and other items to be recycled. Proceeds will be used to cripple children.*
21) *The Lutheran men's group will meet at 6:00 p.m. Steak, mashed potatoes, green beans, bread, and dessert will be served for a nominal feel.*
22) *Please place your donation in the envelope along with the deceased person you want remembered.*
23) *Attend and you will hear an excellent speaker and heave a healthy lunch.*
24) *The church will host an evening of fine dining, superb entertainment, and gracious hostility.*
25) *Potluck supper Sunday at 5:00 p.m.—prayer and medication to follow.*
26) *The ladies of the Church have cast off clothing of every kind. They may be seen in the basement on Friday afternoon.*
27) *This evening at 7:00 p.m. there will be a hymn sing in the park across from the Church. Bring a blanket and come prepared to sin.*
28) *Ladies Bible Study will be held Thursday morning at 10:00. All ladies are invited to lunch in the Fellowship Hall after the B.S. is done. The pastor would appreciate it if the ladies of the congregation would lend him their electric girdles for the pancake breakfast next Sunday.*
29) *Low Self-Esteem Support Group will meet Thursday at 7:00 p.m. Please use the back door.*
30) *The eighth-graders will be presenting Shakespeare's Hamlet in the Church basement Friday at 7:00 p.m. The Congregation is invited to attend this tragedy.*

31) *Weight Watchers will meet at 7:00 p.m. at the First Presbyterian Church. Please use the large double door at the side entrance.*
32) *Mrs. Johnson will be entering the hospital this week for testes.*
33) *The Associate Minister unveiled the church's new tithing campaign slogan last Sunday "I Upped My Pledge—Up Yours."*
34) *Our next song is "Angels We Have Heard Get High."*

DAY 25—Wednesday, August 27, 2003—Elk Hart, Indiana to Lake City, Minnesota

As we leave the Day's Inn at 6:15 a.m., the golden sun is shining in all its glory. Getting rid of the accumulation of thunder, lightening in the atmosphere, probably made the sun feel better. The mileage is 155,128 as Marnie drives onto the Interstate Nos. 5 and 90 as we wave goodbye to Elk Hart.

South Bend, the city of Notre Dame, is reached in a short time and George's cursory glance from the freeway revealed little damage.

It appears that the people in charge have put freeways 80 and 90 together, so traffic is light as this hour. It is cursory glance day, as Gary, Indiana, the home of "Music Man," received the same treatment.

There was not even a glimpse of Chicago as the freeway passed to the south of the famous city. The threesome are great fans of the academy award-winning movie of the same name. Would you believe that George and Nan have a DVD player, and the picture is better than in the movie house. Next step for the old man is HD TV, as he can see the stitches on the baseball, which is awfully good for eighty-seven year old eyes. George saw little of Joliet as Marnie sped by the prison city.

A town by the name of Morris received a closer look as the Volvo was thirsty, Nan needed a cappuccino, Marnie and George settled for coffee.

Moline, Illinois gave way to Davenport, Iowa on the way to Cedar Rapids, which was honored by our presence at a MacDonalds. George is a big fan of Macdonald's "fruit and yogurt," and also their washrooms.

At Waterloo, George suggests Highway 63 which is a secondary road but which travels in a straight line, almost. Highway 63 passes close to Kent and Patty in the city of Amery, Wisconsin. Marnie is on the cell phone to Kent who tells her that it is a long drive. "It's a long way, Dad. We had better stay on the freeway to get there by 5:00 p.m."

"I hear you, but let's try No. 63. It's a much more pleasant drive."

George was both right and wrong. For some reason, the stoplights in the small towns are all red, and workmen are fixing No. 63 in places. There is nothing worse than a guy or gal holding a red flag when one is in a hurry.

It is almost five o'clock when the famous city of Rochester, Minnesota is reached. It is the home of the Mayo Clinic, and is much larger than George envisioned. IBM also has a facility in Rochester, causing even more traffic. The city is swarming with motels and hotels. It is a beautiful but busy city.

There is still about a hundred miles to travel to reach Amery, the home of Patty and Kent.

Marnie suggests a stop for the night at Lake City about thirty miles ahead. On the map it appears to be on the bank of the mighty Mississippi.

Marnie apologizes to Patty and Kent. We will see them early tomorrow. There are many motels overlooking the river and Marnie chooses "The Lake City Country Inn" a small but fancy place.

Lake City has many restaurants, Port O Call is Marnie's choice, and she is right as usual. It has two sections, one with an upscale menu, almost empty, the other full of people, eating hamburgers, etc. We want to be in the hamburger section, which is full, but waitress Lacey says, "No problem" and leads us to the almost empty section, with hamburger menus.

Lacey, the waitress, is a native of Lake City, has finished one year of college, and is very personable. In answer to George's question, "Do you have many boyfriends?" she replied, "Not many. I'm too strong for them."

Lacey and Marnie have a long and strong talk on education.

Day 26—Thursday, August 28, 2003—Lake City, Minnesota to Amery, Wisconsin

The sun is back where it belongs but it may be temporary. The pleasant lady who owns the Lake City Country Inn has coffee ready as we prepare to leave. She says Lake Pepin is 85 miles around and it is the widest part of the Mississippi. The opposite shore of the lake is Wisconsin.

Water skiing was invented in this area in 1922. The original boards are displayed at the Chamber of Commerce Office in Lake City. The Hale Irwin Jewel Golf Course will open in 2004, joining many others in the 85-mile circumference. Early in May each year, the folks hold an 85-mile long garage sale around the lake, lasting three days.

Marnie is very familiar with Highway 63 from Wednesday's long drive. At Red Wing, a pretty town at the end of the lake, we cross the Mississippi and are going north on Highway 63.

The town of Ellsworth proclaims that it is the curd capital of the world. Marnie stops at Brad's Liquor and Cheese Shop for natural cheese curd, buffalo jerky, and coffee. Brad produces a bottle of Nan's favorite Lambrusco wine.

In an hour, we are at Amery, and there is Patty standing in front of the house waiting to greet us. Kent shows Marnie where to park the Volvo, as he is having a new driveway installed. Due to the holiday weekend, the concrete will be poured on Tuesday. The driveway is completed with the rebar and stakes in place, so the workers can screed the cement after it is poured. The driveway drops from the street in about a five-foot gentle swirl. The cement layers are artists.

The Volvo has a fault. One of the headlights is not working, as it has evidently burnt out. The headlights have not been used on this trip, so the only thing we don't use is broken. Kent says it is caused by vibration, so he replaces the defective headlight. Thanks, Kent. He also paid for the bulb.

Kent has recently returned from an annual fishing trip with a group of his old friends. A fish fry makes certain all the fish are disposed of in a tasty manner. Patty and Kent are out for the evening but entertainment is supplied in the form of a DVD of "Chicago," the award-winning movie. The Wescoombes and Marnie have seen it, but are glad to see it again.

The DVD of "Chicago" contained the "out takes" and comments from the director and producer. A great evening's entertainment.

Day 27—Friday, August 29, 2003—Amery, WI with Patty and Kent

Another fine day! Where has all the rain gone?

Kent has promised to drive the ladies to the Mall of America in Minneapolis, Minnesota. He and George will make the trip. This is scheduled for about 11:00 a.m.

To start the day off right, coffee and scones, bagels and donuts, at Gramma Bonnie's is in order. This shop on the main street of Amery is hot, busy all the time. It is not long ago that donuts were the number one item. Now, there seems to be more of a bakery selection, such as bagels and scones.

The Mall of America is about a 90-minute drive, seemingly in many different directions. One would have to be born in this area to find the Mall. But when it is found, it is the largest mall in the world, probably, four times as large as most malls. It has four sections, North, South, East, and West, so named so the customers may have a chance to find their way out of the place.

Kent stops at the entrance to the North Quadrant, allowing all to enter the Mall and wait for him to park. He is lucky as someone leaves from the front row. George has already found a bench in front of "Victoria's Secret" and is quite comfortable when Kent joins him. The ladies are watching, so the men move about 100 yards to "The Twin City Grill" a high class drinking joint. The ladies promise to return in an hour for lunch.

The waiter, a personable young man named Steve is not busy and is willing to talk, especially as we continue to buy the local favorite beer Leinenkugels Red. The beer company advertises, "It takes a special beer to attract 2,500 men to a town with no women." That was 125 years ago in Chippewa Falls, wherever that is.

Both Kent and Steve were born in the Twin Cities area and swap stories about happenings through the years. Evidently there are only a few dangerous areas.

Steve's wife is an accountant who works for a big firm and George suggests that she start doing income taxes on her own. "Steve, you're the type who could drum up business for her through the bar. If she charged one half of the H & R Block price, she would make a ton of money in four months each year. Then she could do bookkeeping on a monthly fee bases." By the time George left the bar, Steve is about to retire.

The ladies return and have lunch at the bar. They have covered about ten percent of the North Quadrant and wish to do more.

George and Kent got back to the "Leinenkugels" and Steve. The girls return in another hour. Kent starts the long drive back to Amery while George has a nap. Four of those beers are a lot, especially with that long name.

Kent, who knows this area like the back of his hand, does his usual masterful job and George wakes up in front of Meister's Cedar Lake Grill and Bar at 6:30 p.m.

Bernie and Sandy Meister, with their son and daughter, are friends of Kent's and have been in business in this area for fifteen years. They close for a couple of months in the winter and vacation in Florida. George is particularly impressed by their daughter, Jessica, who works as a waitress. She is a lathy young lady and wears her black hair in a French bob. George calls her "Mimi" and gives her a big tip. Old men are allowed to have innocent fun, n'est pas?

At home Patty played a DVD called "Legally Blonde" starring Reese Witherspoon, and it is a funny one, which we all enjoyed.

Day 28—Saturday, August 30, 2003—Amery, Wisconsin to Council Bluffs, Iowa

It is another beautiful day. Mileage is 155,771, as we bid good bye to Patty and Kent. Kent has given Marnie a list of five freeways to use in the 80 miles required to reach Freeway 35 heading south. Minneapolis-St. Paul has a gigantic metropolitan area.

George knows we are heading south as the sun is hitting him in his bad left eye as he sits in his office behind the driver. Marnie follows Freeway 35 due south until Des Moines is reached and old friend Interstate 80 appears heading west.

Our destination for tonight is the Comfort Inn at Council Bluffs, Iowa, directly across the Missouri River from Omaha, Nebraska.

The State of Iowa is evidently big on gambling. Council Bluffs has three Las Vegas style casinos, Harrahs Casino and Hotel, Isle of Capri Casino and Hotel, and the Ameristar Casino and Hotel. There is evidently a law that the casino part of the hotel must be floating on the river for some part of each day.

The Comfort Inn is not far from the Ameristar Casino and Hotel, so Nan will do her gambling in that location. It is a luxurious, 160-room hotel with live entertainment, 1,500 slots, 35 table games, and four places to eat.

While Nan loses her quota, George and Marnie decide to have supper at the Prairie Mill Café, which extends into the walkways so one may watch the passersby while eating. George enjoys a steak, and Marnie has her favorite, liver with onions.

It is not long before George is amazed at the size of the men and women passing by, near where he and Marnie are sitting. Although it is none of his business, George is concerned about the size of the people he has seen along the way. Last evening at the Ameristar Hotel was the epitome. Casual observations indicate that the people in the east or west of the country are not as heavy as those in the center. George guesses that on the average, the people in the east and west are overweight by 25%, but in the center the unhealthy condition rises to 50%. This guess applies to both sexes over the age of 30. Sometimes the big ladies have a trail of big kids following them.

Later, George relates his observations to Nan. She says, "What's the problem. I remember movies from the 17, 18, 19 centuries in which the people were extra large and nothing untoward happened. Do you think these folks are going to explode or something?"

"It looks like that could happen, but I am more concerned about the general health in our wonderful country. It is unhealthy to be overweight. It is hard for me to believe in the last five years, I've gained 15 lbs., making me 10% overweight and I don't like it at all. As we get older, it is more difficult to loose the extra pounds. To me it is a serious problem, not as much as the terrorists, but close. If we kill ourselves by overeating, it will save the terrorists the trouble," George replied lengthily.

Nan inquired, "You must have some wild solution, as you usually do."

George has only a top of the head answer, "Well, it is not easy. We certainly couldn't incarcerate everyone who is more than 20% overweight. We do not have enough jails. I think we would be better off as a country to let out the ones in jail for marijuana, and try to turn the overweight folks around. This is a funny subject. Maybe Jon Stewart could handle it."

"Do you have any more fantastic solutions?" answered Nan, who is used to George's fantasies.

"Why not hit them where it hurts, in the pocket book. Everyone would be weighed every two weeks and pay a fine of $20.00 for each pound overweight. A person 25 pounds overweight would owe $500.00 payable in twelve months. He could recover the fine monthly, as the extra weight was lost. A double premium would be paid to those who got back to normal."

Nan says, "Are you nuts? Keeping track would be a lot of work."

"We have a serious unemployment problem, also. Let's put people back to work and make the country healthier at the same time."

DAY 29—Sunday, August 31, 2003—Council Bluffs, Iowa to Ogallala, Nebraska—Mileage 156,600

At last, a rainy day. The first one in 29 days. The sky is completely overcast and it is drizzling, not raining. The tap is not fully turned on but it is enough to need the windshield washers.

Marnie is proceeding west on that old standard, Interstate 80. There is little traffic and despite the annoying drizzle, driving is easy.

Lincoln, the capital, is the cultural center of the state and also has the Cornhuskers, always one of the best college football teams in the country. Every home game has been a sellout since 1963.

The city of Grand Island appears about five miles north of Freeway. 80. Marnie thinks she has been there sometime in the past. George says, "Drive the five miles to it, maybe you will recall." Marnie couldn't recall the city, but found excellent bagels, coffee, etc.

George has been sniffling and coughing, so Marnie calls on her medical ability and buys him some Night Easy with instructions to take a couple of swigs later tonight.

The drizzle continues as we drive across America's heartland, over mostly level plains and ranch land, which can grow anything the farmers want to grow. The day of the small farmer is gone, and the ranches we are passing are mostly owned by large corporations, who probably are paid whether they grow anything or not.

The Indian town of Ogallala is reached, and the Comfort Inn is our home away from home for tonight. There is little to see or do in Ogallala, so George's choice of a venue is a dud. This time he blew it.

For excitement, there is an immense antique store, which is next to a large Dollar Store. The ladies are tired of the splendid shopping in a few minutes. It is time for dinner and Taco Bell is the only choice.

George has taken two swigs of Night Easy as Marnie suggested. His idea of a swig is overly large and the nine percent alcohol content cured his cough but knocked him out. He slept from eight o'clock straight through to five in the morning. Marnie, who has no problem, is up and in great spirits for a six o'clock departure.

Coffee and cereal helps the old folks get started. In fact, they are as good as new when Marnie reaches the freeway.

It should be remembered that on August 31, 1823, Lewis and Clark, famous explorers, set off from Pittsburgh, Pennsylvania on the expedition that opened the American west. Pittsburgh is hosting a gala in celebration today.

DAY 30—Monday, September 1, 2003—Ogallala, Iowa-Labor Day—Salt Lake City, Utah—Mileage 157,234

Marnie is up early this beautiful morning and raring to go at 6:00 a.m. Her three little grandsons are only a couple of days away and she is anxious to see them. They are the light of her life.

Clear blue skies have replaced the overcast condition. Traffic is light except there are a few more trucks than expected—still a great day to drive on Interstate 80 past or through Cheyenne, Laramie, Rawlins, Rock Springs, Little America, and Evanston, all in Wyoming. George is not sure this is America's heartland but it must be a part of it. What a beautiful, beautiful country we live in!

Little America is a large hotel complex, which attracts customers by advertising ice cream cones for 35 cents on billboards along the highway, the same way Burma Shave used jingles. Does anyone remember Burma Shave?

As we approach the great city of Salt Lake the traffic thickens, but as this is our destination, it is no problem. The reservation is at the Comfort Inn but evidently Salt Lake City does not approve of signs. Marnie was lucky to see the tiny sign. We wonder if the people who run Salt Lake City know how difficult it is to find the location of hotels in the city. Finally, we found half a dozen all together in an area that looks like a classy industrial park. The hotel signs are very small giving the impression that hotels and visitors are not really important to the city. A few strategically placed directional signs would solve the problem.

The Comfort Inn is a beautiful hotel but not at all busy, nor are any of the other half dozen hotels including the Hilton, next door. They are crowded together in something like a hotel park. George reasons that the hotels are basically for business in Salt Lake City.

The ladies utilize the pool area while George sips on a vodka tonic and thinks about this long trip which will soon be over. Imagine 30 days without a problem to anyone or to the eight-year-old Volvo. George's guardian angel, Mabel, must be in charge. Thank you, Mabel.

A Perkin's Coffee Shop, attached to one of the hotels, supplied all the sustenance necessary to get through the night.

When one travels 8,000 miles on America's highways in 34 days, one stops, if one is adventurous, at a few truck stops. George and Nan have great respect for the gentlemen who drive the behemoths of the roads. Nan has been known to flirt with one or two on occasion.

Like most industries, the trucking business has several throwaways, "if anything is free, George reads it." From reading the throwaways, George discovers:

1) Be more than an employee, be a part of the company.

2) Average annual pay $50,000—signing bonus---2-years experience $1,500—under 2-years experience $750.00.

3) Must be 21 years old, high school diploma or G.E.D. equivalent.

4) Benefit plan includes: medical, dental, life, disability, 401K, stock purchase plan.

5) $400.00 year safety bonus. Regular home time.

6) Plus .01 per mile for running over 120,000 miles per year.

In several states, the highways seem to be in need of maintenance as George, in the back seat, has been bounced around unnecessarily, almost hitting his head on the roof a couple of times. And Marnie is a careful, considerate driver. Everybody seems to be paying a lotta taxes. The money is not being spent on the highways, evidently. George could say it is being spent on Bush's war, but that is a federal drain, not a state problem.

In any event, it seems there is something radically wrong with our wonderful country. In George's opinion, it had better be fixed soon, both at the state and federal level. He thinks there are too many uncontrolled hands in the till.

DAY 31—Tuesday, September 2, 2003—Salt Lake City, Utah to Winnemucca, Nevada—Mileage 157,600

It is a beautiful morning in Salt Lake City as we vacate the Comfort Inn and attempt to find Interstate 80 west. It is easy to proceed back the way we came, but it is nearly five miles before we are able to turn around and drive westerly. George was reminded of one of Al Barclay's chestnuts, "We are going the wrong way, but we are making good time."

Highway 80 soon reaches and crosses the Great Salt Lake Desert. Bonneville Salt Flats State Park is part of the desert.

Wendover is a border city located in Nevada where that gambling state abuts Utah. What a surprise! George cannot remember the last time he was in Wendover, but it was not like it is today. Four large casinos rise in the clear blue Nevada sky. They are not of the magnitude of Las Vegas, but they are impressive. They are the Montego Bay, the Peppermill, The Rainbow, and the State Line Nugget Hotel and Gambling Hall. There are also two 18-hole golf courses.

Nan chose the Nugget as the casino to which she will contribute this day. Casinos specialize in low-priced breakfasts. The Nugget provides a regular $5.98 breakfast for $1.98. Both Marnie and George take advantage of the special, so as a group, we are $8.00 ahead. Meanwhile, as Nan has lost $10.00, we are $2.00 behind. She will probably blow $30.00 total. George and Marnie figure they will have to eat four breakfasts to break even. No way, let Nan have her fun.

Elko, also on Interstate 80, has grown into a gambling center. The population of Elko is near 20,000, about five times that of 10 years ago. Where is this gambling frenzy taking our wonderful country? George is much against casino gambling.

Winnemucca, named for an ancient Indian chief, has been a favorite stopping place for the Wescoombes for at least thirty years. It has always been a gambling town and Nan won occasionally in this friendly city, which has a population of over 7,000 western folk. Through the years, a few upscale hotels have appeared, such as the Red Lion, Quality Inn, Holiday Inn, Day's Inn, and two Best Westerns. George and Nan usually stay at Scott Shady Court as Nan likes the slots at the Winner's Casino, nearby.

So it's Scott's this time. It has been upgraded through the years and charges $45.00, which is more than the rate at the aforementioned national chains.

Nan and Marnie, after a swim, head for the Winner's Casino, still the biggest in town after more than sixty years. Nan has been up and down all afternoon, but escapes with only a $20.00 loss. Marnie lost $5.00. They pick up George when it's time to eat at Grandma's House in the casino.

In this part of the world, the Giants are on TV most of the time. George follows the Giants because of Barry Bonds, son of recently deceased Bobby Bonds. The Bonds family was raised in Riverside, California when George lived and worked in that pretty city of old trees.

The Giants are headed for the National League pennant and hopefully for the World Series. They were beaten by the upstart Angels last year in seven exciting games.

The Angels are George's home team, but they usually are a less than .500 team due to poor management, in George's opinion. George does not really care which team wins anymore. He still loves the beauty and intrigue of the game, the ballet of the defense and the power and concentration of the hitters.

DAY 32—Wednesday, September 3, 2003—Winnemucca, Nevada to Incline Village, Nevada—Mileage 157,816

Interstate 80 beckons as Marnie guides the Volvo from Shady Rest Motel along the short main street. It is 7:30 a.m. and the freeway is completely devoid of vehicles, just as the sky is completely devoid of clouds.

The destination today is Incline Village in Nevada where we will change vehicles and pick up two passengers. Devun age 4, and Tre age 3, will stay with their doting grandmother Marnie for a week in her home in Thousand Palms, California. Mary Jane, Marnie's daughter and the boys' mother, suggested that Marnie drive her Ford Excursion, which is complete with all the accoutrements necessary to guarantee the boys comfort and safety to Thousand Palms. Janie will drive the Volvo to Marnie's home in a week to pick up the little boys. Janie's older son, Holden, 7 years old, will travel with his mother.

Surrounded by slot machines, crap tables, etc., breakfast is at the Ramada Inn at Lovelock, Nevada. Nan lost $3.00, but enjoyed it. The little city looks bedraggled.

In Reno, we say a fond farewell and thank you to Interstate 80 and switch to Highway 395 to Mount Rose Highway to Incline Village.

Mount Rose Summit is at 8,900 feet. Marnie and her friend Helga enjoy hiking to the top of Mount Rose, which is at least 11,000 feet above sea level. There is an outstanding view of Lake Tahoe as we find the entrance through the trees to Janie's house in Incline Village. It is not easy to locate, but Marnie usually finds it.

Incline Village is an upscale area with many eateries having excellent views of Lake Tahoe, which is a deep turquoise, sparkling in the crystal clear sky.

Janie is fashionably late for the luncheon date, but as we are in no hurry, we do not let her know we noticed. Janie's business card reads: Mary Jane Smith, Sales Manager, Hyatt Vacation Marketing Corp., Incline Village, Nevada. We know she is a busy lady.

While Nan and Marnie do shopping for the boys and themselves, George does what he does best, napping.

We are to meet Mary Jane (her grandfather is the only one who calls her Janie) and her fiancé, George Walters (nuptials, November 15, 2003) for cocktails at five, at the Biltmore. She will bring her three handsome boys.

Nan has met Walters on a previous visit and speaks highly of him to Wescoombe. And Nan is a great judge of people.

A well-dressed couple with three beautiful little boys in tow should draw attention and, indeed, they do.

Walters and Wescoombe greet each other cordially and like each other immediately (I hope).

With three lively little guys scampering all around the cocktail lounge, it is not an opportune time for serious conversation, if any is necessary.

The little ones are the center of attention in the bar and Wescoombe is impressed by the manner in which George Walters did his share in the controlling (?) of the energetic youngsters.

Janie is smart to keep it a short get-together, by taking the boys away to be fed, at home. It was a fun but somewhat hectic hour.

Nan and Marnie, along with George, have a snack in the Biltmore. The ladies want to win money at the slot machines, but George knows that is impossible and devotes his time to baseball on TV.

DAY 33—Thursday, September 4, 2003—Incline Village to Thousand Palms, California—Mileage

It is up early this a.m. as Marnie wants to arrive in Thousand Palms by 5:00 p.m. It is a 500- mile trip.

A change in plans, the ladies have decided that it would be easier to put the boys car seats in the Volvo than to move all the stuff to the Ford Excursion.

George doesn't really care as long as they tell him where to sit and buckle him up. He ends up in the front seat with the driver, and Nan has the two boys with her in the back seat. The Volvo doesn't care, and that is what counts. The boys are buckled into their individual car seats, also a good thing. It was not long ago that seat belts were not mandatory. George can remember when kids were allowed to wander all over the car while moving. Wonder if statistics show how many lives are saved by seat belts.

It is crowded in the Volvo with people who love each other, which made it enjoyable. The little guys had toys, books, etc. to keep them occupied. They are both great conversationalists (George wishes they would shut up sometimes) and they know a great deal for their age group.

Little boys have to pee a lot and as George was once a boy, he enjoys the stops, for the same reason.

Nan is happy to reach the half-way point in Bishop, at MacDonalds. She will get a half-hour break from the boys. MacDonalds has one of the contraptions that keep the youngsters entertained by climbing, sliding through tubes, and almost every form of exercise. Let's hope it puts them to sleep, the little (monsters) darlings. At MacDonalds, George has his favorite, fruit and yogurt parfait. What made

MacDonalds come up with something so completely different from the product line that made them so well known and profitable?

Everyone is tired by the time Marnie comes to a halt in front of 32381 San Miguelito Drive in Thousand Palms, California, where the old folks live. It is normally a quiet peaceful part of the world, no speeders, very little traffic, and in the summertime, half the population has left for cooler areas.

In no time, Marnie has unloaded the Volvo and leaves for her home at 33416 Lisa Court, about a mile away, with the boys who have had a long day and are ready for bed.

George and Nan are also tired but thank Marnie for the wonderful job she has done in driving 8,700 miles with absolutely no problems. Thanks to the 1994 Volvo, which has now covered in its lifetime, 158,868 miles. The only thing replaced in 8,700 miles is a headlight bulb, which the dashboard light told us about. Kent replaced the bulb and when George tried to pay him, Kent said, "It was less than $10.00. Forget it." Thanks to Kent and Patty, and all the others along the way who put up with us.

The most important thing about a lengthy trip is that one gets away from the regular, day by day, hammering by newspapers and TV of all the bad things that are happening to our wonderful country. It is nice to get away from all that crap, but it is still there.

The headline in this morning's paper screams out, "Bush to seek $87 billion for effort in Iraq."

George has been operating in the financial world for 87 years and doesn't have the foggiest notion of what 87 billion dollars is and does not believe anyone in government has a clue either.

George is 87 years old, the Volvo went 8,700 miles in 33 days, and Bush is screaming about needing 87 billion dollars.

Let's take another trip.

ROUND-BOUT ENGLAND AND SCOTLAND

This narrative relates the adventures of two odd and old fictitious couples, George Wescoombe and his wife Nan, and Barclay Allan and his wifey Juney, on a recent motor trip through England and Scotland. There is no way one could write about Great Britain without mentioning Round-Abouts.

Juney is George's young sister, which makes Nan and Juney, sisters-in-law, Barclay and George, brothers-in-laws or thereabouts.

Any resemblance to anyone living or dead is purely coincidental.

D. Wesley Coombe

DAY 1 – MONDAY – JULY 24, 1995
LAX TO HEATHROW, LONDON

(WARM AND SUNNY)

Daughter Pat picked up George and Nan Wescoombe at the Stardust Motel ($50.00) on Wilshire Blvd. in Santa Monica at 9:00 AM in order to move them to LAX to catch United Airlines Flight 934 leaving at 12 Noon to London.

Pat knows her daddy is a bagel freak and suggests "Bagel Nosh" on Wilshire Blvd. for a breakfast snack. Bagels are making a major impact into the donut business., George has a cinnamon raisin bagel with almond nut cream cheese; delicious. Pat has a plain bagel but Nan passes as she thinks bagels are too chewy. George is looking forward to scones for breakfast in England. Incidentally, scones are also doing well in California.

In order to conform with regulations, Pat delivers her parents to LAX exactly two hours before flight time. Pat has called United and is informed that Flight 934 will depart Gate 68. Thanks, Peeps. The folks at inspection have never heard of Gate 68 and suggest George and Nan go to Gate 78 as most international flights leave from Gates 74-78. Sure enough, Gate 78 displays a sign, Flight 934, London, 12:00 Noon.

Soon, Nan is enjoying her favorite location, an airport cocktail bar, sipping a glass of wine, waiting to go anywhere.

George finds the duty free shop and purchases a bottle of Canadian Club for about 30% more than it would cost in the local Thrifty or Longs Drug Store. Duty free means that the people who own the duty free shops buy the goods duty free not sell them for less. Caveat Emptor, whatever that means.

Flight 934 starts boarding at 11:00 AM and George wonders why. It turns out everyone has to be transferred by bus to Gate 68 in the Continental area as United has run out of gates and is borrowing Gate 68 from Continental.

The Wescoombes have not flown on United since the employees bought 55% of the company in July 1994, in exchange for wage reductions and other concessions.

United, in spite of a revenue of 15 billion per year and flying to 150 cities in 30 countries, was losing 300 million per year and was in great danger of going belly-up.

The employees took pay cuts of $2.00 - $3.00 per hour but still are paying themselves $12.00 to $22.00 per hour. After one year, it looks like the (ESOP) employees stock ownership plan has a great chance to succeed.

Incidentally, the flight attendants did not come in on the original ESOP. They will be asked to join in March, 1996. If they refuse and go on strike, they will probably be replaced by foreign workers.

At least, if United is borrowing gates, business must be booming. Flight 934 leaves only 10 minutes late, even with the dislocation and is 95% full. The flight will take 10 hours and 8 minutes and cover 5,800 miles.

George and Nan, with very few exceptions, always fly coach, tourist or economy, whatever the airline chooses to call it. Wealthy people refer to it as "cattle class."

Maybe when the flight is announced and the mob of people in the staging area dutifully arise and surge toward the gate in a straggling line, there is a resemblance to a herd of cattle.

Once enclosed in the metal tube, then sorted and packed into one's allotted slot, George is reminded of a can of sardines. Wonder if a sardine cares if he is in coach class.

United is a good name for an airline. When an aircraft is completely filled, it seems like all on board are united. George has heard of couples whom, when the aircraft has empty areas, actually stretch out on the seats, and fly united. They are usually modest enough to cover themselves with blankets.

Until a better, safer, less expensive way to get around

the world is developed, it is hard to improve on flying coach.

The folks in first or business class are more comfortable and pampered, for a short while, but their baggage arrives on the ground at the same moment. At that time, they have nothing to show for the excessive difference in price.

One thing United could do is pump more fresh air into the economy section and why does it have to be so dry?

Many years ago, 1979 to be exact, when George was working for a living and the company was paying for coach fare, George and Nan paid the difference and flew from London to New York on the Concord. It was a beautiful, quiet and speedy flight. In fact, the Wescoombes reached New York before they left London. They had to wait in New York for five hours for their flight to Los Angeles.

George asked one of the crew why they didn't fly on to Los Angeles. The officer had, what may have been a facetious answer, in his haughty English accent, "It would have only taken an hour or so, but your government doesn't want this aircraft flying over the United States as the aircraft was not designed and built in the U.S.A."

George realizes that our government acts that way so there was no need to reply.

Don't forget when flying coach to walk around as much as possible and also bring a folding toothbrush. George forgot his. Also, set your watch to landing time.

Drinks are free and plentiful. George enjoys the (Four) small bottles of Crown Royal. Nan is into wine, as usual. If one is not an expert on food, airline meals are satisfactory.

George and Nan are in that category. They eat to live rather than live to eat.

It is now 11:30 London time and there are only 7 hours to go before meeting with the Allans at Euro Dollar Car Rental.

George is also anxious to read what the London tabloids have to say about John Daly's great victory in the

British Open at St. Andrews on July 23.

DAY 2 – TUESDAY – JULY 25. 1995 LONDON-TUNBRIDGE WELLS

(WARM AND SUNNY)

United Airlines, Boeing 767, lands at Heathrow precisely at 6:40 AM, as advertised. The new owners are showing off.

Fortunately, Terminal 3 has many moving sidewalks so George and Nan were able to manage the one-mile trip to passport clearance.

Most international airlines land at Terminal 3. The English arrange for several large aircraft to land simultaneously so passport clearance has at least 2,000 people in line at the same time. They have 25 inspectors on duty but to clear 2,000 people takes at least 45 minutes.

George figures the inspectors are paid for 1 hour, then laid off for an hour until the next shipment of passengers arrive. By scheduling the landing in that manner, they need to pay for only 12 hours to cover 24 hours.

Nan is impatient, as usual, as the passengers are herded round and round for almost an hour. Now, she understands where the term "like cattle" comes from. The wealthy folks are in a line labeled "By Invitation Only."

George thought of getting in that line and telling the inspector, "The invitation must have got lost in the mail." Probably would have worked, too.

The Euro Dollar Car Rental booth is in the "Arrival" area. The young lady says, "Go outside to Stop 19 and the bus will pick you up in 10 minutes and take you to where the cars are kept. "

George's guardian angel, he calls her Mabel, prompts him to ask the following questions, "Do you have more than one area in Heathrow where you keep the cars?"

"Oh yes, British Airways, which uses Terminal 4, also has an area where cars are kept."

"Does this Euro Dollar bus that you are putting us on also go to the storage for Terminal 4?"

"Oh no, you will have to take the bus, which circles Heathrow and have the driver drop you off at Terminal 4 then go to the Euro Dollar booth in Terminal 4, and they will direct you to a Euro Dollar bus. It's all free."

George says, "I'm glad I asked."

Believe it or not, Heathrow Airport is so large, it takes 30 minutes to get from Terminal 3 to Terminal 4. Around and Around, the British do not like straight lines.

Although the Wescoombes were scheduled to land 80 minutes prior to the Allans landing, the 80 minutes has been used up going round and round in the passport clearance line and round and round on the free airport bus.

Luckily, the Allans are at the curb outside Terminal 4, waiting for the Euro Dollar bus when George and Nan get off the airport bus. Thanks, Mabel.

Of course, everyone is happy to meet, as if by chance, so far from home. The Euro Dollar car storage was to be the meeting place, but who would have known there would be two storage areas. Mabel knows everything.

Euro Dollar has a brand new Rover for Barclay to drive. They put the steering wheel on the wrong side and forgot the air conditioning, but other than that, it is a beauty. The boot holds all the baggage easily.

Then the fun begins. The girl says, "Just get on the M25, go east to A21, then straight to Tunbridge Wells." When George heard the word" straight" he knew there would be a problem.

When driving in England, George figures on being lost at least one hour per day. If it is planned for in advance, it is no big sweat. George sometimes gets lost in the hotel. Nan is like a will-of-the-wisp. If George takes his eyes off her for a moment, she disappears. She always knows exactly where she is, "I was in front of W oolworths." But where is

Woolworths, relative to the Tower of London.

Whoever laid out the roads in England, whether it was the Romans, Celts, Saxons or Normans, they had no conception of straight lines or right angles. The English, to this day, do not believe that the shortest distance between two points is a straight line – nor do they give a SH--.

The classic round-abouts are a throw back to ancient times. If one knows where he is going, they are an engineering masterpiece.

If one doesn't know where he is going, aha, he should circle around as many times as necessary until he finds the correct off-road or runs out of gas, whichever comes first.

North American drivers should always "think left," and when entering a round-about, "give way to the right."

The few tense moments when driving are worth it, as one has the freedom to stop whenever and wherever, and can also meander along the winding country roads, looking for a place to get lost.

England may be small, but its distances are deceptive.

The M25, the circle road around London, passes close to Heathrow but getting on it is not easy.

Barclay driving on the wrong side and George, navigating with only one good eye, screw up the round-abouts and take two or three passes before making the correct guess. Another thing the English enjoy is one way streets. How are they able to have the streets going in the wrong way every time?

After an exciting hour, Exit 21 is reached and Tunbridge Wells is within 12 miles. Yes, miles, the English do not use kilometers.

Ephriam Lodge is purported to be just off Ephriam Road, one of the main streets of the town. After traveling circuitous Ephriam Road a couple of times with no luck, Mabel tells George to look on the back of the lodge's card, and sure enough, there is a map. Ephriam Lodge and a couple more fancy Bed and Breakfasts are located down a lane, impossible to find without the locator on the map.

Ephriam Lodge, dating back to 1650, is charming. The Wescoombs get the best room, as it is the one with twin beds. Nan does not sleep with George anymore. She says, "Been there, done that."

The room is huge, with simulated Doric pillars and panels and large windows overlooking the grounds complete with a fireplace. The room not the grounds. Both rooms have private bathrooms. Also, there is a breakfast room and sitting room.

It is a warm day and after checking in, the travelers are thirsty. Next door is the Mount Edgecombe Hotel, which has a lounge and a garden drinking area. A pint of bitter each for the men and shandys for the ladies slake the thirst.

The main reason for visiting Tunbridge Wells in Kent is that June wishes to check on her dad's ancestors and relatives. John, the proprietor at Ephriam Lodge, has lived in T. Wells for many years and is a former architect. He is able to easily locate the address in an area of Tunbridge Wells called Rust Hall nearby to the lodge.

It is a short drive to Rust Hall, and the residences are located easily. As usually happens, an elderly neighbor, Dennis, who knew the Ashby family, is very friendly and loquacious. He is able to answer most questions in his interesting accent.

It turns out one of June's uncles was the best plumber in town and another owned one of the local pubs, the White Hart.

Dennis suggested that Roy, whose family had owned the bicycle shop on the main street for several generations, also knew the family. Roy was happy to put down his wrenches and converse for a spell. English people love to talk. Roy said there was a large family and he could name most of them. He also pointed out the way to White Hart Public House.

The present owner of the White Hart had only been there three years but had records dating back to 1650. The place burned down in 1911 but was immediately rebuilt as the thirst of the neighborhood had to be continually quenched.

On the main street of Rust Hall, George found a bakeshop, which among many delicacies featured his favorite, scones. Two made a nice snack. The others say they will wait for dinner. Ha Ha.

By 5 o'clock, all are hungry, but in England, Tunbridge Wells anyway, don't try to get food at that hour. They don't have Denny's in England or any of the other popular, open-most-of-time restaurants as in the US and Canada. Pub food usually starts at 6:30 PM.

Glynn, the proprietress at Ephriam Lodge, volunteers to make sandwiches for the tired and hungry travelers. The food is delicious and copious and goes well with wine and Canadian Club.

The Marathon Bridge Tournament begins, but tonight's short session does not count, according to Nan who plays all the time. She figures the rest should have a practice round.

The men let the ladies win, as it doesn't count.

Someone asked Bill Clinton what he was going to do about "The Prostitution Bill." He said, "Don't worry, I'll pay it."

DAY 3 – WEDNESDAY – JULY 26, 1995 TUNBRIDGE WELLS – BRIGHTON

(WARM – ONE HOUR OF RAIN)

Another beautiful day dawns in jolly old England. The table in the breakfast room is set splendidly. As there is plenty of orange juice, good morning England's are in order, as they will be from now on.

Grapefruit are already in place, followed by eggs, prepared as one wishes, and Canadian or back bacon. There is lashings of toast and an always full coffee carafe. Home made preserves, especially George's favorite, raspberry, complete the proper English breakfast. Thank you, Glynn and John, for tastefully serving this repast. These folks go out of their way to make one welcome.

Promptly at 9:00 AM, Ann, from the Chamber of Commerce appears at the door. Barclay arranged the stay at Ephriam Lodge through Ann. This gracious lady volunteered a tour of T. Wells, somewhat beyond the call of duty. Barclay accepted, providing she would lunch with the group at a location of her choice.

As this attractive lady has lived in T. Wells for most of her sixty (guessing) years, she knows every nook and cranny. Whizzing about in her Peugeot, listening to her descriptive chatter was a treat. T. Wells is an ancient old town/elegant city and as it is hilly, has many steep slopes and partly hidden, older but well maintained homes and buildings. Like most small English cities, it was busy, crowded, and lacked parking. Without Ann, this trip was not possible.

The highlight was a visit to an area known as "The Pantiles." A bubbling spring was discovered in 1606, and from that simple beginning, it became fashionable even for royalty to "take the waters." The Chalybeate spring, as it was known, became surrounded by upper and lower walks. Princess Anne fell on the slippery ground and donated funds to have the whole area paved with small square clay tiles, known as Pantiles. Only a sampling of the original tiles remain, as the now five-block area is covered with flagstone.

The Pantiles is very popular with the locals and tourists. Many speciality shops, restaurants, public houses, theaters, meeting rooms, etc. are available for common people and the gentry.

The group paid for a dipper of water from the well, as is the custom, but George thought it tasted as if the pipes were rusty. Jane, the dipper lady, was pretty and was able to sell George a book, which she was pleased to autograph.

The daily 11:00 AM show, with actors in period

costumes, was about to start when down came a rain shower. The nearby Swan Hotel was an excellent retreat from the culture and the rain.

Ann, who is in business as a public accountant, took the travelers to her home on the way to lunch. It is not often one has a chance to visit an English home especially one 100 years old as the majority are.

This splendid place, only probably 20 x 20, was four stories high and reminded the Wescoombes of Judy Ryan's former home in downtown Toronto. Ann has her office on one floor, complete with a computer, word processor, fax and all the latest electronic toys. She also has her own parking area, which probably doubles the value of the building.

It's a short distance to the classy public house, "The Hare," in an area known as Langton Green. The food, although known as pub food, is excellent. George has corn beef with a special type of beans and potatoes.

The English desserts were much fun. George had no idea what it was but ordered a "spotted dick with custard". It turned out to be raisin suet pudding with a lemon custard.

The highlight was when George innocently asked the others, "Would anyone like to try my spotted dick?"

Nan said, "Not if it has spots on it."

Barclay said, "If it's got spots on it, we better get you to the hospital."

Ann said, "If the spots get bigger, let me know."

June declined to embarrass her brother any further.

Ann drops the group off at the Ephriam Lodge, at which time they thank her profusely. She will not even consider reimbursement for the time away from her work.

It is still early, so a drive, 30 miles, one hour to Brighton on the coast is maybe a good idea. The drive through the countryside is fine, but the resort town of Brighton is a mad house. Mostly young people starting on a fun weekend. The Brits do have fun.

George wanted to visit Brighton to see the world

famous Royal Pavilion. The following blurb in the travel section sparked his interest.

The **Royal Pavilion's** Indian-style exterior with its minarets and spires, floodlit at night, creates a uniquely romantic picture. Step inside and enter a fabulous world of luxury and extravagance: this is truly one of the most exotic buildings in Europe. The interior is Chinese in style – and magnificent in effect. The beauty of the Music Room is said to have moved the Prince Regent to tears. The Pavilion contains many royal treasures on loan from the Queen. A guided tour is recommended.

Around the block a couple of times in the car was the closest this group got to the Royal Pavilion. Parking was used up for at least a mile. Too far to walk, but the idea was good.

The Red Lion, in Rust Hall where June's father lived as a boy, is the choice for supper. The bartender made a few inquiries and came up with the address of Roy, who is June's cousin. They had never met before.

After eating, the group located Roy's home nearby. He was delighted by the visit and suggested the travelers call on Maureen, his spinster cousin, who also lived close by and said he would come to Maureen's shortly. Later, Roy cxplained that he and his missus are not completely compatible to say the least.

Maureen, also June's cousin, welcomed the visitors and produced drinks and biscuits. When Roy arrived she brought out an ancient album, thoroughly enjoyed by all. She also presented June with a group photograph, which she removed from her wall. It's hard to beat the hospitality and friendliness.

Roy's wife probably had a reason for the incompatibility as he admitted he spent many hours at the White Hart. As he is retired, he works only a few hours a day as a gardener.

Maureen has worked at Marks and Spencer for many years.

Roy insists the party adjourn to the White Hart so he may treat for drinks. Everybody at the White Hart knows Roy as it is his second home. Barclay tried a well worn joke on the party:

> *Chap was at dinner with a group and he broke his bottom plate.*
> *The fellow next to him asked, "Don't you fancy pheasant?"*
> *The chap answered, "Yes, but confidentially, I just broke my bottom plate."*
> *This fellow said, "Here, try this one."*
> *"Okay, but it's too tight."*
> *" Well, try this one. "*
> *"Okay, but it's too loose. "*
> *The helper reached in to his back pocket and handed the distraught chap another plate. "Oh," said he, "this one is perfect: You must be a dentist. "*
> *"No," was the answer, "I'm an undertaker. "*

June will not let Roy pay and the group manages to escape before he orders another round.

What a delightful visit.

DAY 4 – THURSDAY – JULY 27, 1995 TUNBRIDGE WELLS TO CREDITON

(WARM, OVERCAST)

This is a travelling day – 165 miles – estimated at 6 hours using the secondary roads.

John and Glynn of Ephriam House provide a super English breakfast with, as John says, "lashings of everything."

The English use strange words to confuse visitors. Furthermore, they have a lot of trouble with pronunciation, maybe because they do not move their jaw muscles sufficiently. Visitors barely get used to one dialect before trying to understand another. It is not necessary to fully understand, as their warm smiles, kindliness, friendliness, and good humor say it all.

The travelers are very comfortable with the people in this land of their ancestors.

The road system is another matter. Today we will stay off the motorways and use the highway system. These are mostly two lane roads passing through towns at least every five miles. In the towns, the roads practically touch the buildings and in the country do touch the hedges. Sometimes trees overlap the road, making almost a beautiful tunnel.

Barclay, now in his fourth day, is becoming an expert on round-abouts. The secret is to keep circling until finding the proper exit. Taking the wrong route leads to a complicated mess.

Everyone helps with direction, but poor batteries in the hearing aids are a problem. When June says "Go" and Barclay hears "Whoa", there is a major difference.

Barclay has overcome his initial problem of hitting the curb with the left front wheel. He says it's the Rover's fault as the car is wider than it looks.

One way streets are major obstacles. It's embarrassing to come face to face with another driver. Most drivers are very courteous except young girls who are very quick with the finger.

By using the 31 and 303 for the trip today, the M25 was avoided.

Back in 1989, England planned to spend $3.5 Billion a year on road building. "The greatest road building since the Romans."

However, studies at Oxford University showed that "no realistic main road program can keep pace with a forecasted traffic growth." The Oxford study plus the environmentalists caused the government to throw in the towel.

The ring road, the M25, which circles London and connects the motorways heading out of the capital, was designed to carry 100,000 vehicles per day. It is now burdened with about 165,000 daily, and the number's increasing rapidly. Traffic on the M25 slows to a crawl several times a day. The public opinion is that building new roads generates more traffic so it's a no win situation.

For a country so green and beautiful and small, it would not take much to cover all of it with concrete. Maybe improving public transport is the answer.

An hour and one half lunch stop at the Pembroke Arms Hotel in Salisbury was a welcome break. Fortunately for the English, in the country at least, they do not have the fast-food joints so rampant in the US and Canada. They are better off "brown bagging it."

After twisting and turning through the pretty countryside and making no more than the allotted wrong turns, the Coombe House Country Inn, Coleford, Crediton, Devon was reached at 5:00 PM and everyone knows what happens at 5 o'clock

The lounge bar with its ornately carved wooden mantle-piece was ideal for a libation, okay, two.

The "Cellar Bar," serving a la carte meals, opens at 7 o'clock. The manager, Anne, brought menus and offered to have the food ready in the "Cellar" when it first opened at 7:00 PM. That was a nice touch, as this old group prefers to eat early.

The main dining room looked beautiful but only served lengthy, five-course, expensive meals. When George sees the prices, he quickly loses his appetite.

Coombe House Country Hotel is some 200 years old, but the foundations and cellars (now bars) are reputed to be 700-800 years old. Thus it is full of character, atmosphere, and intrigue, and is listed as a protected building of historic interest. During the Civil War some of Cromwell's men supposedly hid in the cellars and escaped, via a secret tunnel, to Crediton, 3 miles or more away.

The present building was originally the Manor House of a large country estate, with sufficient and spacious rooms to accommodate a large family, servants, and visitors, so lending itself to becoming a small, friendly country hotel. The bedrooms are commodious and have bathrooms en-suite, colour TV, tea and coffee making facilities, and direct dial telephones. Central heating has been installed throughout the hotel.

Two young men in the bar were from New Zealand. They worked for a New Zealand company, Bierton Downs, which is establishing the ostrich raising business in that country.

Dr. Les, the senior of the two, told how his company bought ostrich in Zimbabwe but had to ship them to England for six months quarantine before the birds(?) would be allowed into New Zealand. Evidently Newcastle disease is affecting the poultry (ostrich is poultry) business worldwide. The quarantine area is at Lapford, nearby to Coleford.

Thus, the birds have to travel almost around the world. It's a shame they can't fly. George is imagining a big flock of ostrich flying by, like Canada geese.

Ostrich raising is becoming big business world wide as the meat is as good as beef without the fat and cholesterol. George ate an ostrich steak in Capetown and could not tell the difference. South Africa is the leading country in the ostrich raising business.

Dr. Jim told about the predecessor of the ostrich called a moa, about three times the size of an ostrich, once a native of New Zealand, but now extinct. A New Zealand eagle with a 20- foot wing span ate all the moas but also became extinct from severe stomach pains.

George asked Dr. Jim, "How do you move these creatures around the world?"

Jim replied, "We fly them."

George: "What do you do, buy a bunch of coach class tickets." George had a vision of sitting next to an ostrich on United Airlines.

Jim laughed a little, "No, believe it or now, we charter a 747 and fly a hundred at a time-carefully crated of course."

George still curious, "What is the mix of ladies and gentlemen ostriches?"

Jim's answer: "Domesticated, we like the male to serve two females, but in the wild state, he handles about five."

George stated, "That's a dirty trick, reducing their fun."

The group had chicken prepared a fancy way, which was enjoyable. There was steak on the menu, but George is afraid to sink his teeth into a thick, juicy steak as they may stay there. The English usually serve French fries which they call chips. Potato chips, they call crisps. Whatever the name is, they are still fattening.

The lounge has tables suitable for bridge, so the marathon tournament is under way.

Life is really a funny old dog.

DAY 5 – FRIDAY – JULY 28, 1995
COOMBE HOUSE – CREDITON

(SUNNY AND WARM)

Another beautiful sunrise in green, gracious England. Good morning England's accompanied by a Sunday brunch type breakfast got the day off to a splendid start.

George and Nan have been to Devon several times before, but a trip to Okehampton where George's grandfather, great grandfather and great, great grandfather were born is a must.

The great, great grandfather was born in 1784 and it is difficult to go further back. These ancestors became Methodists in John Wesley's time, thus breaking away from the Church of England. It seems the Methodists did not keep very good records until the eighteenth century for some reason, probably political.

Okehampton has been a busy farming center since Roman times mainly due to its location at the confluence of the Oakmont and East Oakmont Rivers.

George heard his grandparents speak of Tiverton, a town about 10 miles distant. George should have asked them how they got there, as it is a long walk. Another good question would have been "How did you meet?" They were born 40 miles apart, a tremendous distance 150 years ago.

Tiverton is larger than Okchampton and has a walk around central market.

A bloke, Douglas Fletcher, claims he is the world champion town crier. In his uniform, he is paid 10.00 an hour to shout out advertising for whatever. Douglas has appeared in many parts of the world and makes a fine living by shouting. Barclay hopes he has him on the malfunctioning camcorder as Douglas announced to the townsfolk that Canadian and American visitors were in town.

The Mormons have a booth in the central market and give away Mormon bibles to anyone interested. According to reports, religion is not doing well in England with attendance declining steadily. Maybe the Mormons can attract some business.

Lunch is at the White Ball Hotel, near the car park.

People recognize the group as tourists and wish to talk. Maybe its because Barclay and George are the only one wearing shorts – its warm in this country.

Now, it's time to go to Grandma's house. She was born in Sidbury about 5 miles inland from the famous coastal resort town of Sidmouth. Sidmouth has a boardwalk and beach stretching for miles, lined with mostly expensive hotels and shops. It's like a very small Miami Beach. The place is crowded on weekends and Friday is the beginning of the influx.

Back to Sidbury, Sidmouth is at the mouth of the Sid River and Sidbury is at the bury of the Sid River. It is a small town with a church and only two pubs. Grandma's father worked at a dairy in the late 1800's. The dairy is closed down, but the buildings have been converted to dwellings so it is easy to see where she lived as a child.

The church school built in 1837 is still in use. As she was born in 1854, she probably attended the fine old school.

One of the pubs is operated by an owner who has his own hours and this is a closed period.

The other pub has been bought by a young couple who have converted the building to a storage and national sales office for commercial ovens. The attractive lady said they got a good deal on the pub as it was about to go belly up and their business could be conducted from anywhere. What could be better than the peaceful little town of Sidbury.

She directed the group to a new spot, the Sid Valley Country Hotel, about a quarter mile out of town. Stephen and Sarah have taken this mid 17th century "E" rated property and updated the inside to a first class small hotel. It has eight luxury rooms with gardens on 5 acres. It has a heated pool and charges $110.00 per night. It is a very pleasant place to spend a relaxing hour in the lounge.

The Brits love their flowers. Everywhere, flowers are blooming in all colors. Every house seems to have a flower garden and public areas are full of flowers. Roses grow in profusion.

Back on the motorways, through Honiton, Tiverton, Crediton to Coleford and more practice on the round-abouts for Barclay.

Back to Coombe Country House Hotel for excellent food, good drinks, and a couple of hours of bridge.

It was a smashing day.

DAY 6 – SATURDAY – JULY 29,1995
CREDITON TO BRISTOL

(SUNNY AND WARM)

Another beautiful day in the Motherland. Barclay is driving with much more confidence, handling the round-abouts easily to Tiverton, where the on-ramp to the M-5 is located. Barclay has completed over 100 round-abouts to this point and the right side of his brain has taken over. That's the side that controls things one does automatically, almost without thinking.

It's a strain when one has to figure out what has to be done at each round-about. The Englishmen and women, too, speed into a round-about, sorting themselves out with no trouble. In America, that exercise is accomplished by overpasses consisting of millions of tons of concrete or by a series of stop and go lights. The English do not have the room for the concrete, nor the patience for the stoplights.

Barclay is rapidly developing the English, in-born trait, of always looking right. That is the secret of the round-abouts. All must give way to those on the right side, otherwise, a serious cock-up could result. Barclay, being Canadian, drives with the car headlight on in the daytime. The Brits are continually blinking to let him know something he already knows.

Older folks have trouble changing the habits of the right brain. George has to use the left cortex of his brain to go up and down stairs safely. A slight misstep could break one's ass.

It has become apparent to Barclay, driver, and George, navigator, that an ordinary road map (gas station type) will not suffice in this country of a million or more roads.

Along the major motorways or carriage ways are

stopping points every 20 miles or so. These are called "Welcome Breaks" and besides petrol, sell everything imaginable for traveling.

Let's stop and buy a map with more definition. It's Saturday and the English are driving about with their families. The "Welcome Break" parking area is immense but parking is at a premium.

Inside the sales area are several hundred people queued up waiting to pay their money.

George and Barclay find the "Road Atlas of Great Britain" – 21/2 miles to the inch. It is perfect except it costs $20.40 US and weighs 20.4 lbs.

The conversion rate is $1.70 US to the pound.

The travelers go to the end of the queue for what appears to be a long wait. The three English ladies at the cash registers are very fast and polite. The fifteen-minute wait allows George time to check his research on queuing.

The queue, the traditional first-come, first-served, file of customers has been faithfully observed in England almost forever.

"An Englishman even if he is alone, forms an orderly queue of one."

Oxford University psychologist, Peter Collet, sees queuing under threat from within. Queue-jumping is becoming more frequent, examples are:

1. Jockeying consists of shifting from one line to another to find the faster line.
2. Colonizing is keeping a sharp eye open for another cashier or ticket window to open and dashing for the head of the new queue.
3. Transgressing is pretending not to notice a queue and slipping into an up front gap in the line.

For the British, a queue is a cameo of an idealized society where everyone knows their place, accepts it, and doesn't try to steal an unfair advantage over others. People are treated as equals and espouse the equalitarian ideal.

The British need to know where they stand and what to expect, orderliness and predictability is essential.

Sometimes the British form invisible queues, expecting the person behind the counter to remember who is next to be served. Often an orderly British customer will point to another person to indicate the first" in-line."

The word queue is from the French word meaning, "tail." Somehow the cultural habits got reversed. The French consider a queue an imposition, an unwarranted form of regulation and interference, like the government. The Latins say, "it is debasing, regimented and it prevents individuals from using their intelligence and initiative to personal advantage."

George, who has been on Englishman for many generations, is both an equalitarian and an elitist. He is of the opinion that queuing is indicative of politeness and fair play.

After that interesting half hour it's back on the M25 for the mad dash to Bristol. There does not seem to be a speed limit. There is some slight slowing approaching Bristol for the usual invisible reason, too many cars for the road, momentarily.

The new map book works perfectly. Off on 4018, winding and twisting and gyrating through the round-abouts, it's not long until St. Pauls St., near the B.B.C. is spotted.

Seeley Hotel has been built inside the shells of about six joined together stately homes. According to the National Trust, one can do anything inside but don't change the outside.

This place is quite modem, and has 55 rooms, a restaurant, 24 hour bar lounge and a fitness centre. The highlight is the rear patio and beautiful garden.

As soon as the travelers are settled in, it's to the patio for a libation and a planning session.

George and June's grand parents lived in Bristol around the turn of the Century and raised seven children at 25 Badminton road. Rachel, the Receptionist, suggests a taxi and calls Leon, who happens to be black. Leon, who has a big smile and one gold tooth, has friends who live on Badminton Road and he himself lives nearby. You guessed it, this part of the city, which is close to downtown, is mostly black.

One would not know that fact from the appearance of the large, joined together, houses which have been well-maintained for the last 100-150 years. Most of the faces on the street are black, however.

Hopefully, all the folks are as happy and pleasant as Leon, who waited for 15 minutes while the visitors took pictures and cased the place. George hoped somebody would come out of No. 25 but if they saw the group, no one stirred. That was to be expected. Maybe George looked like a taxman.

It was possible to visualize this area, a hundred years ago. Only horses and wagons, no paved road or sidewalks and poor people walking all over the streets. George's ancestors were neither rich enough or crooked enough to be important. What a wonderful look into the past. A similar house across the street had a "for sale" sign on it. George called the broker, who confirmed the houses were about 120 years old, had 4 bedrooms on three floors and were priced at $75,000. Grandpa probably paid $750 for it in 1890.

Le Chasseur restaurant serves only full course meals but the lounge bar has a limited menu of al-a-carte items. This is a neat little hotel. The ladies have a bottle of wine with their meal in the lounge bar. The remaining wine comes with them to the patio, which is ideal for bridge. A balmy evening in a garden seating.

George had a feeling there may be mosquitoes. No, but the wasps were a nuisance. There is always something. These were not the stinging type wasps but they enjoyed sitting on the edge of the glasses and drinking wine and beer. Maybe wasps eat mosquitoes in England when they get drunk.

DAY 7 – SUNDAY – JULY 30, 1995
BRISTOL

(SUNNY, WARM)

A proper English breakfast in the dining room at 7:30 AM. So far, the breakfasts have been complete, well served with table cloths and flowers. George eats too much, as it is available.

The M32 leads quickly to the M4 which leads to the massive suspension bridge over the Severn River and into Wales. Cardiff is the destination.

It soon became evident that Wales is not England as all road signs are posted in English and also in a strange language. Cardiff is spelled Caerdydd in Welsh and probably sounds as strange as it looks.

The massive castle in downtown Cardiff is an item of interest. The original building dates back to Norman days. It presently covers several walled blocks and part is in use as a concert hall.

Shirley Bassey appeared last evening and drew 12,000 people. In an adjacent parking area, George and Barclay chatted with the leader of a convoy of six trucks carrying portable loos from Coventry in England. He had no use for the Welshmen.

"The rotters ordered only six loos for the 12,000 people and should have ordered nine or ten. What a mess this morning. "

Caerphilly, the city where the great Welsh cheese is produced is nearby, but as this is Sunday, nothing is open.

Back to Seeley's Hotel for a light lunch.

About a mile walk, in the sunshine, to the floating harbor where the regatta boat show and other entertainment is taking place.

Tied up in the harbor, being restored, is the SS Great Britain, the first propeller driven ironship built in Bristol in

1845. After many years of ocean service, it was abandoned in the Falkland Islands in 1886. Contributions from citizens of Bristol resulted in bringing the SS Great Britain on a Barge to Bristol. It is now in use for special events and is a landmark. A welcome taxi brings the group uphill to the hotel. A mile downhill is one thing, uphill is a struggle.

George is aware that "Harry Ramsden's" is the world's most famous fish and chip restaurant. There are fifteen locations in Britain and around the world and maybe the reputation is justified. The fish was perfect, but for George, the chips were a little soggy. Maybe the British like them that way.

The restaurant holds about 500 guests, has glass chandeliers, oak paneling, stained glass windows, wall to wall carpets and ample parking.

They also serve chicken faggots.

It is a beautiful evening so bridge outside on the patio is most pleasant.

Daylight begins at 5:30 AM and continues to 9:00 PM. Why are there no flies or mosquitoes in this country?

These old folks start to burn the midnight oil at 9 0' clock and so to bed.

DAY 8 – MONDAY – JULY 31, 1995
BRISTOL – FARINGDON – STROUD

(SUNNY, HOT)

What a beautiful day in the U.K. After the usual morning ritual (too much food), it's on to the M4 for an hours drive in the direction of London to the town of Faringdon.

The road atlas is a big help in sorting out the multitude of roads. The group is well under George's quota of one hour lost time per day.

Faringdon is reached about an hour before the appointed time. Like most English towns, it has a center, lined with shops, restaurants, etc. There are usually many people walking about in a relatively small area. As most do not have cars, what else can they do?

The Portwell Hotel Coffee Shop is open. George has his usual scone and the others a choice of eccles cakes, sticky buns, date squares, ginger squares, truffle logs, butter tarts, iced tea cake, cheese pasty, and other English delicacies. The English have not caught on to doughnuts.

George spends an hour with Keith at his factory. Then the group moves to the small city of Stroud about 30 miles distant.

Its lunchtime so the Bell Hotel on the main street near George's next meeting is ideal for a light snack and libation. George and Barclay enjoy splitting a ploughman's lunch, great old cheese, rolls, sliced onions, cucumber, and peppers. Today the choice of cheese was Stilton.

George has a meeting with Stephen and Belinda for an hour while the rest check into the Apple Orchard House in Nailsworth, a pretty town on the outskirts of Stroud.

It's laundry day. There are not many Laundromats in England, but fortunately in Stroud, there is a "Fluff and Dry" not far from where George has his meeting.

While the ladies figure out the coins necessary to activate the equipment, the men search out a pub in which to sit whilst the clothes are cleaning.

Not far away is the Duke of York, 22 Nelson Street, Stroud, Glos. The ladies, after getting the machines in motion, are tired and also find the Duke of York. It's only a couple of doors away, so it's easy to slip in and out, checking on the progress in the laundromat.

The pub is not busy, so Mike, the owner, has time to talk. George has been drinking the English standard, Bitter, but is amazed to see in the lager section, Red Stripe, his very favorite Jamaican Beer.

"Mike, it's so nice of you to have my favorite brew. How did you know I was coming to Stroud?"

"Twas a coincidence." Mike replied. "I have it on tap

most often. This is a free house, not beholden to any brewery, so I can buy and sell what I wish. I get good deals from small or foreign breweries. Have to do it to make a living with business down."

All of the above in a colorful Irish accent.

Beer sales are down in the pubs for two reasons. Stricter drunk driving laws are forcing people to drink at home, and the breweries are stocking the supermarkets with cans and bottles to take advantage of the trend.

When people do go out, they have a meal with their drinks, so only classy pubs with food are busy.

Mike paid £235,000 for the Duke of York three years ago and now could get only £185,000, a loss of £50,000.

This is a problem all over England. Prices are down on the average, 20% for almost everything. America is about the same or maybe worse. It's a period of adjustment from the highflying Reagan and Thatcher years. One can only live on borrowed money for a limited time.

Mike gave George a Red Stripe glass mug and Barclay a bar size coaster. George promised Mike a copy of this story. Mike pretended that he would like that. Barclay thought he would try an old standard on Mike.

The wife asked her husband to bring home a live chicken.

After buying the chicken, he decided to see a movie, so he stuffed the chicken inside his pants. The lady sitting next to him said to her friend, "This man is exposing himself."

The friend said, "If you've seen one, you've seen them all."

The reply was "Maybe so, but this one is eating my popcorn."

The laundry is finished. A supermarket is nearby so coldcuts, rolls, cheeses, fruits and beer and wine are purchased for in-room consumption.

Nailsworth, a suburb of Stroud, is the location of Apple Orchard House. The Cotswolds are a beautiful part of England with green trees, green fields and gentle hills.

Apple Orchard House has fine ensuite rooms with a country view from the large windows.

Victoria is a good business woman, but her hasty cooking is not up to prior locations. You can't win them all.

The back patio is ideal for a continuation of the bridge marathon. Nan is keeping score, but that is not helping the ladies get good cards. Somehow or another, Nan is able to make the scorecard disappear.

Did you know that thirty percent of the children in the USA are born out of wedlock?

DAY 9 – TUESDAY – AUGUST 1, 1995 STROUD. WINDERMERE

(SUNNY, HOT)

The Brits are complaining about the hot weather. They should go to Palm Springs at this time of year.

After good morning England's and a proper English breakfast, it's time to get on the M5 motorway and join the excellent drivers (mostly) for a speedy 180 mile race northward.

The drivers on the M5 take their work seriously, change lanes politely, and are willing to momentarily give way before resuming their 80 MPH speed. Barclay misses the round-abouts when driving on the motorway, but says he would rather pay attention at 70 than loaf along at 50.

A couple of "Welcome Break" stops during the three and a half hour drive are, indeed, welcome breaks. The English tell it like it is.

Windermere is the most popular resort in the Lake District. It would be foolish to arrive on a weekend. This is Tuesday, and still the whole area is very busy. If one does not have a reservation in England, one goes to the Big I sign and within 15 minutes, suitable accommodations will be found by the efficient young ladies and gentlemen. The Big I people charge 10% of the room rate for this service, which is absorbed by the hotel, guest house, B & B, etc.

The Coppice, a B & B in a beautiful house, is located close to town center going down town, but not so close when walking back uphill.

Windermere, in fact the whole Lake District, appears to be mainly hotel and other type accommodations, fancy shopping areas, restaurants and pubs, the same as any popular resort in the world. Parking is at a premium but is always there if one looks hard enough. The fee is high, however.

Lake Windermere, the largest lake in England, is about 12 miles long and about 1 mile wide and is interspersed with small islands, some privately owned. Small boats, powerboats and most other watercraft are in view. Lake Windermere became known throughout the world when, in 1930, Sir Henry Seagrave was killed while breaking the world water speed record.

Sir Malcolm Campbell was killed while trying to break Seagrave's record in 1967 on nearby Coniston Water.

The travelers opt for an hour's cruise around the lake on an open topped ship with about 100 other tourists. A bloke with a pleasant accent continually chattered. This area has been popular for about 200 years. The time scale is different in England.

A double-decker bus is available for a 90-minute tour of the whole district for $8.00 each. Would you believe after ten minutes, the bus developed a fault (overheated). The driver gave the folks the option of waiting 30 minutes for another bus to be brought or money back. 30 minutes usually becomes 60 minutes, so money back was the choice.

A ready taxi moved the travelers to Bowness where the car is parked. The town of Bowness adjoins Windermere and a stranger would not be able to tell the difference.

Bowness has the usual promenade along the lake and

features the" Aquarius Center and Restaurant."

June has been anxious for shepherd's pie and sure enough, it's shown on the outside menu. It's pleasant enough overlooking the lake to spend an hour. Of course, the Aquarius serves beer and wine.

Back to the Coppice where Bob and Christy, owners, set up a bridge table so the tournament may continue.

Bob and Christy were in the restaurant business for many years, and about five years ago when prices were high, got a chance to sell for a good price. The English tax system says if you have a capital gain, the tax is not payable if you roll the principal and profit over into a new venture.

Thus, they moved into the Band B business. The English system has another feature, which would go over big in America. After a taxpayer reaches the ripe old age of 55, the tax on capital gains is forgiven. Bob and Christy have about five years to wait.

The travelers are tired, so after the men win a 700 rubber, it's time for sleep. The men had all the good cards, which is the way it should be. George bid a small slam but went down on a distribution fluke. June led her ace to Nan's singleton and then, of course, led the same suit again.

George feels like the guy who was doing push-ups and forgot about the mousetrap on the floor.

Tomorrow is another day.

DAY 10 – WEDNESDAY – AUGUST 2, 1995 WINDERMERE – CARLISLE

(SUNNY, HOT)

Another sparkling day in the U.K. It had better rain soon, or this cannot be England.

There is nothing prettier than an early morning drive through the lake country in bright sunshine. Rain would dampen the pleasure.

Ambling through Ambleside, stopping at Grasmere and Keswick before reaching the A595 to Carlisle, is an easy drive early in the morning on a Wednesday. It would not be fun to visit these tourist towns on a weekend in the rain.

At least every fifth building is a hotel, guest house, or a B & B. The Brits believe in holidays, and this country is either affluent or has a great welfare system.

There must be a dozen small lakes, so there is plenty of room for the visitors to enjoy aquatic adventures. All in all, it is probably the prettiest part of England.

Lake Windermere area has the scenery, but Carlisle, about 60 miles north, has the history. Carlisle, 10 miles from the border of Scotland, is an ancient city.

Hadrians wall was built in the second century A.D. by the Romans. IT is a most impressive landmark, but George has been unable to find out why Emperor Hadrian had it built or whom he was trying to impress. He must have had a lot of people looking for something to do. Houstrads, a fort which is part of the wall, had a garrison of 1,000 and was laid out with rows of streets and public buildings. George will buy a book on this subject, as the Romans must have had a reason other than to extend their empire from Mesopotamia to the north of England.

Carlisle Castle, only a thousand years old, dominates the city and had a practical use. Most castles began as fortifications and this monstrous group of walls was continually in use as the tribes from the north, probably Scots, Picts or whatever name they used at that time, battled the English or whatever to the south.

Next to the castle is the cathedral, founded in 1122. This is a splendid example of the ability of the stone masons of that time period. They had plenty of time to hammer, chisel, and carve as there was no T.V., movies, or holidays at Windermere.

All the ancient history made the travelers thirsty, so the outside bar at Yates' Wine Lodge was a welcome stop. Watching the busy folk scurrying along the street is a change from old buildings. George was able to pick up four buttered scones from a nearby bakery. It's a treat to see small butcher shops and bakeshops along the streets. Incidentally, milk is still delivered by an early morning milkman.

The people of Carlisle are not ancient. They have developed an extensive shopping area, part of which is covered. No motor cars are allowed, parking is adjacent. Nan and June need to visit the shops while the men sit in the shade on one of the many benches throughout the area. This is a neat city.

Eastview Guest House on Warwick Road is only five minutes from the shopping area, has parking and en suite rooms. Alice, the proprietress, is able to supply ice, a precious commodity in England.

Also, on Warwick Road is the Casa Romana, advertising, "the essence of Rome in the heart of Carlisle." This is a true Italian restaurant featuring, along with the food, Roman archways, pillars, and marble statues. George expected to see a pink flamingo or maybe a cement mixer. The place is typically Italian.

The spaghetti and lasagna were excellent, washed down with Chianti. The ladies needed a "finale" and Nan chose Tiramasu and June, Zuccotto. The men were allowed a spoonful each.

Back to Eastview House, where Alice supplied a bridge table and ice. The ladies, after losing 500 points in penalties, were able to win a 500 rubber to even tonight's match.

Love will find a lay.

DAY 11 – THURSDAY – AUGUST 3, 1995
CARLISLE – EDINBURGH

(SUNNY AND WARM)

After 10 miles along the A7, Scotland is reached. At

once, Barclay feels better as this is the home of his ancestors. George would not know the difference, except the folks talk funnier than they do in England. Isn't it amazing that only Americans speak perfect English.

The A7 passes right through the busy center of Hawick, Galashiels, and other smaller cities. Parking is difficult except in a car park and unless one is staying "long. Term" it's too far to walk.

Edinburgh is reached by noon and Strathmohr House, at 23 Mayfield Gardens is found easily. George's Guardian Angel, Mabel, said, "turn here." Sure enough there was a postman delivering the Royal mail, who knew Mayfield Gardens like the back of his hand.

Strathmohr is rather a classy B&B, in a cluster of classy B&B's. Stuart, the proprietor says, "Don't drive your car. Take either the 3, 31, 69 or 81 bus which passes right in front every five minutes for only $1.80 US return."

Strathmohr has large windows and the window in the Allan's bathroom facing the bus line is stuck in a wide-open position. June cannot wait until Stuart fixes the window. She spends a few minutes on the throne waving to the folks on the bus, in a queenly manner. The bus driver backed up for a better look.

Each of the four, took a bus number and a one pound lottery was held, paying off to the holder of the number of the first bus appearing. In five minutes, Nan was richer with a ticket on No.3.

Princess Street is only twenty minutes away. This famous busy thoroughfare is lined with shops on one side. On the other side many ancient buildings may be seen including the well-photographed Edinburgh Castle on the Rock. Barclay has his camcorder operating and records a description of the castle in his Scottish accent. George MacWescoombe also commented on the grandeur of the scene.

The way to the castle is all up hill so this ancient group gave up after 10 minutes and returned to the shops on the main street.

Milnes, "a must in Edinburgh" has been on Hanover Street since 1790. There is no seating on the main floor, nor on the next floor down, nor on the next floor down, but four floors below street level, the travelers settle down for a libation. The ladies have the usual wine, but Barclay finds "Tennants" on tap, the beer his father used to drink. There is a bar on each floor. The Scots must be experts on burrowing.

Haggis Pie is on the posted menu so George, who has heard of, but never tasted Haggis, ordered one pie with four forks. Haggis turns out to be spicy meat, with vegetables, under a flaky pastry. It disappeared in a short time. Maybe it had oatmeal to add body. It tasted better than it sounds.

Back on Prince's Street where the castle dominates the skyline. This landmark has been in use for 3000 years, added to by each Scottish king or conqueror. It has been a fortress, barracks, or a royal residence. It is also the home of the Scottish crown jewels.

Nan wins the lottery again, as a No.3 bus is the first to appear. The bus knows the way to Strathmorh House. June and Nan sit at the front on the top of the bus and are excited by the driver's near misses.

Across the street from the Strathmohr is Arthur's View Court, a licensed and classy B&B, a great place for dinner.

"Steak and Ale" for four was the order plus the usual libations. The men won a 700 and a 500 rubber so Nan conveniently lost the scorecard.

DAY 12 – FRIDAY. AUGUST 4, 1995
EDINBURGH – ABOYNE – CRUDEN BAY

(SUNNY AND MILD)

It is a gorgeous day in Scotland. After a petite cock-up (10 minutes) the travelers find the A90 which leads to the magnificent suspension bridge across the Firth of Fourth.

The destination today is the Arbor Lodge in the town of Aboyne. Barclay chose Aboyne as it is central for three small towns where his parents were born and raised. The Arbor Lodge was chosen from an advertisement and Barclay has spoken to Sheena, the proprietress on the telephone. Sheena, whose husband has access to the Internet and also a special software package for travelers, volunteered a computerized routing, Edinburgh to Aboyne. On the following page is a sample of what a computer can provide for a traveler.

AutoRoute Express V3.04 (UK+Irl 03.94)
Route: 'Edinburgh,Lothian' to 'Aboyne,Grampian'
Quickest: 122 miles, 2 hrs 47 min, £7.86

Time	Dist	Instruction	Road	For	Dir	Towards
00:00	0.0	DEPART Edinburgh (Lothian)	A90	2 miles	NW	(Blackball)
00:05	2.1	At Blackball stay on the	A90	2 miles	W	(Crarnond Bridge)
00:11	4.6	At Cramond Bridge stay on the	A90	6 miles	NW	
00:17	10.5	Stay on the	Forth	1 mile	N	
00:19	11.6	Stay on the	A90	2 miles	N	. (M90 II)
00:22	13.4	At M90 JI stay on the	M90	27 miles	N	(Milnathort)
00:45	40.0	At M90 JIO turn off onto	M85	1 mile	NE	*C;heck access.
00:46	41.4	At M85 JI stay on the	A85	1 mile	W	
00:48	42.4	Bear right onto	A94	½ mile	N	
00:50	43.0	Bear left onto	A93	5 miles	N	Braemar
01:02	48.4	At Guildtown stay on the	A93	4 miles	N	Braemar
01:07	52.1	At Cargill stay on the	A93	6 miles	E	Braemar
01:16	58.2	At Blairgowrie stay on the	A93	1 mile	NE	Braemar
01:18	59.4	At Rattray stay on the	A93	6 miles	N	Braemar
01:25	64.9	At Bridge Of Cally stay on the	A93	29 miles	N	Braemar
02:06	93.5	At Braemar stay on the	A93	9 miles	N	(Ballater)
02:19	102.9	At Crathie stay on the	A93	7 miles	E	(Ballater)
02:30	110.2	At Ballater stay on the	A93	7 miles	NE	(Banchory)
02:40	117.0	At Dinnet stay on the	A93	5 miles	E	(Banchory)
02:46	121.8	Turn right onto	B968	½ mile	S	(Aboyne)
02:47	122.2	ARRIVE Aboyne (Grampian)				

AutoRoute Express (0 NextBase Ltd.
Maps (0 Ordnance Survey 1994

The time, 2 hours and forty-seven minutes, to cover 122.2 miles on the winding, narrow roads of Scotland is what Jackie Stewart did in a practice run. The Scots are excellent drivers and most think they are Jackie Stewart. Barclay is a fine driver and after 300 round-abouts can give-way, step-on-it, and circle a round-about in a semiprofessional manner. George estimates that four hours would be achievable, and also safe.

The A93 winds through rolling hills, with picture postcard scenery on each side. Barclay stops so the ladies may pick a bit of heather from the hills. As usual the road passes through the center of several old towns, the largest, Raftry and Blair Gowrie.

Wonder what Jackie Stewart does in those towns. He would need more than a scatter sign, as the roads are crowded with cars and people

This is mostly farming country. Many fields have hay neatly bundled in rolls. Each roll contains exactly the same number of blades of grass. Machinery is the answer

After Raftry, there are fewer pastoral settings, as the landscape becomes more rugged in the foothills of the Grampion Mountains.

Braemar is a center of tourist activity. Skiing at Glenshee, golf at Braemar's many courses and possibly the finest salmon fishing in the world, on the River Dee. The elegant Invercauld Arms Hotel makes a perfect pit stop.

The town of Petercutter is on the A93 – George figures maybe Lorena Bobbitt came from that town.

Aboyne is reached in three hours and fifty minutes, only one hour more than the computer estimate.

Arbor Lodge is an absolutely beautiful, four-year-old, modem house. What a change from all the prior, ancient, B&Bs. After 11 nights of fifteen-foot high ceilings, tiny recently installed, bathrooms, windows hard to close, this place, is really a palace.

Sheena, whose husband is the computer expert and also a building contractor, designed and built this beautiful house. The couple also have a home in Florida, where they spend three months in the winter.

The grounds and flowers indicate a gardener has been on the job. An outstanding display of many varieties, including roses.

George commented, "I think these people have a bob or two." Nan, whose hearing aid is not connected, replied, "I didn't see a barbecue."

During the conversation with Sheena, a handsome 45-year-old (guess) lady, Barclay mentioned that tomorrow, Saturday, the group would travel to Cruden Bay where his father was born. In a few minutes, without being asked, Sheena returned with a computer printout of the quickest way to Cruden Bay. It was only 60 miles and the computer estimated that Jackie Stewart could make it in 1 hours and 43 minutes.

"You could do it this afternoon," Sheena suggested, "It is daylight until 9:30 P.M."

George, the navigator, used the printout in conjunction with the $20.40 AZ map. Barclay made it in 2 hours and 15 minutes without a problem. The roads are winding but the traffic was light. In the bright sunshine, the green fields were even greener. In some places the hedges were high, causing Nan to remark, "They should cut down the trees, they're blocking the view."

The townof Ellen, where Barclay's mother was born is reached first. Then, Hatton, where she lived as a teenager.

Cruden Bay, near the top of Eastern Scotland, is a small pretty town on the North Sea.

St. James Scottish Episcopal Church where Barclay's parents were married in 1908, is in good condition and is very active. The church was built in 1843 and celebrated 150 years in 1993. According to legend a church has been on that site since 1012.

In the town center stands the Kilmarnock Arms Hotel where the young couple spent the first night of their married life. Naturally, the group had a fine meal in the dining room.

The hotel was quite busy and is in good repair.

After dinner a drive to the Harbor, which in olden days, was reputed to be a smugglers haven. Bram Stoker, author of Dracula, wrote a novel about the smuggling in Cruden Bay and about Slaines Castle nearby. The book is "The Watter's Mou," whatever that means.

George is a smart-ass on the return trip and uses the computer printout without the map. A wrong turn resulted which caused a delay of half an hour. All was not lost, however.

Barclay and George went into the "Cross Roads Filling Station" at Newmachar to get back on track.

Fergus Hood, the proprietor, pointed out the problem in a few minutes. Fergus was also in the Honey Business and insisted on giving each a jar of his honey. Barclay put five pounds on the counter, but Fergus said in his sweet Scottish accent, "No way, I had a good year and I like you two gents." Maybe Fergus changed his mind, after Barclay told him this old clunker:

"Three guys met a hooker. She said she would do anything for $100.00 if they asked in 3 *words. The Welshman said – "Come to bed." She said, "You got it."*

The Englishman said, "kiss my butt" she said, "You got it."

The Scotsman got all excited and said, "Paint me hoos."

Despite the delay, Arbor Lodge was reached long before dark. No bridge game tonight. George picks up the brochure on Arbor Lodge which describes the place as follows:

> *Arbor Lodge is a large luxury home standing in over an acre of land, with a formal garden to the front and natural woodland to the rear. All bedrooms have walk-in dressing rooms and en-suite bathrooms containing both bath and separate shower*

enclosures. Tea making facilities and colour T. V. are in all rooms. A lounge and reading room are available for the exclusive use of residents. Car parking.

DAY 13 – SATURDAY. AUGUST 5, 1995 ABOYNE

(SUNNY AND WARM)

Another cloudless day in the UK. What's going on? This can't be Scotland.

Arbor Lodge continued to amaze. George saw something this morning that he has never seen before or heard of.

In the large shower enclosure, is a small panel, where by simply pushing buttons, one can control the type of spray, the amount of pressure, and also the temperature of the water. The temperature is displayed on a digital readout. George can handle 41, which is probably centigrade. The temperature goes up and down like the volume on a T.V. remote control.

One of the problems with foreign travel is finding a receptacle for an electric razor. This place has a panel in the bathroom that will accept any style plug. Also, lighting in the hallways is activated by a person's presence.

The Queen Mother was 95 years old yesterday and the telly covered all the activities. Everyone seems to love that grand old lady.

The rest of the Royal family is not so fortunate. One of the tabloids conducted a poll a couple of months ago. The result showed that people under 30 wanted to discontinue the Monarchy, people over 60 wanted it to continue. Those between 30 and 60 years were about 60-40 in favor of discontinuing. It was only a poll, nothing will change. This story is very old as it relates to the wedding night of Diane and Wales.

Wales knocked on Diane's door and announced, "I *offer you my Honor."*

She replied, "I *honor your offer."*

So it was on'er, off'er, on'er, off'er all night long.

It is a super day so let's try to get a starting time at the Aboyne Golf Club, established in 1813.

The pro turns out to be Innes Wright, father of tour player, Pamela Wright. Pamela was club champion at this club for several of her younger years. Pam's mother, Janet, also works at the club with her husband.

Innes arranges a starting time, in an hour, for nine holes. George asks for an electric cart, which got a few laughs Trolleys and hired clubs will be provided. Total cost for four, $98.00 US.

The course is short, 5910 yds. With a par of 68, and lots of roll. George bounced a few iron shots onto the green instead of stopping short and had a reasonable 42. Barclay did 47 and the ladies each broke 60.

On one green Barclay said to George, "I hit a couple of beauties on that hole." George "I was watching you and I didn't see anything special." Barclay – "You weren't looking when I stepped on a rake in the trap. "

It was a wonderful day, not a cloud in the sky and very little wind. The clubhouse and bar were quite comfortable. The drinks welcome.

Sheena, owner of the Arbor Lodge, has a thirteen handicap and teed off two groups ahead of the travelers. She has a 13-handicap swing. Sheena and husband, Bill, play golf in Florida at their home on Marco Island for three months in the wintertime.

The Highland Games are in Aboyne today. It's a fun show if one can stand continual bagpipes. An hour is enough for the Wescoombes. The games feature the Big Men, tossing the caber, a tree trunk, which weighs 132 lbs and is 20 feet long. They also whirl around and throw the hammer. George figures if he tried that stunt, the hammer would stay there and he would sail through the air.

Tug of war is another featured event. These giants tugged each other for 10 minutes and nothing happened.

And, these big dudes are all wearing skirts.

The young ladies have several dancing competitions, pipers play individual solos, it's like a three-ring circus.

About 100 booths line the perimeter of "the Green" selling various wares. The woolen clothing drew a blank on this hot day. One can't say the same about the beer and whisky concessions. It was apparent that the throng of a couple of thousand would have a riotous time tonight.

The Charleston Hotel nearby was the choice for supper. Barclay is a hit with his Scottish brogue and Scottish sayings. "Och aye" is alright, "foo the noo" means had enough or full up. The proprietress, Mamie Murray, a fun lady, tells Nan and June to ditch those two old guys and come back tonight and meet the Highlanders. Of course, Nan and June are wary and really don't care what the Highlanders wear under their kilts. Barclay told Mamie the one about the 70-year-old lady.

There was a lot of traffic through the old gal's hotel room – men going in and out all night.

In the morning the woman in the next room asked, "What was going on?"

The reply was, "When I was young, I sold it. When I was middle aged, I gave it away. Now, I'm buying it all back. "

It's bridge tonight at Arbor Lodge and as the ladies win by a 500 rubber, the scorecard is not lost.

It's necessary to close the windows as the pipe band a few blocks away is making so much noise.

Did you know in 1985, in the United States, 10,728 people were killed by handguns, in Great Britain, only eight.

DAY 14 – SUNDAY – AUGUST 6, 1995
ABOYNE – ST. ANDREWS – MOFFAT

(SUNNY AND WARM)

These fine people put on an excellent Scottish breakfast. The best so far. Sheena has a lady to help her.

George, nosey as usual, is with Sheena alone, and asks, "it's obvious you have a few bob, why do you open your fine home to strangers?"

"Yes, we have plenty of bob's. I started it as a hobby thinking it would be fun, but now we have so many customers, it's a pain and a nuisance. I don't know what to do."

"The easy way to reduce business is to double your rates."

"I'm thinking about it." She charges "$75.00 per room and it's a great bargain.

Bill, on his computer, has produced a printout showing roads, miles, and time from Aboyne to Heathrow Airport. He will take no money for this most useful information.

This is the day the trip passes St. Andrews.

As the Scots tell it, "The Gaemme of Gouf originated in Scotland, probably at Sintondress, in 1502. As the worst-ever war with the English had just ended and the fields were no longer needed for bow and arrow practice, King James the Fourth of Scotland bought himself a set of clubs and balls. He then married Mary Tudor, daughter of the English King and peace was assured." It was time to play around a little.

George has been playing at golf for nigh on seventy years. Seldom in that long period of time has there been a round from which he did not derive pleasure. George equates golf with life and marriage. If one takes the good with the bad, there is much pleasure to be found along the way.

As the trip nears St. Andrews,' George is wondering

whether the sight of that hallowed ground (to golfers, that is) will have the same affect on him as it did in 1984 when George and Nan played St. Andrews with Gary and his wife.

As Jim Murray, the L.A. Times sports writer says, "If you're a golfer when you walk on St. Andrews, you kind of get the bends. It's like a Catholic entering the Vatican for the first time or a Muslim reaching Mecca. "

Eleven years ago, it was not easy to get a reservation to play on "the old course" at St. Andrews. Gary, entrepreneur and industrialist that he is, was setting up a banking relationship with Barclay's bank in Edinburgh. One of the unspoken but implied conditions of the placement of the account was a tee time at St. Andrews. The banker was able to comply and has had a satisfactory banking relationship for many years.

At that time in 1984 the British Open was due to be played in about a month. The grandstands were already in place around the first tee and along the fairway. George was afraid he might do a Gerald Ford and hit someone in the gallery. Actually, he remembers fading the ball into the stands but that didn't bother the workmen.

At St. Andrews there are no electric carts and everyone has a caddie. The main reason for the caddie is to get the foursome around the course in four hours exactly. It is easy to imagine a group of Americans without a caddie playing St. Andrews and being lost for days.

The course is wide open and nary a tree lines the fairway to aid direction. Many holes have double greens, which would only add to the confusion without a guide. The fairways are so close together that a sign is posted, "Homeward players have the right of way."

George asked his caddie on one tee, "which direction?" The answer was "Laddie just hit it to the right of the church tower in the town below and ye'll be fine."

The caddies were mostly old men who had held the job for a lifetime. They were graded as to ability, somehow, and each foursome had one *of* each grade.

Nan had a great old gentlemen, maybe 80, named John, who thought she was a beautiful young chick. On the first tee she said, "I cheat." His reply was "Don't worry, Ma'am, I'll help ya." She was never in the gorse nor had a bad lie for the entire round. She had a wonderful time.

Gary had the grade "A" caddie, a young lad of about 60 who steered him around to a fine 85. The man had a great knowledge of the "potato chip" greens and had Gary putting with much success.

George was recovering from arteriosclerosis surgery at that time and was still weak. He hit a shot into one of the many five-foot deep pot bunkers. Getting into the bunker was not much of a problem and advancing the ball about 20 feet was accomplished. Getting out of the bunker was another matter. Gary and the "A" caddie had to lift George out. The other caddies couldn't help. They were all so old that they wouldn't have been able to get out themselves.

On another hole, maybe the sixteenth, George found himself, in two, comfortably thirty feet from the cup. About to putt, he was respectfully reminded that he should putt to the other cup. George was just able to see the other flag on the green, which appeared to be at least a quarter of a mile away. In between was a green that looked like a roller coaster. George, carefully worked his way up and down, across the fast surface and finally managed a treacherous three-footer for a satisfactory four putt.

What great memories. There is the Royal and Ancient headquarters just as it was 11 years ago. Many other buildings have changed. The large hotel has had a face-lift and a couple of new smaller hotels have been built. The old pro-shop still sells souvenirs, but the activities and caddies have been moved.

Nothing has changed on the "Old Course." It is closed for today and many tourists are walking the fairways. It is still very difficult to get a tee time on the "Old Course," but there are three other courses nearby. Old Tom Morris' large souvenir shop is doing a land-office business. St.

Andrews, the town itself, seems to be the same, very busy at this time of year.

Lunch and drinks at the Niblick Bar were a treat.

There is no reservation for tonight so it was decided to drive south for a couple of hours. Daylight is from 5 am to 9:30 pm, about 3 hours longer than in California.

Across the famous bridge over the Firth of Forth, then south, between the great Scottish cities of Edinburgh and Glasgow. The computer routing is along the motorways, which are crowded with Sunday afternoon traffic.

George makes a calculated guess and a secondary road takes the travelers to Lanark. That splendid town is full so the lady at the information center obtains a room at Moffat, 30 miles further along.

Eileen, the proprietress of Thai-ville is a charming lady in her mid-seventies (guess). The name arises as Eileen and her 81-year-old husband, John, have wintered in Thailand for the last 17 years. The sprawling, one floor, corner home is elegantly furnished and the en-suite rooms are commodious. All B and Bs which are en suite are very satisfactory, but scarce. There are many available without private bathrooms. Eileen serves a plate of pastries for a bedtime snack.

Bridge and Euchre in the lounge bring this fine day to a close.

DAY 15 – MONDAY. AUGUST 7, 1995
MOFFAT. SCOTLAND
LEYBURN. ENGLAND

(OVERCAST AND WARM)

This is the first morning with clouds in the sky, but no threat of rain.

Eileen and Bill prepare a Scottish breakfast, a feature being kippers. George makes Eileen's day by asking her if she was ever in the movies.

Their home is elegant with many Eastern objects d'art. The breakfast is served on Paragon China, 1758, Belinda pattern. Now, that must be class. .

Eileen suggests that the travelers stop at Station Park on the way out of town. The park is ablaze with colour having been a finalist in "Britain in Bloom" and "Scotland in Bloom" for many years. The park was planted in 1888 and covers 4.726 acres.

Back on the M74 south. Soon the town of Lockerbie is reached. The area where the Pan-Am jet crashed on December 21, 1988 has been made into a pretty park with a memorial to the victims. It's quite obvious where the six homes were wiped out, only 200 yards from the M74.

Further south off the M74 and close to the border of England is the tourist town of Gretna Green. This is the place where young English couples could slip across the border and be married at 16, by the blacksmith. Since kids sleep together at any age these days, it is not necessary to be married at Gretna Green. Tourists, such as the travelers, make it a busy spot.

One of the souvenir shops sold Haggis so George made a note of the contents. Minced lamb, beef, oatmeal, onions, spices filled into a natural bag then fully cooked. Serve with potatoes and turnips. Tatties and neeps in Scotland.

Off the M74 on the 684 for 35 miles of winding roads to Leyburn. It's a slow, pleasant drive through pretty farmland. Along side the road, a tall purple flower grows in abundance. It is a weed, knows as "Fireweed" and requires no care.

The town of Garsdale Head features a hotel with an interesting name "The Moorcock Inn." It was time for beer and wine with cheese and onion sandwiches. English words mean many different things. A Moorcock is a bird.

Further along the country road is Hawes, the market town for the area. Hawes is quite busy and one of its attractions is the Wensleydale cheese factory.

This interesting place converts milk into cheese while you watch. A half-hour in the viewing gallery displays the whole process. Cheese made "by hand" is an entirely different procedure from that used by "Kraft" cheese. Kraft would turn out this small plants monthly production in an hour.

Cheese was first made in this location by the Cisterican Monks in the fifteen century.

The travelers purchased a pound of mature Wensleydale for later use. George scarfed up samples of many types, including blue. An interesting visit. .

In a short while Eastfield Lodge at Leyburn is reached. It has been modernized since Lisa and Pat were there in 1990, by new owners. Every room is now en suite. The dining room has been closed, being unprofitable, but the bar and lounge continues.

The travelers, in the center of the busy town, at the supermarket, pick up cold cuts, fruit, a French stick, scones, and, of course, beer and wine. All of which complements the fine Wensleydale cheese.

The travelling bridge tournament continues but not for long as the ladies are getting all the good cards. The men, being poor sports, switch the game to Euchre.

The only thing wrong with being a good sport is that one has to lose.

After the others retire, George needs a cold beer. The bar is only a floor below and Barry, the owner and bartender is alone. Barry is one of those Englishman who sound like they have a mouthful of marbles. After a few moments, George was able to understand and Barry was talkative and interesting.

Janet and Barry bought Eastfield Lodge in order to roll over their capital gains from a busy pub, which they had owned for many years. This is common, due to the tax laws.

They paid 185,000 pounds for this place and spent 50,000 pounds to modernize. The English seem to have tons of money. Those sums are way over George's head but he pretends they are not.

The breweries are selling the Englishman's favorite pub drink "Bitter" in cans, for home consumption. This is a result of the strict drunk driving laws. The pubs are suffering. In the cans of "bitter" is a gadget known as a widget, which gives the beer a head when it is poured. Each brewery has a different widget but they produce the same result. John Smith Brewery call their invention, the "cask pour system" and Bodingtons call theirs the "draught flow system." Sales have been brisk as much more beer is consumed at home.

The chat with Barry reminded George of a full-page story in the Times about drinking in Ireland.

Why not paraphrase the newspaper article. It is both sad and comical.

Ignatius Murray, owns and operates Iggy's Pub in Kincasslagh, somewhere in Ireland. Business has gone sour at Iggy's since the government lowered the blood-alcohol limit to .08% and stiffened the penalties.

This standard is seen as absurdly low by most Irish drinkers to whom a gallon of beer is a typical night out. Joe McFadden says "The law may make sense in America, but the Pub's the national pastime here."

Pat Berry of Ireland's largest brewer Guinness says "Business was off at first when the law went in last December, but drinking patterns are moving back toward the usual."

In Ireland, driving tipsy is a tradition. Ireland's road fatality count is 12 for every 100,000 people compared to England's 7 for every 100,000 people.

Publicans and customers blame the pot-holed, narrow roads for the driving deaths, not the potted drivers.

In January 1995, Murray, McFadden and 3000 other pub landlords and beer distributors marched on the Dail, the Irish Parliament. Politicians invited the proprietors in for drinks at taxpayer's expense. They drank the Dail bar dry and nearly wrecked the place.

Environment Minister Brendan Howlin pledged to keep the new standard but would consider reducing the punishments.

Pat (Manos) O'Donnel attributes his ninety plus years to regular consumption of beer. When asked about the new drunken-driving law, Pat said, "I ne'er learnt to drive, but you'd have to have plenty of drink in you to see straight down these Donegal roads."

DAY 16 – TUESDAY. AUGUST 8, 1995 LEYBURN. YORK. NEWARK-ON-TRENT

(OVERCAST, THEN SUNNY AND WARM)

The proper English breakfast is supposed to last to tea time and probably would if the many street-side bake shops didn't display the following mouth-watering delicacies: eccles cakes, butter tarts, lemon tarts, caramel krispie, iced tea cake, Cornish pasty, cheese pasty, ginger squares, truffle logs, cheese straws, fruit rolls and, George's favorite, scones with currants. These goodies sell for about 50 cents each. Good thing they are not available in the U.S.A. The bakeshops are crowded.

Back on Country Road 684 for twenty miles, then to York. There is a contrast in fencing between North and South England. Barclay, who is from the stone age, wrote the following.

In Southern England, the fields are divided by hedges as are the road sides. In Northern England and Scotland, the hedges are non-existent. In stark contrast, dry walls of stone are the separators. Rocks and stones are abundant and, of necessity, must be cleared from the fields.

These rocks are piled in rows one to one and one half foot thick to heights of four to six feet. As no mortar is *used to bind the stones, care must be taken to fit the various pieces in order to bind them into an integral unit. These rows of stone have been standing for hundreds of years.*

The ancient city of York has also been an attraction for many, many years. The Romans, in the first or second century, built a wall around the city for defensive purposes. Much of the wall is still standing and can be walked upon. Of course, the present city encompasses the wall and has many mall type streets with very attractive shops, for blocks and blocks. The city has developed a park and ride system otherwise it would be impossible to move in the down town area.

The world famous York Minster dominates the city. This overwhelming architectural giant rates with the Taj Mahal as either number one or two.

George has been to Westminster, St. Pauls, Winchester, the Sistine Chapel, Salisbury and others, but in his opinion, York Minster gets the nod.

On this site, religion has been practiced since 314 AD, when Christianity invaded England with the Romans. There was a gap of about 200 years when the pagan invaders controlled the north of England.

In 625, things improved, and a wooden church, followed by a stone church were erected on the site. Around 1100, with the advent of the Normans, a vast new minster was constructed. Additions and improvements continued for hundreds of years until the present edifice as consecrated in 1472.

It is hard to describe the huge stained glass windows, the 200-foot high central tower, the intricate carving on the pillars, the decorating on the ceilings and so much more. The building is 518 feet long and 250 feet across.

No one knows for certain how the engineering was accomplished to raise pillars, blocks, etc. to such a height. Probably thousands of men worked for years on the construction, being paid only their food and a place to sleep. How they did it doesn't matter. It is there for all to see.

In addition to the Minster, another magnificent structure is along side. This is the Chapter House where the business of the Minster is conducted. Around 1300, the forty or so officials of the Minster decided they needed a conference room to conduct their meetings.

As there was an abundance of cheap labor and as the Minster was progressing famously, they caused to be constructed, attached to the Minster, the Chapter House, 63 feet across and 66 feet high. It is certainly as magnificent as the Minster in every way. These days, it has a practical use, as concerts are held there occasionally.

All of the beautiful workmanship is worth at least two or three hours of viewing time as it is unforgettable.

McMillan's Café and Bar is only a few blocks away and is excellent for lunch and libation. All that culture makes this group thirsty.

Back to the motorway south to the city of Newark-on-Trent, which is the stopping place tonight at the South Parade Hotel. George has trouble getting South Rampart Street Parade out of his head, but there is no connection.

The hotel has 14 bedrooms, plus a dining room, lounge and bar. The appearance is Georgian and is a Grande II listing.

Owners and operators are Phyllis and Robert with their three daughters.

Five minutes to the city center, which is the usual in England walk-around type. Unfortunately, this is not a market day but there is plenty to see and do.

The Queens Head Inn has an outside patio facing market square. It is delightful sitting under an umbrella watching the townsfolk bustling about doing their shopping and other errands. Wine is \$2.50 per glass and beer from the barrel \$2.80 for 20 imperial ounces. That is quite comparable with a similar location in California. Thankfully, something is comparable, as most items are 50% higher after eliminating the exchange. The only way this group can afford to travel in England is to use the Bed and Breakfast system and mostly eat pub food. As this record indicates, there is nothing wrong with doing just that. There is a listing at the end showing the cost of lodgings in US dollars at an exchange rate of $1.70 to the pound. Yet the English appear so well off. Their cars, houses, and clothes are either modem or in good condition. Maybe it's the Welfare State. Incidentally, they use miles for distance instead of kilometers, which is a help when traveling.

A card table is set up in the lounge at the South Parade Hotel. The ladies win at first, but the men, after another beer or two, charge from behind for a narrow victory. It would have been nice to have had more time in York.

DAY 17 – WEDNESDAY. AUGUST 9, 1995 NEWARK – SUDBURY

(SUNNY, WARM)

Breakfast in the dining room was more than adequate – one of the daughters was a pleasant server.

Barclay was reminded of another old gem as he saw George eating cereal:

A doctor told a guy he had sugar in his urine, so he peed on his corn flakes.

The A-I south appeared out of nowhere as the motorways seem to do when one has plenty of time.

A stop for petrol at Texaco was necessary. All the biggies are in the UK – ESSO, Mobil, BP, of course, and they all take American Express. After allowing for the larger gallon, gas (petrol) is $3.66 for an American gallon. The Brits have their own oil from the North Sea. The price is mostly tax. What else is new.

The town of Sudbury is reached by noon and "The Old Bull" is discovered easily. They have the reservation, but the rooms are not ready until 2 PM.

The Old Bull was originally a 16th Century coaching inn and retains much of its "Olde Worlde" charm. There are 9 bedrooms, each unique, with open beam ceilings. The logs bend and twist as they have not been replaced since at least 1649.

The restaurant called "Trivets" surprisingly has a large collection of trivets. The owner, Ian Taylor, is also the chef. The "Old Bull" has its own car park, very important in England.

Almost across the street, on the bank of the Stour River, is the "Boathouse" a restaurant with umbrella tables on the lawn. In the bright sunshine, it is a pleasant place for a libation. George wonders if rain would put a damper on things. Don't worry, it's not going to rain during this trip. The ladies decide to try a Pimm's #1, which is gin with lemon and lots of fruit.

The girls had spotted a Fish and Chips shop on the street only a block or so away. It must be a good one as many cars are parked on the street in front. This ties up the traffic on a narrow street, but the English do not seem to mind.

The busy shop features haddock as a special, 10-minute wait. Where will the group sit. The nice lady says there is a park with benches a couple of hundred yards further along. The roads wind about so much it is impossible to know what is 200 yards ahead without going there. Sure enough, the park is overlooking the Stour and a farm across the river with a herd of cows close by. It is a pretty place, again with bright sunshine.

Next to the park is a classy hotel and restaurant called the "Old Mill." The lounge facing the river is ideal for a drink, but after looking at the prices on the menu, George was most happy with the fish and chips on the park bench. When one looks at prices, at first glance, they appear about the same as California. In reality, they are 70% higher, which is getting close to double. Never the less, the dining room is crowded.

City Center in Sudbury is the usual walking mall with little motor traffic. The travelers had no further use for the AZ road atlas, which to now, has been invaluable. It was decided to mail it to Ann, who was so kind to the travelers in Tunbridge Wells.

Back to the "Old Bull," George calls Kenny whom he has talked to on the telephone but hasn't seen since 1984 in Auctermuctee in Scotland. They agree to meet at 7:30 PM at the "Henny Swan" for dinner. George then called Lorraine whom he had met last Christmas at the "Henny Swan" during his visit with Gary. Lorraine and her husband Steve had booked the "Old Bull" for the travelers and also made reservations for a party of eight at the "Henny Swan."

Kenny, an entrepreneur, and Lorraine, who is a graphic artist, both do business with Gary's company in California.

Lorraine and Steve pick up the travelers at the "Old Bull" for the short but complicated trip to the "Henny Swan." Lorraine doesn't want the group to get lost, so she and Steve each bring a car. Thanks, Lorraine.

Kenny and his pretty, brown-eyed Scottish lady, Donna, arrive very soon. George is happy to get hugs from both young ladies, Lorraine and Donna.

The restaurant is full which is a tribute to its excellent food and drinks. George, at Christmas, enjoyed the pork chops, with a cheddar cheese and wine sauce. Barclay joined George for a repeat performance.

Barclay saw an opportunity to spin one of his yams:

Couple at breakfast:

Wife – What are you doing today?

Husband – Going fishng.

Wife – I'd hoped you would repair the tap in the bathroom.

Husband – Look at my forehead, do you see the word plumber?

Wife – Would you change the light bulb in the kitchen?

Husband – Look at my forehead, do you see the word electrician?

After fishing, husband said he had had a great day. How was yours?

Wife – I had a handyman in and he fixed the tap and the light bulb and all he wanted was sex or cookies.
Husband – I hope you gave him cookies.
Wife – Look at my forehead, do you see the word Betty Crocker?

The Wescoombes and Kenny recalled the visits to Scotland in 1984 and 1985. Lorraine and Donna are both pretty and smile all the time. They are business ladies. Nan and June enjoyed chatting with them. Kenny and Steve are entertaining but only have one drink. The strict driving laws cause people to save money.

The travelers have no such restrictions and make up for the others. It was a cracking good evening with old and new friends in Sudbury.

DAY 18 – THURSDAY – AUGUST 10, 1995 SUDBURY – LONDON

(SUNNY, HOT)

The folks at "The Old Bull" did the usual good job on the proper English breakfast. Only a few more to go and then George can return to a small bowl of Raisin Bran.

Another cloudless day as Barclay drives flawlessly to Euro Dollar storage area at Heathrow Terminal 4. It was necessary to circle the airport twice before finding where Euro Dollar was hiding. That is what is known as a petite cock-up.

Barclay has driven 2278 miles on the wrong side of the road and is now a master at round-abouts. He has also perfected a reverse ewe turn. Thank you, Barclay, for an outstanding performance. He is very impressed with the English Rover, which also performed perfectly. George likes the large boot, which holds the bags for four people with ease.

An Indian taxi driver, Raj, charged $60.00 to move the group from Heathrow to the Majestic Hotel on Cromwell Road, in London, a half an hour trip. The airline bus charges $10.00 per person, so the extra $20 was for the convenience. Not bad at all, especially as he was an interesting Hindu.

When crossing the street in London, it is necessary to look in the proper direction. In America, people drive on the right side of the street, whereas in London, they drive on both sides of the street. Some tourists handle the problem by remaining on one side of the street for the entire visit and see the other side on another trip.

Nan can hardly wait to walk the half mile along Cromwell Road to her favorite pub" A Bunch of Grapes" which is close to Harrod's. George and Barclay escort the ladies to the proper side before releasing them. June has never been to England before so Nan takes her to Harrod's for "just a look."

The Bunch of Grapes has great pub food. Cottage pie was the choice, with beer and wine. Shepherd's pie is now known as cottage pie for some reason.

Down the underground station at South Kensington,. Then the District Line to Victoria Station.

The travelers have vouchers for 3-day passes on London Transportation, and the vouchers are exchanged at Victoria Station for passes. These passes cost 10.00 for 3 days but must be bought outside England. A single tube, or bus, ride costs a minimum of 2.00.

It's a perfect day to sit on the top of a double decker bus, catching the breeze and going where ever the bus travels and back again to Victoria Station.

After two hours of traveling, it's time for a libation at the Shakespeare Pub, close to Victoria Station. The ladies have switched to Pimm's No.1.

Another tube ride to Cromwell Road, where the Forum Hotel is perfect for a light supper and drinks outside on the patio.

It's been a long, fun day and the group is slowing

down by 8 PM. It's a short walk along Cromwell to the Majestic Hotel.

The Majestic is a typical medium-priced hotel of which there are many along the main streets of London. Toward the end of the 19th Century, when England was at its most affluent, the gentry lived in 5-story flats joined together with space at the rear called the mews, where the horses were kept. Those folks also had houses in the country for summertime use.

In the last 30 – 40 years, entrepreneurs have purchased partial blocks of these former palatial dwellings, gutted them and converted the inside to hotel rooms.

The Majestic has 83 rooms and cost 95.00 US dollars. The rooms are small but adequate, certainly not in a class with the Bed and Breakfasts mentioned previously. George's main complaint is that the bloke who installed the bath made the level of the bottom of the tub about 4 inches higher than the surrounding floor. One slip and there go the family jewels. Not that they are important when one is approaching eighty, but who needs to be disfigured. George does a belly-roll over the site of the tub and once more escapes disaster.

An old man, in a retirement home, walked into a ladies room.

"I'll bet you can't guess how old I am."
"Take off your pants." He did as she asked.
"Take off your shorts." He did as she asked.
She looked him over carefully and finally announced.
"You are 92."
"That's amazing, how did you figure that out."
"You told me yesterday."

And so to bed.

DAY 19 – FRIDAY – AUGUST 11, 1995 LONDON

(SUNNY, HOT)

The Londoners are hoping for a thunderstorm or anything to break, what they call, the heat. The Californians and Ontarians are quite used to it.

The Majestic serves a continental breakfast, which is quite sufficient. George has had his fill of bacon for a while.

The tube takes the group to Picadilly Circus in a few minutes. Trafalgar Square is nearby, featuring Nelson's column.

Some important streets fan out from this location, such as the Strand and the Mall. Glimpses of St. Pauls, the Parliament Buildings and Big Ben can be seen.

This is where one has the feeling of what a powerful, dynamic city London really is. One can almost feel the throbbing. George found a short article on the history of this great city and it is worth recording for posterity.

London – Capital City

> London had been a major Celtic settlement for centuries before the Emperor Claudius founded the military camp of Londinium. The Romans fortified an area of about one square mile, which coincides roughly with the boundaries of the square mile of the City of London today. After briefly being captured by Boudicca (aka Boadicea) during the rebellion of 61 AD, London became an important port and the capital of one of the four Roman provinces of Britain.
>
> The Roman withdrawal left London to be settled by waves of Angles, Saxons and Jute and laid waste by hordes of Danes and Norsemen, but Alfred the Great, who took London in 886, began a period of growth, consolidated by Cannute and Edward the

Confessor, who both made Westminster their residence. William the Conqueror was crowned in Westminster Abbey, and built the White Tower at the Tower of London, though London did not replace Winchester as the English capital until the reign of Henry I in the twelfth century.

From then on, London developed as the principal trading city in England, with a population that rose to half a million by the sixteenth century. The Plague slashed the population by 70,000 in 1665, and the Great Fire of London destroyed three-quarters of the city the following year. Yet that catastrophe merely spurred London to a great rebuilding programme in which Christopher Wren was the dominant architect. London grew to be the heart of the Victorian Empire and has remained by far our largest and most important city to this day, surviving the destruction brought about by the Battle of Britain and at least some of that wrought by property developers.

The underside of London must be a veritable warren. The tubes seem to run everywhere at various levels.

The Circle line takes the travelers to the Monument Station in a few minutes.

The Monument is a 300-foot high tower designed by Christopher Wren and built to commemorate the fire of 1666. Much of the city was destroyed by the fire.

London Bridge is nearby and affords an excellent view each way as it crosses the Thames. This bridge was built in 1973, when the original was moved brick by brick to Havasu City, in Arizona.

The south side of the city across the bridge is appropriately named Southwark, pronounced Southark. This area has many buildings at least 700 years old, including Southwark Cathedral, which is still an operating church.

Shakespeare, Dickens and many other notables attended Southwark Cathedral including a man named

Harvard, who founded Harvard University in the USA.

The north side of the city, at that time, was very conservative. Southwark was where the action was, hence many notables hung out in that area.

The travelers are interested in lunch at the George Inn. The brochure says it all:

> The George Inn is one of London's most magnificent pubs and yet it hides shyly down an alleyway off the A3, once a vital coaching route to the ports of the south coast. That same route also brought hops from Kent to the capital with the result that the borough of Southwark became a vital and vibrant brewing area of London, based around the Hop Exchange, a vast and ornate building now being restored to its former grandeur. Courage, Barclay Perkins and Thrale all had breweries in Southwark and Dr. Samuel Johnson, a regular visitor to the George before dining with the Thrales, was profitably involved in the sale of his friends' Anchor Brewery to Barclay Perkins.
>
> Southwark was an area of entertainment as well as boozing. Shakespeare's Globe Theater was close by and it is reputed that his strolling players performed in the courtyard and from the galleries of the George. The original inn was destroyed by the Great Fire of 1666, which also ravaged most of Southwark (the spot where the fire broke out in Pudding Lane is marked by the Monument on the other side of London Bridge). The inn was rebuilt in 1677 and is the last surviving Elizabethan galleried inn in London. It once occupied three sides of the courtyard but when its owners, the trustees of Guy's Hospital, sold it to the London and North Eastern Railway Company in the nineteenth century, the railway barons thoughtlessly reduced the inn in order to use some of the buildings as engine sheds. They

> have long gone but the inn, its presence marked by a sign in Borough High Street, remains in galleried and beamed glory.
>
> A visit to the George is a memorable occasion, recalling the heady times of the first Elizabeth. The pub is owned by the National Trust, but it is a living pub, not a quaint museum piece.

This unique place is as good as its publicity. By noon, the place is crowded inside and outside by office workers enjoying their lunch break.

The travelers along with beer and wine, partake of the English pub lunch, sausage and mash. The Old Thames Inn, where a bloke drank George's beer on a previous visit, is only a few blocks away.

A double decker bus stop is nearby. No one in the group knows where a Number 15 bus goes to, but it doesn't matter. The bus winds through the city, stopping at almost every stop, allowing plenty of time for sightseeing. After about an hour, it stops at a place called Aldgate. There was probably an old gate at this spot centuries ago. The English are not particular about spelling

There was a bookstore nearby, so George tried to buy the Charles Dickens book, "The Little Dorrit," in which he talks about the George Inn and Southwark. No luck.

A tube station is close by and as luck would have it, one of the lines passes by the Gloucester Road Station, which is near the Majestic Hotel.

Believe it or not, about 300 yards from the Majestic, the Holiday Inn Company has gutted at least six of the old mansions and inside, is the Holiday Inn Kensington, with 160 rooms. It is a beautiful hotel, but no one would know from the outside.

One drink is enough as the wine is $9.00 per glass and the beer over $6.00. There are not many people around. The rooms are $290 per night and breakfast $25 additional.

The Forum across the street is crowded, but the group

is able to get their favorite table on the patio. This is the best spot for a light supper and drinks for a high, but reasonable price, served by Cora, a young Canadian gal from Huntsville, Ontario.

Many friendly Americans are at tables nearby.

The Majestic is about 200 yards from the Forum. Both last night and tonight, Sainsbury's, a store with a large parking lot, is on the way.

Sainsbury's turns out to be one of the finest supermarkets the travellers have ever seen, and it is busy. Food from everywhere in the world at prices only about 10% above California prices, which is a bargain in England.

George and Barclay pick up a few snack items, including fancy crackers and caerphilly cheese. George is a raw peanut freak and, sure enough, there they are, from China, no less. They are not in supermarkets in California.

It's been a long, fun day and it's up early tomorrow for Paris.

Did you know that there are 5 million people in prison in the United States and more prisons are needed.

DAY 20 – SATURDAY – AUGUST 12, 1995
LONDON – PARIS

(SUNNY, HOT)

Euro Star, the tunnel train, departs Waterloo Station at 6:50 AM for Paris, if it's running. The French engineers are on strike.

The travelers are up at 5:00 AM (it's broad daylight) to catch the District Line to the Embarkment station and then the Northern Line to Waterloo Station.

An announcement is made that the train direct to Paris at 6:50 AM will not run, but the ticket holders will go on the 7:25 AM train to Brussels.

This promises to be Le Grande cock-up, but everybody

has to be somewhere and Brussels is a fine city.

Euro Star is a beautiful train, which speeds across the English countryside, Kent, in particular, and then dips into the tunnel for about 20 minutes before bobbing up again in France. It is smooth, quiet, and comfortable. More so than a jet aircraft. Stewards bring drinks, etc. on carts along the aisle, the same as on an aircraft.

It's usually a three-hour trip with speeds up to 180 miles per hour in France. After about two hours, the train glides to a stop at Lille in Normandy.

The Euro Star people announce that the Paris passengers will get off the Euro Star and transfer to a high speed train from Lille to Paris. That doesn't sound too bad, except that it is about a mile walk, up and down stairs, and takes almost an hour. George is not good at walking a mile, but finally makes it, hoping for a cool beer on the new train. Alas, the bar car and the dining car are closed, so it is a dry trip. Barclay and George decide to sue, but the ladies talk them out of it.

The conversation got around to whether France is a welfare state, such as England.

George made a comment, "Maybe they have the Dole, as in England."

June doesn't hear her brother too well and inquired, "What does DeGaule have to do with it?"

Hearing aids hear funny things sometimes.

Gard De Nord in Paris is reached an hour late, but who is in a hurry. A friendly black taxi driver knows where the Hotel France Eiffel is located at 8 Rue Saint-Charles. His English is on a par with George's French. The hotel is small, only 36 rooms, but is neat, clean, and comfortable with a nice patio.

One room is not ready until 2:00 PM, but there is a café only a block away on Blvd. De Grannelle. There is always a café in Paris.

This is a Lebanese café run by Stephan. The ladies have to buy a bottle of Lebanese wine each, which holds three glasses. The beer is German.

George and Stephan chat about Beirut, as it was, about twenty years ago. Stephan escaped but remembers the beautiful city, destroyed.

It is too early to eat, but a plate of chewy, flat Lebanese bread soaks up the beer and wine.

Nan remembers Paris as the place where one sits in sidewalk cafes in the sunshine. A French man once kissed Nan on both cheeks. The only problem was that she was bending down tying her shoe at the time.

After getting the room keys, a taxi takes the travelers to the Arc De Triumph, a monument at one end of the Champs D'Elysees.

Thirty years have passed since George first visited the Arc. At that time it was life threatening to cross the street as traffic came from every direction at 90 miles an hour. George thought the monument was in honor of the brave folks who died crossing the street. Now the only way to get to see the Eternal Flame is through a tunnel and pay $5.00. Paying $5.00 is a lot better than nearly getting killed.

There is a lot of history in this part of the world. Today, it is wall to wall people. George estimates that maybe one in ten is French. Ninety percent are tourists from all over the world, some wearing their native garb.

Strolling along the shady side of this very, very wide street is most interesting. The shops are of every kind, and the sidewalks and street are crowded with other strollers. No one is in a hurry.

This group is getting hungry. Nobody in Paris eats until 9 PM except old North Americans.

Henri, at the Chez Clement, is, of course, not very busy at 5 PM. He sets up a fine table right at the edge of the sidewalk. A few drinks start the meal off on the right or left foot. This is on the right bank.

The group decides on the mixed grille, consisting of roast beef, pork ribs, and half a chicken with mashed potatoes. One may have as much mashed potatoes as he wishes. There is far more delicious food than anyone can eat. The large salad has an excellent cheese dressing.

Yes, Barclay started off with 9 oysters on the half shell. No one joined him.

Henri vigorously promoted desserts which were tempting, but where would one put more food. All of the above for $150, not bad for Paris. Of course, the choice was near the lowest price on the menu, being by French standards, rather ordinary.

There are taxi racks along the Avenue Des Champs D'Elysees, so after a short stroll, a taxi takes the group back to Hotel France Eiffel for $15.00 rather than the $2 .00 charged to get to the Arc D'Triumph. Taxi drivers seem to know if a person is a stranger. Wonder why. Everyone seems to have a little larceny in them. Like the bank manager who was caught stealing pens.

In London, it was mentioned that the Brits do not believe in straight lines. There is not a straight road in that city...Paris is exactly the opposite. All the streets in Paris radiate from various centers as they do in London. However, in Paris, the streets are straight and join together at sharp angles. A psychologist would probably say it's a reflection of the character of the English and French. Quite a contrast.

It is a beautiful night on the patio. The ladies have had sufficient French wine and it improved their bridge. They played the first 8 hands and made a 700 rubber. The men suddenly get tired.

DAY 21 – SUNDAY – AUGUST 13, 1995 PARIS – LONDON

(OVERCAST – WARM)

It is a continental breakfast at the Hotel France Eiffel – cereal, rolls, toast, jams, cheese, eggs (boiled), croissants, and scotch in the plentiful coffee. Elegant sufficiency.

The Eiffel Tower is only a few blocks away. A stroll along the Seine leads to the large square on which the tower has stood since around 1890. Paris was the locale of the World's Fair.

Walking across the river on a nearby bridge afforded excellent views of the Paris skyline in each direction.

As it is not sunny, it is much cooler and crowds are gathering for a Sunday along the river. This is the special Sunday in August when large areas are marked off for pedestrian and bicycle traffic only.

Not wishing to be hemmed in by a horde of Frenchmen, the group checks out of the Hotel France Eiffel and by taxi, ride to the Sacre Coeur (Sacred Heart). There is another horde of people of all nationalities at the Sacred Heart.

For extra francs, the driver stalls for a few minutes so pictures can be taken (probably of a lot of strangers and little of the famous church). Incidentally, a Franc is 23 cents: at this time.

Sacre Coeur sits atop a hill and on a clear day offers a view of the entire city. Yesterday would have been perfect. George remembers 30 years ago buying a set of pornographic slides from a vendor on the steps of Sacred Heart. That was years ago, when George had a dirty mind, or dirtier mind.

As the church area is too crowded to get a comfortable look, the taxi driver, whose meter is running, moves the group to Le Gare Nord where they will wait for the Eurostar departure at 5:10 p.m.

The area around the North Railway station has blocks of outdoor cafes, souvenir shops, etc. etc., so the group picked a likely spot for a libation and some people watching.

The waiter recognized tourists immediately and charged $20.00 for two glasses of French wine. Barclay wanted to challenge him, but George said, "Let's not get incarcerated in the Bastille."

The Eurostar section of Le Gare Nord is quite new and has a fine restaurant named L' Alize with table cloths, etc. The Wescoombes have grilled salmon at $19.00 per plate and the Allans have poached halibut at $17.00 per plate. Some may say, "what is high about $19.00 for lunch." Remember to add to that an appetizer (starter), soup or salad, vegetables, a finale (dessert) and with a couple of glasses of wine it is easy to reach $50.00. The food was first rate as were the bread sticks and fruits. Incidentally, the same wine was $10.00 for two glasses. Classy places do not cheat for $10.00.

The London Sunday Times and the International Herald provide plenty of reading material. There was some kind of a cock-up at Dodger Stadium and the Dodgers were forced to forfeit the game. Must have been the umpire's fault. It is only the middle of August but it looks like all divisions are settled except for the Dodgers and Rockies. Somebody must have had foresight to put in the wild card play-off spot.

The 5:10 Eurostar leaves Le Gare Nord at 5:11 so one might say the train left on time. There is no stop at Lille on this return trip as the strike has been settled. George is pleased about that, as the one-mile walk is too much.

The last time George made this trip, he sat with a charming English lady, Eileen North. Mrs. North is also an amateur writer as George is, and they agreed to swap stories. Eileen did much more research on the technical aspects of Eurostar. With Mrs. North's permission, the following is taken from her writing.

Technological Information

The "Tunnel" is a realization of more than two centuries of dreams and incomplete plans. In 1750, a geologist named Nicholas Desmarets discovered that thousands of years ago, man could walk across what is today the Straits of Dover. He suggested a bridge or tunnel could reconnect us to France, and his early projects have culminated in today's Tunnel. In 1802 it was suggested to Bonaparte that a tunnel be dug under the Channel, but fighting between France and England broke out again, so it was abandoned.

In 1834, Aime Thome de Gamond was the first to put forward a plan for a tunnel with concrete vaulting, and earned Gamond his title of "Father of the Tunnel." In 1880 work was actually commenced on tunneling, then abandoned. More trials were held at Folkstone in 1922, then with much improved technology from 1960 onwards, some serious thought was given to the idea, but it was stopped for financial reasons.

At a Franco-British summit between Mrs. Thatcher and President Mitterand in 1981, four plans were chosen for further consideration in 1985. They were a bridge, a tunnel for road and railway, two twin road and railway tunnels and the underground railway for Le Shuttle and The Train. The last idea was adopted, and its development was agreed by the signing of a FrancoBritish agreement in Canterbury Cathedral on 12th February 1986. On the 14th March 1986 a 55-year concession was signed by the two Governments and France Manche and the Channel Tunnel Group.

On the 6th November, 1986, work started at Sangatte near Calais. Construction work on the Tunnel began on 15th December 1987. On the 1st December 1990, the French and British broke through to join up in the service tunnel. The 22nd May 1991 saw a join up in the northern railway tunnel. Tunneling was completed on 28th June 1991 when the machines met in the southern tunnel. Between 1992 and 1993 the fixed equipment was installed, i.e. tracks, catenary, signals, electricity, ventilation, etc. On the 6th May 1994, the Queen and President Mitterand inaugurated the Tunnel, but it wasn't till the 24th November 1994 that the first Eurostar ran its first service from London to Paris, and shortly afterwards 'Le Shuttle' from Dover to Calis for cars etc. began. Several trial run-throughs had been done before, and in March 1994 people walked the 26 miles through the Tunnel to raise money for charities.

The Tunnel comprises three tunnels, one for the journey each way and a service tunnel. After extensive geological research, it was decided to dig the tunnels in a 20-30m thick layer of impenetrable chalk, 40m below the sea bed. The huge boring machines, more than 8m in diameter and 260m long drilled the tunnel at the rate of 800-1,000 meters per month. The French machines drilled, removed spoil and laid the tunnel wall at the same time. This was precast concrete segments reinforced with steel bars, which sounds a bit safer than the method recently used at Heathrow airport. Eight million cubic meters of chalk was either made into an artificial hill in France, or used for agricultural purposes in England.

The main cross-Channel railway tunnels are 7.60m in diameter, and are connected every 375m to the service tunnel, 4.80m in diameter in between the two, which is used for ventilation, safety and maintenance. The railway tunnels, which are single track and one-way are about 50k, long, of which 38km is under the sea, 3km on French soil and 9km in England. At 38km under the sea, it is the longest underwater tunnel in the world. Le Shuttle runs 24 hours a day right through the year, and completes the journey under the Channel in 35 minutes with an approximately time of 1 hour from motorway to motorway. Generally car drivers and passengers stay in their cars, but may stretch their legs. Smoking is prohibited.

The Eurostar Train from Waterloo is passengers only, and now runs four trains a day to Paris, with 5 on Fridays. It also goes twice a day to Brussels. In 1996, it is hoped to run right through to Amsterdam. It is a very comfortable way of travelling. It is run by British Rail, SNCF (France) and SNCB (Belgium). Each train cost 24 million pounds and carries 794 passengers. (584 2nd class, and 210 1st class). As first class passengers pay another 100 pounds, they have far greater comfort and lunch is served en route. The Train has 18 carriages, including two for Bar/Buffets. It is 394m long (1,292 ft), and 2. 8m wide (9.2 ft.) It weights 800 tons when loaded, and has a tractive power of 12,200kw. Maximum speed is 300kph or 186mph, but only in France at *present. There is a tri-lingual computerized system in the driver's cab, and he has to check everything out like an aircraft. During the journey, the driver has to operate three different signaling systems, and adapt to varying platform levels. (You'd think they'd have them all the same height!). The driver sits in the middle of the cab to solve the problem of left or right hand drive. All information comes from the control centre at Lille, and is shown on a digital display in the cab to help the driver keep to the different speeds. Instructions are displayed tri-lingually, but the driver and crew use the language of the country they're in. They may use their mother tongue on the shore to train radio. Uncoupling takes less than two minutes. If the Train passes through a smoky area, it is hermetically sealed from the outside air. It has three braking systems; rheostatic, shoe and disk. All three are used in an emergency (thank Goodness!). When the Train brakes from 186mph, it absorbs as much energy to run a domestic electric fire, non-stop for two weeks!*

And if that isn't enough information about this Tunnel and Train, well, find some more yourself!

Mrs. North did an excellent job on the technical stuff. Her last paragraph is a gem. George knows more about Eurostar than he needs to know. Thank you, Eileen.

Interesting to George is how are they going to make a profit on a project of this magnitude. Although the Train has been running for 9 months it has not paid a dime on its fixed interest load of 3.5 million dollars per day. Bankers do not take kindly to that sort of result.

For London-Paris business people, the Eurostar must be a dream. It is competitive price wise with all other forms of transport between the two cities and is more comfortable and faster. But 20,000 business travelers each week seems like a bunch.

Holiday people have to fill up the trains. $150 U.S. return is good value. Eurostar should start selling along with the fare, packages for 2, 4, 8 hour sight-seeing trips in each city. Throw in lunch at varying prices and also hotels for people staying one night or more.

This would require marketing expertise, but one would think major tour companies would be happy to pay a high commission to Eurostar for the built-in business. It could be marketed and packaged under the Eurostar label.

George knows all the answers, but nobody asks him the questions.

Another solution would be for the three governments to each take a huge equity position using taxpayers money. But don't let the taxpayers vote on that proposition.

The three-hour trip is quickly completed as the Eurostar glides to a stop at Waterloo at 8:15 pm, 5 minutes late.

The Northern line to Embankment station, the District line to Gloucester station and after a ten minute walk the travelers are back at the Majestic Hotel.

There will be no bridge tonight as the Wescoombe have to be at Heathrow by 9:20 am tomorrow, Monday.

DAY 22 – MONDAY – AUGUST 14, 1995
LONDON – L.A. – INDIAN WELLS

(SUNNY AND WARM)

The airport bus leaves from in front of the Majestic at 6:45 am for the one-hour trip to Heathrow. The bus charge is $10.00 per person and is very convenient. Barclay is in the lobby waiting to help George carry the two bags to the bus stop. The Allans do not leave until tomorrow, Tuesday.

George will not be able to help Barclay. Thanks again, for helping an old fellow across the street.

The Wescoombes are at the bus stop for only two minutes when an empty taxi pulls up. The driver has a fare to pick-up at Heathrow and offers to take the Wescoombes to

Heathrow for the same fare as the bus, rather than drive dead head. George gives him a $5.00 tip.

As the Wescoombes have not seen a T. V., the driver who is a golfer describes the closing holes of the PGA Tournament, which Elkington won yesterday at Riviera. The man plays two times a week for $20.00 per round pulling a trolley. Buggies are not available at his course. He has seen the last 10 Ryder Cup matches in England and one in the USA.

The Wescoombes were lucky and won the right to have their bags checked thoroughly. It's a random check. George was somewhat surprised that the checker was a swarthy Pakistani, with scars on his face. Nan was leery about giving him her passport. The man was very pleasant and is no doubt a loyal British subject. He asked the usual, "has anyone had possession of your bags since you packed them" at least 3 times in 5 minutes. Maybe a guilty person changes his answer, from "no" to "maybe" to "yes." They are very careful.

Flight 938 due to leave at 9:20 am is late coming in from San Francisco, and is now scheduled for 10:50 am. Time for breakfast and the newspapers.

Two of George's favorite people left this week. Phil Harris – 89 on August 11, and Mickey Mantle – 63 on August 13.

There is not much to do, sitting comfortably in a B767, streaking through the sky at 600 miles per hour, except think and sip on Crown Royal.

George tries to think of what may have been the highlight of the trip. Everyday was a highlight.

One thing comes to mind. For 3 weeks the travelers were not exposed to the ubiquitous Simpson trial. That's a relief. The newspapers and TV in England report the farce sparingly, the group is told.

When asked the English say, "Simpson is guilty, but he will get off."

A sad commentary on the American Justice system.

George feels sorry for the people on the jury. Of the people in the courtroom, O.J. is fighting for his life, the judge and the attorneys are very well paid.

The jurors on the other hand are paid very little, yet have to sit there day after day watching the attorneys preening their feathers before the TV cameras and supposedly pay attention to the continuous drivel.

Of course, a juror has a chance to be a celebrity. It is a difficult call, would a juror prefer to become famous by suffering on the Simpson jury for two years and then help someone write a book or take the faster route, become famous by giving head to a celebrity in his car. Not much of a choice, but it's a fact of life, in these times

A London newspaper had an article on juries. George liked the article as it reflected his negative opinion of the jury system.

Here are a few of the salient points, taken from the article.

The jury system originated in England around the twelfth century. Today outside of some English speaking countries there is less recourse to a jury and more voices are raised about eliminating it.

When juries were first used, Jurors were locked up without food or water to encourage them to render a speedy verdict.

If they brought back the wrong verdict they could be charged with the crime of "attaint" (Disgrace-dishonor). Judges could empanel a second jury to try the first without food or water, of course.

What reason could there be for using a number of naturally biased and mostly undereducated persons to follow the complicated advice and incomprehensible instructions given by the bench.

Also, why should a jury of 12 *people offer always a unanimous decision when the nine members of the Supreme Court almost always express a dissenting opinion.*

The English, whose jury model the US copied,

abandoned juries years ago as too costly and cumbersome in most civil cases.

It would be more efficient and cost much less to have a panel of three judges as is done in many parts of the world.

George considers himself to be an optimistic, carefree traveler. After intensive and extensive planning, it is expected that everything will happen as predicted. If there should be a cock-up, George is very surprised. Pre-planning allows the planner to take the trip, at least, twice. This does not mean that one should travel without sufficient, built-in, safeguards. For every 14 days of travel one day of slack is included to be used at anytime.

The day of slack was used for the stop at Newark, thus cutting the trip from York to Sudbury in half.

Most of the success of the trip was due to the ability of Barclay to adjust to the English style of driving. Thanks, Barc, for a job well done.

The excellent weather was a prime factor in reducing problems. Imagine only 30 minutes rain in 21 days in Great Britain. Unbelievable!

Also, no one was ill at any time, thankfully.

The old timers may have started burning the midnight oil at 9:00 pm, but they got underway early each day.

Nan, who was scorekeeper, only kept the score sheets on the nights the ladies won, so there was no official result. George kept a running total in his head. Ha, Ha. The ladies won by a thousand points.

Flight 938 was 90 minutes late, but daughter Pat was a welcome sight at the gate. Thanks, Peeps, we love you.

HOTELS – ROUND-ABOUT ENGLAND AND SCOTLAND
July 25, 1995 to August 14, 1995

Date	Location	Hotel	Lbs.	$US
7/25 & 26	Tunbridge Wells	Ephraim Lodge	42	72
7/27 & 28	Crediton	Coombe House	58.5	100
7/29 & 30	Bristol	Seeley Hotel	44	75
7/31	Nailsworth	Apple Orchard	35	60
8/1	Windermere	Coppice Lodge	40	68
8/2	Carlisle	Eastview House	30	51
8/2	Edinburgh	Strathmohr	60	102
8/4 & 5	Aboyne	Arbor Lodge	44	75
8/6	Moffat	Thai-Ville	34	58
8/7	Leybum	Eastfield Lodge	36	61
8/8	Newark-on-Trent	South Parade	40	68
8/9	Sudbury	Old Bull	44	75
8/10 & 11	London	Majestic		95
8/12	Paris	France Eiffel		110
8/13	London	Majestic		95
				1582
	Conversion rate – English Pound		= $1.70 US	
	Average cost per night		20 x $79.00	

PETROL Round-About England and Scotland

July 25 to August 14, 1995

Date	Liters	English Pounds
7/28	29.64	15.98
7/28	30.58	18.01
7/30	28.81	15.53
8/1	31.22	18.39
8/3	29.98	17.36
8/4	32.42	17.80
8/6	27.38	15.31
8/8	27.99	15.09
8/9	22.44	14.59
8/10	26.02	14.65
	286.46 Liters	162.71 Pounds
	63.0 UK Gallons	276.60 US $
	75.6 US Gallons	

Conversion Rate – English Pound = $1.70 US

Miles Traveled	2,278
Miles per UK Gallon	36.16
Miles per US Gallon	30.13
Cost per liter-Average	56.8 UK
Cost per Gallon US	$3.66

Nan and Geprge proving they visited Scotland.

LA JOLLA TO CINCINNATI

JUNE 5 TO JUNE 13, 2004

Including a visit to John T. Kitching

On June 8, 2004, in Andrews, Texas

By Wescoombe

PREAMBLE

On Friday, January 4, 2004, Sally and John Coombe paid a visit to the parents in Thousand Palms.

Bernice and Wes had been recently informed by Frank and Vicki, their next-door neighbors, that they were willing to sell their house to them.

The old timers were unwilling to make such a momentous decision without the guidance of John and Sally. Hence the most welcome visit.

Wes and Bernice, age 88 and age 85, think the most of the luxurious house situated behind their present house, on the shore of a small lake and also on a golf course. It would be ideal to spend a few years in that location. However, as their tenure in this world will be limited, it is necessary that John be willing to dispose of both them and the house when the time comes, for the benefit of the family.

DAY l-Saturday, June 5, 2004 - Thousand Palms to La Jolla

For a couple of important reasons, our trip to board the Mississippi Queen in Cincinnati, Ohio, begins in La Jolla at Lisa and Rob's house on Avenida Alamar.

Katy, our beautiful ten year old Burmese, will be living in Lisa's guest house until our return on July 1 or thereabouts. Lisa promises to clean and feed her every day. Rob will fall in love with Kate, so we will be lucky to get her back.

Maty Kay Burke, an ardent baseball fan has procured five tickets, one each, for Nana, Grandpa, Bette, Marnie, and herself to see Milwaukee play the Padres at the new Petco Stadium. Grandpa comes up with the $140, which is as it should be.

Lunch is at the upscale restaurant, George's, on Prospect Avenue in downtown La Jolla. The view of the Cove is magnificent as is the food and service. Thank you, Lisa and Rob, for the treat.

Mary Kay shows up and directs Marnie, who is driving the Volvo, to within a couple of blocks of Petco Stadium. Our seats are on the sixth floor with an unobstructed view, straight down onto the playing field. Using a 1930 motif, the designers have omitted a center field wall, thus giving the impression that the stadium is situated in a factory district close to downtown. It is clean and open rather than the glob of concrete so prevalent in recent ballparks. It is easy to purchase hot dogs, nachos, beer, wine, peanuts, etc., etc. at the usual exorbitant prices.

Wes enjoyed the old fashioned game, as it was played in two hours and fifteen minutes due primarily to Ismael Valdez shutting out the Brewers, 4-0, on four hits.

Marnie and Bette left the Volvo on the eighth floor *of* a nearby high-rise parking building. Their only complaint was about the time that it took to unload the building with only one downward road

Lisa and Rob had been to the wedding of Bill Canning's son and arrived home about the same time as the baseball watchers.

Mary Kay poured Wesley a nightcap of Crown Royal, which put the old guy in the mood to crawl into bed with Nan and Katy. Thanks everyone for a delightful day.

DAY 2-Sunday, June 6, 2004 - La Jolla, California to Tuscon, Arizona

Sadly, after coffee with Lisa and Rob, we say goodbye to Katy. Of course, she knows what we are saying. It is a beautiful but hot day as Marnie drives the old Volvo along Highway 8, easterly (can't go far westerly) to El Centro where a breakfast stop is made at IHOP.

As golf is on TV this p.m., our objective is to reach a venue around 2:00 p.m. in order to watch the finish, if our timing is right. When we stop at Mr. K's Bar in the Holiday Inn in Casa Grande, it is disappointing to find that Ernie Els won the Memorial Tournament twenty minutes ago. As there are very few places with TV along the freeway, one has to be lucky to find one. Els was first, Freddie Couples second, and Tiger Woods third. Ernie had only 100 putts for 4 days, making him 44 under par in the putting department. Putting still wins tournaments even though most of the players drive 300 yards these days. It is still drive for show and putt for dough.

Word came down that Ronald Reagan has left us at the age of 93. He had Alzheimer's for ten years, a terrible way to die. Ronald was too nice a man for that. I always liked him, not because of his brains, but because of his acting ability. He had the trained ability to follow a script, right or wrong.

Basketball playoffs have been on for about six months so there must be a game on tonight. I only watch the last three minutes so it doesn't matter if there is a game or not.

Nan always goes to bed early so she doesn't have to watch this nonsense. She likes Sport Center, however.

DAY 3-Monday, June 7, 2004 - Tuscon to El Paso, Texas

Marnie has us moving speedily along Highway 10 on a hot morning. Thankfully, the air conditioner has been restored, by Pete, to its former glory, for only $810.

I was attracted by a big ten-pound bag of pistachios for a reasonable price, which just about took the place of lunch for Bette and Wes. Nan is always happy with a milk shake, and Marnie enjoys a salad.

The Comfort Inn in El Paso has a cool pool and a sad-looking hot tub. Cool, in this case, means "not hot." Sad looking means it has leaves in it.

In the bar attached to the hotel is advertised a Happy Hour with appetizers at half price. The appetizers were delicious enchiladas plus Mexican buffalo wings. After a couple of each, it was decided to have more and more drinks thus making it easy to dispense with a dinner altogether.

In fact, I forgot whether I was watching hockey or basketball, which is hard to forget as the players are different colors in each sport. I think it was hockey as it was a sad night for 30 million Canadians. They have not won the championship of their game for many years. They should have won this time except the Calgary team forgot to light the flame until it was too late. Imagine a team from Florida winning at ice hockey. It shows what money can do. Here I am sobbing when I think of Auntie Eileen and my sister, June, crying real tears. It's getting too late to think about next year.

Nan fell asleep early, but I woke her up when Calgary scored their goal with ten minutes to go and I shouted "hurrah." But it was in vain.

The USA is becoming on a par with the third world countries, and the Canadians are sinking also. Let's hope we win an event, or maybe two, in the upcoming Olympics in Greece.

It is time to forget all these sad things and hit the sack.

Nan insisted that Bette and Marnie have their own room on this trip. She said, "They are too old to listen to their dad's snoring and farting all night long."

Dad said, "They will be in our room anyway, I hope. That's where the booze is."

DAY 4- Tuesday, June 8, 2004 - El Paso to Andrews, Texas

Marnie moves the Volvo, on a beautiful day, along Highway 10, in an easterly direction. Highway 10 goes to San Antonio, so at Van Horn, she takes Highway 20, which goes to Dallas.

The objective today is Andrews, Texas, where Wes's old friend, John Kitching, lives with his wife Gloria. John and Wes met in Riverside in 1966. John, an insurance agent, was helping his old friend, Mervyn Flory, locate an accountant to set up a record keeping system for Flory's real estate business in Riverside. Efficient John put an advertisement in the Riverside Press Enterprise. Wes and Bernice had bought the Avalon Hotel in Palm Springs in 1964. Bernice, as president, was completely in charge. Wes, as vice-president of trash removal, sometimes became bored. He saw the advertisement, made a phone call, went to Riverside, and the rest is history. John and Wes have been friends ever since.

The meeting place today is the Barn Door Steak House in Odessa, Texas. This is a nationally known operation. Wes had seen the advertisement probably in an airline magazine. Full up, 350 diners can be seated comfortably. The decor ranges from checkered tablecloths to an elegant, white table clothed formal dining room. As we arrived at 2:30 p.m., the checkered area was in operation. Wes had to try the steak, so he and John shared a top sirloin--delicious and plenty.

After a nap, the travelers drove the couple of miles to Gloria's house, where she lets John live if he is a good boy. Her house is commodious, but she makes John have his office in the backyard under the pecan tree.

Gloria produces homemade ice cream and cake for dessert which was absolutely delicious but too much. The two old timers huddled under the trees and made their usual attempt to solve the problems of the world.

"John, now that the local editor-publisher has asked you to do a commentary, you should assume a neutral stance. A journalist is required to present his message with provable facts to present an unbiased opinion. I will ask you for your opinion on certain matters and we can search your answers for evident of bias. Let's try it.

The last time we passed by, on the ground anyway, was about 22 months ago, in August, 2002.

John, you had strong feelings about what was going on in our country. So I am sure you have kept track of all the happenings since.

An undeclared war with Iraq was started about March 19, 2003, 15 months ago, 7 months after we were here. Moving to Baghdad was easy, like an elephant crushing an ant, and in June, 2003, after about 3 months, Bush declared victory.

Now, about 12 months later, fighting is still vicious with soldiers killed and injured since the war was officially over.

What is your opinion of all this bad stuff? I have set the time frame only. Let's hear it from an expert commentator. "

John removed his pipe and began, "I had hopes for

Bush at first, but my mind has changed. It's the arrogance that is appalling as well as the incompetence. The war has been under funded, poorly planned, and a sham to begin with. If this administration was a department in a private company, the whole lot of them would have been fired."

"That's a good start, John. How is he doing in the War on Terrorism?"

"I'm glad you asked. I can't name one Al-Qaeda terrorist that has been found in Iraq. Jordan and Italy have found several. Bush bungled the job when he didn't finish up in Afghanistan and began the futile war in Iraq. Previously, we declared a war on poverty. Result: there are more poor people in America, not less. Then came. the war on teen-age sex in an effort to reduce pregnancies. Result: there are more teen-age pregnancies and more abortions than ever before. Congress declared war on illegal drugs. Result: there are more drugs everywhere and somebody is making money from that despicable business. Every war our government has declared makes things worse, not better. The declared War on Terrorism will result in more terrorism in America, I am afraid."

"John, if what you say is true, things are worse than I thought. You must do a lot of reading and studying."

"All one has to do is read the newspapers and I have plenty of time to do that," John continued. "Have you noticed Bush's devastating environmental record?"

"Tell me about it, in a few words."

"Well, he has cancelled 200 Federal environmental laws, cancelled global warming treaties, allowed arsenic in drinking water, allowed power plants to spew mercury, allowed mines to pollute rivers, sold federal forests for clear cutting, sold wilderness for road building, gutted the Clean Air Act, halted toxic waste clean-ups, and dismantled 30 years of environmental progress."

"Well, John, that's more than a few words. It's terrible, but how do you know your comments are true?"

"Wes, it is all part of the public record. Anyone can

verify everything I said. The sad part is no one is making a fuss about how our great country is being destroyed from within."

"John, are you saying that Bush is intentionally destroying our country?"

John took a long drag on his pipe before replying. "That is a very grave charge, but I didn't know any other way to put it. Maybe it is just his mannerisms that throw me off. Such as, 'Your either with us or against us.' There is no middle ground--George has that special type of arrogance that assumes that any fair-minded person must think as he does. However, his swaggering, sneering, tough guy attitude is turning the whole world against us."

"Well, John, it's obvious that you don't think much of George Bush. Remember when all we had to worry about was a president's sex life?"

"It was a simpler time. Now everything is life and death. I don't hate George Bush, but I do hate the things he does, and the obvious lies and deception that got us into this mess. It will be almost impossible to come out clean."

"Thanks, John, for your insights. Personally, I don't think invading Iraq and capturing Saddam was worth the wounding of one American soldier, let alone their death. Let's go on to something we talked about 22 months ago--the rotten, greedy, bastards that stole from their company, their employees, and their shareholders. Has anything happened in that unpleasant area?"

"I'm sorry to say, not much. A few have had their wrists slapped, and there is hope that more may even visit a prison for a few years. The real big guys are still living in their mansions. I hate to think that George Bush is protecting them. That's a terrifying thought, almost as bad as lying to start a war. No, stealing is a lesser crime than murder. I'm sure you read that Martha Stewart may be incarcerated for lying."

"Yes, I read the headline. Was Martha's lie bigger than claiming there were weapons of mass destruction when there were none?"

"Oh, no. Martha just made a silly mistake trying to save a measly fifty grand. All she had to do was say sorry and return the paltry sum of money. I read that she is not a nice person so maybe 'they' had it in for her."

"That's too bad. I do not know much about the lady. Maybe she should serve six months for not being a nice person. I read that the President claims he has not been given reliable information from his agencies."

"I can believe him on that issue. He has the CIA, FBI, and the National Security guys and they all seem to be inept and don't talk to each other. All I can say is that it is unbelievable how badly we are screwed up."

"John, you have brought me up to date, as far as I want to be anyway, except on the most important subject of all. Is it true that there will never be peace in the Middle East until the USA settles the Israeli-Palestinian thing?"

"Yes. "

"John, we were upset because Saddam tortured prisoners. Do you think we would do the same?" "Perish the thought. We would never do anything like that."

"John, I read in the newspaper that the Mideast contains 75% of the world's oil reserves. Yet the USA, home to about five percent of the world population, consumes about 25 percent of the world's oil production while possessing only about two percent of the world's oil reserves. That makes us look like greedy bastards. Is there anything that can be done?"

"Well, you know our scientists could come up with a fuel equivalent that would relieve us from our reliance on Mideast oil. However, we have never really put that statement to the test. It seems that every time we make a serious start, more oil comes from somewhere, the price goes down, and we back off The Arabs and Dick Cheney are very smart and they know we love big cars."

"There is one simple thing we could do, but our oil

companies (Cheney) would not approve. If we raised the fuel efficiency standard for light trucks to the same standard as other vehicles, it would cut consumption by one million barrels per day and reduce carbon dioxide emissions by 240 million tons per year."

"Cheney dismisses those who advocate conservation and/or alternatives as dreamers. I think an administration that ties us to a medieval monarchy, with a king who has lost most of his marbles, which cares little about what is happening worldwide, where corruption is rampant, from where we have asked Americans to leave, whose educational system advocates hatred for America is reckless and dangerous, to say the least."

"When the 9-11 Commission completes their work, I am hoping for an explanation as to why on 9-11 when all airline traffic was on hold, a planeload of Saudis was allowed to leave, including members of Bin Laden's family. I wish I knew the answer to that one, but it may be too close to the top."

"John, I just wrote about our scientists developing a substitute for oil and now I read that our great country is losing its global dominance in scientific studies. Are we really becoming a third world country?"

"You are kidding when you say we are 'third world' but it is true that China is gaining by leaps and bounds. Scientific publishers reveal that in published research, China is submitting more than 1,000 papers a year. On the other hand, American papers fell, in two decades, fell from a majority to a minority, last years total was just 29%, down from 61 % in 1983. We are also falling in the number of patents won. The Asians are very active and in some fields have seized the innovation lead. In Nobel prizes won, we peaked in the 1990's. But we have fallen in the 2000's, to about half, 51 percent. We are in a new world, Europe and Asia are ascendant."

"John, how do you keep up with all this important stuff I will bet that there is no one on George Bush's staff that is as knowledgeable as you. I find the newspapers are a great source of information. Here is a little something I noticed. George Bush and I have one thing in common, we both love baseball. Bush knows how to make a fast buck by having the right connections. In 1989, his group paid $83 million for the Texas Rangers. He put up $600,000 of the $83 million. Texas taxpayers built a brand new stadium, financed by a higher sales tax. Bush's boys sold the Club for $250 million, George's $600,000 became $15 million. What a sweet little capital gain without lifting a finger. It is easy if you are in the right place at the right time, and know the right people."

"I read the newspapers from stem to stern but I didn't notice that gem. It was not on the front page, I'll wager. We both know, it's not against the law to take advantage of who and what we know. Just because he knew they would get a new stadium paid for by the taxpayers doesn't make it 'inside' knowledge. Of course not."

"John, you are right. Of course, it's not against the law but it is taking advantage of one's position. There is going to be an election soon and we will talk about that later. You know I do not vote and the reason for that is simple. I have been in this country from Canada for fifty years. When I first heard about the power of the lobbyists, I decided I would never have the money to make my vote count against that kind of crap. So I love my country but let the chips fall where they may as far as who runs it. That's why I ask you your opinion, as I should not be voicing my opinion. I read there is something called gerrymandering going on. What is that?"

"Well, it seems to me to be a legal gimmick that the politicians use to somehow move the districts around so they will have a majority of their party in each district. It is probably a lot more than local as the maneuvering can add up to a lot of votes and probably decide an election."

"There is another election due in another few months. Will this country, which is a model for the world, be able to count the votes accurately this time?"

John took a deep puff on his pipe and replied, "I'm glad you asked because votes can be bought, stolen, miscounted, lost, thrown out, or sent to Mexico. Nobody knows precisely how many votes are uncounted in an election. What happened in Florida when 19,000 votes were discarded alone is the rule, not the exception.

To many Americans, the right to vote is sacred. However, elections across the country are under funded, badly managed, ill equipped, and poorly staffed. For example, in New York City voters use machines no longer made, as they also do in Louisiana, which can be jimmied with pliers, or a screwdriver, or a Q-tip. In Texas, canvassers or consultants simply buy or steal the ballots.

Alaska has more registered voters than voting-age people. Indiana encourages voting with signups by mail and there are hundreds of thousands of people who should not be on the registration lists. In Oregon, 36,000 voters mailed in ballots signed by someone else. In Wisconsin, many students say they voted as many as four times. In Louisiana, the commissioner pleaded guilty of a kickback scheme."

"Thanks, John, for clueing me in on that travesty. I'm more glad than ever that I don't join the people who are misled. Do you think political consultants who manage legislators' campaigns could also be lobbyists?"

"Of course not, unless there is full disclosure."

"John, why such short answers? Are you getting tired? Here's one you can chew on for hours. What is your opinion of our Secretary of Defense?"

"That is a simple one. I'll make it short. By any normal standard of business or government, Donald Rumsfeld should long since have resigned or been fired from that most important position. His boss has shown that responsibility for disaster does not matter. Mr. Bush says, 'You are a strong Secretary of Defense.'"

"I mentioned earlier that our great country was falling behind in new inventions, patents, etc. Do you know that the highest rate of mental illness is found in the USA? The rate is 26.4 of people in this country."

"No, I didn't know that. It is serious, so maybe 1 should spend more time with you so I may know what it is like in person."

"John, what do you think of the high price of gasoline? Do you know the reason?"

"No, I don't think Mr. Cheney shares his secrets with the common people. It doesn't bother me, as I don't drive very much. But I feel sorry for the folks who have to spend more money to get to work and to pay the prices that will go up on account of shipping, delivery, etc. I don't feel sorry for the SUV users as they can afford it."

"Here's a tough one, John. I know you live in the hot bed of Christianity. I also know you won't agree with me, but let me state my thoughts. Even the most conservative or authority-dependent Christian or Muslim or other believer has chosen his or her authority somehow from among an enormous variety of options, and by that choice is precisely a relativist. There is no absolutely safe and reliable choice to be made, for all who claim that there is are subject to human failure. The best we can do is to use our heads intelligently and make the best judgments that our minds can make, in all aspects of life.

For those who wish to depend on an authority, I hope for the sake of the rest of us that they choose wisely and recognize that it is very difficult to follow an authority wisely. Our own arrogance and needs often get in the way.

Just because we may think we've made a wise choice, that does not give us the right to tell another how he or she must live or believe, without equal respect for the other's judgments.

Thank you, John, for your erudite answers. You sure know what is going on in our country. As soon as we can, let's sit down for an hour or so and analyze if your answers display bias and if so, which way. Thanks, again."

DAY 5--Wednesday, June 9, 2004 - Andrews to Dallas, Texas

Adjacent to the Park Inn, in Andrews, Texas is a large restaurant and bar owned by a couple, Rusty and Donna, and known as R & D's. Wes likes to call it Red's but none of the natives know what he is talking about. John and Gloria arrive at 7:30 a.m. for a farewell breakfast. The place was divided smoking 80% and non-smoking 20%. Remember this is Texas. We were in the 20% section.

Gloria and her first husband owned several businesses in Andrews, such as service stations, hardware stores, and a travel agency. Many of the old-timers having breakfast in Red's called to her by name. It is a regular morning meeting place for all the retired guys. Marnie and Bette want to stay in the old men's section.

Breakfast is a typical Texas feast, including grits, whatever that is. Wes and Nan had California fare, a waffle and cereal. John and Wes thought they were solving the problems of the world, but the ladies knew they were doing just that. John passed out gifts to the ladies, including shelled pecans. Wes is 88 and John is 77. On parting, they agree to meet again in a few years.

Gloria tells Marnie of a shortcut to Highway 20, which meets Freeway 10 at Big Springs, Texas.

A stop for gas and lunch at the Iron Skillet resulted in enough food left over (roast beef and steak) for sandwiches for four of us. No wonder so many in our country are obese. The servings are at least twice as large as necessary. The servings have to be large in order to justify the price. The price has to be large enough for the restaurant to have sufficient profit. It is a never-ending cycle, which results in overweight people.

All of a sudden, shortly after moving to Highway 30, at Fort Worth, the sky opens up and drops a veritable lake on the entire area. Marnie expertly maintains her position on the crowded freeway. Bette locates a Comfort Suite at Rowlett, a suburb of Dallas, and makes a reservation. In about 20 minutes, off ramp 64B shows up and Marnie, with a sigh of relief, parks at the lobby.

It is a classy joint and each room has a separate sitting room, which makes it a suite. Adjoining the hotel is Dickey's Barbecue Restaurant, available for sandwiches and rolls, etc.

The rain subsides for awhile but soon builds another lake surrounding the hotel. Everything is big in Texas.

Baseball on TV is entertaining but only New Yorkers want to watch the Yankees win every night. The Padres beat Boston, but the telecast was pre-empted by the Yankee game. Boo.

DAY 6-Thursday, June 10, 2004 - Dallas, Texas to Little Rock, Forest City, Arkansas

The rain has abated, but the skies are threatening. After breakfast at the hotel, Marnie says, "Let's get out of here" and drives the Volvo eastward along Highway 30.

The rain last evening was not much by Texas standards, earning only a two-inch headline in the Dallas morning news. "Storm not up to usual Texas standards." The Trinity River in Dallas reached 34 feet yesterday, two feet above flood stage. It is expected to crest Friday at 35 feet. We are warned to watch for flooded roadways. Marnie got back on Highway 30 with no problems, not 'wishing to wait for Friday.

Texarkana, our hoped for destination yesterday, was reached at 10:00 a.m. and we stopped for coffee and gas before crossing into Bill Clinton country.

The girls wished to stop at the city of Hope, the birthplace of Bill Clinton, at 117 South Hervey Street. A visit to the Hope Visitor Center and Museum located in the restored Iron Mountain/Pacific Railway Depot has exhibits, which showcase the President from birth through the White

House years. Hope is also famous for its world champion watermelons.

Arkansas is a small state but it is famous for being the birthplace of Walmart, in Bentonville. We see enough Walmarts without going to Bentonville.

Let's go to the capital city of Little Rock, population 183,000. Little Rock is a big little city. The skyline has a dozen or so brand new or nearly new skyscrapers and many office buildings that have yet to show signs of wear and tear. The Capitol Building stately stands out at the end of Main Street. We drove all around the building, which at 2:30 p.m. had the appearance of vacancy. Maybe the politicians park underground where it is cool. Near the Capitol, we found the Sufficient Grounds Restaurant, which was ready to close at 3:00 p.m., but supplied sandwiches, etc. for lunch.

Evidently, the folks who live and work in downtown Little Rock stay indoors in the middle of the day, as the scrupulously clean streets are practically deserted.

Highway 40 brought us to the town of Forest City, not far from Memphis. The usual Comfort Inn appeared, as did the beer and vodka.

This is catfish country, Wes's favorite, and as it is a specialty of Grandma's Restaurant nearby, the ladies let him partake of the delicacy? They had more plebian food.

The Lakers took a night off, as is their custom, and were trounced by Detroit. I'm tired of basketball more than usual. When will it be over?

DAY 7-Friday, June 11, 2004 - Forest City, Arkansas, Memphis, Tennessee, White House, Tennessee

Today is a big day. It is only 25 miles to Memphis and that means Graceland, and that means Elvis. Marnie and Bette are excited to visit the Pricilla Presley memorial to Elvis. Elvis was born in 1935, appeared on the Ed Sullivan

Show in 1954, and died in 1977 at the age of 42. He's said to flash across the sky and sputter out due to alcohol and drugs, so it says.

Nan and I were not great Elvis fans, although I enjoyed his dancing more than his singing. Watching and hearing the young girls mesmerized and then screaming when he twirled his hips in a sexy manner was fun. They were obviously having a good time. I enjoyed Hound Dog, Love Me Tender, and Ann Margaret. Too bad he succumbed to his addictions.

After Graceland, Marnie moved along Highway 40 to Nashville and without stopping at that metropolis, took Highway 65 to the town of White House.

White House is a small town with a large cluster of hotels, motels, and eating places of all types. Believe it or not, I had never eaten a chalupa, nor had I heard of one until recently when I saw on TV, that funny kid on the Taco Bell commercial. Advertising does pay, for sure, when they can get an old man to try a chalupa. And it was good. Nan had a desire for a root beer float. So it's to the A & W place for four of them. And they were good.

We were able to pick out the Comfort Inn amongst the conglomeration at the corner.

DAY 8-Saturday, June 12, 2004 - White House to Cincinnati, Ohio

The sticker on the windshield says it is time for a lube and oil change. While moseying around the shops on the corner last evening, Marnie noticed a fast lube joint. We decided to visit it this morning after breakfast. We were first in line at the second rack. Imagine, this place has a very knowledgeable lady owner, Lisa, who approached Marnie and me, thinking we were a couple, and said, "My mechanic has discovered you have a defective oil drain plug, and I do not want him to take it off in case we can't get it on again, and we do not have another Volvo plug. We will check all your fluids. That's all I can do. Sorry, no charge." That lady could change my oil anytime, but it's a long way to go.

So it's off to Cincinnati with the same old oil. It will do its job unless the plug unplugs.

Marnie has the Volvo dodging the raindrops and splashing through the puddles. If we stay in this part of the world, we will trade it for a boat. Let's hope the Mississippi Queen has umbrellas.

Not only is there continual rain, but the roads haven't been repaired for a long time. One day's war expenses would pave the roads in the whole country. Sometime soon we will have to fix things.

Marnie drove through the rain, splashing her way along 47 to Newport on the Kentucky side.

Cincinnati is a monstrous city and is in Ohio. Directly across the Ohio River are two small cities, Newport, and Covington, both in Kentucky, joined across the river by six bridges.

Comfort Suites is a 120-room hotel, on the riverbank, in Newport overlooking Cincinnati. We are on the second floor and the girls on the sixth floor. It is impossible to tell the cities apart except for the name signs. Evidently, not long ago the shoreline along the three cities was cleared up, cleaned up, and now looks new again. The Great American BallPark houses the Red's in style, the Paul Brown Stadium is used by the Bengals, also a new convention center and a major shopping mall.

In the old days, Covington was a hotbed of gambling, etc, etc. When we came from Burlington in 1953-54 to see the Kentucky Derby, we would visit the Beverly Hills Casino, open for dancing, etc. The Casino burned down in 1977.

The Italian Festival drew a crowd of 5,000 people lining the riverbank, not far from our hotel. We managed to dispose of some delicious Italian food while listening to great music and entertainment.

Nan did not want to face the crowd, so Bette, Marnie, and I frolicked without her. She enjoyed her room and the fireworks from the window.

DAY 9-Sunday, June 13, 2004 - Newport, Port of Cincinnati

From the hotel room, we can see the Mississippi Queen, parked at the foot of Broadway, on the other side of the river. We are excited, but they won't let us on board until noon, or into our staterooms until 3:00 p.m. The important stuff, food, and drinks will be available from noon onward.

We need to breakfast, pack our bags, load the car, and drive to the Queen. This hotel says we can leave the car in its lot for Mary Kay to pick up when she flies into Cincinnati next weekend. Marnie plans to drive us to the Queen, drop us and all the stuff at the dock, drive the car back to the hotel, park it in a space near the door, then she will walk back to the Queen in ten minutes.

We are most happy the girls came along with us.

George, John, Marnie, Nan, Lisa, Patty, and Bette
The Wescoombe Family

George, Nan, The Captain and Marnie
dreesed up on the Mississippi Queen.

STEAMBOATING

ON THE

MISSISSIPPI QUEEN

FROM

CINCINNATI TO ST. LOUIS

JUNE 13-18, 2004

WITH THE

NIGHT BLOOMING JAZZMEN

BY WESCOOMBE

DAY 1—Sunday, June 13, 2004

As planned, Marnie dropped off Nan, Bette and me at the Mississippi Queen at about 12:30 p.m. She then took the empty Volvo back to the Comfort Inn and parked it in its assigned space until Mary Kay picks it up next Friday or Saturday.

One thing cruise companies have in abundance is food and it is available most all the time. They have set up an extensive buffet for the early arrivals. The Steamboat Syncopaters are making sweet music in the Grand Saloon. I may be mixed up on that name. To me it sounds like the Grand Salami.

It's 3:00 p.m. and the cabins are ready. Nan peaks into Stateroom 214 and screams in horror. There is a king-size bed in the middle of the room. We had ordered twin beds. Nan has not slept with me since I dreamt that Mia Hamm was teaching me how to kick a soccer ball (the women's world championships were on TV) and I kicked Nan very hard and my toenails cut her leg badly.

She visited the purser demanding a different room. There were none available but she would be first in line should there be a cancellation. Not even wine tasting made her feel better. Nor did the embarkation celebration with hors d'oeuvres and drink specials in the Paddle Wheel Lounge, but the parties helped pass the time until sailing, scheduled for 6:00 p.m.

Nan is at the purser's office immediately at 6:00 p.m. and is overjoyed when the purser said, "There is one cancellation. Here are the keys to cabin 240." I breathed a sigh of relief as I had already picked out the couch I intended to sleep on for the next five nights.

At 6:45, in the Grand Saloon, we met the cruise staff and were entertained by a rendering of patriotic songs in a show called "God Bless America," for obvious reasons.

We are on late dining at 7:45 p.m. It's called Main Seating, but we don't care what they call it. The dining room holds 220 diners and is a magnificent room.

We meet Bill and Jan Read, Jan's sister Helen and her husband, Harold, who join Bette, Marnie, Nan, and me, at Table 15. Of course, there is the usual hubbub of greetings, hugs, etc. which subside when waiter, Tony, starts to serve a delicious five or six course dinner.

Nan doesn't eat much, but I am sure I had a small portion of some type of beef. I have forgotten the appetizer, soup, salad, but all were first rate. Trying to stay away from sweets, I ordered a cheese plate. Tony gave me an "is this guy nuts" look for two reasons. One, why would anyone eat cheese when all those delicious desserts are right here? Two, he has to go down two decks to get the cheese. Furthermore, food is not my business, so you may not hear any more about the mouth-watering delicacies. Also, if I live to eat, I could fill another book. I eat to live.

Maybe the Night Blooming Jazzmen performed on this day, but if so, it was not on the program. If they played, we missed them, damn.

The Mississippi Queen was built in 1976 and refurbished in 1996 at a total cost of 32.5 million. She is 382 feet long, 68 feet wide, and weighs 3,364 tons. Her peak speed is 11 m.p.h. and cruising speed is 7 m.p.h. She has seven passenger decks, six above waterline, accommodates 458 passengers max, and has 157 in the crew.

DAY 2—Monday, June 14, 2004

Nan enjoyed her bed so much, she slept until 7:00 a.m. Maybe it was the bed, or more likely it was because she didn't have to sleep with me. After 67 years, she has had enough of that action.

Breakfast was in the Grand Saloon where we ran into Bette, Marnie, and the Reads, unintentionally, believe it or not. After breakfast, a visit to the beautician secured an appointment for a haircut at 10:30 a.m. with Barbara.

Bloody Marys and Screwdrivers are $2.50 at the Calliope Bar. Nan and I scurried to that location to get the day started. Believe it or not, sitting at the bar are our two oldest female offspring, Bette and Marnie. They are well trained or they, at least, remembered that their parents usually gravitate toward discounted drinks. Incidentally, the pretty young bartender was named Devin, an easy name to remember, except it is spelled with "i" rather than "u," as in our great grandson's name, Devun.

The ship's horn blasted at 10:00 a.m. indicated that we should be outside Cabin 240 for fire drill inspection. It's not like on a regular ship where all must go to a station. Here, the inspectors march through the passageways, inspecting as they go, the whole process taking only ten minutes and the "all clear" sounds. We have done the drill on at least twenty ships and the thought always goes through my head, "What a sinking feeling it would be if it were real." We don't really want to know.

The beautician is on "Lower Level" and Barbara Brewer-Post is a charming, attractive, personable lady, somewhere in her middle years. Barbara had a shop in San Bernardino for many years where she lived and raised her children with her first husband, until he passed away about four years ago.

She subsequently met Wally Post, trombone player in the Steamboat Syncopaters, and they married. Barbara had a chance to obtain the hairdresser contract on the Queen and now works four weeks on and four weeks off with her husband being on the same shift. They make their home in Palm Bay, Florida.

When I told Barbara that the beauticians on the round the world trip "The Saga of Ocean Explorer I" were from England, she said that is very possible as an English company; Sheldon's, has the contract for the beauticians on most of the cruise ships in the world. This company hires girls who want to be beauticians, trains them, and puts them out to work without pay in money, their training is their pay, while charging the cruise companies for their services. A shady but lucrative business.

Barbara wishes she had a top-level partner, with whom she could share the time on the Queen. But the company wants her to do it alone—a lotta work.

The Night Blooming Jazzmen are on at 2:00 p.m. in the Paddle Wheel Lounge for a one-hour private blast. It was good to say hello and listen to the great group of musicians with whom we spent a couple of weeks in Bavaria. See the narrative "A Fortnight in Bavaria With the Night Blooming Jazzmen."

Chet Yeager, leader forever, raises his hand and the "Canal Street Blues" fills the room. This group of fine musicians has played together so long that they have no trouble moving the melody, what melody, around, seamlessly.

Chet plays the cornet, not a trumpet. The trumpet has a sharper, shriller sound than the more mellow tone of the cornet. Included in this hour is the lovely melody, "That's My Home." I would like to hear Louis Armstrong sing it. Anyway, Chet must have a new mute, as the sound is as pure and sweet as an angel's breath. That man gets better with age.

Captain Gabe Chenbery treats the passengers to a champagne reception by popping open a couple of bottles. Really, there was plenty. He is a generous man with the company's money as he should be. I hope I'm kidding.

The lovely and talented ladies, Laura Sable and Traci Vaughn along with a couple of handsome and talented dudes, Michael and Jim, comprise the Mississippi Ensemble. These people can do everything in the entertainment business. Backing the foursome are the Steamboat Syncopaters, directed by Norman Bergan, at the piano.

Original choreography and costume changes make the presentation of a dozen Broadway tunes in a show called

"Take Me To the River," well worth the watching. I enjoyed watching the ladies especially.

We are eating dinner at 7:45 p.m., which is known as Main Seating. Bill and Jan Read, and Jan's sister Helen with her husband Harold join Bette, Marnie, Nan, and me as a pleasant eightsome.

The Night Blooming Jazzmen love their work as they are on again at 11:00 p.m. in the Grand Saloon.

Chet evidently likes to start with a powerhouse and "Beale Street Blues" is no exception.

The front three have fun doing their melodic bits. Another exceptional musician, Lance MacLean, does wonders on the banjo and guitar. His work on "Sweet Georgia Brown" ranks on my top ten.

The ever-popular "St. Louis Blues" closes the set with at least ten minutes of excitement. Jim Richardson plays two horns at once, and Dick Doner joins Les Deutsch in a sparkling piano duet.

DAY 3—Tuesday, June 15, 2004 – 333 Miles at Henderson

I was not aware that there were so many locks involved in the movement of water along the Ohio River. Oh well, one can't know everything. For some reason, Captain Gabe goes through the locks in the middle of the night or when something else important is happening, like dinner. Up to now I haven't had the pleasure of a lock passage. I saw a bunch of locks in the Welland Canal and in the Panama Canal, but as hard as I looked, I didn't even find one in the Suez.

The pretty gal, Devin, mixes Bloody Marys and Screwdrivers at 9:30 a.m. in the Calliope Bar for $2.50 a pop. The drinks are great and so is she. It's a half-hour well spent. I am told that daughters Bette and Marnie frequent the

Calliope Bar. There must be other attractions, but I refrain from asking.

Daughter Bette had this to say about the visit to Henderson:

There's not much to say about Henderson—a pretty fountain area near the river for the kids to run in and cool off. We walked up a couple of blocks and saw mainly a few shoe stores, which seemed to beckon all the Mississippi Queen passengers. I walked past the Town Hall, saw many monuments to the Civil War soldiers, so I sat for awhile in the beautiful park surrounding the town hall and read the paper.

Back to the boat by 11:30 for a 1:00 p.m. departure, and not to mention not missing the buffet lunch.

Daughter Marnie enjoyed the visit to Henderson. She said:

Up early, sitting outside watching fellow passengers exercise by continually walking around the top deck of the Mississippi Queen. I realized we were docked at a small town with miles of walking trails lining the shore. I disembarked and walked the paths and streets of the small, not too interesting town of Henderson, Kentucky.

Returning to town after breakfast, the shoe store, the hottest spot in town, was open. I chatted with Jan and Bill and Helen and Harold, all perusing the humungas selection of shoes, with some making purchases. I managed to resist temptation, so the impulse to buy several pairs of shoes soon passed. A brief conversation with the ship's photographer on the way back to the boat revealed lots of gossip about onboard romances, which I promptly passed along to fellow passengers.

At 1:00 p.m. the Queen departs Henderson with a rousing Calliope salute. I wonder who plays that thing.

Captain Gabe invites all those interested to a navigational seminar. His job is easy if you have enough guys helping. Somebody has to be looking at all times. Let's not hit trees, branches, other vessels, or the ground. There are expert lookers called Pilots and one is helping the Captain 24 hours a day with the looking and watching.

At 3:30, Bette, Marnie, Nan, and I are invited to a reception for repeat passengers. This is held by the Paddle Wheel Steamboat Society of America, of which we are members, as about 20 years ago we traveled on the Queen from New Orleans to Natchez and back. The girls were ensconced in the cellar of the ship on that trip, but now they are traveling with the real people. We are able to down some free refreshments but did not win any prizes or awards. On the trip, 20 years ago, we were seated with a couple of fashionable southern ladies. They were either so southern or so fashionable, we couldn't understand a word they said. One was quite pretty and her name was Pearl. The other was not as classy, so we called her Plain, but not to her face. I'm glad I was responsible, as it would have been impolite if the girls had those mean thoughts.

A guy on this ship known as the Riverlorian, Bill Wiemuth, is a knowledgeable and entertaining dude. Bill is a top-drawer actor and plays the one-man part of Sergeant Patrick Gass who was on the Lewis and Clark Expedition and kept a journal of the trip. Bill played every entry in the journal as though he was there. It was a masterful performance. Thanks, Bill.

At 6:45, our favorite jazz band is featured in the Grand Saloon. The Night Blooming Jazzmen are billed in Steamboating Events, as follows: "Like the aromatic night blooming jasmine flower that blooms only at night, our special guest jazz band comes out tonight with a sweet and wonderful bouquet of musical blossoms."

As usual, Chet signals for an up-tempo favorite, Louis Armstrong's "Strutting With Some Barbecue." We must be in Kentucky as the laid back "My Old Kentucky Home" pays tribute to that fine state. "Up a Lazy River" pays tribute to any and all rivers and the dancers find the tempo to their liking.

Bill Keyes, an exceptional violinist and an old friend of the band, joins the Jazzmen on occasion, to add a touch of class. It is an anomaly but that man can sure fiddle.

The band played for the early dinner seating at 8:00 p.m., but as that was my time to take on nourishment, I missed the session. Maybe I should guess the tunes the Jazzmen played. Those guys have a lot of stamina and love their work.

My favorite hour of the day (other than listening to the Jazzmen) is dinner with the usual eightsome. Bill and Jan Read put this adventure together, as they are friends of the Jazzmen and attend most of their outings.

Jan's sister, Helen, lives with her husband Harold in Nebraska. He is still farming with their two sons. The brothers-in-law, for some reason, call each other, Mort. Mort means dead, but these two are far from that unhappy condition. Mort also means dark, so it will remain a dark secret.

Bette and Marnie tell some wild tales about the happenings of the younger set. Some of the young folks in the Calliope Bar tell them, otherwise how would they know?

Jan, as usual, keeps the conversation moving in her inimitable interesting and entertaining manner. The older ladies don't have much to say. They sit quietly and look beautiful.

It's 9:15, so let's pop into the Grand Salami and watch the dancers glide and slide to the smooth jazz of Norman Bergen and the Steamboat Syncopaters. It's nice to know someone in the band, Wally Post, handsome trombonist.

DAY 4—Wednesday, June 16, 2004 – Paducah at 464 Miles

The Queen is docked this morning at the city of Paducah, which dates back to around 1834. I was surprised to hear that monstrous steamboats like the Queen are sometimes driven up on the shore, a short distance. They are pretty well flat bottomed so it may be possible. I don't believe it myself, so don't tell anyone. At Paducah, there is a long steel platform stretching from the ship to the top of a rocky bank. There are no side rails on the platform so the old folks (me) were nervous.

At the top, there is a flat strip of land for about a quarter of a mile, at which point, buildings start to appear. I am unable to walk that far, but my usual luck held and a charming lady in a red coat came up, asking if she could help me. "Yes, I would like to have a look at Paducah, if there is transportation."

She replied, "I am Ann Russell, a member of a group of volunteers. I will get my car and drive you around the city."

I could not turn down that delightful offer, so in a few minutes she was explaining, as she drove, the features of Paducah.

The first step was to see Brenda Taylor, manager of the Convention and Visitors Bureau. This efficient and knowledgeable lady loaded me up with enough literature, that if I read it all thoroughly, I would know more about the town than necessary.

Brenda told me that Paducah, once a thriving riverboat town, had its ups and downs, mostly downs until a lady mayor, Gerry Montgomery, was elected in 1988.

The energetic lady started a program aimed at modernizing the downtown area. Some old buildings were deemed untouchable on the outside, but the inside was open for upgrading. A committee put the stamp of approval or disapproval on all suggested changes.

Daughter Marnie had this to say about the visit to Paducah, Kentucky:

Up early and down the ramp to explore this cute little town. A short walk with my Mom and Jan Read revealed to us the location of the Quilters Museum of America and the beautiful murals that lined the city walls along the Ohio River. After breakfast on board, Jan, Helen, Mother, and I disembarked and entered the hallowed halls of the Quilters Museum, literally enthralled with the artistic design and intricate stitchery on display at the museum. Fabulous to see!

Daughter Bette enjoyed the visit to Paducah. She said:

What a nice town! A few local citizens were at the base of the gangplank in red shirts to welcome the Mississippi Queen passengers and give directions. I set out for the "American Quilt Museum" and spent over an hour looking at the absolutely exquisite quilts—all hanging on the walls according to the type of quilt stitch that was used. So beautiful—breathtaking!! I even bought a "Beginners Quilt Kit" in the hopes of having one of mine hanging there next year.

Back to the MQ by noon—for buffet lunch and a 1:00 p.m. departure.

The Queen does not like being tied to the shore. Sharp at 1:00 p.m., the Calliope does its thing, whatever that is, and the Mississippi Queen haughtily moves from the shore, with disdain. She is a creature of the river.

At 3:30 p.m. in the Grand Salami, lecturer Douglas Matheson tells the passengers about "Humor and Its Effects on Behavior." This erudite young man claims we should laugh at least 15 times a day. I say why stop at 15. Do we have to procure a counter and keep track so when we get to 15, that's it, no more laughing for today.

He is right, though. The USA is far too serious. Our leaders think we have to run the world. We would be better off to send jokes around the world 24/7 in every language. Dr. Matheson could be director of a new department—The Bureau of Humor.

At 5:00 p.m., the Jazzmen swing into action again. As is the Chief's custom, he starts the guys off to the fiery beats of "Lime House Blues." Not many of the dancers can keep up with the torrid pace. There are two couples, however, who like a deserted floor. One distinguishing-looking, serious gentleman and his stately wife probably took lessons from Arthur Murray. They bow to each other, then start striding rapidly in a precise pattern around and across the room. They somehow make their turns exactly in each corner. They resemble ice-skaters doing the compulsory figures, and fascinate me by keeping up with the rapid rhythms of the Jazzmen.

Another couple, usually dressed to the teeth, tails and formal gown with black gloves, twist and turn each other inside out in a small space, with big smiles on their faces. Obviously they are happy and enjoying themselves. They have no trouble keeping up with the Jazzmen's explosive pace. The lady's long black gloves caused Chet to remark, "Sorry you lost your arms."

This set contained a couple of my top ten. Les Deutsch, pianist extraordinaire, grabs handfuls of keys and dispenses them rapidly in "A Nickel In a Slot." Jim Richardson, double saxophonist, brings "Ain't Misbehaving" to a peak in a dazzling display of reed expertise. Where does the time go when you are having fun?

At 6:45, in the Grand Saloon, the ensemble presents a high-energy montage of movie memories in a show they call "The Way We Were." I could watch this foursome all night, especially the two young ladies.

Dinner is the usual, look-forward-to affair. Everybody recounts their activities of the day, if they still have the strength. The youngsters, Bette and Marnie, have their own hangouts. Jan and Helen go to the more intellectual happenings, and Bill and Harold favor the lecture circuit. This double foursome follows Matheson's advice and laughs a lot.

One of the waiters is a purveyor of jokes and usually lays a couple on our table when passing. I'm going to try to recall my favorite:

The Parish Priest had to put up with a drunk who was continually falling down in the streets and embarrassing the father. The father finally thought he had better teach him the power of the Lord.

He took the drunk to the shore of the lake, dunked him into the lake for a few minutes asking, "Did you find Jesus?" The drunk shook his head.

The Priest dunked him into the lake again asking, "Did you find Jesus?" Again the drunk shook his head.

One more time, the Priest dunked the drunk into the lake asking, "Did you find Jesus?"

The drunk shook his head and asked, "Are you sure this is where he fell in?"

Believe it or not, the Jazzmen are performing again at 10:30 p.m. in the Grand Salami. As usual, the energy is high as the band sails through "Muscrat Ramble." The formally dressed lady does not have her black gloves on causing Chet to remark, "Glad you got your arms back."

Another of my top ten is in this set. Dick Doner emotes "Honey Suckle Rose" in his mellow baritone. That guy has a beautiful voice.

I enjoy the way Chet sings, "Is It True What They Say About Dixie" and it is in my top ten. I'll wager that Chet has sung that oldie but goodie, a thousand times.

It's nearly midnight, late for this old man.

DAY 5—Thursday, June 17, 2004

This is a river-boating day. We don't leave the boat. A boat travels on lakes and rivers--fresh water? And a ship sails on the sea--salt water? Somebody just told me that, but it sounds too broad, interesting though.

I have developed a great routine. We are on the second floor, deck that is. The deck with most of the action is Deck O, the Observation Deck, located between Deck 3 and 4, in other words, two decks above where we live or conversely, we live two decks below the action deck.

From Stateroom 240, I walk about 70 yards to the center of the ship where the stairways are located. The stairways have brass handrails, which keep me from falling on my ass. There are four little flights of ten steps each from No. 2, past No. 3, to Deck O, where the dining room and the Grand Salami are located. I can make it in 150 seconds from Cabin 240 to the Grand Salami. Ten times a day gives me an appetite or a thirst depending on the time of day.

There is nothing like steamboating on the Mississippi. Bill Wiemuth, that talented young man, gave a talk about how steamboating began and how these boats changed America. Moving the crops of the field and products of our cities cheaply and relatively quickly is the secret of growth. When someone thought of putting rooms on the second deck, passenger service began. Now, however, massive barges move the commodities, having taken the place of steamboats.

One barge equals 15 coal-hoppers or 58 trucks. One tow equals 2.25 trains or 870 trucks. Or simply, one barge equals 1,500 tons, and 15 barges equal 22,500 tons. A 15-barge tow is a quarter mile long and slips along without any noise.

Bette attended the disembarkation talk at 1:30 p.m. It is necessary to follow the guidelines so they may remove 400 people and bring 400 different people aboard in about four hour's time. It is easy if you know how, and cruise companies do it effortlessly, humorously, and make it enjoyable.

At 4:00 p.m., Creative Traveling, who put this great Night Blooming Jazzmen tour together, are buying all of us a drink or two or three at a cocktail party in the Grand Saloon. Very few people turn down a free drink, even those who don't drink, so there was a good turnout of jazz buffs.

At 5:00 p.m., our heroes (they really are) put down the cocktail glasses, picked up the tools of their trade, and blasted off with "South Rampart St. Parade." In an hour, the musical gentlemen waste little time and usually pour forth about ten jazz gems.

Our chief, Chet Yeager, believes, rightly, that laughter is the best medicine and his one or two-minute asides between numbers are sidesplitting. His humor is only exceeded by his cornet playing, which moves effortlessly from syrup to savage, from song to song, or phrase to phrase, as the need may be.

The remaining sidemen complement the Chief perfectly. They have played together so long, they know exactly what he wants from them. It's second nature. Although he does have signals, that long arm pointing over everyone at maybe Lance, or the finger circling in the air, meaning last chorus.

There is a lot of talent on this ship. Laura Sable, one of the Mississippi Queen Ensemble, shows her class with a single show called "Lady be Good" in which she sings the songs of Garland, Striesand, Cline, Fitzgerald, and even Billie Holiday. She is accompanied by Norman Bergin and the Steamboat Syncopaters. She is assisted by Bill Wiemuth, the Riverlorion, in "Indian Love Call." There is a rumor going around the ship about these two beautiful people. Let's hope it's true.

The usual enjoyable dining hour usually takes an hour and a half. Not that we eat so much, but some have a lotta interesting stuff to say, not that I can recall anything, off hand. Just about everyone on the boat is pooped by 10:30

p.m. But the Night Blooming Jazzmen are raring to go in the Paddle Wheel Lounge. This is a smaller venue and the fans are wall-to-wall.

The Chief raises his hand and the musicians light up "Midnight in Moscow" with a loud but happy roar.

Next is one of my top ten. I'm writing this so I'm allowed to have a top ten. Dick Doner has a beautiful voice and it suits "Do You Know What It Means To Miss New Orleans" perfectly. Another favorite is "Bourbon Street Parade" in which the musicians try to outdo one another with innovation and stamina. They leave me weak, just listening. I do listen hard, though.

In ten hours on this trip, they have played about 100 tunes and only repeated one. I think they doubled on "Avalon" and that's all right, whether it's true or not.

DAY 6—Friday, June 18, 2004 – St. Louis – 691 Miles

This is getaway day. Yesterday, a short talk set the stage. Independents, that is what we are, with yellow tags on our bags, can vacate the boat anytime after 8:00 a.m. Make sure you snag a little or as much breakfast, as you wish. All the goodies are laid out in buffet style. Cereal and coffee are sufficient for Nan and Wes.

It is surprising how many people one becomes acquainted with, in three or four days. Usually short good-byes are all that are necessary, plus promises to see each other again on the Oregon trip next spring. There are about 150 Jazzmen groupies on this trip. The Oregon trip is longer, ten days, and twice as expensive. That may reduce attendance.

The Jazzmen supplied great music over five days, and played many different tunes. I tried to maintain an accurate record, but concentrating on numbers with the Jazzmen's' rhythms buzzing around in my head was a big job for this ancient brain.

If I have recorded a tune on the wrong day or in the wrong set, please forgive me. It was a memorable experience, with a great bunch of people. Thanks to everyone.

ST. LOUIS

TO

THOUSAND PALMS

June 18-29, 2004

With stops at

AMERY, WISCONSIN

BOISE, IDAHO

CARMEL, CALIFORNIA

By Wescoombe

DAY 1—Friday, June 18, 2004 – After Disembarking in St. Louis

Before we boarded the Mississippi Queen in Cincinnati, Bette called Comfort Inn Central to make a reservation in St. Louis for today. Of course, she had no idea where 3730 South Lindbergh Blvd. might be. The reservation people said within 15 minutes of "The Arch." So Bette said, "Close enough." But the friendly taxi man whom we hired at the dock said, "It's farther than that." So away we sped for 45 minutes to an area known as Sunset Hills. The driver had mistakenly taken the wrong route, to the right place.

The hotel is fine and the people friendly, the pool is warm, the grass is green, so "what's the problem."

The girls bring out the vodka, and although it is now 9:30 p.m., there is still time for a heart starter. There is a large desk in the room suitable for writing this manuscript, so that is where I settle. Nan is soon in the hot tub, and Bette and Marnie visit a small market area for subways and bagels.

The U.S. Open is on TV with Lefty at six under and Tiger at three over, but there is a long way to go.

Hey, what is happening? The sky is darkening, rain is descending, and thunder and lightning is all around. The TV guys say a tornado is coming. Hey, guys, it is already here. As quickly as it came, it was gone with little damage in this area except a lotta water. Other areas had things blown down. It was known as a little tornado.

The girls brought back one of the best bagels that I have ever encountered. I will try for another, tomorrow.

Watching the U.S. Open is always interesting, as the people in charge like to show their power by making the course more difficult than usual. Difficult is one thing, unfair is another. The Open requires skill and luck and is usually a good show. Tiger is slumping, so it is wide open. Phil is the big U.S.A. hope. Vijay, Ernie, and the other guy from Ernie's country, are major contenders.

The restaurant beside the hotel offers everything from pizza to steak. Nan and I shared a bowl of spaghetti with meatballs, plus beer and wine.

TV reruns of golf and baseball fill the evening.

DAY 2—Saturday, June 19, 2004 – St. Louis, Missouri

We awaken to a beautiful day in the Gateway City. As Mary Kay Burke will not be here until early afternoon, Marnie and Bette decide to investigate Sunny Hills. Of course, they find a mall and St. Louis Bread Co., which has the best bagels in the world. Dad will eat another. Mother enjoyed the hot tub. Kay arrived around 2:00 p.m., in time for lunch at Spagolas, adjoining the Comfort Inn, pizza and/or Italian specialties.

Cincinnati plays the Cardinals at Busch Stadium at 6:00 p.m. Deciding to get to the game an hour early was an excellent idea as we managed to reach our prearranged seats (by Kay) only ten minutes before game time.

The beautiful, functional stadium is full to capacity as Junior is still at 499, and fans like to be present when baseball history is made. He will be the 20th player to hit 500 home runs in the history of baseball.

Nan has a crush on Tony La Russo and as he is the manager of the Cardinals, she cheers for St. Louis. Bette, Marnie, Kay, and I don't care who wins, but hope to see Griffey make history.

We have reasonably good seats (we can see most of the field) and we are in the shade. $32 per seat x $5 = $160, not bad for three hours entertainment, plus beer, hot dogs, nachos, and peanuts at ball park prices.

The game drags along with Junior hitting the ball sharply for a single and a long fly out, then a strike out, and a line drive single. No home run.

Jim Edwards cracks a homer in the sixth to make it a 1-1 game. In the seventh, the Cards get a couple on, and Pujois wacks a homer to make it 4-1. The Reds get a homer from (not Junior) for a 4-2 score. However, in the eighth, the Cards with Scott Rolen hitting one out, get three more. So we work our way out of the stadium before the rush, and walk about 300 yards to the Marriott Hotel bar for needed libations.

Marnie, who knows St. Louis like the back of her hand, volunteers to walk back to the stadium, and move the car to the front of the Marriott Hotel. Excellent timing allows the old man to meet the Volvo at the curb.

Marnie is an expert at finding the way around strange cities, Fwy. 44 led to Lindbergh Blvd. and the Comfort Inn. Good driving, Marnie.

DAY 3—Sunday, June 20, 2004 – Father's Day, St. Louis, Missouri

Good Morning Americas, then the car is packed and driven to the Arch area, which is crowded. We picked a bad day to show the Arch to Mary Kay as half the people in St. Louis are doing the same. The waiting time for a ride is over an hour. We settled for the museum store and bought Kay a videotape, describing the Arch.

The walk from the car through a beautiful park was about half a mile—four sit-downs on benches for me. They didn't have old people in mind when they set up this outstanding monument in the Gateway City.

Marnie expertly wiggles the car through the traffic toward the airport.

There are great eateries in St. Louis, but none are advertised on the freeway between the Arch and the airport. Kay's departure is at 2:30 p.m. Although we allowed an hour to eat, we have spent that time looking in vain, so Kay has to lunch by herself in the airport. She won't go places with this group again.

After leaving Kay at the airport, we headed along the highway toward Springfield, with Peoria as the objective.

Immediately, we saw "Steak and Bake" advertised at the next off ramp. It turned out to be a high-class hamburger joint (they claimed the ground round was steak) featuring excellent milkshakes. Nan is still having trouble in the eating department, and a milkshake is easy for her to handle; she also shares with one of us.

As golf is on TV while we are driving on the freeway, we are happy to reach the Comfort Suites in Peoria, Illinois, in time to see the exciting finish. When Phil went ahead on the 16th, we thought he would be able to hold on and our country would have its own champion. However, a three-putt on 17 did him in, and the second man from South Africa, Retief Goosen, putted superbly. Putting is the secret in major championships. Goosen earned his second U.S. Open.

Perkins Restaurant and Bakery is close by and it is about the same as Coco's in Palm Desert. It has been a long day, and the beds are welcome. Incidentally, Kay called to say she found a restaurant in the airport.

DAY 4—Monday, June 21, 2004 – Peoria, Illinois--Amery, Wisconsin

Breakfast at Comfort Inn is over at 8:15, and we head for Amery, Wisconsin, to visit Patty and Kent.

About 9:30, the sullen, depressing-looking sky dumps a veritable lake of fresh water damply upon the old Volvo. The floor may be leaking but fortunately the roof is impenetrable. Marnie is now an expert at driving underwater and maintains a steady pace. The rain stops at Dickeyville, allowing us to put gasoline in the car without getting wet. Coffee and a snack are available.

I asked the pretty cashier how the town got its strange name. She smiled, "Don't blame me, I didn't name it." I got the impression that many smart asses had asked her a similar question.

Lunch at the Country Kitchen in Viagra, Wisconsin strengthened us for the afternoon drive, and the rain stopped completely by 2:00 p.m.

We are paralleling our old friend the Mississippi, northward, and actually cross it three or four times. There is no doubt it is the lifeblood of our great country.

Kent is on the phone and advises Marnie to stay on Highway 61 to Redwing, then switch to 63 through Ellsworth, and then 46 to Amery. He is a big help as there is no freeway nearby. 61 and 63 are good roads but visit many small towns, so it's not easy to average 75 m.p.h., or even close.

Since we were last in Amery, Kent's house has acquired a new curved, cement driveway. Patty and Kent greet us warmly with hugs and libations. Patty does typing for her dad, so they exchange work done for work to be done. I am very thankful that Patty does the typing on the narratives, and Bette does the work on the autobiography. They are the only people in the world who can read my handwriting.

It has been a long day for the travelers, so Patty sets out a simple but delicious repast, complete with a menu. Kent has one of those large, flat-screen TVs, which can get channels from all over the world. I took at least 20 minutes trying to surf the channels until I was told that one channel is a directory, which knows everything. How modern!

In front of a large window with an expansive view, there is a conference table with computers, etc. set up on each end, so both can work, talk, and look at each other. Kent is an expert on most facets of computerism and Patty is not far behind. As I know zilch about computers, most people are wizards to me. Nan is a wizard on email and I can barely turn the TV on. If a gadget has more than "on" and "off," I am lost, which is what I am now. Good night.

DAY 5—Tuesday, June 22, 2004 – Amery, Wisconsin

It is a normal day in Amery, half sunshine, half overcast, about 70 degrees F. We intend to change the oil and lube the Volvo this morning. Kent's opinion is that the water on the floor on the passenger's side of the front and back seats is the normal condensation that occurs when the air conditioning is on, and which usually drains to the street. For some reason it is draining inside rather than outside the car. Maybe the oil change man can spot the problem from underneath, but no luck.

Kent was able, by reading the manual, to learn how to turn off the air conditioning system, which should help until Marnie gets the car back to Pete and Rick to rebuild.

The ladies are on their way to Grandma Bonnie's for coffee, etc. Kent and I have a logical man-type reason for not accompanying them. Kent has hired a tree-handling company to remove two or three trees from his tree-covered property, and they have just arrived.

The crew consists of one powerful young man and a helper. She is a smiling, well-built, recent valedictorian graduate from high school. However, they couldn't do the job without special equipment vehicles. A large stake truck with a pneumatic, many directional crane, was the key. Unloaded by the crane from the flatbed were two much smaller pieces of caterpillar-type equipment capable of getting much closer to the downed trees.

Although he could have climbed the tree without the aid of a ladder, the Tarzan-like young man used a ladder for the first 20 feet. He has evidently chosen 30 feet as his pivotal point as he used his climbing gear to raise himself to that point where he established a tether. A sturdy rope is passed through the tether. The girl is an expert with all the levers on the smaller, tractor-like vehicles, and brings them closer to the designated tree.

The boss man has three sizes of chainsaws and used the appropriate size to cut the trunk and notch it skillfully to help direct the fall. The rope from the tether is attached to one or the other of the tractors, and by following the boss's hand signals, the driver lady is able to move the tree forward and side to side with a system of pulleys. Finally, the tree is free of obstruction and is downed by the power of the larger tractor. Once down, the man, with a chainsaw, cuts the tree in pieces, five or six feet long. He picks up the 200-pound chunks like matchsticks and loads them on the smaller tractor. The assistant drives the load to the street where the stake truck is waiting. The boss man with the precision-infinitely-variable crane, with the claw on the end, picks up the logs and stacks them into the massive truck. The process is repeated until the downed tree is completely downsized into the truck.

Tree No. 2 is a sixty-foot high, skinny, dead fellow standing in the midst of several live trees. Tarzan climbs the tree easily, dismembering it as he climbed. Now it is like a pole. By sawing off six feet at a time from the bottom, and maneuvering the ropes, he is able to have the tree drop straight down, becoming finally a pile of ten six-foot pieces, easy to move to the big truck by the small tractor, which is equipped with a carrying device. Imagine doing this four-hour job with a handsaw.

At 4:00 p.m., we travel about three miles to the home of Larry and Joyce, Larry being Kent's younger brother. Larry enjoys boating and fishing and has a 12-passenger pontoon boat docked in front of his house on the lakeshore. It is too late for a spin, but there is always time for libations of all kinds.

Bernice and Wes invited the party of eight to the newest restaurant in Amery by the name of Camelot. The restaurant is well appointed, but not well attended. The food is varied and well prepared, but is not in the same class as Caulderwood. I would have preferred the place, which featured the French waitress, Mimi, but it was closed.

The Wisconsin beer, Leinenkugel's Red, "Leinies," was most enjoyable.

DAY 6—Wednesday, June 13, 2004 – Amery, Wisconsin--Dickinson, North Dakota

This is get-a-way day from Patty and Kent's home in Amery. Kent has had a new driveway installed since our last visit, and it is spiffy with a concrete bench along one side overlooking one of the two creeks. Patty has taken up bird watching as a hobby and knows many of the birds personally. The blue heron is known as Big Blue, which makes sense.

Marnie checks under the car and decides there is no oil leaking, so the rumor of a cross-threaded drain plug is false, at least for now.

Kent has given Marnie a computer-prepared routing from his house to Mike and Sharon's house in Boise. It is 24 hours total, or 8 hours per day. Marnie says 9 to 5 is easy.

Within an hour, it is gas-up time at the town of Taylor Falls, Minnesota. Across the main drag, a sign says, "Rocky River Bakery" and the raspberry scones are delicious. I also buy a baklava pecan tart for later consumption.

I have been upset at my cell phone for about a week as it keeps turning off after only a minute operation. (See Father's Day card that Marnie gave me). Kent said "Let's get a new battery and it will be as good as new." I asked, "It lives in its little nest every night, how could it run down?" An unexpected reply, "You are charging it too much."

At the nearest Wal-Mart store, we found something Wal-Mart doesn't stock—a cell phone battery for a Verizon-served phone. Verizon is not big enough in Wisconsin for Wal-Mart to recognize them. Don't let them know.

On Freeway 94, at 12:30, the usual rain descends in copious quantities, and it has been saving up all morning. By 1:30 p.m. it has had its fun. So we are able to move from the Volvo to Mulligan's in Moorhead, Minnesota, on the border of North Dakota. Mulligan's Stew was perfect for lunch. Moorhead is across the Red River from Fargo, North Dakota.

Marnie says, "Let's motor down the freeway toward Bismark, North Dakota." We reach Bismark sooner than expected. There is no traffic and the speed limit is 75 m.p.h. Marnie and Bette decide to continue to Dickinson about 90 miles farther along 94. Bette reserves the last two – two-bed rooms in the Comfort Inn in Dickinson.

There is a waterpark in Dickinson and the whole town is overrun by happy kids. Also, the Comfort Inn has a Happy Hour from 5 to 7, with free wine and snacks.

It also has a Radio Shack, but the Radio Shack does not have a battery for my Verizon cell phone. There are many stores in the large mall, so the ladies shop until an Applebee's appears, with only four empty seats. The place is full of kids, cute, but crying.

The ladies thought the pool or hot tub would be pleasurable before bed, but, you guessed it, both were full of kids.

When I first saw the name of the town, I hoped it would have a museum of Emily's work, not a waterpark. However, the waterslide brings in much more revenue, no doubt.

DAY 7—Thursday, June 24, 2004 – Dickinson, North Dakota--Butte, Montana

The breakfast room in the Comfort Inn was crowded this morning with children of all sexes, shapes, and sizes, all reasonably happy. All we needed was coffee and orange juice for Good Morning Americas.

Marnie has the Volvo (182,265 miles this a.m.) back on Freeway 94 for a short run across Montana, to Billings for lunch. We are the only people using this highway today. Volvo for life is our slogan.

Montana is the fourth largest state, but has less than one million people. It is the home of the Rocky Mountains, the Missouri and Yellowstone Rivers, Custer's last stand, and a lot of cold weather. It is not cold today, but not many are driving. Freeway 94 has changed to Freeway 90, but it is still devoid of traffic.

The close to a million people are always in the same restaurant as we are and they bring their kids. We get the last four seats in the diner and they gave me what seemed like two servings of corn beef hash. If I lived in this part of the world, I'd become fashionably large.

Bette, on her cell phone, called the Ramada Inn in Butte, Montana. Triple A has it listed at $65, which is less than the Comfort Inn. It is a monstrous place and is obviously being renovated. Ramada is selling the property to a private group. They are still using one end, which includes the restaurant, bar, pool, and hot tub, and we are fine in rooms 112 and 114.

Although the Copper King Lodge (new owners) has a large dining area, Bette and Marnie decide to visit downtown Butte. They pick up, among other things, WD40 and black tape, which Marnie and I will use to repair the Volvo. They have a desire to eat in Room 112 and return, laden with a barbecue chicken and other goodies.

Around 1900, Butte was a mining metropolis with a population of some 100,000 hardy adventurers. Gradually the mines closed for various reasons, until today it has less than 30,000 hardy souls, plus many memories and momentoes of its illustrious past.

After eating, Bette and I need a drink while Nan and Marnie visit the hot tub. In the immense lounge, we soon become best friends with the bartenders, Kevin and Michelle.

After learning we are going to Boise, Michelle writes out directions as to how to reach Highway 15 (yes, it is our Highway 15) bypassing a half-hour's worth of construction. It turns out to be worth the extra $1 tip.

Thursday is comedy night in the lounge, starting at 9:00 p.m. Supposedly, some folks from "Saturday Night Live" are on tour and are appearing tonight.

Bette turns up at nine, finds the joint packed, buys a drink at the bar, gets tired of waiting as the actors are late, and leaves at 9:30 p.m.

Nan and I have been watching baseball on TV, my favorite pastime.

DAY 8—Friday, June 25, 2004 – Butte, Montana--Boise, Idaho

Breakfast in the dining area is either cooked for $4.95, or uncooked for free. We chose cereal and coffee and leave a $2 tip.

I use the WD40 on all the door hinges of the Volvo and they stop squeaking immediately. Marnie replaces the small piece of windshield molding, which has disappeared, with electric tape.

The directions to Highway 15 are perfect. In five miles, on 15, we pass the Continental Divide but don't know what to do about it, except wave at the sign.

We stopped at Dillon (a town being repaired) for gasoline, necessities, and a 30-pack of Montana beer to give to Mike later today. Bette seems to be very happy now that she is back in Idaho, where the Burke family spent many pleasant years.

At Delco, we stopped at Jake's Joint for sodas, milkshakes, hamburgers, and a raspberry tart for me--a much-needed stop. As Bette is now in her beloved Idaho, she will take us on into Boise.

Mike Burke reserved a suite at the Red Lion Hotel for Nan, Wes, and Marnie. Bette will stay at Mike and Sharon's home to visit with 12-year-old Erin and 10-year-old Matt. The youngsters love to have their Gramma visit.

Mike and Sharon have a favorite Mexican restaurant, La Tapatia, which is near the Red Lion. Boise, the capital of Idaho has a population of about 180,000 busy people. The city is clean and orderly with enough new buildings to hide the downtown, which dates to the thirties and forties. The Boise River cuts a swath through the middle of the city.

All eight of us enjoy Mexican food at a round table in the middle of La Tapatia. A guitarist barely makes himself heard. Mexican beer and California wine helps to wash down the well-prepared tacos, enchiladas, burritos, taquitos, and quesadilla. Several boxes of leftovers were carted away.

A nightcap at the Red Lion got the group in the mood for slumber. Great-granddaughter Erin surprised everyone by being able to read her great-grandfather's funny writing. Not many have been able to accomplish that amazing feat.

DAY 9—Saturday, June 26, 2004 – Boise, Idaho

Breakfast at the Red Lion is an elaborate affair, but we stick to cereal and coffee hoping Mike will take us to a scone store later. Bette, who spent the night at Sharon and Mike's, did my laundry. When we got back to the room, there it was, neatly folded, on the end of my bed. Thanks, Bette.

On a closed-off main street, a large crowd attends the Boise Saturday morning Farmers' Market, which displays the freshest fruits and vegetables in the world. Stores along the street have outside seating, giving it a festive feeling.

The scone store does so much business that they serve coffee in one store and pastries in the next. It was fun sitting outside, eating an excellent raisin scone, and watching a composite of Boise passing by, including every breed of dog. The ladies wished to become passers-by, leaving Mike and I to defend their chairs, an impossible task. Grandpa Wes gave Erin and Matt some "walking around" money.

The Burkes came to the hotel and used the swimming facilities for a couple of hours. They are water people, for sure.

Kinko's produced five advance copies of the first third of this trip, which Patty had already completed, thanks Patty. One copy I sent to John Kitching for approval and one went to Mike, leaving three on hand.

I have been having difficulty finding a new battery for my Verizon cell phone. Mike took me to a store in Boise, owned and operated by an Asian lady. She did not have the battery in stock but was able to remove one from another phone. It was not quite the same, as it will not fit into the charging nest. It is a sales and engineering trick to sell more product by making items slightly different, size wise. I did not know, at the time, that it would not fit, but probably the genius lady did, as she sold me a connector to use to charge the battery in the cigarette lighter. No harm done, the phone works again. Money usually comes through in today's world.

Golf is on TV and an Aussie, Adam Scott, is running away from the field. The Dodgers are getting whacked by the Giants again. They will need help.

We are invited to Mike and Sharon's house for pizza, beer, and wine. They have made extensive changes to their fine house, and it is more attractive and functional than ever. Plenty of room both inside and outside.

Also, in the gathering are Elizabeth French, Sharon's mother, looking fit, and John Burke, Mike's dad. It was great to see those old friends once again. John is sporting an attractive beard, quite fashionable. His stories of the trip to Ireland rivaled Nan's stories about the Mississippi Queen.

Patty Burke is absent as she is competing in her favorite event, one-third running, one-third swimming, and one-third cycling. She scored her best time. Congratulations, Patty.

Bette is staying at Mike and Sharon's house to look after Nala and the cat for a weekend longer. We will miss her after the long trip we had together. She will enjoy Boise, no doubt.

DAY 10—Sunday, June 27, 2004 – Boise, Idaho--Reno, Nevada

The breakfast at the Red Lion is scrumptious and leads to obesity. When something is free, people tend to eat more.

We depart early. Marnie overcomes a few wrong turns, and soon we are speeding along Highway 15 toward the objective of Reno. It is a beautiful day, so much different from the dismal, dreary, depressing skies of the east and middle of our wonderful country.

The speed limit is 55, and the troopers are lining up the folks along the roadside. A sign says, "Sucker Gulch." I am usually fond of Oregon. Jordan Valley area must be an anomaly. I am told the sign refers to the fish caught in the streams, not the out-of-state drivers.

The old Volvo climbed the 4,600-foot grade and is relaxing on the level plateau toward Jordan Valley, with its 40 m.p.h. speed limit.

Mcdermott is soon reached, and Nan has half an hour of fun gambling away her twenty-dollar quota. Marnie and I had one egg each, and one order of toast between us, plus a beer each.

There is very little traffic, so Winnemuka is soon the repository of Nan's twenty-dollar donation. Marnie had a scoop of spumoni, and I, a scoop of chocolate, while Nan satisfied her addiction at "The Winner's Club."

Our intention is to stay at John Ascula's Nugget as we have several times before, but it is so crowded, we decide on the Quality Inn nearby. There is no casino in the Quality Inn, so Nan has her pleasure time at Silver City, and we also have dinner at that nearby location.

Before we have time to order, Nan comes back with the news that she had won $40 and wants to go back and lose it instead of eating. Marnie's arguments prevailed, and Nan put away a half a bowl of soup.

Marnie and I ordered pot roast and received more food than we could eat in two days. People who eat large portions usually become large. It seems a shame to waste such good food, but I feel as though I am carrying sufficient bulk already. Marnie is small and dainty.

Back to the hotel for Sixty Minutes, which had three segments including Michael Moore, the Bush-hater. He has a lotta nerve and must be a Democrat.

Fortunately, we have something sensible to watch next—baseball.

DAY 11—Monday, June 28, 2004 – Reno, Nevada--Carmel, California

We are up early for the drive over Donner Pass (7,239 feet) toward Janie's new domicile in Carmel.

Before attacking the Pass, a welcome stop is made at Truckee Bagels, a shop frequented by Marnie when she lived and worked at the medical office in Truckee. I remarked that Nan and I would probably never visit Truckee again. Nan figured Marnie would go through there on her way from Palm Desert to Carmel. Marnie said, "No, Mom."

Freeway 80 is the only way to reach Sacramento, where Swartznegger reigns supreme. Californians love celebrities. I wish Snoopy were running for president. I would probably vote for the first time.

Let's switch to Freeway 5 south, past Stockton, almost to Los Banos, and then Highway 152 west to Highway 101. What a difference in the traffic from the highways we have been traversing the last several days.

Gasoline is 35% more in California than in the states we have just left. But it is worth it, of course?

The grass is a golden color, as California has much gold. We were in Idaho yesterday morning where the grass was a deep green color. Take your choice.

We come to a fork in the road, and decide to take it. Highway 156 is the choice, but unfortunately, it is closed. The city of Salinas is a puzzle, but Marnie solves it by finding Highway 68, south.

Finally, Highway 1 leads to the special town of Carmel-By-The-Sea. Marnie knew how to find Janie's house at 2960 Cuesta Way, in the Carmel Meadows. We drove to the house, but no one was home, not even the dogs. Driving back down the street, we meet Jane and Tre coming back from the beach, walking uphill against the strong wind.

Jane shows us through the spectacular house, which has a 180-degree view of the Pacific Ocean. It is on the edge of a rise with nothing between it and the beach, which can be reached by the street in front of the house, which has access to the beach about 200 yards distance.

Jane and George Walters, her husband, are in the process of furnishing the house, which is now in escrow. Jane has the day off, and George is working at the Hyatt, where he is a sales executive.

We have a room reserved at the Carmel River Inn on the banks of the Carmel River. The people at the desk asked why we are not staying at the Hyatt, and I had to say, "I don't know." It is a fine room with a view of the river, for $90 per night, plus tax.

Jane drives us around Carmel in her Lincoln, which does not take long, as it is a tightly packed village of around 4,000 wealthy people. Five o'clock arrives, so drinks are in order at Clint Eastwood's restaurant known as "The Mission Ranch, Inc." because it is also a hotel or ranch.

It is decided that the appetizers are better at the Rio Grill, a few blocks away, at which point we are joined by

Robin, an old friend who works for Jane as a salesperson at the Hyatt.

George, Janie's husband, arrives with a real estate man who has papers for Jane to sign. It's none of my business but I am happy that Jane is signing something. The men leave, and we finish dinner. Incidentally, we have handsome, but noisy, 3-year-old Tre eating with us.

Janie is conducting business continually on her cell phone and, as usual with that energetic young lady, there is not a dull moment. She looks great and is obviously very happy.

Marnie is staying at Janie's home tonight, and as Nan is fading, we are dropped off at the Carmel River Inn.

Nan hits the sack about 8:30, and I realize that Mike Tonti lives in this area. Sure enough, I dial 484-1999, and my former tennis partner is on the phone. He wants us to stay for a couple of days, but when I tell him we have been on the road for 29 days straight, he let's me off the hook.

Mike sounds real well and tells me things are fine with him. He is getting in some golf and also tennis. The tennis club he owns, on eight acres, has become very valuable and he is tempted to sell.

Mike said he had visited John and helped him move furniture in his new condominium. It was great to have had a chat with Mike Tonti.

DAY 12—Tuesday, June 29, 2004 – Carmel, California—Thousand Palms, California

A beautiful morning in Carmel-By-The-Sea when we awaken in the Carmel River Inn. There is no morning fog or wind.

Marnie spent the night at Jane's, but arrives at 8:00 a.m. with 3-year-old Tre, who will be my seatmate today. He is a handsome youngster in every way. By the time we get to Thousand Palms, I will have figured out what he is saying, and he will have figured out what I am writing.

Marnie has left old Highway 1 and has pointed the old Volvo southward on old Freeway 101. At Paso Robles, she heads eastward on Highway 46 toward Freeway 5 at Lost Hills. As it is early in the day, Marnie decides to take the Grapevine Route on Highway 5, as the traffic is reasonable.

At Freeway 210, traffic becomes heavier, but as we have the Diamond Lane all to ourselves, we pass hundreds of slow-moving cars until the freeway flashing light comes on "Accident Ahead." In 20 minutes, the police have the two cars disentangled and we are full speed ahead in the Diamond Lane. However, another sign reads, "Move from 210 to 10--due to congestion. Marnie takes Freeway 15 to 10.

The freeways are clear, so a 30-minute stop at Bakers in Beaumont for milkshakes, hamburgers, and salads is welcomed. We arrive at Tri Palms at 5:00 p.m.

Marnie drove nearly the entire 6,680 miles. We used 260 gallons of gas at a total cost of $520. The average cost was $2 per gallon and the Volvo averaged 26 m.p.g. There was not a major problem.

Thanks to Bette, Marnie, and Mary Kay, and to all those we visited or met along the way. It was an unforgettable experience. A special thanks to Patty and Kent for putting the whole story together. Love and all the best.

The following was copied from a newspaper found in a restaurant lobby—without permission:

WHY DID THAT CHICKEN CROSS THAT ROAD?

GEORGE W. BUSH

We don't really care why the chicken crossed the road. We just want to know if the chicken is on our side of the road or not. The chicken is either against us or for us. There is no middle ground here.

COLIN POWELL

Now to the left of the screen, you can clearly see the satellite image of the chicken crossing the road.

HANS BLIX

We have reason to believe there is a chicken, but we have not yet been allowed to have access to the other side of the road.

JOHN KERRY

Although I voted to let the chicken cross the road, I am now against it!

RALPH NADER

The chicken's habitat on the other side of the road had been polluted by unchecked industrial greed. The chicken did not reach the unspoiled habitat on the other side of the road because it was crushed by the wheels of a gas-guzzling SUV.

PAT BUCHANAN

To steal the job of a decent, hardworking American.

RUSH LIMBAUGH

I don't know why the chicken crossed the road, but I'll bet it was getting a government grant to cross the road, and I'll bet that somebody out there is already forming a support group to help chickens with crossing-the-road syndrome. Can you believe this? How much more of this can real Americans take? Chickens crossing the road paid for by their tax dollars. And when I say tax dollars, I'm talking about your money, money the government took from you to build a road for chickens to cross.

MARTHA STEWART

No one called me to warn me which way that chicken was going. I had a standing order at the Farmer's Market to sell my eggs when the price dropped to a certain level. No little bird gave me any insider information.

DR. SEUSS

Did the chicken cross the road? Did he cross it with a toad? Yes, the chicken crossed the road, but why it crossed I've not been told.

ERNEST HEMINGWAY

To die in the rain. Alone.

MARTIN LUTHER KING, JR.

I envision a world where all chickens will be free to cross roads without having their motives called into question.

GRANDPA

In my day, we didn't ask why the chicken crossed the road. Somebody told us the chicken crossed the road, and that was good enough.

BARBARA WALTERS

Isn't that interesting? In a few moments, we will be listening to the chicken tell, for the first time, the heartwarming story of how it experienced a serious case of molting, and went on to accomplish its life long dream of crossing the road.

JOHN LENNON

Imagine all the chickens in the world crossing roads together – in peace.

ARISTOTLE

It is the nature of chickens to cross the road.

KARL MARX

It was an historic inevitability.

RONALD REAGAN

What chicken?

CAPTAIN KIRK

To boldly go where no chicken has ever gone before.

SIGMUND FREUD

The fact that you are at all concerned that the chicken crossed the road reveals your underlying sexual insecurity.

BILL GATES

I have just witnessed eChicken2003, which will not only cross roads, but will lay eggs, file your important documents, and balance your checkbook...and internet explorer is an integral part of eChicken.

ALBERT EINSTEIN

Did the chicken really cross the road, or did the road move beneath the chicken.

BILL CLINTON

I did not cross the road with THAT chicken. What is your definition of chicken?

AL GORE

I invented the chicken!

THE BIBLE

And God came down from heaven, and he said unto the chicken THOU SHALT CROSS THE ROAD. And the chicken didst cross the road, and there was much rejoicing.

COLONEL SANDERS

Did I miss one?

George and Nan…somewhere.

DAY ONE
Thursday, June 13, 1996
Newport Beach, CA - Anchorage, Alaska

George and Nan Wescoombe are up at their usual 6:00 a.m. starting time. Last evening was most enjoyable at Sally and John's. There is never a dull moment with Julie, now 18 and Brian, who will be 16 on June 25. Both those young people are very busy with athletics and studies.

Julie will enter the University of Oregon this fall to study Gen. Ed. and boys. She is a slim and attractive volley ball player, maybe not quite tall enough to play college ball. George thinks she plays well enough, but height is so important.

Brian is a handsome, all-round jock. Six feet and still growing. Brian does baseball and basketball, but specializes in the 5K distance on his high school track team. George recommends to Brian that he pick one sport and work toward a scholarship. Brian's excellent reply was, "No problem, Wes, I'm going to get an academic scholarship."

Tracy, temporarily living at home while completing a commercial real estate training course with Coldwell Banker is now 25 and beautiful. She is very serious about her career and works from 7 A.M. to 6 P.M. six days a week. When George sees her leaving for work, he comments, "Trace, you should be a model, showing what the junior business lady should look like." Her slim figure displays the classy clothing perfectly.

Sally and John have a bulletin board on which their upcoming social events are displayed. Nan notices several invitations are for affairs scheduled for the same night. Nan remarks "What a busy schedule. I'm glad we have been there and done that, to a certain extent. It's so nice to not have to go out at night."

The Bulls have won the first three games of the NBA Championship but it will not be a sweep as the Sonics are much the better in game four.

George and John enjoy the action while sipping on Canadian Club.

The Wescoombe flight on Reno Air is not scheduled to depart until 10:30 A.M. But as is customary with old people, they do not mind being early. John Wescoombe departs for work at 7:30 A.M. and drops his Mother and Father off at John Wayne airport at 7:45 A.M.

Check-in goes smoothly and the Reno Air people have seats available on Flight 689, which leaves at 8:30 A.M. This means the Wescoombes will wait in San Jose airport until Flight 649 leaves San Jose for Anchorage at 1:05 P.M.

George knows everybody has to be somewhere, so the 8:30 A.M. flight is the choice.

What does it matter, Orange County airport or San Jose Airport.

The equipment on Flight 689 is the new MD90, M.D meaning McDonnell Douglas. This aircraft has been in service for about 5 years but the one Reno is using is only 6 months old. The plane is much quieter than most older aircraft. Evidently the builders have eliminated one of the most distressing things about flying - cabin noise. This is done mainly by quieter and more efficient jet engines.

This is especially important in Orange County where ordinances prohibit jets from taking off before 7:00 A.M. and landing after 10:00 P.M. Also, outgoing aircraft are required to fly without turning on their engines until they reach 10,000 feet. This is done slowly and quietly so the Orange Countians will not be unduly disturbed.

The MD90 climbs to 10,000 feet at which time the captain turns on the power and the thing moves ahead like a rocket to the cruising altitude of 35,000 feet. This aircraft has a capacity of 128, comfortably, and is a virtual gem.

The smooth flight to San Jose takes only an hour. Coffee and an apple cinnamon snack bar are served free of charge. George would have preferred a cinnamon raisin snack bar, but was not given a choice.

As usual, San Jose airport has the usual plethora of eating and drinking areas as well as an assortment of shops. Prices are higher in airports but if one needs a drink or two and some food, it's cheaper than taking a cab to McDonalds. Whoops, here's a McDonalds right in the airport. It's hard to escape those places.

Anyway, Nan and George find a quiet bar which features clam chowder served in a hollowed out chunk of special bread. George forgets the name of the bread, but it is not Webers. Draft Bud and White Zin complement the chowder.

There is lots of action in an airport so the Wescoombes have no trouble passing the waiting period.

Flight 649 to Anchorage is boarding at 1:05 P.M. and George and Nan are pleasantly surprised to find that they have been bumped up to First Class. Thank you, Reno Air. Reno Air uses the slogan "Discover a Better Low Fare Airline. "

Cocktails and wine cost $4.00 and beer $3.00, about the same as at Indian Wells Country Club.

Shortly after taking off, the pretty ladies presented everyone with a package (box lunch) containing a Croque Monsieur, small carrots and dip. After nibbling, George decides that it is time for a one-hour nap until Flight 649 lands in Seattle to pick up more passengers for Alaska.

This aircraft is a MD80 which means that McDonnell Douglas built it in the eighties; making it at least 10 years older than the MD90 used on Flight 689. There is no doubt this thing is 10 times noisier than the MD90. There is hope for quiet flights in the near future.

George is able to sleep in any kind of noise and does not hear the racket for long.

The stop in Seattle is 30 minutes, then it's away for the three hour leg to Anchorage.

A new crew distributes another food package. This one contains thin slices of cold beef in a terriyaki sauce along with a cold pasta. George asks Nan what the dish is called. Nan is never at a loss and promptly replies, "Cold Beef."

V. O. and Baileys do a lot for the meal. Time for another nap. What a wonderful world.

Flight 649 lands at Anchorage smack on time at 6:05 P.M. Those two weird and wonderful wacko's Marnie and Pat Wescoombe are waiting at the gate. What a splendid reception!

The two adventurers had left the real world(?) of Palm Springs on May 22 and drove in Marnie's Honda over 4,000 miles through California, Oregon, Washington, British Columbia, Yukon and finally after 23 days reached Anchorage. They have had an exciting trip - more later.

As the Honda is full to the brim including the "S" cargo, it is necessary to rent a car. Hertz has a dozen Ford Escorts available at a reasonable price. George, of course, asks for a further discount. The clerk, John, says "maybe you could get a discount by calling advance reservations and taking delivery tomorrow. He connects George to Hertz reservations, who admits they should give George a 20% discount, but get out of it by stating, "we do not have any Ford Escorts in Anchorage." George is looking at a dozen available cars but decides not to get into a useless argument. It is less trouble to write a personal letter to the President of Hertz after arriving home.

Pat has been looking at the Anchorage map, and as she is an expert map-reader, knows the approximate way to the motel for the night. Pat and George are in the lead car, and within 15 minutes are within a quarter mile of the Merrill Field Inn, where George made a reservation.

It takes 5 minutes to pinpoint 420 Sitka Street. Not bad. The motel provides a large room with all necessary amenities, including a Chinese restaurant next door. Marnie scoots over to the restaurant and for $20.00 returns with more than enough Chow Mein and Fried Rice.

The girls look more beautiful than ever, as when they were in White Horse, they took jobs as models at "Cut Loose Studio" and have very becoming, new and different, hair styles. They tell their parents of many hilarious happenings.

And so to bed.

DAY TWO
Friday, June 14
Anchorage

Cloudy - 62°

George and Nan usually retire and arise with the sun. But in Alaska that is virtually impossible. If Alaska used daylight savings time, they would have 25 hours of daylight. The sun has no place to hide, as the Arctic Circle is the only part of the earth pointing toward it.

At this time of year, near the summer solstice, the sun seems to set in the north and rise in the north, a few minutes later.

The owner of The Merrill Field Inn agrees to allow the Honda to remain on the hotel lot as the Wescoombes make a reservation for one week hence.

The plan is to travel the George Parks Highway to Fairbanks, a distance of 358 miles. Marnie has purchased a marvelous book, the Milepost, which describes all the highways (not many) in the Yukon and Alaska, mile by mile. It is an outstanding guide; no self-respecting traveler should be without one. It lists even the railway crossings and scenic view turn offs.

The highway named for George Parks, the territorial governor from 1925 to 1933, travels between snow capped mountain peaks reminding George of Colorado. George is told the mountains in Arizona are dry and those in Alaska are wet, whatever difference that makes. The road is generally smooth except for occasional heaving caused by the winter frost.

There is not much in the way of human endeavors after passing the town of Wasilla; no billboards, no fast food outlets, no Dairy Queens, only spectacular scenery and a B&B every 10 miles or so. The idea is to stay close to Denali National Park tonight (250 miles) and visit the park tomorrow.

Mount McKinley can be seen at times and looks very impressive in the sunlight. Approaching the town of Talkeetna, George spots a sign advertising flights to Mt. McKinley, "Let's go see how much they charge."

The first air service asks $100 per person. George decides to try a new tact. At Hudson Air Service, George asks for a group rate. "How big is your group?" "Four", says George proudly. Business is slow, so after a few minutes of friendly dickering, it is settled at $216.00 for four people for 75 minutes.

Don Bowers, in his fifties, a Vietnam veteran is to be the pilot. The aircraft is a bright red, 32 year old, Cessna 185. Marnie is in the front with Don, George and Nan are side by side and Pat is in the back seat. Modem headphones are in place and in a few minutes, Don has the craft in the air and heading for Mt. McKinley, probably 40 miles away.

In the clear air and with so much snow, distances are deceptive. Things look much closer. It is soon evident that the pilot is an expert who has made this flight maybe a 1000 times in the last 20 years. He keeps up an entertaining conversation with all four passengers.

At 10-11,000 ft. and at about 10 miles from the mountain he levels off and circles about for picture taking.

Of course 10 miles looks like one mile and the majestic peak seems right beside the aircraft.

Don points out the Ruth Glacier, which trends through the Great Gorge for 31 miles. The Great Gorge was named by mountain climbers, and is known as the Grand Canyon of Alaska. Don says, "We are going to go into the Gorge, find a location known as the Amphitheater, and land on the Glacier." Everyone says, "Kak Tovik", Eskimo for "Let's go."

The man wiggles the plane through some small openings into the narrow gorge where each side rises 5000 feet.

The biggest thrill is when the little craft lands on the glacier and virtually skis along to a stop in the level amphitheater. Don seemed to turn the plane sideways, just before landing, to reduce the speed.

It is a beautiful, sunny day and walking on the packed snow is "out of this world." Also in the amphitheater area is another Cessna and also a group *of* 20 climbers and skiers who are camped at that spot. Skiers are coming' down the long slopes to join the group.

Time to go. The little craft jumps off the snow like a ski jumper. Don follows the glacier downward at a height of 100 feet. George thinks it is more like ten feet especially when the wings seem to be so close to the cliffs.

Don is an expert and the old ship responds to his tender touch.

On the way down, Don points out many moose, but only one bear. The ice formations on the glacier were interesting. Don explained those developed over the eons. A very knowledgeable dude.

It turned out he was a single man who lived with his team of dogs which he raced in the Iditorad each year. George gave him a large tip, which may feed his dogs for a week or maybe only a day.

Back on the George Parks Highway, northward to the entrance of Denali Park. As it is getting late, most of the motels are full.

At one place the room was so small, George remarked, "We will have to take turns sleeping." Marnie added, "You can get into the bathroom, but you will have to back out."

Not much farther along, the Denali R.V. Park and Motel appeared; there were 100 RV spaces with six motel rooms in the middle. Room number three was ideal.

As it was a beautiful evening, the outside table seemed perfect for Scrabble. The group got their initiation to mosquitoes in Alaska. In two minutes the game moved inside.

Next door neighbor: "The mosquitoes start feeding around sundown."

George: "What time is sundown in Alaska."

Neighbor: "Oh, figure about the same time as where you live."

George: "You mean those voracious bastards know where I live."

George has made it a rule not to kill any living thing, but he draws the line on mosquitoes.

The Stampede Lodge, featuring the Buckmaster Grill was 3 miles further north. Nan and George split a prime rib, which with beer and wine was excellent. The girls had a fishwich and barbecued beef.

It was been a long and exciting day.

DAY THREE
Saturday, June 15
Denali Park – Fairbanks

Sunny, Warm.

It never gets dark in this part of the world, at this time of the year. The sun shines for about twenty hours and the remainder is made up of a two-hour sunset and two-hour sunrise.

The idea this morning is to take a three-hour tour at Denali Park. As the flight yesterday had covered the whole park from the air, there is no need for an all day bus trip. Cars are only allowed in the park up to the 15 mile gate. Visitors are loaded on buses at a reasonable rate ($10.00) and drive about the park. This provides revenue and greatly reduces traffic.

All the three-hour tours are booked so the 30 mile drive is the only remaining option. Marnie is able to locate Rocky's brother Roger's friend, Frank, who drives a bus in the park. They had a short chat trying to figure out who was who.

Marnie, who was driving, followed a tour bus. Many mooses (meese) were seen and also a lynx. The scenery is terrific as the park is bordered by the Alaska Range, featuring Mt. McKinley. Marnie and Pat needed to use the facilities; in order to gain entry, they applied for summer jobs at the park. That is getting two things done at one time. Very efficient young ladies.

Back on the George Park Highway to Fairbanks by 1:00 P.M. The Klondike Inn at Fairbanks has a two bedroom suite available which fills the need and then some. There is a shopping center nearby so Nan and George buy Raisin Bran and milk for breakfast.

Marnie and Pat got a ton of info on Fairbanks at the Visitors Center, plus Raisin Bran and milk for breakfast at a nearby supermarket. It seems to George that he just wrote that. There should be plenty of action tomorrow.

Fairbanks' premier attraction is "River Boat Discovery", Alaska's most memorable adventure. This three-decked, six hundred passenger sternwheeler sails at 8:45 A.M. and 2:00 P. M. On Saturday there is also a 6: 15 P. M. Midnight cruise. George is able to get a 20 % group discount, for his large group. It pays to ask.

The Binkley family has operated Sternwheel River Boats in Alaska since the Gold Rush of 1898. Jim and Mary first offered riverboat tours in Fairbanks in 1950 and the business has grown ever since. The present vessel, Discovery III, uses the latest technology. The paddle wheel is activated by diesel power, close circuit on 20 T. V. sets gives all passengers a view of everything that can be seen on either side of the river.

The commentator, a retired radio broadcaster, is smooth and knowledgeable and loves his work.

Some of the features: a view of several outstanding log cabins near the landing; a pilot demonstrating short takeoffs and landings on the bank of the river; the entrance to Cripple Creek, Alaska's richest gold mining stream; historical Pump House Restaurant; but the visit with Susan Butcher, who lives on the river, was the most memorable.

Susan was three-time champion of the Iditorad race - 1158 miles from Anchorage to Nome. She won in 1986, 87, 89, setting speed records each year. She and retired dogs, 17 year-old Granite, 14 year-old Longhorn, and 13 year-old Mattie sat on the lawn of her estate with her husband and new baby daughter. They chatted with the commentator on the ship. She credited the three main dogs with leading the other dogs to victory. Granite hobbled about like a 17 x7, 119 year-old man and when applauded, seemed to bow. What a great dog athlete.

It was interesting to George to watch the joining of the water from the Chena River with the water of the Tanana River. The Chena is fed by melting snows and run-off and is crystal clear. The Tanana is a glacier river and is loaded with the silt, which a glacier gathers in its travels. The Tanana's brownish color soon over-powered the clear Chena. Thousands of tons of silt will eventually end up in the Yukon River. Nature must have some reason for these machinations.

George had never seen a fish wheel. This contraption, activated by the current, gently rotates. An unsuspecting migrating salmon may inadvertently swim in to the moving basket and be unceremoniously dumped into a tank with many of his friends.

An Indian lady picked a salmon from the tank and in less than a minute she had eviscerated, skinned, beheaded, detailed, deboned, etc. etc. the unwitting fish, and had hung the salmon filets in the smokehouse. They claim she does a thousand a day. George figures he could do one in an hour if they let him wear gloves.

A native Indian girl and a native Eskimo girl led an interesting tour, which traced living conditions from ancient times to the present. They had a few good jokes to lighten the serious subject. Also, they were pretty. The Indians in this area are Athapaskans.

Back to the Klondike Inn for nightcaps and Scrabble.

DAY FOUR
Sunday, June 16
Fairbanks – Paxson

Sunny, Warm.

Another glorious day, 70 miles south of the Arctic Circle. It is so strange as the sun rises almost in the same place as it set a few hours before. It sets in the north and rises in the north. George and Nan who are daylight people are confused, as there is so much daylight. When does one go to bed and get up. The locals say, "they soon get used to it".

This is Father's Day and along with a beautiful card, George is presented with a can of Captain Jim's Gourmet Alaska Smoked Salmon from Marnie and a couple of cinnamon raisin bagels from Pat. Thanks, girls.

Sunday is church day for Nan and Pat at the Church of the Immaculate Conception, which in 1906 was slid across the Chena River on the ice from the east side to the west side and 400 feet up stream. "If your parishioners won't come to you, move the church to them" was the priest's slogan. There were many gamblers in the early days and much money was wagered on the success or failure of the move. The odds favored failure, but God and a very resourceful priest, Father Munro, beat the odds. The church stands today, very impressive with its, later added, tall steeple.

George and Marnie, not so Holy, drive 10 minutes to North Star Golf Club, the worlds northern-most golf course.

The clubhouse is not much, about like Indian Springs, but the course, a par 36, is 3,280 yards long. Their slogan is, "If your game goes south, come north to fix it."

George chats with the pro. Tom Mulka, who is a friend of Mark Wurtz, one of the pros at La Quinta and also a friend of Rich Fehr who is on the tour. Tom works at a course in Seattle in the wintertime but loves his North Star summer job. George springs for a North Star sport shirt as a souvenir.

As it is such a beautiful day, 75°, and not a cloud in the sky, George realizes he has made a mistake in not planning a game for the foursome. Tom says "What's the problem, we have Starting times up to 10 P.M." No shoes or equipment maybe caused George to be a chicken - some other time, right!

The Richardson Highway, named for the General who had his men build it, goes from Delta Junction to Valdez, Fairbanks to Delta Junction is part of the Alaska Highway. Whatever they are called, the highways are almost devoid of traffic.

Nan is interested in Sunday brunch, as it is Fathers Day. Does that make sense? The town of North Pole, about 20 miles along the road from Fairbanks, is her choice.

The Elf's Den features a Sunday brunch, which includes champagne, and is picked by Nan. The girls and George order from the menu. As the chef is Greek, Tommy Tsakalos, George opts for the Souulaki, which he has never heard of, but which is a featured item. The marinated pork, broiled, and served with diced onions, tomatoes and parsley wrapped in pita bread, was delicious. Nan has the champagne, champagne, and champagne brunch.

The U.S. Open is on TV, but only the first nine is

completed at this time. Tom Lehman has a 2 stroke lead with several others breathing down his neck. George will try to pick it up again along the road, if there is a bar. Fat chance, in this beautiful but desolate country.

The Trans-Alaska pipeline parallels the Richardson Highway, sometimes close to the road, other times along the side of the adjacent hills, and often out of sight. There are turn-offs when the pipeline is near the road for close-up viewing. A four-foot diameter pipe is pretty big, close up, but it's still a pipe.

There are very few businesses - like none - for miles and miles. One has plenty of time to absorb the grandeur of the rugged peaks carved out against the azure sky.

The Paxson Lodge appears out of nowhere. Fortunately, they have a restaurant and plenty of space, with tables for Scrabble.

Even George manages a short walk in the warm sunshine.

DAY FIVE
Monday, June 17
Paxson – Valdez

Sunny, warm.

Paxson Lodge is the only building in town(?) except the gas station. This area is the junction of the Richardson Highway and the Denali Park Highway. The Denali Park Highway runs through the park from the George Park Highway, 136 miles to this spot. The highway through Denali Park is washboard and not for regular people.

Other than in Anchorage there are no motel or hotel chains as in the U.S. and Canada. In Anchorage there is a Hilton, Sheraton, Holiday Inn, a Comfort and a Day's Inn. George notices that many of the privately owned hotels are owned by Orientals, rather than by Indians as in the U.S.A.

As it is a very short season, June 1 to Sept. 15, the few establishments triple their rates. A $60.00 rate becomes a $180.00 during the 14 weeks. Something like Palm Springs used to be. It's the only way the owners can survive.

Prices in general, except for gasoline are about 25% higher than in California, including beer. Liquor is nearly double. A 750ml in Alaska is about the same as 1750ml in California.

The high prices do not seem to deter the Indians, as there seems to be a problem of drunkenness among the young people. What else is new!

The Paxson Lodge, built in 1958, has 19 rooms upstairs with restaurant, lounge, pool tables, and stores on the ground floor.

The restaurant opens for coffee, etc. at 7 A.M., then the group's off on the Richardson Highway to Valdez (pronounced Valdeez).

Alaska has a plethora of creeks, rivers, and lakes. Everywhere, at this time of year, there seems to be a running stream or maybe a waterfall. Actually, there are 3,000 rivers, and more than 3 million lakes larger than 20 acres; it is a land of water.

The road passes through a continual series of snow capped mountains. Mt. Hess at 11,940 ft., Mt. Hayes at 13,832 ft, Mt. DeBorah at 12,339 and a whole raft at lessor heights. It is a beautiful clear day and the snowcaps stand out against the azure blue .sky. As usual, there is very little traffic so it's a pleasant drive except for the frost heaves every few miles.

A short stop for coffee at the historic Copper Center Lodge (since 1899) was a pleasant break from continually looking at snow-capped peaks. People named Ashby, who had no relatives in Canada of whom they were aware, owned the lodge.

The Worthington Glacier, a small one starting at 6,815 ft is 2,600 ft. at roadside. The rock piles on which the visitors stand are brought down the mountain by the glacier and are called moraines. One hundred years ago, Worthington was 1000 ft. longer and 100 ft. higher, but the highway was not there, so very few could see it up close. This state is almost completely glacified.

The Thompson Pass, only 2,791 feet, is steep and very narrow. This is the part of the Alaska pipeline that caused the most problems. Because of the steep incline, the 80 foot joints of pipe weighed 30,000 pounds and had to be winched up the mountain on elevated cable systems. At places the pipeline rises at a 45-degree angle. Heavy blasting of solid rock was required for several miles.

The pipeline has traveled beside or close to the highway since Fairbanks. George and the others have become quite accustomed to the ubiquitous pipeline, zigging and zagging along one side of the highway or the other.

As Valdez is nearby, George suggests a visit to the pipeline marine terminal. The nice folks say all arrangements concerning pipeline visits are handled at the Valdez airport. There they had beaucoup brochures and also a one-hour video.

The best synopsis of the whole project is from a brochure put out by the city of Valdez. A few important points are missing. The owner and operator of the pipeline is Alyeska Pipeline Service Company, a consortium composed of Arco, Exxon, British Petroleum, Union, Phillips, Amerada Hass, and Mobil.

This group got together in 1970.

At that time, gasoline was around 35 cents a gallon in the U.S. In 1973, almost the same group of major oil companies, conspired, in George's opinion, with the Arabs to raise the price of oil, so gasoline could cost about double, 70 cents per gallon. This increase, in George's opinion, was the major cause of inflation. It was further exacerbated in 1979 by another increase in the price of gasoline to about $1.40, again doubling.

The oil companies are continuing to screw the American people. As this is written the price of gasoline is about $1.70. They probably have $2.00 in mind.

The pipeline cost 8 billion dollars in the 1970s. A guess in 1996 prices would be 100 billion. Does anyone remember when a million was a great deal of money?

Incidentally, all the pipe for the pipeline was supplied by Japanese companies.

The following is from the City of Valdez propaganda machine.

Welcome to Valdez

Home of the terminal for the Trans-Alaska pipeline and loading point for the tankers carrying Alaska crude to the lower forty-eight. The port of Valdez is a protected ice-free fjord about 12 miles long, 2 1/2 miles wide and over 750 feet deep. It is large and deep enough to accommodate the largest of tankers. The narrowest portion of the Valdez Arm is several times wider than the ship channels at New York, Philadelphia and Houston.

Getting the crude oil to Valdez was and is no easy project. Construction of the four foot wide line through 800 miles of Alaska wilderness (408 miles buried, 382 miles above ground) began in 1975. Two years later the biggest private construction effort in the world reached completion with the first barrel of oil reaching Valdez on July 28, 1977. During construction, approximately 22,000 workers were needed to weave the pipeline over, and under and through three major mountain ranges and several large rivers, including the 2,000 foot wide Yukon River. Twelve large pump stations exist along the line to provide the "push" needed to get the crude oil to Valdez.

When the oil reaches Valdez, it is stored in one of the 18 tanks, each as large as a football field, until it can be loaded aboard tankers for shipment to West coast ports. The Valdez terminal site encompasses 1,000 acres and tours are available to the general public for viewing the facility.

The Pipeline Inn, on the Main St. in Valdez, is ideal for a two night stay. The library, museum, stores, and even a Laundromat are close by. The Pipeline Restaurant is adequate to satisfy the group who split two entrees. Scrabble and bed complete the day.

DAY SIX
Tuesday, June 18
Valdez

Overcast, then sunny and warm.

George has booked a cruise through Prince William Sound, the feature of which is to view the Columbia Glacier, first hand.

Boarding time is 9:15 and the 70 ton, 150 passenger, "Glacier Spirit" leaves the dock promptly at 9:30 A.M.

The ship is owned by Stan Stephens Charters and Cruises. This is a lucky day as Stan Stephens will be the pilot and commentator. His wife, Mary Helen, co-owner with Stan, will be part of the crew and will mingle and chat with the passengers.

It is an 8-hour trip and will cover 90 miles of Prince William Sound's 3,000 miles twisting coastline, longer than the California coast.

As we entered Prince William Sound,
The sky cleared, disclosing to the West
One of the richest, most glorious
Mountain landscapes, ever behold.
Peak after peak, dipping deep in the sky,
A thousand of them, icy and shining.
Rising higher, higher beyond, burning
Bright in the afternoon light.

No, George is not trying to be a poet. The above was written by naturalist and poet, John Muir, who died in 1914. George thought the sentiment was apropos.

Many bald eagles live in this area. They put their name on the huge nests and use them for several years. A fully developed eagle's nest weighs half a ton.

George, who doesn't know a parrot from a pigeon, is introduced to, among others, Tufted Puffins, Mergansers, Harlequin Ducks, Cormorants, Kittiwakes, Grebe, and Scaup. This is a bird fanciers paradise.

The sea is infested with adorable sea otters frolicking around the boat. The cruise company probably pay them for entertaining the visitors. George can't tell for sure, but they look about as long as a four-foot putt.

Prince William Sound has thousands of small bays, which will be swarming with spawning salmon in July and August.

Many waterfalls shower the shore from a great height.

Last winter 140 inches of snow fell in 5 days and the mountain was unable to hold it. Fallen trees indicate the paths of the avalanches.

The ship parks beside a buoy, which has several sea lions resting on it. George suggests that the Captain tie up to the buoy so the passengers may enjoy a swim.

Captain Stan is doing a fine job of describing the happenings. Nan is fully dressed as she has on her hearing aid. George is wearing his Captain's hat, hoping for a little respect.

The lengthy tanker "Arco California" is moving out with a load of crude oil, heading for Long Beach.

The Glacier Spirit is approaching the Piece D'Resitance, the Columbia Glacier.

This royalty of glaciers has been developing for 10,000 years, is 32 miles long, 5 miles across, 200 feet showing above the water and approximately 1000 feet below the surface.

In the year 1982 a strange thing happened. Columbia started retreating. A glacier is actually a large river and must be moving forward, but this one is also moving backward. The face is actually 6 miles back from where it was in 1982. The glacier experts are trying to figure out the reason for the phenomenon.

The six miles is now covered by ice floes or icebergs. George is not sure which. Up to now, George thought ice was something one puts in his drink.

The Captain is threading the boat around and through the innumerable icebergs. George hopes the captain knows that icebergs are 90 percent under water. George is thinking about the Titanic.

Many seals and eagles are cooling off on the icebergs. They are also paid by the cruise people to entertain the visitors.

The icebergs vary from icy white to delicate and dark blue. The coloring, George is told, varies with the amount of oxygen in the ice. George wonders if the amount of hydrogen in the ice also has an effect.

It's time for lunch on Growler Island, a facility owned by the cruise company. Everything is well organized and the sixty or so folk pass through the. buffet line quickly. This is an "all you can eat" affair, featuring salmon, halibut, roast beef, chicken, soup, salad, beans, rice, etc.

Salmon is very expensive in California so George is able to eat about fifty dollars worth of salmon at restaurant prices, in a very enjoyable hour. No doggie bags allowed, unfortunately. Great lunch, thank you.

The Captain brings the boat close to Bull Head Point, where 161 sea lions, some weighing almost a ton, are cavorting on the rocks.

They appear to be fighting but George soon realizes they are doing something much more fun than fighting.

The mating calls reverberate along the shore and are clearly heard on board the Glacier Spirit, parked 100 yards away.

This is a once in a lifetime sight. George wonders what the odd numbered lion is doing. Maybe he is 80 years old.

The Captain points out a marker buoy, which is located at the spot where the 989-foot super tanker, Exxon Valdez, rammed into Bligh Island Reef on March 23, 1989.

The 125 million-dollar tanker was carrying a million and a quarter barrels of crude oil from Valdez to Long Beach.

A river of crude oil rushed into pristine Prince William Sound causing immeasurable damage to the environment. Although only 20% of the cargo was spilled, in two weeks the damage covered 2,600 square miles. Carelessness on the part of Alyeska was to blame. The people of Alaska made them pay in money but the oil companies got the money back quickly by raising the price of gasoline, one cent per gallon. Furthermore, even at this date, Exxon is trying to make secret deals with those damaged for less than the punitive damage award. The court caught Exxon making an undercover deal with seafood processors; thus saving themselves about 745 million dollars. This is against public policy, according to the *Anchorage Daily News,* dated June 17, 1996.

Mary Helen points out that eight times the 258,000 barrels, which poured out of the Exxon Valdez, is spilled every year by the oil companies in many minor spills, throughout the world.

On the way back to port, the Captain pointed out

many eagles, seals, sea otters, and endless birds, but no whales.

The pipeline terminal can be seen in all its glory from the water, a tanker eyes view. Extensive blasting with solid rock was obviously necessary, as was adequate earthquake protection. There are five berths capable of fueling five 1000-foot tankers with a million barrels a day.

Just before docking, a strong breeze develops, which makes the boat rock and roll and made Nan slightly sick. Thank goodness, it's only five minutes to landing.

Thanks to the Captain for excellent leadership. George also thanks Mary Helen for chatting with him and supplying most of the statistics for this narrative.

Word has just been received that the first red salmon have been sighted. This is very important as the salmon industry is the largest in Alaska and many people are employed.

Nine hours at sea makes the travelers tired but happy.

A few drinks plus Scrabble complete the day. The girls have the latest official Scrabble dictionary and if your word is not in it, forget it. An iron clad rule. The new dictionary 'has 3,000 more words than the old one, so Nan and George are at a disadvantage. George says if he learns one new word a day for the rest of his life, he will catch up. By that time there will be another new dictionary.

No problem. George's definition of happiness is, "continually gaining on a continually receding objective."

DAY SEVEN
Wednesday, June 19
Valdez – Anchorage

Overcast, warm.

Nan has been in Alaska for a week and admits she has not been cold. Of course, she has not been outside at night. On second thought, neither has anyone else in Alaska at this time.

Today is a travelling day. Valdez to Anchorage is about sixty miles as the eagle flies. The road travels 300 miles around a dozen or so mountains, lakes and the usual glacier or two or three. George read that there are 1500 glaciers in Alaska, 150 in Prince William Sound alone. Do they really need that many glaciers?

The coffee maker in Room 12 at the Pipeline Inn has a mind of its own. This morning not even Pat, the mechanic, can get it to work. George is sent across the street to the Apple Valley Trading post for the necessities.

It is necessary that the group retrace it's tire tracks for 115 miles on Highway 5 to Glenallen. Anchorage is 200 miles from Glenallen on Highway 1.

Travelling through the Thompson Pass then viewing the awesome Worthington Glacier without stopping was easy this time. The group is becoming blase about glaciers. The way some travelers become disenchanted with cathedrals in Europe.

A quick stop on the Tiekel River to view a beaver dam, with huge beaver homes a hundred feet long and up to fifteen feet high. Everything in Alaska is bigger than anything in the world, even Texas. Beavers are the largest rodent in North America and are very industrious and family oriented.

Very thick forests are on each side of the highway. The animals probably think the forests are great, but Nan says they spoil the view.

The Hitching Post in Glenallen serves egg dishes to all except Pat who has two tacos for breakfast.

Glenn Highway winds it way up, down and around the awesome snow capped peaks of the Chugach Mountains. There is so much snow and ice around. George thinks he is back in the ice age.

There are many small insignificant glaciers, but finally approaching the town of Palmer is what must be a

Japanese glacier named Matanuska.

Matanuska is still 27 miles long and is an awesome sight. The guidebook states that 18,000 years ago, Matanuska was 87 miles long, averaged 21 miles in width and was 4 miles high at its terminus. Now, that is a big one.

At this time, the last 60 miles has become Matanuska River flowing through the Matanuska Valley.

Passing the town of Chickaloon, Marnie says if there is a Chickaloon saloon, she will stop.

No saloon in Chickaloon, so its on to the lounge at the Gold Miners Hotel in Palmer. This place was written up in the National Geographic travel section. The potato skins and mozzarella cheese sticks were quite palatable. But the lounge would not rate in the George Wescoombe travel journal, as the service was so poor.

On to Anchorage, only forty miles away. Pat finds the Merrill field Inn with no difficulty as she has been there before.

Marnie and Pat have shared the driving, but Pat likes to take a nap every couple of hours so her stints are shorter.

A couple of drinks at the "Irish Setter," a local pub nearby, Chinese food from the Imperial Palace, then a couple of Scrabble games complete the day.

While playing Scrabble, George is able to watch the Wednesday baseball double header on ESPN. It's a small world.

DAY EIGHT
Thursday, June 20
Anchorage

Overcast, sunny, warm.

The group is back in Anchorage at the Merrill Field Inn. Merrill Field is a busy airport for private aircraft, and this classy 40-room hotel picks up a lot of business from people who use the airport.

The information center in Anchorage says the population of Alaska is 606,000. The population of Anchorage is 226,300. About 40 percent of the people live in Anchorage.

There are 100,000 glaciers in Alaska or one for every 6 people. There are also 100,000 private aircraft, again one for every six people, approximately. There are 586,412 square miles in Alaska, one square mile for each person. It is not crowded.

The nearest glacier to downtown Anchorage is only 40 miles distant. It is known as the Portage Glacier. George thinks a good way to raise money would be to charge folks $100.00 to have a glacier named after them. The same idea as having a star with your name on it for $25.00. Some years ago, George bought a star for Nan. It doesn't look like they will reach the star in this lifetime.

Back to glaciers for just one more time. Over 5 percent of Alaska is covered by one of those things. After one week, George is up to his ass in glaciers -- if you have seen one, you've seen them all, kind of thing. However, George has to admit that when he is near one, he can't take his eyes off it. Some kind of attraction.

There is fun work to do today. Marnie has decided she would like to take all the stuff out of her Honda, have some work done on it and clean it up. At the "Irish Setter" last evening, George asked if anyone had a small storage area to rent for a few days. One guy had a brother in the storage business and arranged for a week's storage for ten dollars. After all, it is only the Escargo and a couple of tubs.

The brother in the business thought it was a lot of stuff for $10.00 but took George's money anyway. The girls had everything in the little car except the proverbial "kitchen sink." The girls have named the car "Bettlee" in honor of their two sisters Bette and Lisa, thus having their sisters with them, in spirit, at all times.

Marnie called the Honda folks to service the car and to fix the taillights, which are under warranty. No car dealership in its right mind is going to let anyone get away with only a $32.95 lube job even if they do pick up some warranty money. As George had agreed to pay, he was lucky to escape with a bill for only $107.15. They washed the car, and it was red once again.

As the remaining traveling time with the parents will be only a couple hundred miles, it was agreed to give the rental car back to Hertz and use "Bettlee."

While waiting at the Honda dealership, the foursome played Scrabble in the showroom. As it was approaching noon, George got hungry for fish and chips. The Nordstrom Mall nearby is always an attraction for the ladies.

George found a restaurant with excellent halibut fish and chips. Fish in Alaska has to be good.

It is necessary to have a rest, as George wants to celebrate tonight with the Alaskans, as this is Solstice Day. Officially the sun reaches its peak in the Northern Hemisphere at 6:25 PM, June 20, today. Tomorrow, June 21, will be the longest day of the year, 19 hours, 21 minutes.

The Alaskans celebrate all day and all night. Some places have a three-day holiday. In Fairbanks, the regular professional baseball game starts at 10:30 PM and is played without lights. The sun drops below the horizon at 12:48 AM and rises at 2:59 AM, but there is plenty of light.

In Barrow, the town furthest north, the sun rises on May 10 and sets on August 1. There is no doubt all this daylight warps one's sense of time. George and Nan stay up til midnight and don't know it.

The "Irish Setters" across the street has entertainment and dancing starting at 9:30 PM.

A young guy playing a keyboard with all the accoutrements is very good. Brian plays every rhythm and also sings on key.

George asks him to play "Rock Around the Clock" and then puts on an 80-year exhibition for 3 or 4 minutes along with Nan, who is in rare form.

George also dances with Marn, who is a virtual whiz

at zipping all around the floor. As usual, some guy, Walter, notices her and joins the table. He is also an expert, and they have many good dances. Walter has to dance every dance, so Nan fills in capably while Marn takes a beer break.

A guy in the audience, Chuck, joins Brian and plays great jazz harmonica. They have the joint jumping, so generous George, instead of a tip, buys them both a beer. Alaskans love their beer. Alaskans also smoke a lot, percentage wise; about twice the Californians. Maybe word that smoking kills has not as yet reached the frontier.

At 11:30 PM, the Wescoombes, George, Nan, Marnie and Pat bid goodnight to all their new friends and in broad daylight walk back to the motel.

A taste of night(?) life in Anchorage and all for $30.00, including tip.

DAY NINE
Friday, June 21
Seward

Sunny, warm.

Merrill Field Inn is completely booked for Saturday and Sunday nights. Marnie finds the Mush Inn nearby and makes arrangements at that location.

She and Pat mostly stay at campgrounds. All she has to say at these places is, "I've got a tent and I want to pitch it." They have had interesting experiences. Campgrounds usually have showers for rent. Marnie says, at one place, she and the lady in the next shower traded their life experiences without even seeing each other. The girls met Renee and John, teachers from Davis, in a campground in the Yukon. Upon meeting them again in Skagway, Renee said she recognized them from their clothes. The same as in the Yukon.

They also met a young man, Christian, who had just graduated from McMaster University where George earned his accounting degree about 100 years ago.

George and Nan are giving the girls a change by having them stay in motels with regular beds and bathrooms. Next Monday, they will go back to the wilds.

The Seward Highway to Seward is named after William Seward, the former Secretary of State who arranged the purchase of Alaska from Russia in 1867.

In some places the highway actually becomes three lanes. This area seems to be more civilized. At least there are more business areas, resorts, etc. along the 127 miles; maybe a dozen in all.

The first stop, only five miles from Anchorage, is at Potters Point, a marshy area with a stream running through it. The grapevine said there would be salmon running today. If they were running they were also hiding. Many people were on the viewing area but only geese, tern and swan were displaying themselves; no salmon. Tiny goslings scurried around their mother.

Seward Highway travels along the Kenai Peninsula passed and through the Chugach Range which features the Portage Glacier at the 40-mile point.

The water on the right side is Turn Again Bay so named by Captain Cook in 1778. No one knows why he had to turn again. Maybe it had something to do with the 33-foot tides, which follow the six-foot bore in this constricted area.

There are many dead spruce, an aftermath of the 1964 earthquake which dropped the land over six feet and exposed the roots of the spruce to seawater.

Seward, a tiny seaport perched on Resurrection Bay, is surrounded by mountains. In the summer the bay is full of giant halibut and huge salmon, some weighing 300 pounds, but not even one tiny perch.

The Good Friday Earthquake of 1964 completely destroyed the harbor area. The violent quake caused the shoreline to drop more than six feet in 30 seconds. A few properties survived the quake but were washed away by a series of tsunamis. The entire harbor had to be rebuilt.

Thirteen people died and many were injured. The group took an hour to watch a video of the disaster at Seward and also a video of Valdez. It was so frightening they all needed a drink before proceeding to the three-bedroom suite Marnie had obtained at the Taroka Inn near downtown. Taroka is an Indian name for a coastal brown bear.

Rebuilt Seward is more cosmopolitan than Valdez with many classy boutiques, eating places and lounges. The harbor area is full of private craft of all descriptions, but today the whole area is overpowered by a cruise ship from Carnival line.

In the Yukon Inn, Nan and Marnie are picked up on by Jules Burgert, a hunter, fisherman, guide, trapper, artist, etc., etc. His shop, "Feathers and Fur Ltd.," is nearby so Marn goes with him to see his etchings. Nan makes a date for tomorrow morning. George is happy sitting in the window looking at the pretty town, surrounded by snow-capped mountains, brilliant in the sunshine, drinking his beer. That's a mouthful.

George has never had fish and chips with the fish being salmon. The group also has halibut, which gets the nod over the salmon. Both were delicious.

Scrabble at the Taroka. George is able to play with one eye on the baseball game and the other on the Olympic trials. The ladies always win, as they are smarter.

DAY TEN
Saturday, June 22
Seward

Sunny, Warm.

If George was moving to Alaska, Seward would be the place. Breakfast at Dons was regular, except for Reindeer sausage, which George tried. The sausage was spicy and tasty but somewhat tough. Maybe it came from an old Caribou.

A lady barber, who cut George's hair, came from

Michigan 20 years ago. She would never go back, as Michigan is colder in the winter, hotter and more humid in the summer. George asked her if she was paid by the Chamber of Commerce.

On a bright sunny day such as this, Seward, on the Gulf of Alaska, is 'indeed a jewel. Wonder what it's like in the rain?

In Alaska, many times when one takes a trip, it is necessary to retrace one's tire tracks. Usually, there is only one road. It is 127 miles, Seward to Anchorage, and 127 miles Anchorage to Seward. Just read "the mile post" backward.

Not a cloud in the sky as Pat drives 80 miles to where the town of Portage used to be. The 100 or so inhabitants were driven out by the flood caused by the Good Friday earthquake in 1964.

George suggests ice cream at the Tidewater Cafe located where Portage used to be. Everyone agrees, and the cafe is found to be a happy, friendly place. A smiling waitress to George, who has a dish of vanilla ice cream, "Would you like jam on your ice cream?" George, smart asses, "Yes, I'd like some chocolate jam." Waitress, "We don't have brown, only red and orange." George settles for the delicious strawberry.

The Alaska railroad has a shuttle from this location to Whittier, which is 12 miles away on the Gulf of Alaska. There is no road. The fare is $16.00 return and there are 5 trips daily.

The real reason for the spur is to carry people and their cars to Whittier to board the ferry to Valdez. The ferry ride is 7 hours through awesome scenery, including the Columbia Glacier. The train is just leaving with 5 passenger cars and many flat cars carrying about 50 automobiles.

The Alaska railway covers more than 500 miles, including spurs, and is very important in the development of this frontier state.

Marnie finds the Mush Inn in Anchorage, with no

difficulty.

Anchorage is a small (226,000) city and very easy to get to know. The rebuilding, after 1964, straightened out a few glitches. Mainly, it has a grid pattern; numbers one way, letters the other.

It is Saturday and Pat wishes to go to church at the Cathedral downtown. Mass is at 5:30, the middle of the afternoon in Alaska. Nan accompanies Pat, so Marn and George hit the bars.

The Captain Cook Hotel, Anchorage's finest, is named for Captain James Cook, who in 1778, anchored his ship, "The Resolution", in what is now known as Cook Inlet. The hotel displays a large painting of the captain on one wall and on an adjacent wall a huge drawing of the world, depicting all three voyages Jim made to the New World, before being murdered in Hawaii.

The hotel favors an up-scale English atmosphere. Fletcher's Pub uses warm, friendly mahogany and stained glass to emulate the Savoy in London.

George and Marn pretend that this is their normal habitat and quench their thirst with an excellent English Ale. In true tradition one may purchase a yard or half-yard of beer.

Across from the cathedral is a new building covering half a city block, which looks like a green house. This turns out to be the Glacier Brew House. It is extremely busy.

Marn finds seats at the bar from which she can see the doors of the church across the street. When Pat and Nan come out, she runs to get them.

As they move to the bar where George is waiting, Nan spies a table, which has just been cleared and sits down. There are twenty people in line but no one notices or objects.

About 20% of the space is given over to the latest beer brewing equipment and the remainder has seating for 280 beer loving folk.

Salads with great dressing, then an order of nachos and an order of a cheese pot, with tasty crackers, then an excellent bread pudding with four spoons, has everyone stuffed.

Anchorage is a cosmopolitan, sophisticated city with many new buildings, wide streets, and lots of room.

The group wonders around the downtown area for an hour before returning to the Mush Inn. Tomorrow will be a sightseeing day in Anchorage.

As usual, Pat wins the Scrabble game, but the rest are used to it and contest for second place.

DAY ELEVEN
Sunday, June 23
Anchorage

Sunny, warm.

Another clear sunny day in Alaska. The group is not in a hurry, as this day, Sunday, will be spent looking around Anchorage.

A large park runs along Cook Inlet not far from the center of the city.

At the end of the park stands the restored home of Oscar Anderson, who was the eighteenth person to settle in Anchorage. He lived in the house for sixty years and acquired through the years, a cold storage plant, meat market, a bakery, a coal mine and other assorted goodies. The area is known as Bootlegger Cove, so maybe he handled a little hooch on the side. The sign says the famous man supplied food and fuel to the settlers.

The ladies took a walk around the park in the bright sunshine while George finished reading the Sunday paper.

The Anchorage Museum opens at 10 A.M. so the time has come to soak up a little culture.

It's the typical museum, tracing life in Alaska back to around 10,000 B.P. The land bridge from Asia brought mammoths, bison, horses, and man to North and South America.

There were many Eskimos and Indian tribes in the

area. The principal Indian tribe was the Athapaskans who in Canadian high school were called Athabaskans. George decides not to make a big deal about it.

The Aleuts from the Aleutian Islands were also big timers in the long distance past.

The living conditions and culture of the ancients was displayed in great detail. The making and wearing of masks was explained. George particularly enjoyed the exhibit of carvings of walrus ivory. The work was complicated and precise considering the tools the people had at their disposal. They had plenty of time without T.V. and VCR's.

The best exhibit was that of Alaskan art, particularly the room devoted to the work of Sydney Laurence. He has marvelous paintings of Mt. McKinley, glaciers, and other Alaskan specialties. Nan bought George a 1997 calendar containing twelve reproductions of his work. An exhibit indicated that 60% of the land in Alaska is owned by the Feds, 28% by the State, and 12% by private interests.

George suggests that the federal government sell a small percentage of their holdings throughout the country. That would raise enough money to payoff the national debt and allow taxes to be lowered twenty percent.

Lunch in the museum was served by a young Brazilian who was pleased that George and Nan had visited his hometown of Tabatingo, deep in the Amazon jungle. He was also very happy to be in Alaska rather than Brazil.

The ladies hit the Fifth Avenue Mall while George hunted for a scrimshaw, the tool presently used for carving walrus ivory. Eventually George found the tool and also complete instructions. That doesn't' mean he will ever use them. Brother-in-law, Al Barclay will probably be the recipient.

Phyllis' Cafe and Salmon Bake has an outdoor restaurant under a big tent across from the mall on Fifth Avenue. They claim to be the "Home of the Scone," so George has to find seats for four in the crowded bar area. Visualize sitting outdoors on the main street of Anchorage, Alaska, temperature eighty degrees, quaffing an Alaskan amber from the tap, followed by a delicious scone smothered in raspberry jam. The rest of the group enjoyed the drinks and scones so much, George ordered a couple of scones to go.

Back to the Mush Inn for a nap, Scrabble, golf, and baseball on T.V. Just like in Indian Wells.

Everyone is tired so it's takeout from the nearby Imperial Palace, Chinese restaurant. The shrimp fried rice is especially good.

DAY TWELVE
Monday, June 24
Anchorage to Orange County

Sunny.

Reno Air flight 224 is scheduled to leave Anchorage at 12:01 A.M. Marnie and Pat drive their parents to the airport by 10:30 P.M. Sunday at which time, goodbyes, thank you's, and hugs are exchanged.

George and Nan were glad to find the girls in such good spirits and also to have them do all the driving for 1550 trouble-free miles. Sadly, the time has come to release them back to the wilds.

Flight 224 is delayed for 40 minutes due to a fault with a landing gear light. They managed to get the light to show green, but did not say they had cured the problem.

As George writes this, the aircraft is at 3500 feet on its way to Seattle. George is sipping the Canadian Club that Reno supplied free, due to the delay.

No one will know whether they fixed the landing gear or only the light, until the aircraft lands in Seattle. No problem, that is four hours from now.

It is now 1:40 A.M. and sunset and sunrise can be seen on each side of the aircraft. It is one of nature's miracles.

Nan is enjoying a coffee and Baileys. She is quite

comfortable as the Captain has thrown another log on the fire, and warmed up the plane.

The landing gear works perfectly as the MD80 lands in Seattle at 5:00 A.M. Reno Air is trying to make up time so Flight 224 is on its way to Portland by 5:30 A.M.

By 6:30 A.M. Flight 224 lands in Portland and is on its way to San Jose by 7:00 A.M. Reno Air is doing well as every flight has been at least 90 percent full. Most economy airlines sell their space for 7-8 cents per mile. The big carriers cannot compete on a price basis. The next stop is San Jose, which is reached by 8:30 A.M.

As Flight 224 is late, there is only ten minutes to catch the flight to Orange County. The Wescoombes made it. But did the bags?

The aircraft is the new, quiet MD90, which makes the run to Orange County in ninety minutes arriving at John Wayne airport at 9:55 A.M.

The entire flight took nine hours, Anchorage to Orange County, including three half-hour stops.

Reno Air does a great "no frills" job. George and Nan say, "Thank you very much."

Daughters Marnie and Patty having fun in Alaska.

A BUSINESS MEETING IN ENGLAND

A BUSINESS MEETING IN ENGLAND

George and Nan Wescoombe have been invited by Gary, their long-time friend, to travel to England with him and his lady, Lisa, for X-mas week, leaving December 25, 1994 and returning January 2, 1995.

Gary Bukamier is a prominent Orange County industrialist and entrepreneur. George has been a director and officer of Gary's company for almost twenty years. There are some business meetings scheduled in England, which the two will attend.

Nan said, "Gary, if you had said Jamaica, I would have been the first on the airplane. England, at this time of year, is miserable. It is cold, damp, overcast and rainy most of the time. I have to pass on the invitation, with regret. "

Gary replied, "Sorry, but I don't have any business in Jamaica. It must be England at this time.

George and Nan agree that she will be better off in the warmth of California. She will have for company her new pussy cat, three month old" Angel.

Come along with George, as he recalls the happenings of this short, but delightful visit to the land of his ancestors.

DAY 1 – SUNDAY - DECEMBER 25, 1994 CHRISTMAS DAY

In order to prepare George for the rigors of a December day in England, the weather in Palm Springs changed from the usual sunshine to clouds and steady rain.

Rain started about mid-day on Christmas Eve and continued all night. Santa got soaked as he made his deliveries.

As Flight 5203 waits on the Palm Springs runway to take off at 2:00 p.m., it is raining heavily. This aircraft is the

Jetstream Super 31, which has been banned from flying in the Northeast, due to problems with icing.

George hopes the navigational system is OK, as it is completely socked in, as the aircraft takes off. This area is almost completely surrounded by 10,000-ft. mountains, which are probably quite solid, if one should run into one.

George is the only passenger. Coming aboard with the pilot, George commented, "Not much profit on this trip." His fare is $40.00, Palm Springs to LAX, on Christmas Day.

The pilot responded, "Everybody wants to go to Palm Springs."

George, shaking the water off his 40 year old Aquascutum, queried, "Wonder why."

It has taken twenty-five minutes to write thus far. The aircraft has cleared the mountains and is descending into the Los Angeles area. Why did it take so long to write so little? This tiny aircraft has been bouncing around like a cork in a heavy sea.

It's 2:35 and downtown L.A. appears to the right, bathed strangely enough, in bright sunshine. Los Angeles is a veritable sea of houses, on a maze of streets, in grid form. The aircraft is about to touch down at 2:37 a.m.

It's great to have one's own private jet on Christmas Day.

George is wondering whether to tip the two young pilots, but decides that they may not appreciate the humor. They work a ten-hour day but do three different routes to alleviate boredom. Commuter lines are presently getting a lot of flack due to two crashes. Maybe the pilots are working too many hours per shift. Fatigue could be a problem in this line of work.

American Airlines Flight 136 LAX to Heathrow leaves at 5:25 p.m. so there is plenty of time for a beer or maybe more.

George is sound asleep, nursing his drink in the lounge at LAX, when Gary, accompanied by Lisa, sneaks up and awakens him with a bear hug, from behind.

Gary and Lisa were delivered to LAX from Gary's home in Orange County by a hired limo. Traffic is usually light on a holiday and today is no exception.

There is time for a libation and a chat before heading for the departure gate. All agree that it has been a merry Christmas with many enjoyable gifts and celebrations. The annual Christmas party at Gary's factory, held a few days ago, was a huge success. Work stopped at 11:00 for the fifty employees. Gary gave a short speech, followed by a employee gift exchange. Then most employees went home to pick up their families.

By the time they returned, the parking lot was set up with fifteen tables with seats for ten at each table. A buffet table was loaded with all traditional Christmas food, plus specialties for the Oriental and Mexican employees.

The many children were entertained by a Jumping Jack house and a balloon lady. Santa Claus appeared with a gift for each child. Most employees are young so there are lots of kids. George spent his time visiting each table and kissing the new babies.

The stringent penalties for D.U.I. in California have caused many businesses to go to daytime parties with no alcohol.

There are a few dark spots on the horizon. Orange County has filed for bankruptcy as the county treasurer made a few risky investments and lost Two Billion Dollars of the taxpayers' money.

The decline of the Mexican peso has cost U.S. investors up to Ten Billion Dollars. Remember when a million was a huge number. The Mexican economy has always been unstable so investments in that wonderful country are bound to be risky.

Sol Kerzner, lauded by George after George's recent visit to South Africa, is under investigation for bribery, corruption, fraud, and perjury. Behind every fortune lies a felony.

But who cares about the problems of the rich and

famous? Let's get on Flight 136, have dinner and a drink or two and sleep our way to England. It's about a ten-hour flight in the dark most of the way.

George is able to find an empty seat elsewhere so Lisa can stretch out beside Gary. Before long, breakfast is served and the attendants are preparing for landing.

DAY 2 - MONDAY - DECEMBER 26, 1994 BOXING DAY

Overcast with showers - 45°F

Smooth landing at Heathrow. It's amazing how the English get the bags on the turntable in the reclaim area before passengers arrive. The folks at Denver would be advised to see how this is accomplished.

Clearing customs is a snap as there are plenty of lines. Who said the Brits are slow, stodgy, and incompetent. Not this day anyway.

The car rental company Euro Dollar uses a minibus from the terminal to their location in the airport loop. Gary has made all arrangements in advance by fax, so the 4-door Vauxhall is waiting, complete with gas and maps. The only problem is that the steering wheel is on the wrong side.

The ladies at the Euro Dollar office have a plate of mincemeat tarts on the counter for the customers. George has one and it is so good he has another. The pretty accent says, "You like those, don't you." George replies, "Very much, but they would be better warmed up." The next one is perfect. Thank you, thank you, nice lady and the microwave.

Gary is not about to worry about the location of the steering wheel. Short sighted George is the navigator with Lisa in the back as spotter.

The objective for today is the city of Bath with a stop at a rocky place called Stonehenge.

The map indicates that the M4 is the desired motorway. As our travelers have plenty of time, they immediately get lost in the airport. This causes much hilarity as they pass the same place several times.

The English have never heard of right angles or rectangles. They use a method called a round about in order to change direction. From a round-about there are at least four exits departing in different directions. It is necessary to read a sign with many names on it in five seconds to determine if it is the way one wishes to go; usually snap judgment results in failure, with resultant back tracking.

After a couple of mistakes, Gary realizes that he can circle the round-about as often as necessary in order to make an intelligent selection. The English are born with this instinct, so Gary may be excused if it took him 30 minutes to master something the Brits have been doing for 2,000 years.

When the proper off-ramp is located, Gary puts on the "scatter" sign and goes for it. The English are not overly pleased by this maneuver but they are not heavily armed like the motorists in Los Angeles. They are well versed in the Italian salute. However, no one has ever died by the finger, as far as George knows.

The M4 is a splendid motorway. By traveling 80 miles an hour, Gary is able to keep up with the traffic on this 4-lane speedway. The straight away is easy after one has mastered the turns.

The off-ramp to Stonehenge appears as promised. One cannot get near the big stones as the exhibit is closed due to the Boxing Day holiday. Gary's ubiquitous camcorder records the short visit. It is three-thirty and almost dark, in any event. No one knows much about Stonehenge so looking at it in the dark won't help. The travelers buy a book to file away probably without reading.

It is raining heavily when the ancient city of Bath is reached.

Gary has made a reservation at the Royal Crescent Hotel. The crescent shaped complex in which the hotel is located is so old that it is a national monument. This means the outside of the buildings cannot be changed and only very small signs are permitted.

After several passes, it was decided to try the area with the most lights, Voila, success. The Royal Crescent is a high-class hostelry, Gary having seen it on T.V. in a documentary. It is elegantly furnished and staffed by well dressed but surprisingly friendly Englishmen. They should be friendly for the price they charge.

Drinks are served upon request in the drawing room. George is the first to return and upon entering this formal room, passes a gentle fhart.

Although no one is present, George is so impressed by the grandeur, he says, "Excuse me."

When Gary and Lisa arrive, a houseman appears who is able to produce drinks in a matter of twenty minutes. Gary asks David, "Why so long." The reply was, "I had to go 100 yards across the lawn to the building where the lounge is located."

As the group should have gone to the lounge in the first place, they decide to go there in the second place, and there is David again. It still takes twenty minutes to get another round. David has one speed.

The lounge has many Christmas cards decorating the tables. George opens one and finds it addressed to "Mr. Coombe." "That's class" was George's comment. "How did they know I was coming. "

Upon questioning, David reveals that the general manager of the hotel is "Mr. Coombe." Very interesting.

The dining room at the "Royal Crescent" has been booked for weeks. The food and service is reputed to be in the top ten in England. They do not take kindly to Gary's suggestions of room service and offer to book the group into a fancy French restaurant nearby if seated by 7:00 p.m. It, too, is completely booked for 8:30 p.m.

A taxi splashes through the rain on time. It is also an elegant layout and charges accordingly.

As main dishes, Lisa chooses venison, George opts for pheasant, and Gary remains a steak eater. The starters, desserts, and French wine are most satisfactory. The pretty French waitress was also entertaining.

Lisa was the star, as when leaving the Royal Crescent, she picked up a brochure. The brochure indicated that guests of the Crescent were entitled to a 10 percent discount at the Clos Du Roy. It was enough to pay for a bottle of French wine.

George's room at the Royal Crescent had an antique, four-poster bed complete with frills and flounces. The only problem was that if one descended from that height without being careful, an ankle could be broken. George thought of calling David to lift him in and out of bed, but realized that that gentleman might get the wrong idea.

DAY 3 – TUESDAY - DECEMBER 27, 1994 BATH

Overcast - showers - about 50°F

George is seated in the drawing room at the Royal Crescent enjoying scones and coffee, waiting for Gary and Lisa to arrive.

A young man, about 40, appears and introduces himself as Simon Peter Coombe, General Manager of the Crescent. He had heard that a guest had the same surname.

A long chat revealed similarities that might indicate a relationship.

George's great-grandfather was named Simon. Simon Peter's ancestors came from Tiverton in Devon only a short distance from Okehampton where George's forbearers lived.

Both families were Methodists having broken with the Church of England in John Wesley's time.

Simon Peter's ancestors were millers in the Tiverton area, a much more distinguished occupation than George's ancestors, who were stone masons, mainly.

Simon Peter had a great sense of humor and allowed that possibly his side of the family had absconded with the family funds to buy the mill. George could only comment, "What funds? "

It was decided to keep in touch should other interesting developments arise. Simon Peter is a handsome, knowledgeable young man and George would be pleased to have him as a distant relative. Wonder if the reverse is true; depends on the distance.

The Royal Crescent is the crown jewel of the Summit chain of small upgraded hotels throughout the south of England, and has upgraded guests.

George, then engaged in conversation with two ladies who were present and overheard George's conversation with Simon Peter (they were all ears).

Sybil and Anne were from HopHouse, in Kent. As they were both in their seventies, Gary plied them with questions about ancient England in a humourous way. They stood their ground, especially Sybil who Lisa said reminded her of Mrs. Doubtfire (Robin Williams).

This fun could have continued all day but it is necessary to see the Roman Baths located about a quarter mile away in downtown Bath.

Equipped with umbrellas supplied by the hotel, our adventurers decide to walk to the Baths in the rain.

George's umbrella is quickly blown inside out so he decides, after straightening it out, to use it as a walking stick. It is not cold so the rain is no problem as evidenced by the multitude of shoppers taking advantage of the day after Boxing Day sales.

The Roman Baths constructed in the first century A.D. are well worth visiting. The engineering is on a par with anything done prior to the twentieth century.

In fact, these ruins were only discovered and uncovered about a 100 years ago. It is fortunate that they were buried for 1900 years, and thus were out of the reach of religious fanatics who may have destroyed this priceless treasure.

After leaving the Roman Baths, a pint at the "Angel"

pub was in order before climbing the hill to the Royal Crescent.

The travelers had packed their bags before going to the Baths, but did not expect that the bags would be moved to the car and that the car wold be in front of the hotel with the engine running (no, not quite).

Either they wish to be rid of us or they are expecting a big tip. Gary responded with the latter.

Back on the M40 with a stop at Oxford to see the university. As it is the day after Boxing Day in Oxford also, the city is crowded with shoppers.

In response to the question, "Where is the university," the replies are, "Well, one college is down the street a few blocks, another is to the right about the same distance."

This city is one big university with maybe twenty colleges. Nobody knows the location of the principal campus, but everybody knew where the pubs were.

It's about two hours to Braintree in Essex, where most of Gary's business friends are located.

The M40, to the M25, to the Mll, then the 120 to Braintree. The 120 was a bit of a problem as were the one-way streets in Braintree.

The White House Hotel was in plain view but how to get to it was a mystery.

Gary called his friend, Sid, from a pub nearby. Sid and his lady, Joan, came to the second pub and led the Vauxhall to the White House, the only hotel open for food at this hour.

Gary, master steak eater had a T-bone as big as his plate. George had the combo, a small filet and salmon. Lisa had the salmon and a salad. Great food, atmosphere and friendly people.

Sid had been drinking so his wife Joan returned to guide Gary to the home of Gary's good friend and business associate, Kenny.

Kenny and his lady, Donna, are in India on a well deserved vacation. They volunteered their house at 172

Church Street, Bocking, to Gary while they are away. They will land in Heathrow, from India on January 2, 1995, two hours after Gary departs for L.A., so they will not meet at this time. Sid, who Gary met with earlier, is a director of Kenny's company and helps to carry the ball in Kenny's absence.

Kenny's house has two bedrooms upstairs but George thinks a better idea would be for him to sleep on the spacious sofa downstairs. As usual in England the house has only one bathroom.

Thoughtful Kenny has a refrigerator full of beer, wine, scotch and Hennessey's and has also left the heat turned on. Thank you.

It's been a long day so after a nightcap it's time to sleep.

DAY 4 – WEDNESDAY - DECEMBER 28, 1994 BRAINTREE

Overcast - showers - about 50°F

Another typical English day. Maybe they don't have a sun in England. Fortunately, it is quite comfortable with a raincoat, a cap, and a muffler.

George walks about 400 yards to the small shopping area on Church Street to buy milk, cereal, scones, eccles cakes and chewy french bread. Must not forget a jar of raspberry preserves (Jam).

The lady clerks are very friendly. One had been in California this last summer, traveling from Los Angeles to San Francisco, with her husband.

"And how did you like it?" George inquired.

"Oh, it was so beautiful and it was so warm and comfy, not miserable like here. And the people were all so rich, not poor like we are. They had everything. "

George said, "I like it here, too."

"Yes, but you are only staying awhile. You know

you- are going to leave."

All the above and more, in a soft, pleasant, English accent. George chatted with Mary Ann or Marian every morning, when in Bocking, as he picked up the "London Times," a tabloid inappropriately called "The Sun" and necessities such as milk and beer.

The tabloids are a kick. Each one screams out with a catchy headline describing last night's murder. England has only one murder per day so the papers can concentrate and give each one plenty of ink. Wonder what they would do if they had hundreds as in the good, old, U.S.A. Each paper also has a large photo of a scantily dressed lady on the second page. George wonders what she has to do to get the publicity. Maybe she delivers the papers.

The Brits finally caught a serial killer who had done away with at least a dozen females, raped many more and was a bit of a nasty fellow.

He was being held in the highest type of security prison. The English are much more practical than the Americans. Somehow or another, a rope and a convenient hook appeared in his cell.

He took the hint and hanged himself last night, thus avoiding an 0.J. Simpson type of trial and saved the population from an increase in taxes.

The press like to interview the common folk. One lady made an astute observation, "That's the first decent thing that bloke did in his life."

George is reading all this great stuff, enjoying a coffee and an eccles cake, awaiting the arrival of Gary and Lisa from upstairs.

Gary said he slept in because he had a marvelous dream. All his prior girlfriends passed in review and as there were beaucoup, it took quite some time.

Today features a visit to Windsor Castle, publicized as, "the most romantic castle in the world." It is, indeed, an outstanding, massive, unforgettable display of architecture. For romance, George thinks a smaller more intimate setting would be more appropriate, but the Brits think big. It would be difficult to keep track of someone in this gigantic joint. A lady could have a hundred lovers in this place at the same time and they would never see each other. Now, that's romance.

The castle originated with William the Conqueror who came across the Channel from Normandy in 1066, and took over the monarchy and also the country.

In the succeeding 1000 years there have been about fifty kings and queens who have added their individual buildings. Now the monstrous structure covers 5.25 hectares or 13 acres whichever one prefers.

The proletariat are only allowed into a small part of the castle which is really a good thing as one would have to stay a month to see all of it.

There are 350 people (the staff) who live in the castle permanently. George was wondering why anyone would want to live inside this gloomy looking place (it's raining) until he bought the official guide book which shows in flaming colour how beautiful many of the rooms are or were.

The Royal Standard is not flying so the Queen is not in residence. George does not know where she was for Christmas holiday. For sure, she's not at Kenny's place in Bocking, Braintree, Essex.

St. George's Chapel is done in perpendicular gothic (guidebook) and is well worth the visit. The Chapel and the Queen's dollhouse are about the only places of interest available to the public.

In 1992, about five percent of the castle was destroyed by fire, evidently caused by defective wiring. The Queen wants the public to pay for the rebuilding. However, some nasty twit figured out that she has more money than 95% of the people all together, so why shouldn't she pay. George will lay two to one she doesn't pay but the bookmakers have it at even money.

On this particular day, a ray of sunshine was provided by the smiling faces of 120 American high school cheerleaders. They were All-stars, both boys and girls, and will put on a massive demonstration this weekend. They do not mind the rain as many come from the north and east of the U.S.A. Many parents are with the group.

All in all, it was a well worth while visit. Gary and Lisa are in the photograph business and everything has been recorded on film. The pictures plus this story will bring the trip to life (hopefully) as Gary camcords his comments into the microphone so humor can be expected.

The town of Windsor, which surrounds the castle, is quite busy and has many public houses. A visit to the castle is dry business so the pubs are crowded.

George prefers the British standard drink, known as "bitter" which is not pressurized and is drawn by hand from the keg. Gary has taken to the lagers which are the most famous worldwide brands brewed under license in England and pressurized which makes them last longer in case the Brits don't buy them.

The Brits are too proud to brew their own lager, as does most of the world.

For a complete discussion on "beer in England," please see, "England, Green, Gracious, Grandiose," dated 9/1/90, Page 9.

All we know for sure is that there are at least 77,000 public houses in England. That was at last count.

The pubs are now open from 11:00 a.m. to 11:00 p.m., if they so desire. No more of those weird "closed" hours during the day. It is rumored that the breweries bribed Margaret Thatcher, but that is preposterous.

It is now 3:30 p.m. and quite dark so it's time to put the Vauxhall on the motorway for the two-hour trip to Braintree.

Gary is now an expert, once he fmds the way. And evidently the Vauxhall is a gem to drive. It has all the features of an expensive American or Japanese car including electronic door and trunk locks.

It also has intermittent windows (inside joke).

Occasionally the windows go up and down without apparent activation. The English maybe have a use for this feature, but Gary has not as yet determined what it may be.

Back at Bocking, Gary calls Richard, one of his business contacts. The idea is to invite Richard and his lady, Pamela, to dinner. Richard will have none of that and insists that his house be the venue for the meeting. Incidentally, Bocking is a residential area of Braintree.

A Blue Star taxi is the conveyance to Richard's home. The D.U.I. laws in England are so severe that the taxi business is flourishing. Most business people have an account with a cab company, as does Richard.

In a few minutes, the taxi is at Richard's door. Richard is a somewhat large, lovable, loquacious gentleman with a hearty, friendly nature. George is right at home with Richard in a few minutes.

Obviously Richard loves to eat and after pouring drinks, he chooses an adequate lamb roast from his well-stocked larder, seasons it appropriately and plops it in the oven.

"I don't know how to cook, the oven does the work," was Richard's humble explanation.

The house is on a large lot and very spacious. It is several hundred years old, but the series of owners have made many upgrades. Richard has been the owner for many years and has capped it off with a Jacuzzi on the third floor. It is most comfortable with several fireplaces.

Richard and Sid have recently sold their joint business for many coins of the realm and now, among other things, are directors of Kenny's company.

Richard and Gary sidle off to a quiet area to discuss mutual items of interest. Lisa is examining the house, leaving George to examine (verbally, that is) Richard's very attractive and charming, red-haired lady, Pamela.

George doesn't remember what they talked about, but that is not important.

Richard had available every kind of libation so by the

time he added vegetables to the roast and he pronounced dinner ready, everyone was quite happy.

Gary and Richard were quipping back and forth and Lisa insisted on putting the remarks on paper, which caused much merriment.

George was content to flirt with Pamela. For George's definition of flirting, please see, "______________," page.

Much wine was consumed during and after the most enjoyable meal. The meal concluded with a small round of excellent Stilton.

What a great business meeting. A Blue Star taxi driver had no trouble finding 172 Church Street, Bocking, Braintree, Essex, England.

Richard invites Gary, et al., to a New Year's Eve Party at his house. The invitation is accepted providing all are still awake after a day in Paris.

DAY 5 - THURSDAY - DECEMBER 29, 1994 BRAINTREE

Overcast - showers - about 50°F

It's 8:00 a.m. when George takes his morning stroll to chat with Mary Ann and to pick up the morning papers and supplies.

An interesting item in the business section of The Times headed, "Boxed Wine Kits For Canada." This should be of major interest to all wine lovers who feel it necessary to have on hand, many bottles of different types of wine.

The item continues, "The wine kits produce quality wines, but without the hassle. There is no bottling or siphoning, you just add your favorite tap water to the spray-dried wines and voila, you have French, German or Italian wine."

The company has obtained an order from Safeway for what they call, "a considerable quantity of kits."

Just think of the consequences of this British

ingenuity. Napa Valley could be history, as well as many other grape-growing areas. Bottle and cork companies would have no business.

A major loss would be the conversation generated when tasting wine, gently poured from a bottle.

A wine cellar would consist of a few hundred kits of spray-dried wine. A glass of wine would be as readily available as "Kool-Aid."

Thankfully, England doesn't rule the world anymore so they can't force people to drink this stuff. Generally speaking, the Brits don't know anymore about wine than George does.

Gary has been on the phone with Lorraine, a young lady who neither Gary nor George has met. Lorraine does graphic artwork for Gary's company. She is an expert on the production of catalogs and brochures.

An arrangement is made to meet Lorraine and her husband, Steve, at the Swan Hotel in Lavenham, at 6:00 p.m.

Steve suggests a tour to fill up the day. The 120 to Colchester, A12 through Ipswich, then the 1064 to Aideburgh on the North Sea, then return on the 1071 to Hadleigh and on to Lavenham, about a 100 miles in total.

Colchester is reputed to be one of the oldest cities in England. The Romans, in the First Century, had a thriving port at that location. Many of the original Roman walls are still standing, but are not in use.

The city center is very busy with end-of-year shoppers. This could be a continuation of Boxing Day sales. A packing space is located on the top floor of a parking garage.

Colchester Castle, not far from city center, was built in 1076 by William the Conqueror about the same time as he started Windsor Castle. Colchester Castle was never used as living quarters for royalty but was mainly a fortification. Most of the stones used in the construction came from the ruins of the original Roman buildings.

The castle is now a most interesting museum,

belonging to the city. Through the years the immense building was mainly used for military purposes and also as a prison for the losers.

As is customary, there are many public houses in the vicinity of the castle. The rain is increasing in intensity so nearby "Boars Head" is the choice for lunch. Gary has a slice from the roast with vegetables, Lisa requests a salad, which is a special in a pub, and George has the Ploughman's Lunch, crisp bread and mature cheddar cheese. Very tasty, with a pint of Bitter, Abbot's best, in this house.

The rain is pelting down and everyone has forgotten the location of the parking garage. There are three parking garages in Center City and, of course, the car is in the last one to be located. All the natives are walking in the rain so why be different. George found a butcher shop and had the butcher cut him a slice of stilton and a slice of carephiley, which with a hard roll was delightful to munch on, while lost.

Darkness comes early on a rainy day, so it was decided to abort the visit to the North Sea coast and go directly to Hadleigh and Lavenham.

The Swan, an elegant forte hotel was easy to locate in Lavenham. Before long, Lorraine and Steve appeared and were recognized immediately. Lorraine is petite and pretty and somewhat shy. Steve is the opposite, they complement each other. The Swan does not begin serving food until seven so, after one drink:, Steve suggests a move to their favorite local, The Riverside, closer to their home.

George is sitting next to Lorraine in the car and realizes that she is nervous about meeting her part-time employer, Gary, for the first time. In his best grandfatherly manner, George is able to gain Lorraine's confidence and she quickly begins to relate to Gary's businesslike manner.

The Riverside has a *more* relaxing atmosphere than the more formal Swan. The food is excellent, Gary has a T-bone and George, pork chops, in a sauce of port wine and stilton.

Gary and Lorraine are soon discussing the nature of her work with Gary's company and she is completely relaxed. Modern communications allow her to work easily in a part-time capacity although located 5000 miles away.

George, with Steve and Lisa, are seated at the table far enough away to allow the business conversation to proceed without interruption. Lisa has developed a habit of writing down interesting bits of conversation. The copy seldom comes out like the original, causing much merriment, due to her comedic talents.

Another successful business meeting comes to a close, with Lorraine and Steve guiding Gary in the Vauxhall to the 131, which leads directly to Church Street in Bocking, Braintree.

DAY 6 - FRIDAY - DECEMBER 30, 1994 BRAINTREE, PARIS

Overcast - showers - about *50*°F

George is wondering why he bothers to mention the weather--the word "same" would suffice.

As long as one dresses warmly, wears his English cap and scarf, has sturdy shoes and a raincoat, there is no problem.

The raincoat George is wearing is an Aquascutum that's scutum not scrotum, bought in Canada forty years ago. It could be falling apart from old age, but not from use as it never rains in California. It is the same model as worn by Peter Palk in the TV series, Columbo.

This trip has been really well organized. Gary has spent much time personally and also used his connections to the fullest. When talking about places to go, as recently as three weeks ago, Gary said, "Let's do the Chunnel, it's been open since October." George replied, "The reservation list is three months long. Good luck," that must etc., etc.

The entire trip to Paris has been set-up by Roland, of

Roland's Travel Service. Roland does work for Richard, Sid, Kenny, and Gary and has been in the travel business since the horse and buggy days.

The following has been arranged and ticketed by Roland for this day:

- Blue Star taxi from 172 Church Street in time to catch the 10:02 a.m. train from Braintree to London, Liverpool Street Station, arriving Liverpool Street at 11:06 a.m.
- Ticketed on the Eurostar from Waterloo Station to Paris at 5:15 p.m.,
- arriving Paris, Gare Du Nord, at 9:30 p.m.
- Rooms reserved at the Hotel Sud, 42 Rue Des Petits Ecuries, near the Gare
- Du Nord in Paris.

The only leg not handled is the taxi or underground from Liverpool Station to Waterloo International Station.

Roland has allowed over six hours to accomplish this twenty-minute trip. His reasoning is that there should be sufficient time available for sight seeing in London. Good thinking.

George has plenty of time for his usual visit to Mary Ann's shop to pick up the dailies and supplies. Lisa's coffee, laced with Hennesseys, makes an excellent heart starter. It will be a long day.

All legs of the trip happen with British efficiency and Liverpool Station, completely upgraded, is the place to buy French money. A franc, after commission, turns out to be worth approximately 18 cents U.S.

The Tower of London is the choice for sightseeing and the taxi driver from Pakistan knows where it is located. He has only been in the country for six months and driving for only four, but evidently has the connections or the wherewithal all to obtain a job. London is full of people from former British colonies. Their advantage is being able to speak more understandable English than the natives.

The line for admission to the tower is at least a quarter of a mile long. As everyone has to be somewhere, it makes no difference and the thirty minutes pass by quickly.

The Tower, on an overcast day, looks gloomier than usual. For over 1000 years it has stood on the Bank of the Thames, used mainly as a fort and as a prison.

George's last visit to the Tower was 32 years ago, but he remembers some significant changes. In 1963, the dungeons were part of the Tower exhibit and also the exact beheading spot was in the dungeon.

Sometime during the past 32 years, these two very entertaining exhibits have been moved to a separate nearby location for which another entrance fee is charged. Another example of British ingenuity.

The beheading spot is now indicated by a small sign on the lawn on the Tower grounds. The sign is comprehensive, however, listing the name of the beheaded and the date on which she lost her head. She is the applicable pronoun as most were women who became fully depreciated in their husbands' opinion and were written off. Divorce is much tidier, but perhaps as painful. The axe is speedy.

The Jewel House, displaying the Crown Jewels is still the most popular exhibit and is very well presented.

William the Conqueror built the White Tower in 1078 as a fortress and it is still in use displaying a collection of armor and weapons.

The medieval palace of King Edward built around 1300 is worth a few minutes. The Bloody Tower, where Sir Walter Raleigh was imprisoned for bringing tobacco to England, is worth a walk through. Also, the Royal Armories and the Royal Fusiliers Museum are interesting for those who enjoy wars and death. The Tower is really depressing if one dwells on the horrible things that happened there. They would have happened somewhere else in any event. It's not the Tower's fault.

King Henry III had a private river entrance built in

1216 so he could sneak out without the Queen knowing. The old rascal was a lover, not a fighter.

The Tower is tiring so the nearby attraction, "2000 Years In Thirty Minutes," at Tower Hill Pageant is a good opportunity to sit down and watch the development of Londinium from Roman time to the present.

An almost always-available taxi makes the trip to Waterloo Station without too much extra mileage. One has to expect a little overcharge, being what Londoner's think, wealthy Americans. "Let's stick it to those Yanks," gently, please.

Waterloo has a new international section built especially for the Eurostar. It is an immense futuristic glass bubble and is much brighter than most train stations.

Eateries of all types abound. It's not easy to go wrong with sandwiches and beer or wine, when one is too tired to make a choice.

The fare to Paris and return is $150.00 U.S. on the Discovery Special, if one books 14 days in advance. George is of the opinion that one could get on immediately by paying the standard fare of $250.00 U.S. return, or the first class fare of $325.00 U.S. return, which includes a meal.

The Eurostar is a long train, 18 cars, with 60 places on each Discovery Special. The standard and first class cars may be roomier.

It is much like a small airliner, but much quieter and smoother. George falls asleep within 10 minutes of departure so don't ask him what the tunnel is like. The Eurostar travels 180 miles per hour in France, but much slower in England. The trip takes three hours and George spends two hours asleep. What a great way to go to Paris. Gary and Lisa find the bar car and pass on the sleep department. It must be nice to be young.

Taxis in Paris are plentiful and expensive. At least the driver knew where Rue Des Petits Ecuries was located and 42 was right where it should have been. Petits Ecuries has got something to do with small horses so maybe there were low hitching posts on the street in the olden days so one could park his horse. There is no room to park these days, even the horses would have to walk single file.

Hotel Sud, Hotel South, in English, is in a historical building. The outside may not be changed, but the inside has been gutted and Hotel South is a modem 45-room hotel. Not bad for $80.00 U.S. single and $95.00 U.S. double.

The combination desk clerk, concierge and porter suggests, FIo's, a fancy French restaurant at 7 Des Petits Ecuries for dinner. From 42 to 7 is not far.

George is anxious to continue sleeping and suggests that Gary and Lisa have a romantic evening, together, alone, without his presence.

They reported a delightful time, with French food, French wine, French menus, and a very friendly French couple as table companions.

And also French prices.

DAY 7 - SATURDAY - DECEMBER 31, 1994 PARIS - BRAINTREE

Sunny - showers - approximately 50°F

Hotel Sud offers Petite Dejuener as part of its price. On the Mezzanine is a breakfast room with plenty of cereal, eggs, croissants, buns, rolls, cakes, French sticks, jams and many types of cheese. Also, plenty of cafe au lait.

The combination desk clerk and concierge has arranged a tour of the highlights of Paris by bus, starting at 10:30 a.m. Incidentally there is a one-hour time difference between London and Paris.

The French are as devious as the rest of the world. The concierge asked to be paid twenty percent of the tour price in cash before ordering the tour. The balance could be paid by credit card to the driver. George wonders why this nice young man is so anxious to receive cash. Surely the French pay their income tax. The tour price is $42.50 U.S.

each for 4 hours.

Paris is more expensive than London which is more expensive than Palm Springs. For things other than bare necessities, food and beer, for example, prices in London are approximately 50% higher than in Palm Springs. Prices in Paris are approximately double those in the U.S.A.

A short taxi ride, say 5 minutes, in Palm Springs $6.00, in London $9.00, in Paris $12.00. All, plus tip.

The polite driver and guide is quite ambidextrous, switching from French to English to Spanish without missing a syllable. In the mini bus are 5 Americans and 3 Spaniards.

Paris is bisected by the Seine in the same manner that London is bisected by the Thames. The driver winds from one side of the river to the other over the many bridges.

The Champs-Elysees leads to the Arc De Triomphe to the Place De Concorde to the Tuileries Gardens to the Louvre to the Madeleine to Sacre Coeur, to Invalides (Napoleon's tomb) to the Opera, to the Assemblee National and to many more spectacular landmarks and buildings. The guide is continually pointing out items of interest. Fifteen-minute shops are made at the Eyeful Tower and at Notre Dame to allow closer inspection. George has seen all these wonderful places several times, but it is always a pleasure to see them again. The tour ends at the Hotel Sud, exactly at the four-hour mark, 2:30 p.m.

As the Eurostar does not leave Gare Due Nord unti1 5:09 p.m. there is plenty of time. Gary and Lisa express a desire to see more of Notre-Dame. An almost always-available taxi does the job for about $14.00 U.S. including tip.

Near Notre Dame is a bar-restaurant named for that ancient French hero, Charlemagne. George would rather sit and drink so he volunteers to guard the luggage while Gary and Lisa examine Notre Dame.

It's a pleasure to watch the crowds of people passing by while sipping a large beer, $7.60 U.S., "Biere A La Pression," which must mean "draft."

Many French ladies are wearing hats. The style seems to have the brim fitting straight across the forehead, just above the eyes. There is no need for the lady to have hair, none is showing. Very pretty faces, nevertheless. The ladies also wear long black coats, almost to the ground. Very chic, but they look like large bats.

The difference between the French and English is reflected in their streets. Paris streets are very straight with right angled turns, representing correctness and precision. . London streets wander around in a haphazard manner, as though to say, "Who gives a shit."

The personality of the people is much the same as the streets. The French are very prim, proper, correct, hard to get to know. The English are more likely to slap one on the back before introduction. Take your choice. If one nods to an Englishman usually he will nod back. If one nods to a Frenchman, one may as well be nodding to a statue of De Gaulle--no recognition whatsoever.

On closer scrutiny, the faces of the French ladies passing by are more angular and precise than the more rounded visages of the English ladies. All are beautiful to George who has a great seat by the window and Beaucoup beers. What a wonderful way to see Paris.

The menu in this restaurant shows 18 types of tea, 12 types of coffee, and only 7 types of beer, by actual count, no less.

George is running out of French money. He has only three 20-Franc coins left. A very small beer is 19 Francs, $3.40 U.S. This leaves one-Franc change, which coincidentally is the price to use the washroom where one can get rid of the beer. Great strategy.

George is glad to have to do only No. "un." One must squat to do No. "deux." George would have fallen in, for sure. French people must be acrobats.

George has to pee one more time, but is out of Francs. Gary and Lisa are due momentarily, but George cannot wait. He follows a Frenchman to the loo, grabs the door before it closes and slips in. Necessity is the mother of ingenuity.

Gary and Lisa return as promised at 4:00 p.m. They climbed 300 steps to the top of the Bell Tower in Notre Dame, from where most of the city of Paris can be seen. George would still be going up.

A taxi driver finds the Gare Du Nord with no problem, a half hour before the Eurostar is scheduled to depart. Perfect timing. Gare Du Nord, a historic monument, has had a face-lift in honour of Eurostar. These folks are serious about their train. They even cleaned the glass canopy so light could get in.

The tickets have car numbers with seat numbers thereon so it is easy to find one's place.

It is still daylight and George is determined to stay awake until the tunnel is reached. He thinks maybe the train will go underwater so one can see fish through the train windows.

Gary and Lisa are sitting together and as George is a single, he finds himself next to Eileen a pleasant English widow lady. Eileen's friend is sitting across the aisle with her sixteen-year-old daughter who is on this day trip as a birthday present. Eileen asks George if she can take his picture, as she has never seen an American close up. Her interest seemed to wane after George told her he has been married for 57 years and is nearly 80 years old.

She is really a neat, knowledgeable lady and they do have a great chat about historical England. She also tells George that one cannot see the fish in the Channel, through the train windows.

It is dark by the time the Channel is reached and George has no idea where he is. The train is smooth, quiet and very comfortable and a tribute to British-French engineering. A story went around last May that when Queen Elizabeth dedicated the Channel Tunnel, she departed on a special train, traveled for less than an hour and arrived in another part of England. That's preposterous, at least the engineers would know which way to point the train. .

Smack on time, in three hours exactly, the Eurostar pulls into Waterloo Station at 7:09 p.m. The taxi reaches Liverpool Station in plenty of time to catch the Brit-Rail Inter-city Train, London to Braintree, by way of Witham, which leaves at 8:32 p.m., arriving at Braintree Station at 9:42 p.m.

George loves the way the Brits call their trains by the departure time, rather than by a number. Very clever, and saves a lot of numbers.

It's New Year's Eve and luckily the pre-arranged Blue Star taxi is waiting at the station. In a short while Kenny's home in Bocking is reached.

It is much colder than in Paris. It may be down to 30° F, but fortunately Kenny left the heater on. Thanks very much, Kenny.

A New Year's party is in progress at Richard's house, but no one feels like dressing and taking part in the revelry. No doubt it would be a first-rate affair with many interesting people and accents, in attendance.

It has been a long day and Lisa is off to bed.

Gary and George finish off Kenny's bottle of Hennessey and his scotch while discussing and solving the problems of the world, Orange County and the electrode business.

Midnight passes by and it's an hour into 1995 before the problems are solved and sleep takes over. What a great day.

DAY 8 - SUNDAY - JANUARY 1, 1995
Braintree – HEATHROW

Clear - cold - about 30°F

This is clean up, pack up day at 172 Church Street in the Bocking area of Braintree, Essex. The destination is the Holiday Inn, Crowne Plaza, in the airport loop at Heathrow.

The temperature dropped about 20°F overnight. It took about five minutes to melt the layer of ice on the windshield. Forgot to bring a scraper.

It is New Year's Day and, as usual, the traffic is minimal in the A.M. The two-hour drive, 120, 11, 25 and 4 is easy. Gary has become an expert left-side driver. He says he will be glad to get back to the proper side, however.

The Euro dollar people are out of mincemeat tarts, but do have a car to the Holiday Inn.

It's about noon and time for lunch. Gary and Lisa have not yet appeared so George finds a comfortable chair near the fireplace and enjoys a pint of bitter and two scones with raspberry preserves.

A handsome English couple are sitting nearby with three noisy brats. English accents on adults are lovely, but not from screaming kids. Typically, the parents make no attempt at restraint. In self-defense, George falls fast asleep before the fire.

When he awakens, Gary and Lisa are across the table finishing lunch. "Come on, old man, let's go to downtown London."

The hotel shuttle to Terminal Two at Heathrow. The Picadilly line to Acton Town, then the District line to Victoria Station. The underground is easy if one can read and follow directions. The directions in England are very explicit. For exit they say, "way out," very simple, indeed. One does not need to learn complicated words like "exit."

The last "original London sightseeing tour bus" is about to leave Victoria Station. Last for today, they will be operational tomorrow as they have been for nearly a hundred years. There is a serious problem, however. It is so bloody cold not even Gary can sit outside on the upper-deck. It is the coldest day this winter--29°F.

Inside the bus, it is quite warm. Probably 33°F Brrrrr....

As it is 3:30 p.m. it is almost dark so George will see London at night for the first time. Most of the important buildings and monuments are ablaze with light.

The Parliament buildings, Big Ben, Little Ben, St. Paul's, Trafalgar Square, Picadilly Circus, Westminster Abbey, Southwack, The Tower, Southridges, Harrods, the Marble Arch, to mention a few famous landmarks, all look much different at night. They do not skimp on the power. It looks like Las Vegas.

Unfortunately, the Queen was not at home. When she goes out she turns off all the lights in Buckingham Palace to save money for her subjects.

Most spectacular were the shopping streets with their Christmas lights, such as Bond Street, Regent Street, and others. Very good show, it was, indeed.

The lecturer, obviously one of the boys, did an excellent running commentary. He suggested "Arthur's" as the best place for dinner, about 400 years away on Victoria Street.

Half frozen from sitting on the bus, interruptions are not welcome when striding the 400 yards.

However, a homeless lady is huddled in a doorway. Gary slips her a couple of pounds. A communist-type lady standing nearby sees the action and walks alongside delivering her spiel.

"People like that are a national disgrace," and on and on and on. The gist of her dissertation was that all of England's troubles are caused by the U.S.A.

If it had been warmer, Gary and George would have enjoyed arguing with her, but their mouths were frozen shut. George told her to get a box and go to Hyde Park corner. She had been there all day and was really wound up.

Arthur's was a classy public house completely sold out at 7:30 p.m. "Be out of here by 7:30 p.m. was the proviso." 90 minutes is enough time.

In the carvery, looking and smelling delicious, sits a large prime rib roast, a sizzling pork roast and a fat turkey, Yorkshire pudding, stuffing, potatoes cooked with the roast, succulent gravies, many vegetables are all available. Cold weather makes hot food more desirable.

George stayed with the beef and Yorkshire pudding, but Gary had a helping of each. The starters included great onion soup and among many others, a specialty, mushrooms cooked in port wine.

The dessert tray was hard to resist, but George had several types of cheese with crackers. Lisa eats like a bird, and probably had a small taste of everything. All the foregoing is washed down with wine, beer, and coffee.

It is still very cold. Victoria Station is much easier to reach starting from a warm base and a full stomach. Fortunately, the socialist lady is lecturing somewhere else. Another of her diatribes would be too much.

Retracing the trip to Heathrow takes about an hour, where the Holiday Inn shuttle is waiting.

The fireplace in the lounge is inviting for a nightcap. George has a shot of Hennessey and a pint of bitter, then heads for room 393.

Gary and Lisa are ensconced in front of the fireplace.

DAY 9 - MONDAY - JANUARY 2, 1995
HEATHROW - LOS ANGELES

Cold - 30°F - then 70°F

This is Getaway Day. The Holiday Inn Crowne Plaza has a breakfast buffet featuring just about everything, including bangers and beans and, of course, fatty bacon.

With all due respect to Kenny, this place has a superior shower. It was hard to get a correct temperature mix at Kenny's. Gary, with his natural technical attitude, was able to quickly determine that one of the supply lines was crimped, making it virtually impossible to maintain a steady flow. If he had known where Kenny hid his tool box, the necessary repair would have been accomplished immediately. Kenny, please fax Gary for further details.

American Airlines Flight 137 departs Heathrow at

11:15 a.m. To abide by the two-hour rule one should be checking in at 9: 15 a.m. Holiday Inn has a shuttle every half-hour so there is no problem.

It took an hour to check in, as at every check point, one was asked the same series of questions, who packed the bags, has anyone had access to the bags, were the bags ever out of your sight, etc., etc., etc. The Brits are still afraid of the Irish. That religious war has been on for 400 years.

An hour was left to spend the remaining English money in the many supposed tax-free shops.

Flight 137 left smack on time about 80% full. George was able to switch to the row ahead of Gary and Lisa and had an empty seat beside him. That's the only way to enjoy a ten-hour flight.

Not the only way. The friendly cabin crew were generous with the miniature Crown Royal. George averaged one per hour.

Eating, sleeping, drinking, reading, writing, chatting made the ten hours pass quickly.

George is hoping the flight arrives early. It is scheduled to land at 2:55 p.m. An American Eagle flight is scheduled to leave LAX for Palm Springs at 3:28 p.m. No one has ever deplaned, made the long walk to passport control, passed through to customs, retrieved the bags and walked to American Airlines departure area in the 33 minutes that George has available.

Good news. The captain says the flight is twenty minutes early. He puts the aircraft down and is taxing to the gate and then the bad news. There is an aircraft parked at the same gate that 137 is supposed to use. 137 must wait.

By the time the gate is cleared and the doors opened, the twenty minutes are lost, plus another five. George walks as fast as he can, has good luck at passports and customs. Gary is able to get George's bag immediately, plus a trolley.

George walks as fast as his old legs will allow and reaches Gate 49, five minutes after the Palm Springs flight had departed. Not a bad try. No one is to blame. It would be impossible for the airlines to schedule flights that suited everyone.

The next flight to Palm Springs leaves at 7:15 p.m., almost 4 hours hence. George had expected to have to wait.

The airport bar is comfortable, the second half of the Rose Bowl game is about to start and Florida-Florida State is next. What more could one ask. Everyone has to be somewhere.

Staying awake to 7:15 p.m. was a problem even with football on the telly. George did not have a private jet on this flight, about six in total were on the aircraft.

Palm Springs is about 65°F, much warmer than London last evening. An easy drive to Indian Wells.

Gary and Lisa evidently had fun clearing customs as the inspectors checked her bag completely. George thinks sometimes those gentlemen get a desire to handle female underwear. No problem, just a delay.

What a wonderful trip! Thanks to Gary for a well done organizing job. But thanks, most of all, for doing the driving.

George Wescoombe and Gary Bukamada
London in the rain